A WOMAN OF HER TIME

A WOMAN OF HER TIME

Caroline Gray

·PARRAGON·

This title first published in Great Britain in 1995
by Severn House Publishers Ltd.

This edition licensed by Severn House Publishers Ltd,
produced by Magpie Books Ltd, and published by
Parragon Book Service Ltd in 1996.

A copy of the British Library CIP data
is available from the British Library.

Printed and bound in Great Britain

AUTHOR'S NOTE

I was not privileged to meet Alexandra Mayne until 1957, when she was fifty-six years old. She was then very wealthy, and still an extraordinarily lovely woman, with her figure, tall, slender and yet surprisingly voluptuous, apparently untarnished by either age or excess, her hair as silkily black as ever in her youth, her features, perhaps composed and totally symmetrical rather than classically beautiful, dominated by her amazing, enormous blue eyes. Only the hair, as she later confessed to me, was in any way assisted to perpetuate the illusion of eternal youth; indeed, she dyed her pubic hair as well, which was pure vanity, as in this evening of her life she took to bed only those who appealed to her. But her crowning beauty was her voice, which was utterly liquid, a phenomenon she was herself continually surprised by, and which she attributed to her mixed blood, although the Amerindians from whom she was descended are known more for the harshness than the softness of their tones.

I must confess that when I met her I had no idea who she was. As a very young, and at that time quite unknown, West Indian novelist, I was invited to a party for West Indians soon after my arrival in London, and my hostess, on marching me across the room to meet the Countess, as Alexandra had by now become, gave me a meaningful glance as the introductions were made, which meant nothing to me at all. I was aware that I was in the presence of a remarkably handsome and possibly important woman, but one who was certainly well over twice my age, which was then twenty-two. Equally, she soon made it clear that it was a very long time since she had lived in the Caribbean, nor did she have any desire to return there. I did my best to be agreeable, and apparently succeeded. To my astonishment a few days later I received an invitation to dine at the Countess's flat in Cadogan Square. I accepted with some eagerness, imagining that I was gaining an entree into society which might do my career some good, only to discover, on arriving, that I was the only guest!

If I entered Alexandra Mayne's flat something of a girl, I emerged something of a woman. I visited her again several times, always at her invitation; on the one occasion, soon after our first evening together, that I attempted to call unbidden, I was informed that the Countess did not receive casual visitors. But she did send for me again, and expressed interest in my work as well as myself. Her interest was aroused, I imagine, because my Guyanese background reminded her of her own, even if at some distance in time. Yet she clearly became bored with me, and after about a year the invitations ceased. I was then making my struggling way towards success as a writer, getting married, having children, and was working, and perhaps playing, too hard to miss her greatly, although the memory of our few evenings together were evergreen. But having lost touch, as it were, I was astonished to receive one day many years later a large packet from a solicitor.

Opening it, I discovered that Alexandra Mayne had died, and had bequeathed to me, of all people, her literary estate.

This consisted of several large exercise books, in which she had written down the events of her life as she recalled them, with a wealth of detail. The books are by no means diaries, for they were not written on any day-to-day basis. Rather do they compose a very personal autobiography, compiled, I would imagine, in the last few years of her life, and, it would appear, entirely from memory.

This leaves some of the events she describes open to question, and indeed her whole personal life must be a matter of belief, as there is absolutely no proof as to whether she did the things she said she did, or slept with the men, and women, she claims to have done. All I can suggest is that she certainly could have, and if she did not, then they were the losers.

Her public success is a matter of record.

The notebooks were accompanied by a single sheet of paper, in which, in her huge, bold hand, the Countess had written: *Tell it as a story, but tell it all.* This I have endeavoured to do.

CHAPTER 1

I fell in love for the first time when I was eight years old, Alexandra Mayne writes. *I mean, really. Wasn't I precocious? To tell the truth, I was a little shocked at myself. Put it down to the circumstances of my birth and upbringing.*

Alexandra's father, Jonathan Mayne, was a rancher in the interior of the then colony of British Guiana, situated on the north coast of South America. Guyana, as it is now called, is a relatively large country – it covers an area as great as England – and is best known for its extensive coastal plain, which is flat and in many places below sea level, and in which rice and sugar cane are grown in great quantities. Inland of the plain lie the virtually impenetrable equatorial forests, sliced open by several huge rivers, but beyond these the land begins to rise. Towards the Brazilian border there are spectacular mountain ranges and set in their midst is a large plateau, several hundred feet above sea level, and known as the Rupununi.

Here lived – and still do – the vestiges of the Amerindian tribes which once roamed the entire colony. And here, late in the nineteenth century, several enterprising Europeans opted to ranch cattle, although the grass was poor and the problems, before the coming of the airplane and the refrigeration plant, involved in getting their meat to market immense, as it involved driving the cattle along forest trails for some weeks, with consequent heavy losses.

Jonathan Mayne was one such ambitious pioneer. He assaulted the Rupununi with only native companions, founded his herd, and to an extent prospered. He also took an Amerindian girl to his bed. Alexandra was never sure whether her father and mother were actually married; it seems unlikely. She was, however, certain that they were deeply in love, and equally certain that her mother was a princess, or at least the daughter of an Indian cacique. It is in fact difficult to discover any woman descended from an Amerindian mother who was *not* a princess, but Alexandra Mayne certainly had the presence of one born to rule.

Her father's love for the mistress he lost to a snakebite at a tragically early age, was proven by the fact that he never did remarry.

The Rupununi at the turn of the century, when Alexandra was born, was very much a frontier; in many ways it still is. The "ranch" was a large, unfenced and undelineated area of scrubby grass, teeming termite nests which might stand six feet tall, and the occasional acacia. Being only a few degrees north of the Equator, it was scorched by the sun most of the year, and then inundated by torrential rain for the rest. The ranchhouse was an irregular collection of poorly carved uprights roofed with troolie palms. There were no walls, and the floors were beaten earth, although in places Jonathan Mayne had spread some coconut matting. There were plain, straight-backed wooden chairs, and even plainer wooden tables; sleeping was done in hammocks suspended from hooks in the uprights. Eating was by means of a knife and the fingers. There was of course no sanitation, but at the bottom of the slight hummock on which the house stood there was a stream rippling down from the nearest mountain, and this provided water for all necessary purposes. In this utter lack of privacy Alexandra Mayne was born and grew to girlhood. Each morning she went downstream to relieve herself and then upstream to bathe herself. Everyone else on the ranch, the half dozen Amerindian cowhands and their wives and children as well as her father, were doing exactly the same thing, and as a small girl Alexandra therefore had no inhibitions about nudity or the difference between the sexes – she never noticed them.

She also, in common with the "bucks", as the male Amerindians were called, found herself amused by the antics of the various Europeans from the city of Georgetown on the coast, who from time to time visited the Rupununi, and stayed at the ranch. These included her Uncle Freddie, Jonathan Mayne's younger brother, and his wife Beryl. Freddie Mayne was a lawyer in Georgetown, a handsome, cheerful fellow who readily fell into the primitive Rupununi ways. His wife, the well-bred daughter of a Barbadian planting family – very much West Indian aristocracy – was a tall, slender, blonde woman. Jonathan Mayne once observed in Alexandra's hearing that it was not the slightest bit odd that Freddie and Beryl had no children because he was damned sure she had never allowed "it". Alexandra at this stage had no idea what "it" was, but she was amused by her aunt's insistence on wearing a bathing costume every time she went down to the river, and the way she made her husband stand guard some distance away when it was necessary to pee.

David Lamb visited the ranch with his father, the District Commissioner, early in 1909, just after Alexandra had celebrated her eighth birthday, which fell in December. David was ten, and very pompous. "My father is responsible for all of the Rupununi," he told Alexandra, by way of a conversational gambit. Alexandra was impressed, although she had no idea *anyone* was responsible for the Rupununi. "I live in Georgetown," David continued. "Do you go to Georgetown often?"

Alexandra had never been to Georgetown in her life. "Not very often," she admitted.

"I live in a house, with proper bedrooms," David declared. "And we have a toilet."

Again, Alexandra had no idea what he was talking about. But she got her own back the following day. Donald Lamb had spent much of his life in the interior and knew what to expect. His ten-year-old son did not, apparently, and like Aunt Beryl, he too would not take off his bathing suit. Nor would he come down to the stream when she was bathing, although she could see him watching her from the house. Alexandra was intrigued, wondering if there was something the matter with him, physically, and as he was the first non-Indian boy of her own age she had ever met, resolved to find out. He was certainly suspicious of her, but he had to accept her invitation when, before their respective fathers, she asked him to ride with her.

Alexandra had her own pony, which she rode bareback and astride, in a dress, her ankle-length skirt pulled up to her thighs. David had to be fitted out with stirrups and a bridle as well as a saddle, but he actually rode quite well, and the two of them cantered out of sight of the house to where Alexandra knew there was another stream, which in one place gathered into quite a deep pool. Here she slipped from the saddle, left her pony to its own amusements, and whipped off her dress – she never wore underclothes. "Whatever are you doing?" David cried in alarm.

"Going for a swim." She plunged into the water, swam the dozen yards or so to the other side of the pool, and turned to look at him. "Aren't you coming in?"

"I don't have my costume."

"I'm not wearing a costume."

"I know. I think you're disgusting. You wouldn't be allowed to do that in Georgetown."

"Then I shan't go to Georgetown. I think you're just afraid."

"I'm not afraid. I'm not afraid of anything," he declared.

"Yes, you are. You're afraid of me looking at you."

"Of course I'm not afraid. It's just not proper for girls to look at boys."

"Why not? I don't mind you looking at me. I rather like it."

"Oh . . . you wouldn't understand. You're too young. And you've never been properly brought up."

"Who says so?"

"My dad. He says it's because you have no mother and are living out here in the bush."

Alexandra didn't know what to make of that. She thought she was as well brought up as anyone else. Certainly Father didn't allow her to pick her nose at table, the way the Amerindians did. "All right," she said. "Then I won't look at you. But if you don't come in, I'll tell everyone you're afraid."

David hesitated. "Promise you won't look?"

"I just did." Alexandra turned her back on him, waited, listened to the splash as he entered the pool. She took a deep breath, sank beneath the surface, turned again, and launched herself at him like a torpedo. He gave a shout of alarm and scrambled for the bank, but she was on him too quickly, her arms wrapping themselves round his thighs as her head broke the surface.

"You wretch," David shouted, gripping her shoulders and trying to push her down, but without success, because he couldn't push too hard for fear of hurting himself; her fingers were tight on his penis. "You promised."

"I'm not looking at you," Alexandra panted. She was out of breath from her dive and with excitement at what she felt beneath her fingers, so deliciously like velvet in texture, and slowly seeming to move, and grow. As David was apparently aware. He gave another exclamation and began climbing up the bank, with Alexandra attached. His buttocks moved in her face, and her fingers slipped. He fell to his hands and knees, out of the water now, and she launched herself at him again. He rolled over, and she landed on his chest. For a moment they squirmed together, for if he was bigger, Alexandra, from the outdoor life she had always lived, was at least as strong, then she felt him against her and pushed herself up to look down. "Oh, David!" she cried. "Is it hurting?"

"Go away," he moaned. "Oh, go away."

Instead she grasped it, and a moment later her fingers were covered in a sticky white liquid, while David gave another convulsive heave and a moan. Alexandra was horrified at what she had caused to happen. "Oh, David," she said. "I've hurt you. I know I have."

"You haven't," he gasped. "Please let me go."

She got off him, went down to the water to wash her hands, and then looked back up at him. He was still lying there, panting, but he was slowly getting smaller as she watched. "Are you sure you're all right?" she asked.

He came down to the water beside her to wash himself. "You were horrible."

"Was I? I didn't know what was going to happen. And you said it didn't hurt."

"It didn't." He pulled on his pants.

"Then why are you so angry?"

"You don't understand," he snapped. "You don't

understand anything." He was dressed, and mounting, and riding away.

Alexandra let him go. He was absolutely right. She didn't understand. But she found the whole episode fascinating.

Alexandra dressed and slowly rode back to the ranch. David was already there when she arrived, embarrassed at the sight of her, so obviously that it could not be disguised. Father said nothing, but next day, after, much to her disappointment, the Lambs had departed, he asked her, "Honeychild, that little rascal didn't make a pass at you, did he?"

She was uncertain what he meant by "a pass". As he could tell. "I mean, he didn't . . . well, attempt to touch you? I mean, your body . . ." Father was very nearly as embarrassed as David had been by the pool.

"Oh, no, Father," she said. "I just don't think he likes girls."

"He's a little twit, isn't he?" Father agreed.

Alexandra was inclined to agree. But she couldn't get David out of her mind, began to spend a lot of time day-dreaming about him, and not only sexually. It was David and her doing things together, playing together . . . *I was genuinely in love*, she writes. *There was nobody else in the world, for me, at that time*. She longed for David to come back, quite overlooking the fact that he had been too embarrassed to speak with her on his last evening at the ranch. But she knew he would, one day.

And then, only just over a year after the incident with David, she began to menstruate.

Alexandra was horrified by the pain and the blood, but the Amerindian women, and especially Queenie, who was Father's favourite and almost a second mother to her, were utterly reassuring, and the ordeal was soon over. Only to be repeated four weeks later. But once she understood what it was all about, she ceased to be afraid of it. Indeed, the event heightened her awareness of herself, gave her David-dreams an added intensity. Her body became her closest, indeed her only friend; she watched with eager anticipation the first suggestions of pubic hair, the down beneath her arms, and the slow swell of her girl breasts, which were added areas of sensation. But she was quite taken aback when one day Father said, "Alix, I really think you should start wearing an apron when not actually in the water."

When the next batch of mail arrived – it came once a month – there was a present for her, and when she opened it, she discovered it to be a bathing costume, complete with little apron, just like Aunt Beryl's. Was that how Father wanted her to be? Well, if it was, she was content to obey him; she would always want to obey Father. And besides, suddenly she no longer wanted to be naked in front of the bucks, or any guests who might come by. When she met David again, he would find her a very changed young lady. But that did not seem very likely, as David's father had been transferred from the Rupununi to Berbice, at the very other end of the colony, as far, Father said, as from Brighton to Newcastle, whatever that meant. Alexandra was quite heartbroken. Then there arose the question of her schooling.

Hitherto, Father had taught her himself. He had taught her to read and write, and to add and subtract and divide. He had taught her history, all about the Romans and the English and the Normans and Drake and Wellington and Queen Elizabeth and Queen Victoria. Best of all, he had taught her geography. He drew her a huge map, of a marvellous island, which had in it every known geographical feature, and on which they lived, just the two of them, in a hut in a valley between two mountain ranges. During every geography lesson they made a journey, from their hut to some place on the island, and she had to name all the features through which they passed. The island became a part of her secret world, only less important than her body – she only wished she had someone to share it with, other than Father. Father was always kind to her, seldom shouted at her, and never ever hit her, and she loved their lessons, when they seemed very close, but a lot of the rest of the time she wasn't sure he even knew she was there, especially in the evenings when he came in from the range and would sit with his rum bottle, staring into space.

As she grew older she lost the relaxed intimacy she shared with the Indians. She had no desire to be intimate with the men, or the boys, especially when she remembered David. She began to find the women were fat and lazy and uninteresting. And she was doomed to spend the rest of her life with them. Sometimes she felt quite despairing.

But when she was twelve Father determined that she had to go to a real school, and took her to Georgetown.

This was the first time Alexandra had made the journey from the interior to the city, and a long adventure it was. They went from the ranch to the river, riding horses, with their boxes on a mule led by one of the bucks, Queenie's brother Hopewell.

At the landing they boarded a bateau, a large double-ended canoe, in which they descended the river to the settlement of Bartica, in the mouth of the Essequibo. This part of the journey was terrifying, for the river ran very fast in the interior, and every so often descended several feet in a series of shallow falls, or rapids, at which the passengers had to disembark while the boatmen carried the bateau overland to below the foaming white water.

Bartica was Alexandra's first glimpse of a town, a church, a school; she stood at the roadside and gazed at the little boys and girls, mostly black children, trooping into the squat building at the sound of a bell, and felt suddenly more nervous than ever before in her life – she was at least twice the size of them and clearly several years older than any of them, but most of them had been going to school for more than a year already.

Father was as reassuring as ever. "It'll be different at the convent in Georgetown," he promised her.

But their journey was as yet only half over, in terms of distance, although the hard work was behind them. At Bartica they boarded a paddlesteamer, and in this made the passage out of the river mouth and into the Caribbean Sea, for the voyage round to the capital. Alexandra was awe-struck at her first sight of the ship, so much larger than anything she had imagined, and although Father referred to it as an old tub, so much grander as well. She was equally excited about venturing on to the open sea, of which Father had taught her so much, and was somewhat disappointed to find that it was brown instead of blue, although, more in keeping with Father's lessons, it was distinctly choppy as there was a stiff breeze blowing. Father explained that the brown was because the water was filled with silt brought down by the Essequibo, and it stayed brown all the way round to Georgetown, for the Demerara River was only a little smaller than the Essequibo; apparently one had to venture ten miles offshore for the water to turn blue.

But everything she had seen, heard, been told or imagined, paled into insignificance when they actually entered the Demerara, and she saw the rooftops of the city. She had not suspected that anything so large could possibly exist. She gazed at the neat rows of houses, the huge warehouses along the waterfront, the dominating square clock tower of the Stabroek Market . . . Father explained that only a hundred years before, in the days when the colony had belonged to the Dutch, the entire town had been named Stabroek, and it had only been rechristened Georgetown after the reigning British monarch when the British had taken possession of it following the Napoleonic Wars. Further away still was an enormous structure, which Father told her was the Anglican Cathedral, the largest wooden building ever built anywhere in the world.

The steamer tied up against a stelling, the Dutch word for dock which was still used, and Uncle Freddie was there to greet them with a pony and trap. They drove through wide, spacious, tree-lined avenues, with two-storied wooden houses to either side, built on stilts to avoid flood water, because Georgetown was below the sea level, and although there was a sea wall, it was liable to flood after heavy rain. Alexandra stared at the marble statues which filled the gardens along with the multicoloured flowers. She had never seen anything so grand.

Their destination was the house of Uncle Freddie and Aunt Beryl, on Lamaha Street, overlooking one of the drainage canals which cut across the city. Alexandra was amazed at the luxury of the inside of the house, the sit-down bath and the water closet which worked on the pull of a chain, just as she was terrified at the several black people who were Aunt Beryl's servants – there had been no black people in the Rupununi except for the policemen – and confused by the profusion of knives and forks and spoons and glasses on the dining table.

Uncle Freddie was very kind in explaining to her

what each of them was for, but Aunt Beryl was not so accommodating. "She can't live here," she told Father at dinner.

"I wouldn't dream of imposing on you," Father protested. "She'll board. But if she could come here for weekends . . ."

Aunt Beryl considered. "If she behaves herself," she agreed. Alexandra didn't know what she was talking about; she had never misbehaved in her life, to her knowledge. "And if I have full powers in loco parentis," Aunt Beryl added.

This time Alexandra was even more mystified. She was disappointed that she would not be living in such luxury all the time, but reflected that weekends would be better than nothing. In any event, she was excited about her visit to the Convent, for which she wore the new skirt, blouse and tie Father had bought her, together with the linen drawers and cotton stockings, secured round her thighs by garters, and the stout black lace-up boots. She had never been so well dressed in her life, and the little straw hat with the pink ribbon just set the ensemble off to perfection, she thought.

Aunt Beryl accompanied them, and they drove in a cab to the Convent, which was several blocks away down Main Street, and formed a corner, with high, forbidding walls. To get in they had to ring a bell on a gate which had a little wicket in it, through which a black-robed nun peered at them before admitting them. Inside, however, it was very pleasant, a world totally secluded from the hustle and bustle of the city, of quiet little walks and secluded gardens.

Nor was Mother Superior the least awe-inspiring. She was a short, stout, middle-aged lady with a red face and a ready smile. "What a charming child," she said, holding both Alexandra's hands. "Oh, indeed, how very charming. Yes, indeed, I am sure we can make room for your daughter, Mr Mayne."

Term did not start for another week, which gave Father and Aunt Beryl time to assemble Alexandra's uniform. This consisted of navy blue overalls, in a heavy drill material, which dropped from her shoulder-straps to her ankles. Beneath she wore a white cotton blouse with a navy blue tie, a white vest, navy blue drawers, navy blue cotton stockings, and black elastic-sided boots. She had to have two complete changes of this somewhat repelling ensemble, and two nightdresses, in lined cotton and secured at the neck with a bow. In addition she needed a panama hat with a navy blue band, and a navy blue girdle to tie round the waist of her overalls. Schoolbooks she would obtain from the Convent itself.

Father said goodbye on the day before term was due to start, and Alexandra and Aunt Beryl drove with him down to the dock to watch him board the steamer for Bartica and home. Alexandra was desolate, and burst into tears for the first time in her life. But Aunt Beryl told her not to be a baby, and once Father had kissed them goodbye, had the cab drive her to the Convent to be formally delivered, along with her box. Alexandra felt like bursting into tears all over again, this time with apprehension at the thought of the new world into which she was going to be plunged, but instead found it all very exciting and pleasant.

She had already been given a test, after which it had been decided that although her general level of education was not at all bad, in specialist subjects such as French and Latin, neither of which Father had known enough of to attempt to teach her, she was so totally ignorant she would have to be put into a form two years below her age group. This had not bothered Alexandra, although Aunt Beryl had raised her eyes and remarked, "Good

Lord! How embarrassing." And in fact it *was* rather embarrassing, as the other girls all giggled whenever she failed to answer a question. But the nun in charge of the form was very kind and understanding.

The boarders slept as forms, under the care of a senior girl. Alexandra thus found herself sharing a dormitory with four ten-year-olds, under the supervision of a fifteen-year-old named Rose, who was a fifth former and responsible for their good behaviour at night. Rose was a short, plump girl, over whom Alexandra already towered by at least an inch, but she was also sunny-tempered, and it was a happy dormitory, once Alexandra had got over the initiation ceremony of an apple pie bed and her toes being coated with bootblack. She thought she was going to enjoy herself thoroughly at the Convent, surrounded for the first time in her life by other girls, and with the added interest of going home to Aunt Beryl and Uncle Freddie every weekend, for Aunt Beryl was by no means as fierce as she pretended, and although she maintained strict rules of behaviour, like washing hands before every meal and not allowing Alexandra to leave the table until everyone was finished, she was actually no more severe than Rose, who also tried to maintain standards.

For all the differences in their ages, indeed, Alexandra and Rose Lumley soon became very good friends. "Because you're big for twelve," Rose explained. "And those little ones are such babies. But you could be fifteen yourself. I know, why don't you come to breakfast at my house on Saturday?" Breakfast was actually the midday meal, taken at eleven thirty, because by one o'clock it was simply too hot to do any work, until at least two; breaking the fast first thing in the morning, however substantial a meal, was always referred to simply as "coffee". Work normally ceased in time for "tea" at four, and the short afternoon – dusk was within fifteen minutes of six o'clock all the year round this close to the Equator – was devoted to hockey or netball, with supper following at eight.

Alexandra was thrilled with the invitation, and to her great relief, Aunt Beryl, who apparently knew Rose's parents and regarded them as socially acceptable, made no objection.

Mrs Lumley sat and talked with her before lunch, just as if she had been a grown-up, asking her all manner of questions about the Rupununi, and Mr Lumley, when he came in from his round of golf, was equally charming. The meal was excellent, and Rose smiled at her throughout. Afterwards Mrs Lumley asked, "What are you two going to do this afternoon?"

"Oh, we'll just talk in my room," Rose told her mother.

"Well, mind you don't make a noise. I intend to have a nap." This was a necessary warning, because, as with all the houses in Georgetown, for the sake of coolness there were no ceilings upstairs; the partitions between the rooms ended at the rafters, and above was merely the sloping roof itself. Thus sounds were inclined to travel the length of the house.

Alexandra followed Rose upstairs to her bedroom, which she was envious to discover was far larger than the one she had at Aunt Beryl's, and was filled with interesting looking books and toys. "Help yourself," Rose invited, and sat on the bed to take off her shoes and stockings. "Why don't you make yourself comfortable?"

Alexandra obeyed, sitting in the chair opposite to her, and Rose sighed as she watched the stockings sliding down the exposed limbs. "You have such lovely legs," she remarked.

Alexandra raised her head in surprise. She had never thought of her legs as lovely, nor had anyone ever suggested that they were, before. "So have you," she replied, politely.

"Oh, I don't," Rose protested. "Mine are too short, and too fat."

"Oh, no," Alexandra lied.

"Let's compare."

Alexandra obligingly lifted her skirt again, but Rose was unfastening her waistband. "We may as well take these beastly hot things off. In here we can wear what we like." Her skirt dropped to the floor, and Alexandra followed her example. It felt deliciously wicked to be undressing in a strange bedroom. "See?" Rose asked, standing beside her in front of the mirror. Alexandra had to admit that her legs were by far the prettier shaped, principally by being longer and more smoothly muscled.

"Of course," Rose said, "I suppose I have the bigger titties. But that's only because I'm older. I bet your titties are just as nice as your legs."

Alexandra didn't know what to reply to that. Naturally she and Rose had seen each other naked at the convent, but only briefly, when they had showered or changed into their nightclothes for bed. And she had never really troubled to look because she did think her body was far more attractive than that of any of the other girls. Right that moment she was more afraid that Mrs Lumley might overhear, or come in. Aunt Beryl had a habit of entering her room without knocking. Rose understood her apprehension, and giggled. "She really is as deaf as a post, as long as we don't shout. And we'll just . . ." She turned the key in the lock. "Now," she said, "Let's compare titties."

She took off her blouse. She wore only a vest underneath, and she took that off as well, before drawing a deep breath to inflate her lungs. Her breasts were the biggest

Alexandra had ever seen, except on some of the older Arawak women, and theirs had always hung almost to their waists. Rose's breasts stood away from her chest like a rounded shelf. "You can touch them, if you like," Rose invited. Alexandra hesitated. She had always wanted to touch another girl's breasts, had always had an enormous desire to touch Aunt Beryl's – she had often fantasized about it. It had never occurred to her that one day she might actually be invited to do so. Cautiously she touched the firm flesh, and then cupped it into her hand.

Rose shuddered with pleasure. "Ooh, that feels so good." Her hands stroked over Alexandra's hair, then across her shoulders and down to give her buttocks, guarded now only by her drawers, a gentle squeeze. "I want to kiss you," Rose murmured. Alexandra was taken into her arms, felt her breasts against Rose's, lowered her face and lips for Rose's kiss, was sucked into another embrace which pushed her mouth open and sought her tongue. Her knees felt weak, her entire body began to shudder, as she felt herself drawn forward to the bed. Rose fell over it, taking Alexandra with her, and then rolled, so that Alexandra was on her back with Rose on her stomach, still kissing. What was happening was surpassing her wildest dreams of a shared experience. She had not imagined that any other human being, much less another girl, could possibly want the things she did. But Rose was kneeling at the foot of the bed, and pulling down her drawers.

It was the most exciting day of Alexandra's life. It was intimacy on a scale she had never believed possible. She almost wanted to weep when it was time to go home for tea, and she knew her life could never be the same again. She felt so superior to Aunt Beryl when they sat together at the table; it was impossible to believe that Aunt

Beryl had ever experienced anything like that. Alexandra wasn't even sure if it was possible to experience such total intimacy with a man. Rose had been certain that it wasn't. "You start playing with a man," she had said contemptuously, "and before you know it he's coming all over the place. And then he can't do anything more for an awfully long time."

Which was certainly true in Alexandra's one experience, although remembering the splendid feeling of David hardening beneath her hands was still exciting, but she didn't want to upset Rose by saying so. Nor did it occur to her to ask Rose how she knew about it. She was too happy in their companionship, for now they spent every Saturday together, sometimes at Rose's house and sometimes in the Botanical Gardens on the outskirts of the city, where they could ramble through deliciously deserted little woods, and when they felt like it, and were sure they were alone, stop and kiss.

Their love for each other seemed to grow throughout the next year; certainly Alexandra's did for Rose. She had never before realised what a lonely girl she had been. To have so much to share with someone, who seemed to know exactly how to understand everything she wanted to say, or do, was heavenly. Her only fear was that they might be separated at the end of the school year.

Alexandra had been on the verge of telling Rose about David, but she decided against it. She hated having any secrets from Rose, but she felt it would be some kind of betrayal of their relationship, even if it had happened so long ago – simply because she had so enjoyed it. She was more interested in Rose's confession of how she had longed to share those early experiences – an affair with her cousin who had been seventeen when Rose was eleven and had lasted for some time. "I knew as soon as I saw you that I wanted to make love to you," Rose said.

"You're so grown-up for your age. Why, you're as tall as Betty." Which was the name of the cousin.

Alexandra was enormously flattered, and was utterly relieved when they went up together, Rose into the Sixth Form, and the other five girls into the Third, so that Rose remained their dormitory prefect. "Oh, how I wish the others would all go away or something," Rose grumbled. "Wouldn't it be marvellous if we could have the dormitory all to ourselves. Think of what we could do. I so want to sleep all night with you, Alix. And then," she went on, "if it was just you and me, we could get out."

"Get out? Whatever for?"

"To go places."

Alexandra's imagination could not cope. "We'd be seen. And they'd know we were convent girls."

"Don't be a goose. How could they possibly know, if we wore our home clothes?"

"But where would we *go*?"

"We'd go to Jimmy's house."

"Jimmy?"

"He's my cousin. He lives only two blocks from the convent. We'd go there and have all sorts of fun. He has lots of friends." She winked. "Boys."

"But . . . I thought you, we, didn't like boys?"

"Of course I don't *like* boys, but they're there, aren't they? One day we're going to have to marry one. Each, I mean. So we may as well get to know them," Rose pointed out. "They're great fun, really. You'll have the time of your life." She giggled. "Just so long as you don't let them put their hands inside your drawers."

Alexandra had goosepimples at the thought, but her innate caution immediately surfaced. "There'd be an awful row if Mother Superior found out."

"Oh, she'd whack us," Rose agreed.

* * *

There was a measles epidemic that summer term. Several girls went down, and Mother Superior, to stop the infection taking over the entire Convent, sent every girl with even the suspicion of illness home. This accounted for three of the younger girls in the dormitory, leaving only Rose, Alexandra, and a Portuguese girl named Theresa; there were a large number of people of Portuguese origin living in Georgetown – their grandfathers had come to British Guiana to work in the canefields after Emancipation, but they had quickly abandoned that to become an important section of the business community, and they were, naturally enough, the principal support of the Roman Catholic Church. "A dream come true," Rose whispered as they prepared for bed. "Tonight's the night. Did you see those boys when we were out walking this afternoon?"

"No," Alexandra said. She hated it when the entire convent went for a walk in a long crocodile, accompanied by various sisters; it made her feel like a convict, and she never looked at anyone they might pass on the street.

"Well, one of them was Jimmy, and I signalled him to expect us."

"Tonight?" Alexandra was horrified. She had never supposed Rose was serious.

"At eleven. That'll give everyone time to go to sleep."

"What about Theresa?"

"Theresa? What about her?"

"She'll see."

"She's too stupid to know anything," Rose said.

Alexandra wasn't sure about that. Teresa was not a very attractive little girl, for she wore horn-rimmed spectacles and had pimples. But Alexandra didn't think she was stupid. On the other hand, Rose was so insistent . . . and suddenly she was excited. How wonderful if one of the boys could be David!

As soon as the electric light had gone out, Rose was out of bed. Like all the girls she kept various pieces of candle secreted in her box, and one of these she now lit and stuck on the table beside her bed. "Let's get dressed," she whispered.

Alexander also got out of bed and began putting on her home clothes. Theresa sat up. "Whatever are you doing?"

"Getting dressed, stupid," Rose told her.

"But why?"

"We have someplace to go."

"You're going to meet boys," Theresa complained.

"What's that to you?"

Theresa also got out of bed. "I want to come too."

"You? You're a baby."

"I'm eleven. And I'm in the same form as Alexandra."

"Yes, but she happens to be thirteen. Now you just get back into bed and go to sleep," Rose commanded.

"Shan't," Theresa said. "If you won't let me come, I'll . . . I'll tell."

"Oh, lord," Alexandra muttered. "Look, let's forget the whole thing."

"Because she says so?" Rose was now definitely annoyed. "Listen, you little creep, if you ever breathe a word of this to a soul, I am going to break every bone in your body. Get back into bed, and stay there."

Theresa stuck out her tongue, but she obeyed.

"Come on," Rose whispered, rolling up her blanket and tucking it under her arm . . .

"How do we get out?" Alexandra asked. The dormitory window was barred.

"This way." Rose opened the dormitory door, and sidled into the corridor. Alexandra followed, casting a last glance back into the dormitory, suddenly a place of great security. Rose had killed the candle, and the room was dark, but she could hear Theresa sniffling. How she wished the next couple of hours would just vanish, and she'd find herself back in bed.

Rose knew exactly what she was doing. At the end of the corridor was the fire door, and although this could not be opened from the outside, the bar on the inside was simple to lift. When they were through, Rose took a folded piece of thick paper from her pocket and stuffed it into the hinge; the door closed, but not far enough for the bar to click into place. "Suppose someone comes along and sees it?" Alexander whispered.

"Don't be a goose. Who's going to walk about the corridors at practically midnight?" She continued to be all efficiency, indicating this was not the first time she had left the dormitory at night. They descended the fire escape to the garden, crept along the paths between the rose bushes, and reached the wall. Now Alexandra discovered why Rose had brought the blanket; the wall was only six feet high, but the top was studded with broken bottles. "Mind how you go," Rose whispered, standing on tip-toe to place the blanket, folded three times, on top of the glass.

"How do I get up?" Alexandra asked.

"Just put your hands on the blanket and vault," Rose instructed. "Like you do in the gym."

Alexandra took a deep breath, and obeyed. Her stomach did a roll as she could feel the sharp pointed glass through the wool, but she reached the top, and kept on going, dropping down on the other side. A moment later Rose was beside her. "What about the blanket?" Alexandra asked.

"We'll leave it there, for when we come back," Rose explained. Alexandra felt that was as risky as the door, but Rose seemed perfectly confident, and it was a deliciously wanton feeling to be hurrying through the streets in the dead of night, almost as wanton as taking off her clothes for the first time in Rose's bedroom. "Now listen," Rose told her. "As of now you're sixteen, like me."

"I can't pretend to be sixteen."

"Of course you can. You look sixteen. And if the boys think you're not, they'll be scared off."

Alexandra didn't know why that should be so, but now was not the time for asking, as they rounded a corner and found themselves in the presence of a large black policeman. "Good evening, constable," Rose said without hesitation.

"Good evening, miss," the policeman replied.

Alexandra could only mumble, she was so terrified. But a few minutes later Rose was opening a side gate and they were in another walled garden, at the far end of which were bright lights and the sound of music. There were a dozen people at Jimmy's party, dancing to a gramophone. Seven of them were boys or young men, and the other five were girls, but all considerably older than sixteen, Alexandra estimated. "Thought you weren't coming," Jimmy said. He was no taller than Rose and had freckles.

"Well, we're here," Rose said. "This is Alexandra."

Everyone wanted to look at Alexandra. "Some kid," one of the boys remarked.

"Convent girls," said one of the women, contemptuously.

"You have to dance with me," Jimmy said, putting his arm round Alexandra's waist.

"I don't know how to dance," Alexandra protested.

"I'll teach you. It's a waltz, see? Just relax."

He held her very tightly with one arm, while he grasped her hand with the other, and rotated her about the room, counting for her, "*One*, two three . . ." bumping into several other people in the process. "Won't your parents hear the noise?" Alexandra asked.

"They know I'm having a party," he said. "They won't come down."

Alexandra felt quite battered when the music stopped, but the gramophone was immediately rewound and then she had to dance with someone else. She was whirled about and had hands sliding all over her body, while when she ran out of breath she was given something to drink which had her head spinning, and then she was offered a cigarette to smoke. This caused her to be violently sick, much to everyone's amusement. "We must be going now," Rose said.

Alexandra didn't want to go. She wanted to stay, and have some more of the drink, if only to get the taste of the vomit out of her mouth. She was also fascinated by the way the older women necked with the boys, kissing them the way Rose had kissed her and allowing them to put their hands inside their bodices or under their skirts. She felt that if she stayed one of the boys, Jimmy, certainly, might want to neck with her, and she was desperately anxious to try that too. She was having the time of her life. But Rose wanted to go home, and she couldn't oppose Rose. "You must come to our next party," Jimmy said, and kissed her on the lips. No man had ever done that before, and she felt quite weak at the knees.

"Well," Rose commented, when they gained the street. "Who was the belle of the ball, then? Just remember I took you."

"Oh, yes," Alexandra said. "I'm ever so grateful, Rose."

"Then you can show it by coming to bed with me when we get back to the dorm," Rose said. "Theresa will be fast asleep by now." But when, having scaled the wall without difficulty, they climbed back up the fire escape ladder, it was to find the fire door shut, the wedge of paper having been removed from the hinge.

"Oh, the little bitch," Rose muttered. "Am I going to take the skin from her ass."

"What are we going to do?" Alexandra asked in a rising panic.

"Oh, I'll prise it open," Rose said, producing a penknife from her pocket. But as she tried to force the knife between the door and the upright against which it was settled, it swung outwards, nearly knocking her off the landing.

"You may come in, now," said Sister Anthony.

Alexandra thought the night would never end. Theresa had been removed from the dormitory, and Sister Anthony slept with them instead. They didn't have a chance to say anything to each other, but they managed to exchange a glance and Rose mouthed, "Deny everything." That didn't make sense, as they had been caught red-handed, but when she tried to catch Rose's eye again, Rose looked away. Then the lights were turned off and they were left in darkness, but knowing Sister Anthony was between them.

Alexandra cat-napped from time to time, but at last it was morning, and they were commanded to get up and dress themselves. They were then sent down to breakfast, a hushed affair, as by now the wildest rumours were sweeping the convent. Alexandra was so upset she couldn't eat any "coffee", especially when Teresa wasn't present at the table either, and her stomach churned even harder when, during the meal, Sister Anthony came in to summon Rose to Mother Superior's office. Before Rose could come back the bell sounded for early morning prayers. Alexandra mumbled her way through, wishing Rose would appear and give her a reassuring smile – but she didn't. And when the service was over and they all trooped off for class, there was Sister Anthony, looking grimmer than Alexandra had ever seen her, waiting for her. "You're to report to Mother Superior," Sister Anthony said. "Hurry now."

Alexandra hurried. She just wanted to get the coming interview over as quickly as possible. Deny everything, Rose had told her. That still didn't make any sense. If only she could see Rose for a moment first. "There is no need to knock." Sister Anthony had followed her.

Alexandra hesitated, then opened the door and stepped inside. Mother Superior was standing up, behind her desk, her cheeks unusually red. Alexandra looked left and right, but there was no sign of Rose. And to her alarm Sister Anthony came in with her, and closed and locked the door. She felt she was in the lion's den. With two lionesses. "Wretched girl," Mother Superior remarked, by way of beginning the conversation. Alexandra swallowed. She didn't know what to reply. "Perhaps I cannot find it in my heart to condemn you, utterly," Mother Superior went on. "In view of your background and upbringing. Yet I had hoped . . . now I can see that you are quite impossible."

Alexandra for the first time noticed the cane lying on the desk. She licked her lips. "Please . . ."

"Don't trouble to deny it," Mother Superior said. "Rose has confessed the entire disgusting story. Will you deny that you left my convent in the middle of last night for the purpose of associating with boys, and women of the town? That you intended to have . . ." Mother Superior shuddered. "Sexual intercourse with them?"

Alexandra had no idea what she was talking about. "I had nothing with them," she said. "We went to dance, and to . . ."

"You smoked cigarettes and drank rum," Mother Superior said. "Sister Anthony smelt these things on your breath when you returned."

Alexandra bit her lip. She didn't know what to say.

There was nothing she *dared* say, until she knew what Rose had said. She certainly didn't want to let Rose down. "Please," she said. "We went to Rose's cousin, Jimmy. Just to dance and listen to music. I'm sorry about the cigarette and the drink. I didn't know there was anything wrong with it."

"Jimmy? Jimmy who?" Mother Superior demanded.

"I don't know his last name. Rose must have told you. He's her cousin."

"Alexandra, Rose has no cousin named Jimmy."

"What?" Alexandra shrieked.

"Nor will howlng do you any good. Rose has told us how you made her go with you, to these guttersnipe friends of yours. Now admit your sin."

"The bitch," Alexandra said, using a word Rose herself had taught her. "Oh, the bitch!"

"You are despicable," Mother Superior commented. "I had hoped for some manner of apology. Bend over that desk."

"No," Alexandra shouted. "Whatever Rose told you, it was a lie. She was the one. She . . ." Sister Anthony seized her wrists and pulled her towards the desk. Alexandra wanted to fight them but was too afraid of what they might do then; the convent was full of sisters who could be called upon for aid, and the thought of being held down by all of them was revolting.

Her groin struck the wood and she fell forward, Sister Anthony still grasping her wrists; the sister had gone round the other side of the desk to hold her against it, bent across the surface. And Mother Superior was behind her. Alexandra felt hands raising her skirt, higher and higher, while her legs suddenly felt cold, even in her cotton stockings. Then Mother Superior was tucking the skirt into her girdle, she felt the hands on her drawers, and they were pulled down about her knees. She wanted to scream, and strained on her arms, but Sister Anthony was too strong, and before she could draw breath she felt a most curious sensation, as Mother Superior parted her buttocks and then slid her hand between her legs.

Alexandra was outraged. No one had ever touched her there, save for herself, and on one occasion, Rose. And for it to be Mother Superior . . . Mother Superior straightened. "Well," she said. "It is not as bad as we feared, Sister. Still, a full report must be made to Mrs Mayne."

"Let me go," Alexandra muttered, tugging on her arms.

"Will you use the cane?" Sister Anthony said.

"No," Mother Superior said. "The facts are not proven. But she is certainly guilty of unacceptable behaviour. Now you will go home, Alexandra. Sister Anthony will take you. Your things will be packed up and sent after you. We do not wish to see you here again."

The Countess writes: *I suppose almost every woman has a Rose somewhere in her past; the incident acts as a kick-start, if you like, to her womanhood. But I hope not every woman suffered quite my letdown. Or the consequences. All because I so desperately needed someone to love.*

Alexandra's head jerked. She was being expelled. Expelled! But if that were so, then they had had no right to paw her about as well. She stood straight, shaking with outrage. "You . . . you bitch!" she screamed.

"Take her away," Mother Superior commanded. "Her very presence contaminates the air."

"You . . ." Alexandra tried to think of another word, but Sister Anthony had come round the desk.

"Come along, girl," she said brusquely. "Dress yourself."

Alexandra pulled up her drawers, released her skirt, trying to stop the sobs which wracked her body; Sister Anthony gave her a handkerchief to dry her eyes, and then took her outside. Mother Superior had not spoken to her again. Sister Anthony marched Alexandra downstairs and through the garden to the side gate, where a cab was waiting. It must have been called even before her summons to the office, Alexandra realised: they had been going to expel her whether she had confessed or not. I am being spirited away like a criminal, Alexandra thought, and determined: if they think I am a criminal, then I will be a criminal. As for Rose! She realised that Sister Anthony had got in beside her. The horse immediately moved off. "Why are you coming?" she muttered.

"To deliver you to your aunt. I have a letter from Mother Superior to Mrs Mayne. Your aunt is going to be very angry with you, but it will be no more than you deserve."

Aunt Beryl was going to be very angry! Sister Anthony obviously had a warped sense of humour. But Aunt Beryl was irrelevant. It was what Father was going to say that mattered. Alexandra felt like jumping out of the cab and breaking something – perhaps her neck. But even an ankle or a wrist might earn her some sympathy. Before she could make up her mind to do it, they had arrived. Uncle Freddie was at his office, but Aunt Beryl was home, and gazed in astonishment at her charge being returned to her in the middle of the week. Astonishment which slowly altered to horrified consternation as she listened to Sister Anthony, and then read Mother Superior's letter.

Alexandra shifted from foot to foot as she watched the changing expressions on her aunt's face. Then Sister Anthony finished and departed in the cab. Aunt Beryl stared at Alexandra, and Alexandra stared back. But she was in no mood to compromise. "If you hit me, I'll hit you back," she warned.

"Your mother was a slut. But you are worse. You'll go to your room, miss, and stay there. I do not wish to see you anywhere else in this house. Go there, and stay there, until I can get in touch with your father."

Alexandra was quite happy to obey, at least for the moment. She only wanted to be alone. She threw herself across her bed, listened to the key turning in the lock, and could then give herself up to paroxysm after paroxysm of fear, and anger, and bitterness. But not of guilt. She was too angry. Her feelings for Rose had been the nearest thing to true love she had ever felt for anybody, and she had believed that Rose had loved her back. But Rose hadn't. If she had she could never have betrayed her like that. She could never have lied like that. If Rose had never had a cousin named Jimmy, had she ever had one named Betty? Had anything she had ever said been true? Oh, Rose! She wept to think of the love which had been so horribly wasted. But she knew that if Rose were to walk in here now she'd scratch her eyes out.

To her surprise, she fell asleep – she had been emotionally exhausted by the events of the morning. Then she awoke, at just before twelve, to the discovery that she was really hungry. But no one had brought her any breakfast, nor did she suppose shouting and banging would do any good. She then thought of escaping. Although she was on an upstairs floor she knew she could knot her bed linen together and slide down it with the greatest of ease. Only she couldn't do that until she had had something to eat – and in any event she had nowhere to go. She began to weep again, in sheer miserable anger and frustration. Life had been so absolutely perfect, down to last night. Down to Rose's betrayal. Oh, Rose!

There came a tap on the door, and a moment later it

opened to admit Uncle Freddie. If he had come to add his condemnation . . . but he carried a plate of cheese and biscuits, and a glass of lemonade. "It's not much," he said. "But I thought you might be peckish. Mind if I come in?"

Alexandra shook her head, gazing at the food. Uncle Freddie came into the room and carefully locked the door behind him. "Your aunt telephoned me and told me what has happened. She wants you to fast for twenty-four hours," he said. "But we can't have that. Actually, she's gone out to bridge and thinks I'm at the office, so I sneaked back here."

Alexandra rose to her knees and chewed the biscuits and cheese; she had never tasted anything so good. "You mean you're not mad at me too?" she asked.

"Mad at you? How could I be mad at you, Alicky? What were you guilty of? Trying to have a bit of fun? Yet they expelled you. Well, schools are like that. Tell me, *did* you have any fun?" She frowned at him. "Oh, there's no need to be prudish," he told her. "I'm your uncle, aren't I? I'm talking about what you got up to with those boys. What did you do?"

"Well, we danced, and chatted . . ."

"Kissed?"

"Well . . ."

"Of course you did. And I bet you touched each other too."

Alexandra gazed at him.

"Aha," he said. "I can tell it. That's what the nuns are really mad at, you know. Sheer jealousy." Alexandra was sure he was wrong, but she wasn't going to risk arguing; right now, Uncle Freddie seemed the only friend she had. "Show me how the boys kissed you," he said. "Was it like this?" He lowered his head towards hers.

We can't, she thought: you're my uncle. But she was

still too afraid of antagonising him to turn her face away. He kissed her on the mouth, chastely at first, and then pushed his tongue inside. While he did that, his hands slid up and down her blouse, and came round in front to feel her breasts. "You have the most perfect body," he whispered. "Alicky, would you like to see me?"

Alexandra didn't know what to say, or do. Her problem was, while he was holding her in his arms, nothing else in the world mattered: she felt that she belonged, and she so wanted to belong, to someone – almost anyone. Uncle Freddie took off his shirt and kicked off his shoes. He dropped his socks on top of them and then his trousers. He wore long drawers which somehow looked absurd. But then he took them off as well, and Alexandra gasped; he was so much bigger than David, huge and round and filled with blood. "Doesn't scare you, does it?" Uncle Freddie asked.

Alexandra shook her head. It did, but she wasn't going to admit it. "Do you know what it's for? Apart from peeing, of course."

Alexandra gasped again. She had never altogether believed what Rose had told her, and she believed her even less, now; there was no way that huge thing could ever fit inside her. "Would you like to touch it?" Uncle Freddie asked.

Alexandra licked her lips, because she didn't, really. Not his. One of the boys last night, now . . . Uncle Freddie reached down for his pants, felt in the pocket, and took out a crumpled note. "A dollar," he said. "It's yours, Alix, if you touch it."

"You are just the most beautiful thing on two legs," Uncle Freddie told her, before leaving. "I'm going to come to see you again, next time Beryl is out. And you'll have another dollar."

But he never did, because Aunt Beryl took the key with her when next she was out, and only a few days later Alexandra was on her way up to the Rupununi, travelling with a friend of Aunt Beryl's named Miss Monkton. Alexandra had no idea what Aunt Beryl had told Miss Monkton, but it certainly included the fact that she had been expelled from the Convent, and Miss Monkton regarded her as some kind of evil spirit, judging by both her looks and her conversation; she was clearly very relieved when the ship reached Bartica and there was Father waiting for them.

Alexandra was terrified. The pleasure of playing with Uncle Freddie – and in fact she had enjoyed it once she had started – and having him play with her now seemed an enormously long way away. And what Father was going to say, or do, just didn't bear consideration. Amazingly, he didn't say, or do, anything. He had had her schoolbooks sent up from town as well, and when they got home he merely piled them on the table and said, "You will have to teach yourself from now on, I suppose. At least until I can make some arrangements."

Alexandra drew a long breath. "Couldn't you teach me, like you used to?" she asked.

Father gazed at her. "No," he said. "I don't think I have anything left to teach you, Alexandra."

Once he would have called her Alix, and she realised that she was being punished far more severely than if he had taken his belt to her and then put her on bread and water, because he had withdrawn entirely, drunk or sober. Now she was completely isolated, utterly alone. She longed for Uncle Freddie to pay a visit to the ranch, sure that they would be able to get away together on at least one occasion, but he never did. She had been abandoned by everyone. She turned more than ever in upon herself, spent long days in or by the pool where she had taken David, dreaming the most fantastic adventures, in which she was the heroine, and men, and women, sought to worship at her body.

Strange, she wrote later, *how one can make all one's dreams come true, if one has sufficient determination.*

It was during Christmas of 1914, just after her fourteenth birthday, that Father told her he had arranged for her to return to Georgetown. "I'm afraid neither Aunt Beryl nor the Convent will have you back," he told her, carefully avoiding looking at her. "However, the Girl's High School will accept you . . . as a day girl," he added hastily. "They don't take boarders, anyway. They do not know why you had to leave the Convent, although presumably there have been rumours, so I think it would be very unwise of you to discuss what happened with anyone. I also think it would be very unwise for you to, ah, form any close friendships." He was blushing terribly, it was the first time he had ever actually referred to what had happened. It was only later that Alexandra realised that the nuns might have known more of her relationship with Rose than she had imagined.

"I won't," she promised. "But where shall I stay?"

"I have arranged for you to live with a Mrs Baird. She runs a boarding house on Middle Street, and is prepared to take you into her charge. I'm afraid I have had to put Mrs Baird entirely in the picture, Alexandra. She has promised not to refer to the matter unless forced to do so, but I have also given her complete powers as a mother, if required. Whether she uses them or not is up to you. I must now tell you, Alexandra, that you and I are going to be separated for a few months. I am going to return to England on the first available ship."

"To England?" she shouted. "Oh, can't I come with you, please?"

"No, you cannot," Father told her. "Things are not going to be very nice over there for a while. I don't suppose you understand what is happening, but we are fighting a war with the Germans."

Alexandra had no idea what he was talking about. People didn't fight wars nowadays. At least, not the English. Except against the Indians and people in Africa.

"So I feel I must do my bit," Father went on. "I shouldn't think it will last very long, and then, when I come back, we'll have a long talk about your future. But until then, do please try to be a good girl."

The fact that this was the first time he had actually referred to what had happened was submerged by the stunning news that he was going away and leaving her. To fight in a war? His speech left Alexandra feeling as if a horse had trodden on her. She was, of course, delighted to be returning to Georgetown, but she could not help but suspect that she was in fact being sent to some kind of prison.

Actually, it did not turn out like that at all. Mrs Baird was a small, gray-haired widow, who clearly had what was known as "coloured" ancestry, but who was extremely pleasant, though she could be quite sharp with her servants, and any of her boarders who got out of line. These were mainly young men working in offices in town. Obviously after what Father had told her, Mrs Baird insisted on locking Alexandra's bedroom door every night and taking away the key, and there were bars on her window. This was certainly somewhat like being incarcerated in a cell, but Alexandra didn't mind; she didn't like any of the young men anyway. She had been hoping that as she was in town she might be able to see Uncle Freddie again. When one day he passed her on the street he pretended he didn't see her, and only a few weeks later Mrs Baird told her that Mr and

Mrs Mayne had also left the colony for England, because of the war.

So that was that. She had been deserted by her only living relatives. She had never been able to consider any of the Amerindians as relatives – and she was damned by everyone who knew anything about her. And everyone who didn't know, as well, it turned out. Her appearance at the Girl's High School caused a minor sensation, as apparently it was fairly common knowledge that she had been expelled from the Convent, but as no one had any idea of the real reason, it was generally supposed she had been caught stealing. This did not make her new schoolmates particularly pleased to see her, and some were quite pointed about removing their pencils and erasers from her reach. As she thus found it impossible to make friends with any of them, Alexandra entered into the most lonely period of her life. Had it not been for her dreams, in which she could indulge to her heart's content in the locked privacy of her tiny bedroom at Mrs Baird's boarding house, she would have been utterly miserable.

But she was pretty miserable in any event, until the day, late in 1915, that she again encountered David Lamb.

Alexandra was bicycling home from school one day – her bicycle, bought for her by Mrs Baird with some of the money Father had left for her upkeep, was her proudest possession – when she heard boys whistling at her. Boys often did this, because bicycling into an afternoon sea breeze, which could be quite strong, made it next to impossible to control her skirt, and if her heavy green gymslip adequately concealed the upper half of her body, the flying skirt revealed her legs. Normally she made a practice of ignoring them, and none of them had actually ever attempted to speak to her until today, when this boy, as tall as she was, rode his bike alongside her. "Hi," he said. Alexandra gave him a cold glance and continued peddling.

"I suppose you don't remember me," he said. "I'm David Lamb. I met you, at your father's ranch in the Rupununi. Years ago," he added. Alexandra slowed and shot him another glance. David Lamb! How he had grown. "You're so grown-up now," David commented. "Gosh, you must be fifteen years old."

"I am fourteen years old," Alexandra told him.

"I'm sixteen." She wondered if he remembered that day by the pool? How long ago that seemed, when she thought of everything that had happened since. But of course he remembered that day, or he would not have remembered her. Anyway, he was blushing as he looked at her. "I . . . well, it would be just terrific if you and I could . . . see each other," he ventured.

"I'm not allowed to go out with boys," Alexandra said, but she stopped peddling and slid off her seat; Mrs Baird's house was just round the corner.

"Oh. I thought . . . if you were to go to the Botanical Gardens on Saturday morning . . ." He hesitated, gazing at her. While she gazed back. Shades of Rose. She had no idea what had become of Rose, and she had been afraid to ask. Now he wanted the same thing. She wondered if he was as big as Uncle Freddie, if he would respond the same way, and was suddenly desperate to find out. More important, it would mean she had found a friend. How she wanted a friend; she didn't really care whether it was a girl or a boy. "We could meet, and go for a walk, and . . ." He hesitated again.

"I might be able to get away," Alexandra said.

"Well . . . I'll be there, under the clock, at nine o'clock on Saturday morning. Will you come?"

"I might," Alexandra said again.

* * *

Alexandra was in the habit of going to the library on Saturday mornings. Mrs Baird entirely approved of this, not only because she approved of young girls broadening their minds by reading suitable books, but because the head librarian, Miss Roarke, was a friend of hers. The following Saturday she went to the library as usual, changed a book, and then peddled as fast as she could up Brickdam to the Gardens, arriving only five minutes late. Waiting for her under the clock on the park keeper's office, was David. As one of the park keepers was also there, sweeping up leaves, she cycled straight past them without even a glance, but soon turned down her favourite leafy lane, where she had gone with Rose, and knew he would follow her.

When she had reached an entirely secluded arbour, she got off her bike and leaned it against a tree, heart pounding pleasantly. She had no idea what he had in mind, but just to have, once again, a private friend, a secret relationship, was exciting. He rode his bike through the trees, saw her, and got off. "Gosh," he said. "That was smart. I didn't know what to do about that fellow."

"I'm sure he didn't suspect a thing," Alexandra said.

David leaned his bike against hers and stood in front of her, gazing at her. As it was a Saturday morning she was not in uniform, but instead wore a blue skirt, with a white blouse, and a little tie, with a smart little panama hat; her hair was prevented from blowing all over the place by a blue ribbon tied on the nape of her neck – she wore plaits to school but Mrs Baird allowed her to leave it loose on weekends. "Gosh," he said at last. "You have grown." He was staring at the swell of her blouse.

"So have you," she countered. The small talk of love was something she knew nothing about.

"You're so . . . so lovely," he said, flushing.

"Would you like to kiss me?" she asked.

"Oh, gosh, could I?"

"Of course. We're old friends, remember?"

He came closer, and stood against her. As he didn't seem to know what to do next, she put a hand on each of his cheeks and drew his face to hers; they were about the same height. His mouth was closed when their lips touched, and didn't open until he realised hers was – then she took his tongue into her mouth and discovered it wasn't half as big or as questing as Uncle Freddie's, but rather timid. On the other hand, he tasted much more pleasant. "Gosh," he said again, when she ran out of breath and released him.

"Don't you like kissing me?" she asked.

She held him close again, and put her arms round his neck. He responded, and they hugged each other. Now she could feel him poking against her, and she waited for his hands to move down to her buttocks, but they stayed clasped round her shoulders until they again ran out of breath. "Gosh," he said again. "I'm so glad we got together. I've seen you, several times, on the street, but I never had the nerve to speak to you before."

"I'm glad you did, this time. I always liked you." She gazed into his eyes, and he flushed again.

"Gosh, well . . . shall we sit down?"

"If you like." She smoothed the earth and then her skirt as she sat, legs stretched in front of her so that her boots were revealed and even a trace of stocking – Mrs Baird insisted she wear stockings no matter how hot the day, but here beneath the huge trees it was actually quite cool, and so quiet, with only the occasional bird cry above them.

David sat beside her. "I've heard your father has gone away to fight," he said. "He must be awfully brave."

"Yes," Alexandra said.

"As soon as I'm eighteen, I'm going to go and join up too," David declared.

"Are you? But that won't be for two years," Alexandra said. "The war can't still be going on in two years."

"My father thinks it could be."

"Good Lord!" Even if Father hadn't written her, and had seemed glad to be rid of her, she still wanted him to come back as soon as possible. "Do you really want to go and fight? Mrs Baird tells me it's not very nice – even if you don't get killed."

"I think it's something I should do," David said, earnestly.

They gazed at each other some more, and his gaze kept dropping to her blouse. She knew it was simply a matter of who made the first move, and she knew too that it would have to be her; she simply had no idea how to form a relationship which wasn't in the first place physical. "Do you remember that day by the pool?" She bit her lip. "I was very rude, wasn't I?"

"Yes," he said seriously. "You were."

"And you were afraid," she riposted. "Are you still afraid?"

"Of course I'm not afraid."

"Well, then, would you like to see my titties?" she asked. "I didn't have any, last time."

"Oh, gosh," he said. "Could I? I mean, would you let me?"

Alexandra began to unbutton her blouse. "I might," she said. "If you'll show me your thing."

"Oh, gosh," he said again.

"There can't be anything wrong with it," she explained. "Because we've seen each other before. Let's see how much we've changed."

David licked his lips. "All right. But you must promise not to touch."

Alexandra made a moue. "All right."

"You first," he said.

"But you promise, after."

"Yes," he said. She didn't think he was going to be able to change his mind; his pants had the most tremendous bulge. She finished unbuttoning her blouse, and pulled it out of her waistband. She didn't take it off, not in the Botanical Gardens, but she pulled her petticoat from her waistband as well, and lifted it up to her neck. "Oh, gosh," he said. "Oh, gosh."

"Don't you like them?" She touched her nipples with her fingertips, and they hardened; they had been hardening anyway, with excitement.

"They're just . . . just marvellous," he said.

"Well, you can touch them if you like," she suggested.

"Oh . . . could I?" He held them, cautiously, as he might have taken a pair of cricket balls into his hands. Then he let them go.

"Oh, not so quick," she protested. "Why don't you play with them? You could suck them."

He raised his head. "You mean girls really like that?"

"Of course they do. I do, anyway."

He licked his lips, and played with her nipples, taking them between his fingers and gently squeezing and pulling them; she felt she was going to burst, but then he suddenly squeezed too hard. "Oh," she said, and pulled down her petticoat. "You mustn't hurt."

"I'm sorry. Alexandra, you said I could suck them."

She had changed her mind about that; he might just bite. "After you've shown me your thing," she said.

"But . . . I can't take my pants off, here."

"You don't have to. Just unbutton them and push it out so I can see it." Still he hesitated. "Would you like me to do it for you?" she asked.

"No," he said, and unbuttoned his flies. He fumbled

inside, having to twist his body, his penis was such a size, but finally he got it out. It was even lovelier than she remembered, far nicer than Uncle Freddie's, and absolutely glowing with red blood. "Oh," she said, and dropped to her knees before him.

"No," he said, holding it with both hands himself. "You promised."

"But I let you touch me," she protested.

"I didn't touch you there."

"Then I'll let you. If you let me touch you."

"Do it first," he said.

Alexandra scrambled to her feet. "That's not fair. That's not . . . gosh, there's someone coming."

Desperately David thrust his penis back into his trousers, and Alexandra tucked her petticoat back into her waistband and scrabbled for the buttons on her blouse. But she hadn't got them all buttoned up when the park keeper appeared, pushing a wheelbarrow. He looked at them, grinned, and looked away again.

"Oh, lord," David said.

"He isn't going to say anything to anybody." Alexandra hesitated over her last two buttons.

"But suppose he was looking at us?"

"Then he was a peeping tom."

David was not reassured. "I have to go." He went to the bikes.

"You are the most treacherous beast I have ever known," Alexandra declared.

He turned. "Me?"

"I let you feel my titties, and now you just want to go off."

"I . . . I just couldn't let you, now." He certainly looked scared. "Not now. But Alexandra, I would. If . . ." He licked his lips. "If you'd let me put him inside."

She stared at him. "Do what?"

. . . they'd have to be friends forever after that. "What do I do?" she asked.

"You'll have to take your drawers off," he said. "And lie down. I have to lie on top of you, you see," he explained.

"Oh." She hadn't thought of that. "Suppose the park keeper comes back?"

"You said he wouldn't."

So she had, and she realised she didn't care if he did; they'd just tell him to go away again. But . . . "I'll get dirt up my bottom."

"No, you won't. You'll lie on your skirt, see."

"Oh," she said humbly. She hesitated for a moment, then raised her skirt and pulled her drawers down. When she let them go they fell about her ankles, and she stepped out of them.

"Now you sit down, and then lie down, and raise your skirt," David explained. "The front of it."

"Yes," she agreed, and obeyed. She gathered her drawers into a ball to place under her head, took off her straw hat, and cautiously lay on the warm earth, then raised her skirt. It was the first time since she had left the Rupununi that she had exposed herself in the open air, and somehow doing it when still fully dressed seemed far more exciting that just being naked.

She watched David release his trousers and let them drop, and then follow them with his drawers. He was drooping slightly from the tremendous hardness of a few minutes before, but was starting to lift again as he looked at her thick pubic bush; she was utterly fascinated – to have a part of one's body which had a life, even a will, of its own, as this seemed to do . . .

He knelt between her legs . . . and a twig cracked.

Alexandra sat up so quickly that she bumped into David

and knocked him over, while she pulled her skirt down to her ankles, drawing up her legs as she did so. And stared at a black face, looking down on her from the bushes. “Girl,” the face said. “You ain’ know you are wort’less?”

Alexandra was too horror-stricken to speak. David had risen to his knees again and was frantically dragging up his pants, but now another black boy appeared from the bushes, and pushed him over. He gasped and rolled in the dust. Alexandra’s first reaction had been to tell them to go away – but now she suddenly realised that something terrible was going to happen. She opened her mouth to scream, and a hand closed over it; she had not noticed the third man behind her. “You just keep quiet, eh?” he said. “Or we’ll hurt your friend.” Alexandra gasped. The hand was very strong, and was hurting *her*; it also smelt unpleasant. “Now, you watch,” the man said.

The man who had pushed David over held a machete, known locally as a cutlass, a two-foot-six-inch long cutting knife which all labourers carried – she realised that each of the black men had one. But the man holding her, she realised, was white, even if he looked a labourer, like his friends. “So you do just like I say,” this man told her, “or we’ll cut your friend’s prick right off.” Now it was David’s turn to gasp. The fingers relaxed, and Alexandra could breathe again, but she could still taste him on her tongue. “Please,” she said.

“You can beg,” the white man said. “Fix him up,” he told his companions.

They grinned, and took David’s pants and drawers off; he was too terrified to resist them. Then they dragged him against a tree, still sitting, pulled his arms behind him, round the trunk, and tied his wrists together with his belt. When they were finished he was absolutely helpless.

"You watch," the man kneeling beside Alexandra said again. "We'll let you have her after."

Alexandra screamed.

CHAPTER 2

Alexandra writes: *There will be some who will say I got what I deserved. But no woman ever deserves to be raped. All I was looking for was companionship, someone with whom I could share the turmoil that was my brain and my body. Maybe I had been looking too hard.*

The police inspector was a white man who attempted to look friendly, but didn't quite make it. Mrs Baird wasn't looking all that friendly either, and neither was the doctor who had examined Alexandra. It had been the most horrifying ordeal of her life, and it seemed to have been going on forever. Without an end in sight. The Inspector was looking at his open notebook. "Three men, one white and two black, isn't much to go on," he remarked. "It's an unlikely combination, anyway."

"They were friends of the park keeper," Alexandra said, for the third time. "He told them where we were. I know he did."

"But you say he wasn't one of them."

"No. But he told them we were there. And . . ." her voice faded away, because they were all staring at her, she sank lower in the bed and pulled the sheet to her throat.

"We have to know what you were doing there," the Inspector said. "You and this Lamb boy."

"We . . . we were talking," Alexandra said.

"You, and a boy?" Mrs Baird was scandalised. "Alone in the Gardens? You told me you were going to the library."

"I did. But then I went to the Gardens."

"Why?"

"Well, to meet David. We're old friends," Alexandra said anxiously. "His father knows my father."

Mrs Baird did not look convinced.

"You must have been," the Inspector agreed. "Why were his pants off? That is the most concrete evidence we have. *He* could be charged with statutary rape."

"Of course you can't charge David," Alexandra cried. She didn't want to see David again, as long as she lived, but she didn't want him to go to gaol, especially as he hadn't done anything. "He was tied up. So was I, when . . . when the men left. The park keeper untied us."

"He is a little vague about that," the Inspector said. "That isn't really what he said."

"Because he was lying. Because he's a friend of the three men." Alexandra began to weep, and the doctor intervened. "I really think she should rest now," he said. "Whoever was responsible, she has had a terrible ordeal."

They trooped off, and she was left alone. To wish she was dead. All the pleasure, the enjoyment, the glory, she had felt for her body had been ripped away. She knew she would never be able to touch herself again without shuddering. She didn't even want to think about herself. Her entire life had been ruined. In more ways than one. The Inspector returned once, with a handwritten document which purported to be everything she had said, asked her to read it, and if she agreed it was accurate, to sign it. She did so, and he went away. She never saw him again.

The doctor returned, also once, to give her another

examination. Although there had been a fair amount of bleeding, she had not apparently been seriously harmed. As for anything else . . . he stroked his chin, and said, "We'll just have to wait and see."

Alexandra had no idea what he meant. But Mrs Baird looked even more severe than usual. There could be no doubt that she regarded Alexandra as responsible for the whole business. "I have written your father," she said. "I will, of course, keep you here until I get a reply. But I think you had better stay in your room."

There was no suggestion of her returning to school, Alexandra noted. Presumably the Girl's High School too was now on the list of places where she was not wanted. It was all so unfair – although she had no desire to face any of her schoolmates either, not with the story of her rape having been in the newspapers. But no one even sent her a card of sympathy. Not even Rose. At least Mrs Baird relaxed slightly when a fortnight later she menstruated. "Well, thank God for that," she remarked.

She had collected Alexandra's books from school and suggested that she do some studying on her own, but clearly she was only waiting to hear from Father. However, some two months passed before she got a reply to her letter, and then it was from Aunt Beryl, who informed her that Jonathan Mayne was serving in some theatre with the unpronounceable name of Mesopotamia, and that she had no idea when she would be able to contact him. *As for that wretched girl*, Aunt Beryl wrote – Mrs Baird showed Alexandra the letter – *I am afraid that as my brother-in-law placed you in charge of her, a position you accepted, you will have to make your own decisions until this ghastly war ends and Mr Mayne can resume his responsibilities.*

Mrs Baird looked very thoughtful when she read that latter, and it was only a month later, just before

Christmas, and after Alexandra's uncelebrated fifteenth birthday, that she came into her room, sat down, and said, "Mr Lowndes wants to marry you."

Alexandra was totally taken aback. During her four months' incarceration, her only contact with the outside world, apart from Mrs Baird and her servants, had been with the various lodgers in the boarding house. These young men, all British ex-patriots or the sons of planting families, had shown her great sympathy, and some had even from time to time sat and talked with her in the garden, where she took what exercise she could. They had talked about the War, and the weather, and the War, and the weather, scrupulously avoiding the one subject they all obviously wanted to talk about: Alexandra's rape. Mr Lowndes had certainly been one of them, perhaps, now Alexandra came to think about it, the most persistent of them in seeking her company. He was a thin man, hardly taller than her, with sandy hair and a sandy moustache, who worked as a clerk in one of the Georgetown companies . . . "Marry me?" she asked incredulously.

"He seems to have taken quite a liking to you," Mrs Baird pointed out. "And I cannot help but feel it would be the answer to all our . . . all your problems."

"But I can't marry Mr Lowndes," Alexandra protested.

"Of course you can," Mrs Baird assured her. "I know you are still very young, but you are in your sixteenth year, and you probably know as much about . . . well, *that* sort of thing as most girls of twenty."

"But I don't *know* him," Alexandra cried.

"Well, one seldom gets to know a man until after one is married to him. But as I have said, the important thing is that he knows about you, and therefore if he still wants to marry you, he must be very fond of you. But there is an even more important reason for you to marry him, in my opinion: he is leaving British Guiana."

"Leaving here?" The whole thing was making less and less sense to Alexandra.

"So he can take you with him. He is quite prepared to do that."

Alexandra didn't want to leave Guiana. Whatever had happened, this was her home.

"He'll take you to England," Mrs Baird said triumphantly. "He's going to join the army, you see. So you'll be given a home in England – I believe his parents are quite well off. And there you can see your father when he comes home from Mesopotamia. Your father will like Mr Lowndes, I'm sure. And of course, once you're married, well, all your troubles will be over." She smiled brightly. "Won't they? Now you really must agree this is the best possible thing for you, Alexandra. Indeed, I think you have been a most remarkably fortunate young woman, in view of everything. So I suggest you put on a great big happy smile, and go downstairs, and when he proposes, say yes."

Alexandra wanted to scream. The transparent way in which Mrs Baird was happily washing her hands of the embarrassment of being responsible for her was disgusting. But so was the idea of marriage. Marriage would mean that Mr Lowndes would have the right to touch her, and she didn't ever wanted to be touched again by a man – or a woman – as long as she lived. But she didn't see how she was going to escape it: Mrs Baird had obviously made up her mind. And if it would take her back to Father – she could always run away from Mr Lowndes. So she got up and arranged her features into as pleasant an expression as she could – and then remembered that she didn't even know his Christian name!

* * *

Harry kissed her after she accepted his proposal. She had assumed that accepting his offer of marriage would give him the right to do much more than that, but to her great relief he made no attempt to do anything save hold her hand, although he kissed her once or twice more. They were chaste kisses, and she was almost reassured.

But even if engaged, they did not spend a lot of time together, because there was so much to be done. In view of the slightly irregular situation, Mrs Baird opted against a church wedding, and instead arranged one for her own drawing room; the only guests were her other boarders. But there were clothes to be bought, and made, on which Mrs Baird spent the last of the money Father had left her, and other things to be done . . . Mr Lowndes was leaving for England right after Christmas. "To go and fight?" Alexandra asked him. "I don't understand why you should want to do that."

"It's my duty," he told her. "I, we, all thought the War couldn't last more than a year, and it seemed pretty pointless rushing home if it was going to be over by the time we got there. But now it seems as if it's going to last a good time yet."

Alexandra wondered if, after all, David would get to fight too? But she didn't think he had the guts, not after the way he had cringed before the three men who had raped her.

"Don't worry." Misinterpreting her expression, Mr Lowndes squeezed her hand. "You'll be well taken care of. My mother will just adore you. So will my sisters."

"Do they know about me?"

He grinned. "They don't even know you exist, as yet. I'm going to surprise them."

"Oh," she said, not at all sure that was the wisest course. But it was his family, and he was going to be her husband. And if it meant that she would actually belong to a family . . . the idea quite grew on her as the wedding approached. It was to take place on the very day the ship was sailing, so that they would honeymoon right across the Atlantic. She found that prospect exciting, and in fact her revulsion for the idea of Mr Lowndes actually touching her was beginning to fade, as the memory of the rape faded. He was so very polite in everything he did.

There was champagne with the wedding breakfast, which made her quite tipsy, so that she was more cheerful than she had been for a long time. She submitted to being hugged and kissed by the other guests, even by Mrs Baird, and then rode in a hansom cab with Mr Lowndes down to Stabroek, where the steamer lay alongside the dock, loading sugar, which gave off a sweet smell that quite overlaid the afternoon. The steamer was actually a freighter, and only carried twelve passengers. The other ten were already on board, and consisted of young men also on their way to join the army. When they discovered they were to have an extraordinarily beautiful young woman accompanying them – for at fifteen Alexandra was an eye-stopper – tall, elegant, with a golden-brown body, and long, wavy, midnight hair, and huge blue eyes and her meticulously carved features – they were delighted, even if she was honeymooning.

Alexandra and Mr Lowndes were shown straight to their cabin, which had two somewhat narrow berths, and where, once the steward had left, Mr Lowndes took her in his arms and gave her a proper kiss, but still very gently, stroking her hair and holding her close. Then, just as she was bracing herself for what might be coming next, he held her hand and said, "Come on deck, and we'll wave old BG goodbye."

She had forgotten about that, and found herself weeping as the sirens blew, and the crowds on the dockside clapped, and the steamer was nudged away from the dock by the single tug – really only a large launch with padded bows – and the engines began to throb, the brown water astern churned into white, and she made her way downriver, accompanied by the pilot boat. "Always sad, leaving one's home," Mr Lowndes said. "But I'm taking you to your real home."

"Are you?" she asked, warming to him every moment.

Dinner would not be served until seven-thirty, they were told, and it was still only four in the afternoon. They stayed on deck for another half an hour, watching the roofs of the houses disappearing behind the mangroves while they drank tea provided by the steward, then they looked at each other. "Shall we go below for a spell?" Mr Lowndes asked.

She nodded, and they went down the stairs. He took her hand and she held his fingers very tightly. She was realising with a growing feeling of contentment that this union was now legal. She and Mr Lowndes were entitled to be alone together, to make love to each other . . . and suddenly she was excited again, her fears forgotten, and her nightmares too.

He locked the cabin door. "Don't want the jolly old steward barging in on us, do we?" he said.

Alexandra sat on the nearest bunk, because as it emerged from the river mouth the ship was commencing to roll slightly.

"Well," Mr Lowndes said, somewhat uncertainly. "Perhaps we should get undressed."

"Oh," she said. "Yes." She stooped to unlace her boots, her hair, which Mrs Baird had carefully pinned up for the ceremony, falling down over her ears. Then she took off her dress and petticoat, half turned away from him, not looking at him, her modesty by no means an act. She laid her clothes across the one chair in the cabin, which faced the dressing table-cum-desk between the two bunks, then slid down her drawers. As she stooped to retrieve them from round her ankles, he touched her buttocks, and she straightened with a jerk.

"I'm so sorry, Alexandra." he said. "You are so beautiful."

She laid the drawers on top of her other clothes and turned to face him, stared into his eyes as he took her in his arms and held her close to kiss her, because he was naked too. His hands wandered over her shoulder blades and down her back, slowly and lightly, caressed her buttocks again, and then released her. "I must be the luckiest man in the world," he said. "When I think of those brutes . . ."

It was the first mistake he had made, and it was less traumatic than she had expected. "I've tried to forget about them," she said. "And think only about you."

The next few days were sheer delight, as Alexandra discovered that she could, after all, still feel, and that kindness and gentleness could eliminate even the memory of that terrible day in the Gardens. They made love on every possible occasion, at least three times a day, his delight in her beauty being matched by hers in having such a splendid male body to play with. They rapidly overcame their mutual shyness, and on only their fourth coupling Alexandra had an orgasm. This alarmed Mr Lowndes at first, although once he realised she was not in pain he was delighted; he confessed that he had no idea women ever felt "anything like that", which, as he was really very old – at least twice her age, Alexandra estimated, which made him over thirty – seemed very strange. But, she reflected, maybe Englishwomen *didn't* feel "anything like that". The only Englishwoman with whom she had ever come into close contact had been Aunt Beryl – and according to Uncle Freddie she most definitely had never felt anything at all.

Alexandra bloomed as the voyage progressed, was always surrounded when she appeared in the tiny saloon, by officers as well as passengers, and adored their adoration. This made up for a definite change in the weather. The blue skies and sparkling seas of the Caribbean slowly changed to grey clouds and even more leaden waves, while the temperature began to drop. "We'll buy you some warm clothes as soon as we land," Mr Lowndes promised, wrapping her in his own topcoat to walk the deck. The topcoat had a cashmere lining and was quite the warmest garment Alexandra had ever worn.

The next night it actually snowed. Alexandra didn't see it, and she was amazed when in the morning she found traces of the white powder all over the decks. "Hardly to be wondered at," remarked the Captain, who had by now joined her constant circle of admirers. "We'll be in the Solent tomorrow morning."

She became very excited, almost too excited to make love that afternoon, as Mr Lowndes realised, so they just lay together in the warmth of their bunk, naked, until Alexandra dosed off, to awake to screaming horror. She had no idea what had happened, although she knew it had been a loud bang that had startled her. But the cabin was at an angle and the ship's siren was blowing while the funnel was letting off steam, and there was a great deal of shouting. "Quick, on deck, we're sinking!" shouted Mr Lowndes, pulling her out of bed and wrapping her in the topcoat again.

"I have to dress," Alexandra protested. Since the rape she had lost all desire to cavort in the nude, and she didn't like the idea of going on deck clad only in a coat, even if it was several sizes too large for her and came down to her ankles. But Mr Lowndes was already pushing her through the doorway. She staggered down the sloping corridor, gained the stairs, and crawled up them, holding on to the rail, because the angle was acute. She reached what had been the saloon, but that was now a shambles of broken crockery and frightened men. The fact that she was the only woman helped, because she was handed through the crowd on to the deck, and then half thrown into a lifeboat, which immediately began sliding down the ship's side into the sea. She looked up at the ship, heeling alarmingly, at the frightened faces above her, mouths wide as they shouted, at men jumping into the water, steam issuing from the funnels, and looked frantically left and right to the men on either side of her . . . and realised that none of them was Mr Lowndes.

Alexandra screamed and screamed and screamed. She tried to jump overboard to swim back to the ship, and was prevented by the men around her. She watched the ship slip beneath the waves in a welter of foam, to be replaced by heaving sea, and a bobble of flotsam, including human bodies, wearing lifejackets, but motionless in the water. "Poor devils," one of the sailors said. "That water is so cold they never stood a chance."

Mr Lowndes might have been one of those – if he had got on deck at all, Alexandra realised. She hadn't seen him from the moment he had pushed her out of the cabin, and had assumed he was right behind her. But he hadn't been. Poor Mr Lowndes. But it seemed likely that she would soon join him, wherever he was. She was wearing only his topcoat, and she had never suspected it was possible to be so cold. She lost all feeling in her toes and fingers and nipples and nose, huddled to herself, and made no objection when one of the men put his arm round her and hugged her. There had been two lifeboats that got away, perhaps forty people in all, very nearly the entire ship's complement. But not Mr Lowndes. Alexandra wept, great tears rolling down her cheeks. "She was honeymooning," one of the men said, as if they didn't all know that. "Poor kid."

Darkness fell and it became colder yet. Alexandra nestled against the man holding her, whimpering with discomfort. He held her close and massaged her shoulders and hair, and at some time during the night he put his hand inside the topcoat. She didn't try to stop him, it felt so good; she even fell asleep and dreamed that he was Mr Lowndes. When she awoke it was light again, and they looked at each other in consternation. "I'm most terribly sorry," he said. "I was trying to help."

"You did," Alexandra told him. "I think you saved my life."

Everyone else was very excited because they could see smoke, and soon a destroyer was circling them and, after making sure the submarine was no longer in the vicinity, stopped to let them climb up the net draped down the sides. Alexandra was too cold and numb to climb, so they lowered a rope basket and winched her on deck, from where she was hurried down to a cabin, a place of starched white sheets and the most magnificent warmth. Her topcoat was taken away by a solicitous medical orderly and she was tucked beneath the sheets and given a glass of brandy to drink. With her senses reeling she gazed at the ship's doctor, who pulled away the sheet to examine her. Like everyone else, he said: "Poor child."

The countess writes: *I was never in love with Harry Lowndes. He represented warmth and security, and I needed that, which made his death the more of a tragedy for me. The strange thing is that but for that torpedo I might very well have spent the rest of my life as a contented housewife! I didn't want anything more than that, then.*

The survivors of the topedoed freighter were put ashore in Portsmouth that evening. Alexandra spent the next forty-eight hours in bed, suffering from exhaustion and exposure . . . and shock. For the first time in her life since Father had first taken her to Georgetown she had felt, on the ship, that she belonged – to Mr Lowndes. Now Mr Lowndes was dead.

There were questions, from a hard-faced woman in uniform who did her best to be sympathetic but to whom Alexandra was obviously just another statistic. "Lowndes," she said. "It's not an uncommon name. You'll have to give me your husband's English address so that I can get in touch with his family."

"I don't know his address," Alexandra said.

"You don't know your husband's address?" The woman was scandalised.

"We only got married the day the ship sailed," Alexandra confessed.

"But you must know the names of his mother and father . . . brothers and sisters?" she asked, her expression slowly hardening.

"I don't."

"How very odd," the woman commented, managing to put a load of hidden feeling into the three words. "Then you'll have to go to your own relatives. You do have relatives?"

"I have a father."

"In British Guiana?"

"Oh, no. He's in the Army. In Meso . . . something."

"The Middle East Theatre," the woman said, writing it down. "And his name is?"

"Jonathan Mayne. That's my real name, Alexandra Mayne."

"If you are married, your real name is Lowndes," the woman pointed out, now definitely suspicious. "Where is your wedding ring?"

But there had never been a wedding ring. Mr Lowndes had borrowed Mrs Baird's for the ceremony, and given it back afterwards. He had been going to buy her one in England, he had said. But this woman wouldn't understand that. "I lost it," Alexandra said. "When the ship went down."

"It's all very odd," the woman said again. "Well, I will see if contact can be made with your father. But he is rather a long way away, at the moment. Is there no one at all nearer at hand who can look after you?"

"Well . . . there's Aunt Beryl, I suppose," Alexandra said sadly.

"Torpedoed? Married?" Aunt Beryl was even more scandalised than the nurse. "You really are the most appalling child, Alexandra. How on earth could you be married? You're only fifteen!"

"I shall be sixteen this year," Alexandra pointed out, with dignity. "And it was Mrs Baird's idea."

"Dreadful woman! I always knew your father was making a mistake, putting you in her care. I mean to say, a half . . ." she regarded Alexandra and changed her mind about what she had been going to say. "But what were you doing on a ship to be torpedoed?"

"I was coming to England, with Mr Lowndes. My husband," Alexandra explained, with great patience. "We were going to live in England, with his family."

"Then why aren't you with them now?" Aunt Beryl demanded.

"That's the trouble," Alexandra said. "I don't know where they are."

Aunt Beryl started to look as suspicious as the hard-faced nursing sister; they could in fact, have *been* sisters. "You do *have* a marriage certificate?" she asked.

"Well, we did, But it went down with the ship."

"A passport?"

"I was on Mr Lowndes' passport. That must have gone down with the ship as well."

"Oh, my God! This really is impossible. What am I going to do with you?"

"Do you think you could let me lie down?" Alexandra asked. "I'm not feeling very well."

She was still suffering from shock, and had caught a bad cold; that evening she had a temperature and Aunt Beryl had to call a doctor. Alexandra was in bed for a week as bronchitis developed, and even afterwards was very weak for several more weeks. Aunt Beryl had no choice but to put up with it. Alexandra even sympathised with her, because she was living alone – Uncle Freddie was in France with the army – and she didn't seem to have many friends. That was reasonable, in view of Aunt Beryl's character, but apparently she didn't have any relatives either, close at hand; they were all up in the north of the country and Alexandra gathered that Aunt Beryl wasn't all that popular with them for running off and marrying a "colonial". Aunt Beryl seemed to have made a proper mess of her life. But then, Alexandra realised, so had she, although she suspected she had had more fun doing it than Aunt Beryl. But fun had to be paid for.

Alexandra was just feeling really well again, as the weather began to warm up a little, and was beginning to listen seriously to Aunt Beryl's strictures that she would simply have to get a job or join the Women's

Army or something, and becoming quite enthusiastic about the idea, when she began to feel sick all over again. It took Aunt Beryl very little time to realise that her niece was pregnant. "Oh, my God!" she shouted. "I am being punished. Punished!"

Alexandra couldn't understand why she was so upset. *She* was the one being punished. But Aunt Beryl became quite feverish, and started putting advertisements in *The Times*: *Will the parents of the late Henry Lowndes, drowned 27 January 1916, please contact this address, urgently*. She never received a reply.

That was the most miserable year of Alexandra's life. The summer seemed hardly any warmer than the winter – how she longed to feel just a little Guianese heat on her back – and she grew larger and larger. The war seemed to be going very badly; even the Royal Navy failed to defeat the German fleet, and the government fell. Then news arrived that an entire British army had been forced to surrender at an unlikely place called Kut, and amongst them was Captain Jonathan Mayne. "A prisoner of the Turks," Aunt Beryl moaned. "We'll never see him again."

To cap it all, Uncle Freddie came home from the front on leave and looked at Alexandra as if she were a complete stranger. In fact, he looked at everyone, even Aunt Beryl, as if they were strangers, but Alexandra, who had been hoping for some sympathetic company, was intensely disappointed.

The baby was born in October, in the middle of a storm of wind and rain. Aunt Beryl ordered a taxi to take them to the hospital, and for a week Alexandra was quite comfortable, well looked after by the nurses, who sympathised with her widowhood, and having no trouble at all with the delivery of a seven-and-a-half pound baby girl. "What are you going to call her?" Sister asked.

"Call her?" Alexandra hadn't thought of calling her anything.

"She's a little human being, Mrs Lowndes. She must have a name."

"Oh. Ah . . ." Desperately she thought. The female equivalent of Henry was presumably Henrietta, and she didn't like that. "I shall call her Mayne," she announced triumphantly.

"Mayne?" Sister was scandalised. "That's not a name."

"Of course it is. It's my father's name."

"It's not a girl's name," Sister insisted.

"It's going to be my girl's name," Alexandra said with equal determination. Mayne Lowndes: she thought it sounded rather special.

Aunt Beryl was equally horrified. "You are the most impossible child," she remarked. "I have never heard of such a thing. I doubt you will find a parson to christen the poor little creature with a name like that."

"I shall wait until Father gets home to christen her," Alexandra decided. "He'll understand."

Obviously all thoughts of joining the Women's Army had to be abandoned while Alexandra was feeding Mayne, and however much she disapproved of the whole thing, even Aunt Beryl had to respond to the infant who already gave every promise of having her mother's beauty. Alexandra found her baby a source of delight. They had an almost happy Christmas, even if Uncle Freddie was unable to get home. But then, early in the new year, terrible news arrived: Jonathan Mayne had died in a Turkish prison camp, of dysentery.

The blow, however numbing, was less traumatic than Alexandra had supposed it would be – she had lived apart from her father for so long now she could hardly remember what he actually looked like. The trauma came later, when she realised his death had broken the very last link between Aunt Beryl and herself. Aunt Beryl had also been waiting for Father to come home, to unload the burden of her illegitimate niece and grand-niece. But now Father wasn't ever going to come home, Aunt Beryl had swiftly realised she could be stuck with Alexandra, and Mayne, forever . . . unless she acted promptly. "I have found you a job," she announced one morning at breakfast in the spring of 1917.

"A job?" Alexandra's milk had just given out, and she was spoon-feeding Mayne. "I can't take a job."

"I'm afraid you must," Aunt Beryl said. "It is quite impossible for me to continue supporting you."

"But . . . what about Mayne?"

"Whatever job you do will have to be one which will accept your child," Aunt Beryl told her.

"But . . . I'm not trained to do anything," Alexandra protested, beginning to feel desperate.

"You will have to learn. And as I say, I think I have found you the very thing. Lady Gingham-Gray has been advertising for an upstairs maid. Now, obviously, she is looking for someone with experience and good references – neither of which apply to you. However, I happen to know Lady Gingham-Gray, and I understand something of her, er, circumstances. I have put your name forward, explaining *your* circumstances, and she has agreed to give you a trial."

Alexandra was impressed; she had had no idea that Aunt Beryl had any titled friends, or even acquaintances. In fact, she had no very clear idea what Aunt Beryl did for a living at all in Uncle Freddie's absence. She knew she went out all day to work, in a hospital. But she certainly was not a nurse, and it was not an ordinary hospital. She called herself an almoner, which meant absolutely nothing to Alexandra. But presumably she had met this Lady Gingham-Whatever through her work.

"She will be at her London flat tomorrow morning," Aunt Beryl said. "And will interview you there. It is in Cadogan Square."

"Do I take Mayne?"

"Well, you will have to, as I shall be out."

"You mean you're not coming with me?" Alexandra asked, suddenly nervous.

"I'm afraid not. But Alexandra, I do wish to make it perfectly clear that it is my deepest wish you obtain this employment, and I shall be most displeased should Lady Gingham-Gray decide not to accept you. I hope you understand that."

Alexandra didn't see how she could possibly influence her ladyship's decision, but in the event she needn't have worried. "Alexandra," remarked Lady Gingham-Gray. "What a pretty name. The name of our Queen Dowager, to be sure. And for such a pretty girl. With such a pretty baby. What is he called?"

Alexandra endeavoured to gather her wits. Aunt Beryl had allowed her to ride to Cadogan Square in a taxi because that was how people apparently always went to Cadogan Square. It had been a deliciously wealthy experience – she couldn't remember much about her previous taxi-ride when she had been on the point of delivery – but nothing she had ever seen had prepared her for the elegance of Lady Gingham-Gray's flat, with its deep pile carpets and its paintings. Or for Lady Gingham-Gray herself. Her ladyship was amazingly young – Alexandra did not think she could be a day over twenty-five.

She also could have been quite good-looking, but for her weight, which was in the region of fourteen stone. She was tall, and carried her figure well, but with her flowing yellow hair and somewhat heavy features she reminded Alexandra of a picture in one of Father's books, of the Norse maiden Brunhilde, who had led Siegfried to his doom. But she was quite amazingly charming. "He's actually a she, m'lady," Alexandra explained, having been coached in the right form of address by Aunt Beryl. "Her name is Mayne."

She waited for the invariable adverse comment, but instead Lady Gingham-Gray said, "What a pretty name. And you're an orphan as well as a widow, you poor child."

"Yes, m'lady," Alexandra agreed.

"Well, I shall look after you," Lady Gingham-Gray announced. "You will go down to Southly immediately."

She meant what she said, even if "immediately" had to be in a few days, because apparently Alexandra could not commence work until she had been equipped with several uniforms. This was quite exciting, as the uniforms were totally unlike the heavy gowns and equally formidable caps and aprons worn by Aunt Beryl's black servants in British Guiana. Alexandra had no idea what those women had worn under their skirts, but her underwear appeared to be mainly lace, which was equally unlike the severe cotton drawers and vests she had worn at the convent or to the high school. Her stockings were black silk, and her skirts black linen. Her black blouses were smocked and her white aprons small, also made of lace, and covering really nothing more than her torso. Her boots were black and laced, but light, and her cap merely a circlet of starched linen. She was also required to wear white lace gloves, and had to have several pairs of these, as indeed she was instructed to buy several pairs of everything, Lady Gingham-Gray having provided Aunt Beryl with the necessary funds. "She must be awfully rich," Alexandra remarked, surveying her suddenly extensive wardrobe.

"She is," Aunt Beryl assured her. "Or at least, Sir William Gingham-Gray is."

Her ladyship was paying her new upstairs maid two hundred a year. Alexandra had never in her life had any money of her own before, and the thought that she was going to have two hundred pounds to spend as she chose made her quite heady.

To Alexandra's surprise, Aunt Beryl, having been so eager to get rid of her and Mayne, looked quite upset on the day she left the flat to take the train down to Southly. "I will write," she promised.

"I am sure you will," Aunt Beryl said, without great belief. "Just as I am sure you will make the most of your new position. A life in service, for someone like Lady Gingham-Gray, can be most rewarding."

Alexandra wasn't very enthusiastic about *that*. She had no intention of spending her life in service, and regarded Lady Gingham-Gray merely as a stepping stone to better things – although she had no idea what the better things might be. But she was too excited at the thought of riding in a train for the second time in her life – she had travelled up to London from Portsmouth in a train after being torpedoed – and then at being met at Southly Station by a motor car; she had seen motor cars in Georgetown, of course, and become quite familiar with them in London, but she had never driven in a private car!

Southly was a small village in the Cotswolds, and the few houses clustering to either side of the church and the public house were dominated by the manor, the drive to which lay just beyond the single street. The chauffeur meeting the train, who wore a green uniform and a peaked cap and looked awfully superior, said little on the way from the station, beyond giving a distasteful glance at Mayne. Alexandra was too busy taking in her surroundings to attempt much conversation. She stared at the copper beeches lining the drive, the drive itself, the rows of flower beds beyond which she could see acres of crisp green lawn, the gardeners who straightened to peer at her as the car went by, the gravel which crunched beneath the car tyres as it drew up in front of the house.

This was even more breathtaking than the park in which it stood. The mansion stood on a terrace, to either side of which were formal gardens, a mass of flowers and topiaried hedges and even a maze. The house rose three stories above the terrace and was crowned with innumerable chimney pots; between those and the terrace were a gleam of mullioned windows, mostly bays.

"You'll be Mrs Lowndes," said a very haughty-looking if distinctly overweight man, wearing a black frock coat and a wing collar, who was standing at the top of the steps leading to the terrace.

"Yes, Sir William," Alexandra said, curtseying as she had been told to do when in the presence of her employer, although this was a difficult feat when carrying a small baby.

"I am not Sir William," the butler replied, with some disdain, which increased as he regarded Mayne. His demeanour indicated that he considered himself as a far more important person that the mere owner of the property. "You will address me as 'sir', or Mr Applewhite. Do you understand?"

"Yes, sir, Mr Applewhite," Alexandra said, determined to take no chances.

"Come here, girl."

Alexandra advanced, Mayne clutched against her

breast. But Mr Applewhite ignored the babe. "Hm," he remarked. "A pretty child. We must hope you last. Mrs Luscumbe?"

A tall, thin woman, not wearing uniform but a black gown, advanced from the huge oak doorway behind the butler. She wasn't bad looking, but had an expression of even more extreme superciliousness than Mr Applewhite. "The new girl?"

"Yes, Mrs Luscumbe. Do you think she'll last longer than that Polly?"

Mrs Luscumbe inspected Alexandra in turn, also ignoring the child. "She looks the part," she commented, enigmatically. "If she's a sensible girl . . . are you a sensible girl, Lowndes?"

"I . . . I think so, ma'am," Alexandra said.

"Then you may do well. Remember always, *always*, there is no better employer in the country than Lady Gingham-Gray. Come along now."

Alexandra was led round the terrace and through a side door into the butler's pantry, and thence up a side staircase past the first floor and the second floor to a third floor she had not been aware existed as it was under the eaves. This part of the house was sumptuous enough, compared with any other house in which Alexandra had ever been – saving only the flat in Cadogan Square – but the occasional glimpses she caught through swaying curtains of the family part of the manor took her breath away: she could see suits of armour and priceless paintings and drapes and highly polished wooden panels, wainscoting with intricate designs carved into the oak, and exquisite furniture. She wondered what one had to do to come into possession of such wealth.

Presumably Sir William Gingham-Gray had inherited his. She wondered if she would inherit anything from Father? No doubt the ranch in the Rupununi now belonged to her – she should find out about that. But how primitive and uncouth the ranch in the Rupununi seemed now.

Alexandra was shown to a room which she gathered was to be her very own, in which a cot for Mayne had already been placed and to which her solitary suitcase was now delivered by one of the gardeners. Alexandra was too delighted with the chintz curtains and the bedspread and the amount of space to speak. "You are responsible for the cleanliness and tidiness of this room," Mrs Luscombe told her. "I will inspect it at least once a day. Are you still feeding the baby?"

"No, ma'am," Alexandra said.

"Good. I will arrange for one of the other girls to sit with the child when you are on duty." Mrs Luscumbe stood at the window, and pointed. "Over there, behind that high hedge, is the servants' garden. You may take the babe there on fine afternoons." She went to the door, paused with her hand on the knob. "You are very young to be both a widow and a mother. How old are you, girl?"

"I'll be seventeen this year, ma'am."

"Hm. Still . . . remember what I said," Mrs Luscumbe admonished, and left the room.

Alexandra wasn't sure which of the things she had been told it was necessary to remember, and in any event she was too pleased to be unpacking in a room which was her very own to care. She finished putting away her things, then changed Mayne and gave her a bottle. The baby was still glugging contentedly when there was a knock on the door and a pleasantly ugly face looked in. "Hello. You must be Alexandra. We've been expecting you. I'm Lucy. I'm an upstairs maid too. But not special, like you."

"Hello," Alexandra said.

"Come on downstairs for tea," Lucy said. "You can bring baby with you. Isn't she sweet!"

Alexandra thought she was going to like Lucy, although she couldn't determine what it was that made her a "special maid". But she willingly took Mayne downstairs to the Servants' Hall, where afternoon tea was being served. Here she met Cook and two footmen and the five other maids, as well as the chauffeur. They all seemed quite pleased to welcome her. Like Lucy, the women all made the right remarks about Mayne, and Alexandra enjoyed the tea, which was far grander than anything she had ever had at Aunt Beryl's, but she also observed that there was a great deal of surreptitious exchanging of glances between the other members of the staff, and was aware of a suppressed atmosphere of anticipation. She could not figure out what they were expecting, although she knew it was to do with her, and braced herself. However, the meal passed off without incident, and then she was summoned to the pantry, where she found both Mr Applewhite and Mrs Luscumbe waiting for her: apparently they did not take tea with the other servants.

"As from tomorrow, Lowndes," the butler said, "you will wear uniform at all times in the house. Is that understood?"

"Yes, sir, Mr Applewhite."

"You will be responsible for both the cleanliness and the condition of your uniform," Mrs Luscumbe told her. "I will inspect it regularly."

"Yes, ma'am."

"Should there be any unavoidable damage to any, ah, article of attire," Mr Applewhite told her, "you may apply to Mrs Luscumbe for a replacement. Understood?"

"Yes, sir, Mr Applewhite."

"Very good. Now, your duties will commence tomorrow morning. At eight o'clock you will take breakfast into Sir William. Understood?"

"Yes, sir, Mr Applewhite."

"You will knock once, and then enter the room. You will place the tray on the table by the door, and then you will draw the drapes at the window. You will say, 'Good morning, Sir William,' and then you will draw the drapes from round the bed. You will then . . ." Mr Applewhite stared at her very hard. "Perform whatever other duties Sir William requires of you, until dismissed. Is this understood?"

"Yes, sir, Mr Applewhite." Her brain was teeming with what she had to do, with possible disaster. The room would be strange, and dark when she first entered it, and . . .

Mrs Luscumbe might have been able to read her mind. "Sir William is presently out," she said. "You will come with me and see where your duties lie."

Leaving Mayne with Lucy, Alexandra was led upstairs, and this time allowed through one of the magical curtains, on the second floor, into the gallery which led to the family bedrooms. From the balustrade she looked down on the grand staircase, which began on this floor, but she was more interested in the bedroom into which Mrs Luscumbe now introduced her. It was a huge room, the floor softly carpeted, the two windows with their drapes already closed. Like the rest of the house all the lights were electric, and these glowed to Mrs Luscumbe's touch on the switch. Alexandra stared at the rosewood dressing table and chest of drawers, the comfortable armchairs, the clotheshorse across which some masculine garments were strewn, and above all, the bed, a huge double tester which occupied the very centre of the floor, and was also surrounded by drapes.

While she was still looking at all of this, and marking the table on which she would place the tray before she drew the drapes, she heard a sound. A man entered the room. She was somewhat taken aback by his appearance, for although he was flawlessly dressed in cutaway coat and striped pants, he was rather small and insignificant, certainly when compared with Lady Gingham-Gray, and had a peculiarly mincing manner. She was uncertain whether to curtsey or not, and glanced at Mrs Luscumbe, but the housekeeper merely nodded. "Good evening, Mr Farechild," she said. "This is the new upstairs maid, Lowndes."

"Well, at last," Mr Farechild remarked.

"Mr Farechild is Sir William's valet," Mrs Luscumbe explained.

"Oh," Alexandra said, not at all sure what a valet was.

Mr Farechild stood in front of her and looked her up and down. He seemed pleased. "Well, I declare," he said. "Sir William should be happy with this one. Yes, indeed."

"I am just showing Lowndes the ropes, Mr Farechild," Mrs Luscumbe explained. "Come here, girl." She indicated the door on the far side of the room, through which in fact Mr Farechild had entered. "This is Sir William's bathroom."

Alexandra gazed at more luxury, including a tub large enough to be considered a small swimming pool. "This door," said Mrs Luscumbe, indicating yet another door, facing them, "leads to Lady Virginia's bathroom."

"They have separate bathrooms?" Alexandra asked in amazement.

"Of course they do." Mrs Luscumbe opened the door and showed Alexandra into an even more splendid bathroom, where the decor was pink instead of blue. "And this . . ." she opened yet another door, "is Lady Virginia's bedroom."

Alexandra gasped. Again, it was merely more impressive than the other bedroom, the dressing table being far larger and containing several mirrors, while the room smelt of perfume rather than tobacco. "But are they not married?" she asked.

"What a silly question," Mrs Luscumbe observed. "All the upper classes maintain separate bedrooms. For a variety of reasons. I see you have a lot to learn. Now come with me."

Alexandra was led back through the curtain and upstairs to the servants floor, and then into a rather special sitting room, which she gathered was Mrs Luscumbe's own. "You'll take a glass of sherry," Mrs Luscumbe suggested. Alexandra didn't know whether she would or not, never having been offered such a thing before, but she was not prepared to oppose Mrs Luscumbe in anything at that moment. "Now sit down," Mrs Luscumbe said. "And I will explain a thing or two." Alexandra perched on the edge of a straight chair, and Mrs Luscumbe handed her a long-stemmed glass filled with a deep brown liquid. She had taken one for herself, and this she now raised. "Welcome to Southly Manor."

"Thank you," Alexandra said, and drank – and felt a world of sensation exploding in her throat, then her chest, then her stomach, and then her mind. She had not touched alcohol since her wedding day, but this tasted far more formidable than the champagne she had been given then.

"How long were you married?" Mrs Luscumbe asked.

"Twelve days," Alexandra said.

"And then you were torpedoed. Her ladyship has told

me." Mrs Luscumbe looked at Alexandra for several seconds. "Were they a happy twelve days?"

"Oh, yes," Alexandra said, and then checked herself. From Mrs Luscumbe's expression she might not have said the right thing. "Well, I found them so," she explained. "I had been very lonely before. I have no mother, you see," she added forlornly. "She died when I was born." This was stretching a point or two, but she felt Mrs Luscumbe might not react well to being told her mother had stepped on a sleeping bushmaster.

"You poor dear thing," Mrs Luscumbe said, refilling both their glasses. "And twelve days is not long enough to discover the true nature of the beast that is man." Alexandra drank some more sherry. This, she felt, seemed to be pitching it a bit strong. "The sort of fiend who would leave you with an unborn child," Mrs Luscumbe pointed out.

"Mr Lowndes was drowned," Alexandra protested. "When the ship was sunk."

"No matter. He would have left you soon enough. Men are all the same." From which Alexandra gathered that Mrs Luscumbe's married life had not been a happy one. "Unfortunately," the housekeeper went on, drinking sherry, "it is woman's fate to have to pander to male passion, and suffer at their hands. Lady Gingham-Gray is the most lovely of women, and the most virtuous. It is her misfortune to be married to a brute. Do you understand this?" No, I don't, Alexandra thought. But she nodded, hopefully. "It is therefore our duty to protect her as much as possible. That is why you are here. Do you understand me, Alexandra?"

"Oh, yes," Alexandra said, more interested at being addressed by her Christian name for the first time.

"Do so, willingly and successfully, and you may rise

in her esteem. There is nothing finer," Mrs Luscumbe declared.

"I shall endeavour to do so, certainly," Alexandra promised.

"I am sure you will. You appear to be a dear, sweet child, not yet contaminated by the evil around us." She got up and refilled Alexandra's glass, as well as her own, yet again, which Alexandra found rather surprising, as one of the evils which contaminated the world, at least according to Aunt Beryl, was alcohol. But she drank; she was feeling quite absurdly contented. "But if you fail her," Mrs Luscumbe continued, "she will be very disappointed in you. What is more, I shall be very disappointed in you." Her tone left no doubt which would be the more unhappy fate. She peered at Alexandra, and Alexandra blinked. "Where did you say you came from?"

"British Guiana."

"Where is that?"

"It's in South America."

"South America? Good heavens! Alexandra . . . was your father a white man?"

"Of course he was," Alexandra said indignantly.

"It's just that . . . your complexion is different to other girls."

Alexandra considered telling her that her mother had been an Indian princess, and then decided against that until she knew her better. "I've had a difficult life," she explained.

"You were sacrificed," Mrs Luscumbe said sadly. "A virgin on the altar of the lust of man. It is a sad life. My dear girl. My dear, dear girl."

For a moment Alexandra thought she was going to be embraced, but Mrs Luscmbe merely heaved several heavy sighs. "You are born to make others happy, my dear child. Now run along and have an early night. And remember everything I have told you. I will see you in the morning,"

Alexandra felt breathless. But maybe, she reasoned, it was the sherry.

CHAPTER 3

Alexandra writes: *I was totally out of my depths. This was a world I had never even suspected to exist. There had been nothing in my background to indicate that such a world existed. Thus I was like a lamb led to the slaughter.*

Alexandra hardly slept. She was too excited by everything that had happened, too apprehensive of everything that apparently was going to happen. By Mrs Luscumbe's description of Sir William; by the fear of dropping his breakfast tray or in some other way angering him. What would he do? Judging by what Mrs Luscumbe had hinted he might even beat her. She was up before dawn, feeding Mayne and changing her before putting her down again. This time the youngest of the downstairs maids, Lucy, had been deputed to babysit. "I feel I'm being terribly inconvenient," Alexandra said.

Lucy giggled. "It's a treat. I'm excused housework."

Which was another surprising aspect of her employment, Alexandra thought, that Lady Gingham-Gray would take a maid off housework just so she could serve breakfast to Sir William. In the kitchen she gulped a hasty cup of tea, and was then shown how to lay Sir William's tray by Mrs Luscumbe, who was again the martinet of their first meeting, all thoughts of sherry têtes-à-tête apparently forgotten. Roberts the footman showed her how to carry the tray, while Cook brought the various kettles to the boil. The coffee was made, the eggs, bacon, mushrooms, tomatoes and fried bread served and arranged, the sugar bowl put out and the silver cutlery reverently placed beside the plates. "Who takes her ladyship's breakfast?" Alexandra asked.

"Her ladyship does not breakfast," Mrs Luscumbe informed her. "Now be off with you, it's five to eight. Roberts, you'll see her upstairs."

As it was Alexandra's first morning, the footman actually carried the tray up the two flights of stairs to the gallery. There he handed it over, having to put his arms round her to make sure she was holding it right. Once her hands were firmly clasped on the silver tray she was of course helpless, and he tickled the bodice of her apron. "Oh," she said. "You'll make me drop it."

"You do that," he said, "and old Applewhite will give you six of the best. On your bare ass." He had got beneath her apron and was fondling her breasts through the thin linen of her gown.

"Please stop," she gasped. "Please."

"Just putting you in the mood," he said. "For his nibs. When he's done, maybe you and I could get together, eh?"

"Yes," she said. "Yes. Maybe."

He released her. "Mind how you go."

He went back down the stairs and she was alone, feeling distinctly aroused but even more apprehensive. But the clock in the hall beneath her was chiming eight times. Whatever the ogre awaiting her, she had to face him now. She laid the tray on the table beside the door, and knocked. Then she turned the handle, picked up the tray, and entered. The room was as dark as she had anticipated, but the light in the corridor showed her where the other table was, and she laid the tray down again, took her bearings in a quick glance around herself, and then closed the door.

There was the faintest of stirrings from the bed. Alexandra crossed the room to the window, found the cord, and drew the drapes, blinking in the early morning sunlight. "Good morning, Sir William," she said. There was no reply. She returned to the tray, picked it up, and carried it to the bedside table, laid it down again. Then she opened the curtains.

Sir William Gingham-Gray lay on his back with his eyes closed. His hair was gray and thinning, which surprised her – she had expected the husband of Lady Virginia to be a younger man. His face was not very attractive, especially with the mouth slightly open and the eyes closed, and the chin and cheeks covered in white stubble, although the flesh was firm enough. But he did not look like an ogre. "Will there be anything else, Sir William?" she asked.

The eyes opened, closed again, and then opened again, much wider than before. They were pale blue, and lively. At the same time the mouth closed up, to show tight lips. "Who are you?"

"Lowndes, sir." She curtsied. "The new upstairs maid."

"Christ!" Sir William remarked. "I thought from Ginny's behaviour last night she had something up her sleeve. How old are you?"

"Seventeen, sir," Alexandra anticipated. "Would you like me to pour your coffee, sir?"

"Are you a good girl, Lowndes?"

"I think so, sir." She held out his juice. She thought things were going very well. Sir William sat up, and the covers fell to his waist. Alexandra gulped as she realised he was naked from the waist up – and quite well built, even if his chest had slipped somewhat. But

. . . she could see the curve of his hip, which meant he was naked from the waist down, as well.

He drank the orange juice, handed her back the glass, and gave her fingers a squeeze. “I don’t like girls who are *too* good.”

Alexandra’s brain raced. Shades of Uncle Freddie. But she knew instinctively that this was a far more serious situation. The most important thing was not to annoy him: he was her employer. “I’m not *that* good, sir,” she said.

He gazed at her for several seconds, then released her hand. “There is some money on the dressing table. Go and look at it.”

Alexandra obeyed. There was, indeed, quite a lot of money lying there, at least a dozen pound notes and even several huge, folded fivers. “Would you like one of those pounds?” Sir William asked.

“If I can earn it, sir,” Alexandra said primly. But her heart was pounding: Uncle Freddie had only offered her a Guianese dollar, worth four shillings and tuppence.

“You may have one,” Sir William said. “If you will let me put my hand beneath your skirt.” Alexandra hesitated only a moment; she would worry about the right and wrong of the situation, and the implications of her employment, later. Right now she had not only to please this dirty old man, but also to take him for as much as she could. She picked up one of the pound notes and returned to the bedside, folded the note, and put it in the pocket of her apron. Sir William’s hand slid over her skirt, down the back of her legs to find its way beneath, and then her stockings. He tickled, and she gave a little shiver. “Don’t be afraid,” he said. “I’m not going to hurt you.” The hand found the hem of her drawers and then was inside, on to her bare flesh, caressing and squeezing.

"Did Polly leave because you wanted to touch her bottom, sir?" Alexandra asked, innocently.

"Silly little bitch," Sir William growled. His cheeks had reddened and his breathing had increased. "You're not going to scream and run off, are you?"

She could feel his fingers, sliding up and down the cleft of her buttocks, which she was keeping tightly clenched. "She wouldn't let you go between," she suggested.

The fingers became more insistent, trying to part the flesh. "Would you let me go between?"

"I might," Alexandra said. "For another pound."

"You shall have it," Sir William promised.

"I'll just get it first, shall I?"

"All right, first." His hand slid away, reluctantly. Alexandra went to the table, folded and pocketed another pound, gazed at the fivers. Then she went back to stand beside the bed. Sir William, breakfast forgotten, rolled on his side to use both hands. He fumbled at her drawers, got entangled in the material – and she kept her thighs pressed together. "Damnation," he gasped. "You said you'd let me."

"I will," she said. "But it's the drawers." She allowed the tip of her tongue to show between the lips. "I could take them off. For a pound, sir."

"By God, but you are a mercenary little bitch," he remarked. "All right. Take another pound. But you'll raise your skirts as well." Alexandra had intended offering to do so for another pound. But she knew she couldn't press too hard. She went to the table and pocketed a third note, then she stood in the centre of the room, raised her skirts, and tugged down her drawers. She stepped out of them, returned to the bedside, and raised her skirts again. "By God," Sir William said, reaching for her, and then checking himself. "Are you a virgin?"

"No, sir. I am a widow." She decided against telling him that she was also a mother, right this minute.

"A widow! Hells bells! I want to kiss you."

She realised he was not thinking of her mouth. "Well, sir . . ."

"Don't tell me, another pound."

"Well, sir, if you want to kiss me, there . . ."

He nuzzled her, then suddenly released her and fell back on the pillows. "Take your pound. Then you can go."

Obviously he wanted to masturbate. But that, Alexandra thought, would be a waste in every way. "Don't you like me, sir?"

"Like you? I think you're splendid. But you have to go." His hands were beneath the sheet.

"I could do it for you, sir," Alexandra suggested.

His head gave one of its jerks. "For a pound, eh?"

"Well, sir, that is something special. I'd do it for five pounds. I'll use my mouth, if you like."

"You'll . . . my God! Yes. Five pounds." Alexandra went to the table, took the fourth one-pound note for allowing him to kiss her, then one of the fivers, placed the two of them in her pocket beside the other three. Sir William was panting as if he'd run a long race; he was so aroused it was all very quick and easy. "God," he gasped as he ejaculated. "God . . ." His voice sank to a whisper. "You are magnificent. Lowndes . . . what's your first name?"

"Alexandra, sir." Alexandra went into the bathroom to wash her hands, then returned to the bedroom and put on her drawers; she actually felt quite aroused herself – but she knew this was at least partly because of the ideas which had suddenly started tumbling through her head.

Sir William was sitting up now, nibbling a piece of toast. "No one has ever done that to me before," he said.

"No one, sir?" Alexandra was genuinely surprised. "But . . . Lady Virginia . . .?"

"She won't touch him. She won't even look at him. Lies there with her eyes closed whenever I want to mount her. She thinks sex is disgusting."

Well, what should one expect of a friend of Aunt Beryl? Alexandra wondered. So she hires little girls for you to amuse yourself with. Silly bitch! She felt not the least guilty for what she had done, because it was only what he had wanted – and what his wife had arranged for him. She wondered if Aunt Beryl had known what she was being sent to? But that was unthinkable, when she thought of Aunt Beryl. "You won't leave, will you, Alexandra?" Sir William begged.

"No, Sir William," she promised. "I won't leave."

"Will you show me your breasts, Alexandra?"

"I can't, sir, without taking everything off."

"Then take everything off. Oh, if you want some more money, take it. Take everything off, and come to bed with me. I just want to hold you, feel you . . ."

"I can't, today, sir," Alexandra said. "I've been here too long already. But perhaps tomorrow . . ."

"Tomorrow," he said. "Promise me, Alexandra."

Alexandra drew a long breath. "Twenty pounds, Sir William. For twenty pounds I'll take everything off and get into bed with you." It seemed an enormous amount of money, but he had already given her nine pounds today.

"Yes," he said. "Twenty pounds. Tomorrow."

"Shall I take away your breakfast?" she asked. "It's all cold."

"Yes," he agreed. "Take it away. And send Farechild to me."

Alexandra opened the door, lifted the tray, gave him a little curtsey, and stepped on to the gallery. And gazed at

Mrs Luscumbe and Farechild. "His lordship would like you to go in," she told the valet.

"Forty-five minutes," Farechild observed.

"And not a mouthful eaten." Mrs Luscumbe pointed at the tray.

"You didn't let him have his way with you, girl?" Farechild was anxious.

"No, I did not," Alexandra said. But I will tomorrow, she thought.

"So what did you do that took forty-five minutes?"

"We . . . talked. Now, if you'll excuse me, this tray is very heavy." She made to step past them, and Farechild caught her arm. "I'll drop the tray," she warned. She already almost had.

"If you drop the tray you'll pay for everything that's broken," Mrs Luscumbe told her. "And I'll tan your ass till it bleeds. Where's the money?"

"What money?" Alexandra was trembling, but it was caused as much by anger as by fear.

"He always gives them money," Farechild pointed out, and leered at her. "Think it'll be in her drawers?"

"It'll be in her pocket." Mrs Luscumbe thrust her hand down the front of Alexandra's apron. "Here we are. Nine pounds!" she exclaimed, slowly separating the notes. "God Almighty! What did you let him do, for nine pounds?"

"That's my business," Alexandra snapped.

"I'll talk to you later," Mrs Luscumbe decided. "Right now we'll divvy up." She pocketed the fiver and one of the pound notes. "I'll get the big one changed and split with you later, Mr Farechild." The other three pound notes she replaced in Alexandra's pocket.

Alexandra was speechless for a moment. Then she shouted, "That's my money!"

"Keep your voice down, girl," Mrs Luscumbe snapped.

"You have to share. We set you up, so we get the bigger share. You get twenty-five per cent. Today I'm giving you a bonus."

"You . . . you thieving bitch!" Alexandra shouted.

Mrs Luscumbe slapped her face. Alexandra dropped the tray. Coffee, milk, eggs, bacon, toast, butter, marmalade, shattered crockery, flew in every direction. "You wretched girl!" Mrs Luscumbe cried.

A door opened, and Lady Gingham-Gray was in their midst, eyebrows arched. She wore a blood-red dressing gown and looked more than ever Brunhildian.

"This disgusting child," Mrs Luscumbe said. "Milady, she threw the tray at me."

"I did not," Alexandra snapped. "I dropped it when she slapped my face. She robbed me, milady, of six pounds."

"That's a lie," Mrs Luscumbe asserted. "Where'd a chit of a girl get six pounds?"

Lady Gingham-Gray glanced at the door to her husband's room, which remained firmly closed although the crash of the falling tray had reverberated throughout the house, and flushed.

"You let me deal with her, milady," Mrs Luscumbe said. "I'll teach her her manners."

"You lay a finger on me, and I'll scratch out both your eyes."

Mrs Luscumbe gasped, and Lady Gingham-Gray turned her look on Alexandra. "I'm afraid you will have to go, Lowndes."

"Go?" Alexandra was aghast. Just as she had found the key to untold riches?

"Go?" Mrs Luscumbe was also aghast, as she had also realised just what a source of wealth Alexandra could be for Farechild and herself.

"I'm afraid we really cannot have scenes like this," Lady Gingham-Gray said. "They will upset Sir William."

Why not ask him? Alexandra wanted to suggest. And ask him who he'd prefer to have go, as well.

"But milady, I'm sure I can make her into a good girl," Mrs Luscumbe protested.

"I wish Lowndes to leave, now," Lady Gingham-Gray said, firmly. Alexandra knew the real reason she was being dismissed was that her ladyship was also wondering just what service she could have rendered to have Sir William give her six pounds on her first morning. The poor woman didn't realise it was really nine! But what was to be done now? She just couldn't bring herself to beg for reinstatement. If only the door would open and Sir William appear to insist that she be retained. But Sir William wasn't going to do that. Lady Gingham-Gray could see her distress, and relented, slightly. "You will receive a week's wages in lieu of notice," she announced. "But I will not be able to give you any references, Lowndes. Good day to you."

"Silly little bitch," Mrs Luscumbe remarked when her ladyship had returned to her room. "Thrown it all away, you have. Well, clean up this mess."

"Clean it up yourself," Alexandra told her. "And give me back my money."

"I'll see you damned first. I ought to take the skin from your ass, anyway."

"I would just love you to try," Alexandra said. "You give me my money, and the week's wages, or I am going straight to Lady Gingham-Gray and tell her everything that has happened to me since I came to this madhouse."

Mrs Luscumbe glared at her, but realised she was encountering a character as strong as her own. "You'll have your money," she said. "Maybe it'll pay for your wooden box when they pick you up from the dunghill."

* * *

"What are you going to do?" Lucy asked, anxiously. "Without a reference it'll be hard getting another job."

"I don't want another job," Alexandra told her. "Not in domestic service." She'd hardly find another Sir William, she knew.

"But what will you do?" Lucy asked again. "A week's wages won't last very long. And there's baby to feed." She looked at Mayne, who was sleeping peacefully. "I suppose you can always go back to your aunt."

Alexandra writes: *Obviously, my first venture into prostitution was most unsuccessful. Although it had its repercussions. But I had been acting entirely instinctively, and the realisation that not only Uncle Freddie might want more than his wife was prepared to give him was full of considerations for the future.*

Alexandra realised she had no alternative. But Aunt Beryl was horrified to see her again. "You are the most persistent little wretch I have ever known," she declared. Alexandra, of course, had not told her about Sir William – Aunt Beryl might have insisted she return the money – and had merely explained that she had dropped a laden breakfast tray. "You seem to do nothing but get into trouble. Well, I've done all I can. And I am not going to support you or your brat any longer. I will allow you to stay here for one week, one week, do you understand? At the end of that time you had better have found both a job and a place to live. Because out you go!"

Alexandra wanted to spit at her, but she knew she would then be turned out immediately. And as Lucy had said, there was Mayne to be thought of. So she went out to find a job. But while most of her prospective employers eyed her with approval, they all wanted some proven ability as well as experience, and she had none of either. "Well," said one man, "I suppose I could give you a trial." He ran his hand over her bottom.

"How much?" Alexandra asked.

"Five shillings a week."

"Five shillings?" she cried. "For doing what?"

"Sweeping the floor, mainly." His fingers roamed over her back.

"I have a baby," she explained. "I can't leave her at home. I have to bring her to work."

"A baby? Here? Of course you can't bring your squalling brat here. I've enough of that at home. Off you go, girl. Babies, indeed."

That was a fairly typical response. Aunt Beryl had grudgingly agreed to babysit for this one day while Alexandra job-hunted, but she certainly wasn't going to do it again. Alexandra felt absolutely discouraged. She had had a very light lunch for fear of spending too much of her dwindling severance pay, and she was getting hungry again, but the thought of facing Aunt Beryl . . . she walked disconsolately up the Haymarket, looking at the lights gleaming through chinks in the blackout curtains; several were in restaurants where people were preparing to eat dinner. It was too early for the shows yet, and the streets were almost deserted, save for the occasional woman, mostly just standing around. Alexandra supposed they had been looking for jobs, too. One of them gave her a very hard stare as they passed each other, and Alexandra attempted a smile, but it was not returned. She stood on a corner, trying to make the decision to go home and admit her failure, and a car drew up beside her. The window was rolled down, and the driver, who was alone in the vehicle, asked, "Are you a good girl?"

Alexandra was entirely taken aback, until she remembered that she had been asked that question before . . . by

Sir William Gingham-Gray. And this was an expensive car. "Sometimes," she replied.

"Perhaps I could give you a lift," he invited.

"That would be very kind of you." Alexandra opened the door and sat beside him. The car was warm, and smelt of good tobacco.

"How far do you want to go?" the man asked.

"How far do you want to take me?" she countered.

"You are the answer to a prayer," he told her. "Do you have a room?"

"I'm afraid not."

"No matter." He engaged gear and the car moved away from the kerb. "I know a place." He glanced at her. "You look a cut above the usual sort."

"Do I?" She didn't know what the "usual sort" was.

"You're not . . ." He seemed unable to decide what to say, while she studied him. He was not very old, was very well dressed, and had a little moustache. And he was not in uniform, which was odd, but a welcome change. "You do know what you're doing?" he asked.

"Oh, yes," she assured him. Even if she didn't, for certain.

They were driving down some rather sleazy looking side streets now, and finally stopped in front of a door, above which the word "Hotel" could just be made out by the light of a street lamp, so faded were the green letters. The man opened the door for her and they went inside. There was no one behind the very narrow reception counter, so the man punched a little bell, and again. "All right, all right. Impatient, aren't you?" An elderly woman emerged from behind a curtain, looked Alexandra up and down, and then looked at the man. "Five shillings for the night."

"We don't want it for the night."

"It's for the night or nothing. Here, sign the book."

Alexandra peered over his shoulder as he signed, "John Smith and Mrs Smith". Immediately above him was Mr and Mrs Brown, then Mr and Mrs Green, then two more Mr and Mrs Smiths. The landlady took a key from the board behind her. "Up the stairs, second on the left. You pay in advance." The man handed over two half crowns. "Leave the key on the counter when you go. Don't bother to disturb me again." The woman retreated through the curtain, from behind which there came the sound of a gramophone playing.

"She seems very casual," Alexandra remarked.

"Fortunately, yes." He held her elbow and guided her up the dimly lit stairs. "I presume you *have* done this before?"

"Oh, yes," Alexandra lied.

"I suppose it's a living. But you . . ." They were in the gloom of the corridor, and he suddenly turned her into his arms and kissed her. It was a warm, intimate kiss; she hadn't been kissed like that since Mr Lowndes. She enjoyed it. "You are some*thing*," the man said. "How long have you been on the game?" He released her to unlock the bedroom door, which gave her the time to work out what he meant.

"Since my husband was killed."

He straightened. "Hell! Is that true?"

"Yes," she said. "He was torpedoed, two years ago." She decided against telling him she had also been torpedoed, because that might lead to questions about her Guianese background, and she had gathered that not everyone wanted to know someone with Amerindian blood – not even if their mother had been a princess.

"Two years? And I've only just come across you?"

"I was in . . . Portsmouth, before," she told him.

"Ah." He opened the door and switched on the light, which came from a naked electric bulb suspended from the centre of the ceiling. Alexandra had never seen such a depressing bedroom. It was cold and damp, and the bed was a single iron frame with an uncovered horsehair mattress. There was an enamel washbasin, an enamel ewer half full of water, and an enamel slop bucket; a very well-used towel hung from the rail. There was an equally well-used blanket folded across the foot of the bed.

The man was locking the door again. "I forgot to ask how much you charge."

He looked fairly well-to-do, but was obviously not as wealthy as Sir William Gingham-Gray. And she had no idea what the going rate might be. "That depends on what you want me to do," she temporised.

He turned to face her, looking her up and down. "Just what *do* you do?"

"Anything. Within reason," she added hastily.

"My lucky night." He stood in front of her, slid her cloth coat from her shoulders, let it fall to the floor, while his hands continued to slide down her arms. "Are these real?"

"Of course they are." His hands moved to her breasts, and she stepped back. "You haven't paid me yet."

"All right. What is it? Half-a-crown?"

"Half-a-crown? You must be joking."

"That's what the others charge."

Was it? Half-a-crown? When Sir William had paid her a pound just to feel her bottom? She couldn't believe it. She'd starve on half-a-crown a night. "I'm a cut above the others," she reminded him. "You said that."

"So I did. And you said you did things the others might not."

"That's right." She decided to feel her way. "Ten bob for . . . everything."

"All right. I'll have the lot. Ten bob. If you're worth it. Strip off."

"You'll not touch me until you pay me," Alexandra warned.

He grinned. "You don't mind if I undress?"

"Why not?" She undressed herself, facing him. She knew now that she had nothing to fear about her body: it was perfection. But then, he wasn't too bad, either, and he had an erection already. "Well?" she asked, when she was naked. The chill was striking at her nipples; she could feel them stretching as they hardened. It was giving her goose pimples all over, but she reckoned that too was enhancing her figure – if he didn't keep her standing there too long.

"God," he said, "you are something. You should be on the stage, not a whore."

"On the stage?" she asked, doubtfully.

"Acting. Or just standing there. You'd make a fortune. No one ever made a fortune out of whoring. Well, maybe one or two. Come here." She crossed the room without thinking. He was sitting on the bed, and he threw both arms around her buttocks and brought her against him.

"You haven't paid me," she pointed out, trying to push him away. But he was holding her too tightly. She slapped him on the side of the head, and he turned, carrying her with him, so that they both fell across the bed. "You're cheating," she shouted, as she found herself on her back, with his face still buried in her crotch, as he rose to his knees on the mattress. She exerted all her strength, threw herself sideways, and they fell off the bed together, hitting the floor with a tremendous crash. Then at last he released her and sat up. "Oh, lord," he muttered.

"You up there," shouted the landlady, "any more noise like that and you'll have to go. I run an orderly house."

"See what you've done?" he hissed.

"You were cheating," Alexandra said, and then started to laugh.

"What's so funny?"

"Just us, sitting here, naked on the floor. He's going down."

"Well, I'm not surprised."

"You tried to cheat," Alexandra reminded him. "Like me to bring him back up?"

"I'm not sure you can." The penis was dwindling very fast.

"Give me my ten bob and I'll do it," she promised.

He hesitated, then got up, felt in his pants pockets, and produced four half-crowns. "I must be mad."

Alexandra put the money in her handbag. "I will make you very happy. Lie down." He obeyed her, and she knelt astride his legs, facing him. He was starting to stir again already.

He drove her back to the corner of the Haymarket in his car. She didn't have a watch, but the car clock said seven. She'd been with him about an hour, and she'd made ten shillings. If she could pick up another couple of men tonight, she could make about two pounds. That was about six times her daily wage as an upstairs maid – keep and perks aside, of course. "I may not be able to make it for a couple of days," he said, as the car stopped beside the kerb. "But you'll be right here?"

"Right here," she promised. Presuming she was wasn't with someone else, she reminded herself. But she didn't say it.

"A couple of days." The car drove away, and Alexandra saw a policeman watching her from across the street. She wasn't sure if what she'd just done was illegal or not, but she didn't want any argument with the police, so she turned and strolled away from him, as casually as she could. And suddenly found two women beside her. She didn't know if they were the women she had seen earlier, but she assumed they were, because one asked, "Had a nice time, darling?"

"Yes, thank you," Alexandra replied, politely.

"Staying around here, are you, darling?" asked the second woman.

"Why, yes, I thought I might."

Before Alexandra knew what was happening, she was bundled into a small, dark alleyway, out of sight of the policeman. Neither of the women was as tall as herself, and she struck at them angrily, but one grasped her hair and pulled it so hard her eyes seemed to be starting out of her head, while the other hit her in the stomach with all her force.

Alexandra had never experienced anything like that before. She thought she was going to die. She couldn't breathe, and found herself on her hands and knees, vomiting. The woman was still holding her hair, and the other woman now picked up her handbag and opened it. "That's my money," Alexandra moaned.

"You think you can just come muscling in on our territory? You have another think coming, darling."

Alexandra inhaled, and saw several shades of red. For the second time in a week she was being robbed of money she had worked for, given pleasure for, earned. Still kneeling, she struck behind her with both elbows as hard as she could. The woman holding her hair gave a choking gasp and released her to fall against the wall. The other woman looked up, still rifling Alexandra's handbag. Alexandra reached her feet and attacked her with both feet and both hands, kicking, cuffing, biting and scratching. The woman screamed and fell down, dropping the bag. Alexandra kicked her in the belly and when she rolled over kicked her in the backside. Then she stooped, gathered all the things which had fallen out of her handbag and stuffed them back in, closed the bag, looked at the first woman, who had recovered her breath but remained slumped against the wall, ran out of the alley, and found herself in the arms of the policeman. "Now, then," he said. "What's all this 'ere?"

He arrested all three of them, marched them to the nearest police phone box, and telephoned for a black maria. While they were waiting, several other women gathered round and taunted him. Alexandra thought they might actually assault him and force him to let his prisoners go – they could easily have done so – but they appeared to know him and he them, and contented themselves with remarks. It was Alexandra they clearly wanted to assault. "She has no right," they kept saying. "You give her to us for five minutes, Wally, and there won't be no more trouble."

"And I'd have a murder to investigatc," Wally pointed out.

"No murder, Wally," they promised. "We'll just mark her a little."

Alexandra was so terrified she held Wally's arm. He looked down at her, not unsympathetically. "You've got yourself in a right mess, girl," he said. "All these areas belong. Didn't you know that? And when Tony the Greek finds out . . . listen, I'll give you some advice: when the beak finishes with you, get out of London, fast."

The van arrived, and the three of them were bundled into the back. On Wally's recommendation, a constable got in with them. Alexandra was very relieved to see him. On reaching the station she was put into a separate cell, where there were a couple of other women, but these were both very drunk. It was one of the longest nights of Alexandra's life. She was simply terrified of what was going to happen tomorrow. She ached for Mayne. She was terrified at the thought of what Aunt

Beryl would say on learning that she had been arrested. She was terrified of what Aunt Beryl might be doing, as she hadn't come home, and wouldn't be coming home, until at least tomorrow. And most of all she was terrified at the thought of leaving this place and encountering those women again. As for this Tony the Greek, of whom even the policemen seemed afraid . . .

But eventually it was morning, and she was actually served breakfast, and allowed to use the toilet and wash her face. Then they were all, she and her two companions and several other women, including the two drunks, who were now nursing massive hangovers, put into the black maria and driven off to the Magistrate's Court. It was all frighteningly quick and almost aseptic. "Drunk and disorderly," the Magistrate said, having heard the evidence of a police constable. "Have you anything to say?"

"No, your worship."

"Anything known?"

"Three previous convictions for drink, your worship," said the clerk of the court.

"Ten pounds or seven days. Next." The first of the prostitutes went up, and the policeman named Wally gave evidence.

"Causing an affray. Have you anything to say?"

Alexandra had expected a tirade, but the woman merely said, "No, your worship."

"Anything known?"

"Five previous convictions for prostitution, three for fighting, and one for drunkenness."

"Twenty-five pounds or thirty days. Next."

The second woman, who had a similar record, was similarly sentenced. Then it was Alexandra's turn. Her knees kept brushing against each other as she climbed the short flight of steps to the dock, and she was terribly aware of how unglamorous she must look, her clothes crushed and dirty from rolling in the street and stained with vomit, her hair unbrushed . . . she tried a smile at her friend Wally, but he did not respond. "Causing an affray." The wretched man didn't even look at her. "Have you anything to say?"

Alexandra was tempted to say a great deal, but decided against it. "No, sir." Too late she remembered she was supposed to have said, "Your Worship", and wondered if she had done herself irreparable harm – but he didn't seem to notice.

"Anything known?"

"Nothing, your worship."

For the first time the magistrate raised his head properly to look at her. "You want to think about what you are doing with your life, girl," he said. "Five pounds or seven days. Next."

Five pounds? Alexandra wanted to shout. That would leave her with no money at all. And no job. And no prospects. Leave London, the policeman had said. Oh, how she wanted to do that. But where could she go? She would have to go to gaol. But she couldn't go to gaol. Aunt Beryl would have a fit. But five pounds . . . she found herself in an office off the court, standing before another clerk, seated behind a desk. The two prostitutes who had assaulted her were standing by the door, looking at her. Oh, Lord, she thought . . . when we get outside . . . but they couldn't possibly assault her right outside a Magistrate's Court. All she had to do was get on a bus or something . . . "Sign here," the clerk said.

Alexandra signed, and was given a little bag containing her effects. "I have the money here," she mumbled.

"The money?" The clerk looked irritated.

"For the fine."

"Your fine has been paid, Lowndes. You're free to go."

Alexandra stared at him in amazement, and had her elbow gripped. She turned her head, looked at a man she had never seen before. But he was very well dressed, and didn't look as though he belonged in a police court at all. "Like the man said, you're free to go," he repeated. "So let's get the hell out of here." He smiled at her. "Tony the Greek wants to meet you."

CHAPTER 4

Alexandra's immediate reaction was to run for the door. But the two prostitutes were still lounging there, and she was no longer sure the police would protect her. Before she could think, the man was holding her elbow and guiding her past them and on to the street, where an elegant motor car was waiting, complete with chauffeur. "I need to change," she murmured.

"You can change later," he said, settling himself on the seat beside her. The door closed, the chauffeur engaged gear. The two women had stared at her, but had made no move to interfere with her. "Tony is no man to be kept waiting."

"I don't know him," Alexandra said, feebly.

"Of course you don't. But you will. Everyone knows Tony the Greek. My name is Abraham Martin," the man went on. "I'm Tony's solicitor. That means I'm your solicitor too, now."

"Does it?" she asked, even more feebly. She was looking out of the window at a part of London she had not previously visited, where the houses were just as elegant as in Cadogan Square, and the car was stopping before a block of flats.

"Here we are," Abraham Martin said, and opened the door for her. He was being terribly polite, and she was somewhat reassured. Besides, there was a uniformed doorman waiting to welcome her, and inside, an elevator.

She had never ridden in an elevator before, wanted to scream as the car lifted off the floor. But Mr Martin was smiling at her, so she didn't. They travelled upwards for a few seconds, then the car glided to a halt, the doors opened, and Alexandra stepped on to a carpeted lobby. Before her was a door, but in front of the door was a chair containing a large man with a cauliflower ear, who blinked at her like a sleepy bear, before slowly getting to his feet. "This is Mrs Lowndes, Bert," Mr Martin said.

"Oh," Bert said. "Yeah." He produced a key and unlocked the door. Alexandra hesitated, and Mr Martin held her elbow and guided her into a lobby, elegantly furnished, but containing another man, much smaller than the man outside but far more unpleasant looking. "Mrs Lowndes," Mr Martin said. "Tony is expecting us."

"Yeah," the man repeated and opened a door leading into an even more elegant lounge. This room quite compared with the flat in Cadogan Square for sumptuous furnishings, except that in place of the old masters on the walls there were various studies of nude women.

"Sit down," Mr Martin suggested. "Like a drink?" He had moved to a very well-stocked bar in one corner of the room, and his tone indicated she might need one. Alexandra was inclined to agree with him, although she would have preferred breakfast.

Yet she felt it necessary to show that she was no pushover. "Isn't it a bit early? I only ever drink champagne before breakfast."

Martin turned towards her. "You are a cheeky little bitch."

"Give the lady champagne, Abe," said another voice. "The Bollinger. Come to think of it, I'll have one too." Alexandra turned her head, sharply, gazed at a large but amazingly young man; she didn't think he was a day over twenty-five. His shoulders were broad, his legs long and powerful, and his complexion swarthy; he had a mop of curly black hair which in Guiana might have suggested he was "coloured". He had quite a handsome face, but it was marred by the thin lips, while his black eyes were like pools of angry night. She stood up, and he came closer. He wore a smoking jacket but no shirt that she could see, and pyjama trousers. He stood in front of her. "You stink," he remarked.

She was determined not to show her fear. "I told that man I needed to change," she said. "But he wouldn't let me."

"So take a bath," he said. "In there." He pointed at a door, and she looked at Martin, who was opening the bottle of champagne. "Oh, wait for your drink," Tony said.

Martin gave her the bubbling glass, and Tony raised his. "Here's to friendship."

She drank, then went through the door, and found herself in a luxuriously appointed bedroom, with one of the biggest beds she had ever seen; it was circular and at least eight feet in diameter. Beyond was the bathroom, in gold and silver. She did not suppose the taps were really made of the precious metal, and was more taken by the mirrors which were everywhere, so that wherever she turned she was catching a different facet of herself. She found it exciting. She locked the door, then stripped off her ruined clothes, pirouetted in front of the mirror. She had never realised how lovely she was, seen from every angle. "I love you too," Tony said. "Now try the bath." One of the mirrors opened and he came in, accompanied by Martin. They were both naked.

"You get out of here," she snapped.

"Oh, come now, you're not going to pretend you've never been naked in male company before?" he asked.

"You're a whore, darling. That's what I've been told." He turned on one of the taps in the huge tub. "How long have you been on the game?"

Martin refilled her glass from the bottle he was carrying. "Officially since last night."

"Holy Jesus Christ! My lucky day. How many tricks did you turn before the girls got you?"

"Tricks?"

"How many customers did you have last night?"

"One," she said.

"Slow," he commented. "What did he give you?"

"What I asked for." Alexandra finished her champagne and tested the water. It seemed about right, and she got in, sinking down to the bottom, feeling the heat seeping through her chilled flesh, and soaking her hair. When she surfaced, both men were looking down at her.

"How much was that?" Tony asked.

"Ten bob."

"Ten bob? What the hell did you give him for that?"

Alexandra smiled at him. "So I'm expensive. I once earned nine pounds in half an hour." Tony stepped into the bath beside her, knelt, and began soaping her. "It'll cost you five bob for that," she said. Martin got in as well. "Five bob for him as well."

Tony grinned. "Ever had two men at the same time?"

"Often," she lied.

Alexandra got up and dried herself. "That'll be a pound," she said. "Each." She picked up her clothes, but didn't immediately put them on. Instead she carried them into the bedroom and threw them on the floor. The flat was beautifully warm, and she was starving. She wrapped her wet head in a towel, went into the kitchen, and started breaking eggs.

Tony stood in the doorway, watching her. "Cook some for me, too," he said.

"And for Abe?"

"He's eaten," Tony told her. "He's an early riser."

Alexandra added bacon, served. It felt deliciously wanton to be seated naked at the table, with a naked man on either side of her. "Do you think I'm worth the pound?" she asked.

"You could be worth a whole lot more than a pound," Tony said. "Once you've had a few rough edges knocked off."

"I don't have any rough edges." Alexandra finished her meal, drank some coffee.

"I like my girls to be tough. But not with me," Tony said.

"I'm not tough with anybody," Alexandra said. "As long as nobody tries to cheat me."

"Neither am I," Tony said. "As long as nobody tries to cheat *me*." He stood up, then took the towel from her head. She let him; if he was paying her another pound he could do virtually what he liked. Wet hair cascaded past her shoulders. "Now here's the deal," he said. "If you satisfy me, and I reckon you will, I'll let you work for me."

"For you?"

"It's a good deal for you, Alexandra. I'll protect you, and I'll make sure you don't get any sickness or pregnant. Or if you do, I'll have you fixed up. You've just been lucky, so far. In return, I get three-quarters of what you earn. But like I said, you don't want to try cheating me, if you want to stay healthy."

"You have got to be joking," Alexandra said. "Three-quarters of what I earn?" That was an even bigger percentage than that harridan Luscumbe had wanted, and she had had a slight case, as she had already been the boss.

"That's the going rate," he said pleasantly. "Now, you going to co-operate?"

She tossed her wet hair. "Suppose I don't?"

"If you don't, you're going to get hurt real bad." He reached down and stroked her groin, and suddenly closed his hand, as hard as he could. Alexandra screamed. She struck at him, and had her wrists seized by Abe. Tony grinned at her. "I reckon we're going to have to knock those rough edges off right now, Abe," he said. Alexandra was dumped belly down on a single bed and her wrists and ankles secured with cord to the bedposts. She heard the swish of the cane without seeing it, and a moment later seemed to leap from the mattress as what felt like a knife blade slashed across her buttocks.

The pain was so intense she could hardly take in sufficient breath before she was hit again and again. She gasped and panted, uttering little whimpering sounds, and after six strokes the caning ceased, although the pain continued, wracking her body. "Now," Tony said, bending over her. "Are you ready to work for me?"

I'm ready to kill you, Alexandra thought. Just as soon as I can. But before she could do that, she had to be much stronger, in every way – and he had to be much weaker. "Yes," she whispered.

She was made to bathe herself again, although sitting in the tub was almost unbearable. She told Tony about Mayne and Aunt Beryl, and he asked her if she wanted him to take care of it. She would have loved someone to take care of it, but not Tony the Greek. "Well, just don't stand any lip from any dame," he told her, and gave her fifty pounds. "That's an advance against your first earnings. Go buy yourself some new clothes, and return here this afternoon. With the kid." He chucked her under the chin. "Just don't get any ideas about running off. There ain't nobody cheats on Tony the Greek. You try it, and my friends outside will slit your cheeks and fill them with salt. You won't even want to look at yourself, after that."

She believed him. But then, she had never had so much money in her purse at one time. It did not make her hate him any the less, but it gave her some idea of what she could be earning under his aegis. And she needed a lot of money before she could contemplate bringing him down. She would do that, she swore to herself . . . but in her own good time. She went to a dress shop, moving gingerly in an attempt to ease her pain. The attendants were somewhat snooty when she entered in her filthy clothes, but less so when she bought herself three outfits, off the peg and paying cash, and consigned her old clothes to their bin. Then, wearing her new green gabardine suit over a white silk blouse, with a dark green straw hat, black stockings and patent leather shoes, and equipped with black gloves, handbag and umbrella, she hailed a taxi and drove to Aunt Beryl's flat. "Where in the name of God have you been?" Aunt Beryl demanded. "You went out yesterday morning, you've been out all night . . . and where did you get those clothes?"

Alexandra had already decided that the only way to break with Aunt Beryl once and for all was to shock her out of her senses. "I've had a busy time," she explained. "I went with a man who gave me some money to touch my naked body. Then these two women tried to take the money from me, and while we were fighting, a policeman came along and arrested us." Aunt Beryl's jaw dropped. "So we were taken to the station and locked up for the night."

"Oh, my God!" Aunt Beryl shouted.

"So this morning we went to court, and I was fined five pounds."

Aunt Beryl sat down. "You're a convicted felon," she

muttered, apparently regarding this as more serious than the sexual misdemeanours. "My niece."

"By marriage," Alexandra reminded her, kindly. "Anyway, this man paid my fine, and asked me to work for him. And I agreed." She went into her bedroom. Mayne was sleeping, so she began to pack.

"Work as what?" Aunt Beryl demanded, following her.

"As a prostitute."

"As a . . ." Aunt Beryl seemed about to faint. Alexandra let her get on with it, finished packing her bag, and then did the same for Mayne; their entire store of belongings fitted into one not very large suitcase. "You are obscene," Aunt Beryl said, when she got her breath back. "Obscene!"

"It's all in the mind," Alexandra said. "Just because you don't like sex doesn't make you right, you know. If everyone was like you there wouldn't be any human race."

"Don't you speak to me like that," Aunt Beryl stormed.

"I've decided to speak to everyone as I please," Alexandra said. "Would you excuse me, now? I have a taxi waiting." She scooped Mayne into her arms.

"I forbid you to leave this house," Aunt Beryl said. "A niece of mine, becoming a prostitute!"

"I am not really your niece," Alexandra pointed out again. "And for two years you've been dying to get me out of this house. So now I'm going. Be grateful."

"If you leave, you needn't ever come back."

"I don't intend to," Alexandra said, opened the door and lifted her suitcase; Mayne snuffled against her shoulder.

"You'll be all alone in the world," Aunt Beryl shouted. "You'll wind up hideous and diseased, dead in a gutter."

"'Bye," Alexandra said, and closed the door behind

her. Mayne was awake by now, and Alexandra kissed her. “We’re going to somewhere new,” she said. “You’ll like it there.”

Tony the Greek, it seemed, had a weakness for babies. Or perhaps he saw the daughters of his employees as future employees themselves. He chucked Mayne under the chin and made her cry, and then laughed and wanted to give her gin to drink. Alexandra talked him out of that, and was shown to her flat. It was in a building he owned – where he got all his money from was as much a mystery to her as why he hadn’t been conscripted into the army – and where the other tenants were also in his employ. “You’ll bring your clients here,” he told her. “Here you’ll be absolutely safe. If any of them acts rough you just press the bell and somebody will be along.”

He was very highly organised. The flat was small, just a bed-sitter and a kitchenette, but it was a home of her very own at last – the rent was apparently included in the seventy-five per cent of her income she was to give him – and she was delighted with it. He also arranged for a baby-sitter for Mayne, when Alexandra was working, one of the daughters of a girl who had been “on the game” for a dozen years. Alexandra discovered that she was not required to walk the streets. In the basement of the building where she lived there was a club, frequented by soldiers on leave from the trenches in France. Her business, and that of half a dozen girls, was to sit at the bar in the club, wearing evening gowns which revealed everything except the soles of their feet, apparently drinking themselves insensible. In fact they were always served, no matter what might be ordered for them, with coloured soda water.

They accepted invitations to dance to the wheezing three-piece orchestra from any man who asked them, huddling close on the tiny floor space as they swayed against their victims, and giggling girlishly when their partners' hands wandered, before, equally shyly, accepting the offer of another drink. This was always "champagne", when bought by a customer, which was only obtainable by the glass. Their glass, as usual, contained coloured water. The other glass contained the cheapest possible white wine, into which carbon dioxide had been introduced, as well, Alexandra suspected, as some additional alcohol. Certainly the men all got drunk in record time. Each glass cost a shilling, the equivalent of a day's pay for a private. Many of the men got too drunk to be capable of anything further. For those who did suggest that they "make an evening of it", the girls would hesitantly indicate that they actually lived on the premises, and if they were careful and made no noise to alert their "landlady", they might just be able to sneak up to their room for a few minutes.

It was this aspect of her new employment which very rapidly made Alexandra disgusted with the whole business. It was her job to ascertain, with each prospective partner, whether or not he had the necessary cash to pay for further pleasure. This was difficult to accomplish while maintaining an "I'm doing this only because I love you" facade. Alexandra had always dealt absolutely straightforwardly with her bed partners, from her earliest girlhood. She had told them what she wanted, and in return had given them what they wanted. She hated lying, and subterfuge, and play-acting, and inevitably made a good number of mistakes. Then, when she claimed her money, there might be a scene, and she had to ring the bell, and have the helpless soldier expelled by two of Tony's bouncers. That was distasteful as well, as she could not help but realise that the soldier, in continually risking his life for his country, was an enormously better man than any of Tony's conscription-dodging thugs. Or Tony himself. But there was another aspect of the business which was even more distasteful: there was no pleasure in the sex. It was difficult to enjoy it with a drunken man at the best of times, but Tony insisted that all clients be fitted with a condom before penetration could be allowed – this was to reduce the chances of either disease or pregnancy. Alexandra had looked forward to this too, as giving her endless opportunities for playing with her favourite toy. But she rapidly discovered that fitting a condom on to the half-erected penis of a drunk was an exhausting and passion-killing pastime, and that once the flesh was encased, it became quite uninteresting.

Worst of all was the absence of intimacy. With every previous man, Alexandra had been able to create a real feeling of shared pleasure, mainly because of the enjoyment that she found in all things sexual. But as she was getting so little pleasure out of any of her clients she could convey little. Her customers certainly appreciated her beauty, but she was not there for fun, and confined their activities to the area between her upper thigh and her navel, with the occasional caress of breast or bottom.

For the moment Tony remained her most satisfying mate. He seldom took any of his whores to bed, preferring to discover, and test out, new ones – but he made an exception in the case of Alexandra. Of a totally different sort was Abe, who would often come into the bar and take her to her room. Abe was her one true intimacy, the one human being she genuinely looked forward to seeing and holding in her arms – apart from Mayne, of course. But both Abe and Mayne were aspects of the trap she soon realised she was in. Abe naturally did not pay for her services. Neither did Tony. And for the rest, providing good food and clothes for the two year-old Mayne, meant that she was making absolutely no progress towards anything like financial independence – and she was now nearly eighteen years old.

For the first time she began to feel frightened of the future. It was terrifyingly illustrated for her when she looked at some of the older girls, who, even if they had managed to avoid pregnancy and disease, had lost their figures as the years passed, so that they commanded lower and lower prices, until eventually Tony would decide that they were no longer worth his while.

Without Tony's protection they were forced to abandon the more lucrative areas and haunt the parks, while few of them had places of their own. It was easy to say that their rapid decline was assisted by the amount of alcohol they drank or the drugs they took, and Alexandra rigorously refused to sample either, but it was still a gloomy prospect stretching in front of her.

It was November 1918. Alexandra as a rule paid little attention to the news. It seemed that the War had been going on forever, and that it probably would go on forever; she had never known England not at war and so found nothing terribly strange about it. Even with food rationing most people in London seemed to have a much higher standard of living than those in Guiana. So she was more surprised than anyone when the bells began to ring and the guns to fire salutes, and everyone became hysterical. It happened during the day, and she got out of bed, left Mayne playing with her teddy bear, and hurried down the stairs to find out what was happening.

The bar was packed, although it was outside hours, with soldiers and sailors and airmen, and women. The regulars were quite outnumbered, and Alexandra wasn't even sure that the invaders were prostitutes, although they were behaving like any girl off the streets. Worse, they had taken over the bar for themselves, and were handing out drinks without paying for them. Alexandra simply could not imagine what Tony was going to say . . . but Tony didn't appear. Instead she was seized by two large soldiers and given champagne to drink, and this was the real stuff rather than coloured water. The noise was tremendous and it seemed useless to protest; they wouldn't be able to hear her and they were obviously not men to be crossed. And then, across the room, she spotted a familiar face. That of Sir William Gingham-Gray.

He wore uniform. He recognised her immediately. "Alexandra!" he shouted, and elbowed people left and right to take her in his arms, pushed her into a corner where there was less chance of them being separated by the crush. "What on earth are you doing here?"

"I work here. What are *you* doing in a place like this?" Tony's bar and brothel was surely not Sir William's natural habitat.

"I'm celebrating." He kissed her mouth, her eyes, her lips, her hair. "Oh, Alexandra, how I have missed you."

"Have you, Sir William?" She pulled her head back. "You didn't send after me."

"Oh, I did. I tried to find you. But . . ." He squeezed her against him. "I've found you now. I knew it would happen, one day. This is my lucky day. It's the greatest day in history."

"I'm more expensive, now." She owed him nothing.

"Do you think that bothers me? Listen . . . this bloody noise is frightful . . . you're coming with me."

"Where?"

"Where we can be alone."

"I can't leave Mayne." There was no hope of getting any of the other girls to babysit, tonight.

"Who the hell is Mayne?" he asked suspiciously.

"My baby."

"Well, bring her with you. You are coming with me. With or without Mayne."

She didn't want to argue: Sir William Gingham-Gray promised real money, at last. "Five minutes," she said. "There's a back entrance in the alley. I'll meet you there."

He held her arm. "Promise?"

"I'll be there." She wriggled past him. A man reached for her and she pushed him away and ran up the stairs, scooped Mayne and the teddy bear from the bed.

"Ma?" the little girl asked. "Where gone?"

"Somewhere very nice," Alexandra told her. She didn't doubt that. It might even be a good hotel. She wrapped them both in coats, hurried downstairs again, and out into the freezing November air.

Sir William was waiting, with another, much younger man, also in uniform. "This is Freddie," he explained.

"Oh, yes," Alexandra remarked. He even looked a bit like Uncle Freddie. She was quite happy about that. She'd charge them double.

"It's a bit of a walk," Sir William apologised. "Can't get a taxi for love or money." He led them on to a main street, where there were still crowds of people.

"Ma," Mayne said. "I'm cold." Alexandra hugged her more tightly.

"How long have you had her?" Sir William demanded.

"Well, two years," Alexandra told him. "I had her when I was at Southly."

"Did you, by God! Nobody ever told me."

"Looks a sturdy child," Freddie commented, stroking his blond moustache.

"She weighs a ton," Alexandra panted. "Would you like to carry her?"

"No fear."

"It's not far now," Sir William kept saying, but they walked for a good half an hour, and Alexandra's arms felt like lead, before she realised they were in Cadogan Square.

She stopped. "You're not taking me to your flat?"

"Where else would I take you?"

"You have got to be crazy. What about Lady Virginia?"

"She's down at Southly."

Alexandra allowed herself to be persuaded. They got into the warmth of the building and took the lift. Alexandra became aware that both men were distinctly excited, and they were reasonably sober, too. It could be a very profitable evening – providing she remembered to keep her head. The lift stopped, and Sir William unlocked the door. "All the servants have gone," he announced. "It's going to be just the three of us."

Freddie, obviously feeling very daring, squeezed her bottom, and she smiled at him. "There are four of us," she pointed out. "I have to feed and settle Mayne before I do anything."

"Oh. Ah . . . right ho. The kitchen's through that door. I'll fix us some drinks."

Alexandra took Mayne into the kitchen, sat her in a chair, and hunted through the larder cupboards. There wasn't anything she really would have chosen for the little girl, but she did find a pot of something called Gentlemen's Relish, which smelt quite attractive. She gave this to Mayne, with a spoon and some biscuits. "I'll be back in a little while, darling," she said, and rejoined the men.

Sir William had opened a bottle of champagne, and he poured her a glass; this was Clicquot rather than coloured soda water. "To find you again, Alexandra," he said. "My God!"

She had taken off her coat and was in her evening gown; Freddie's eyes were popping out of his head. "Well, I'm glad to see you again, too," she said. "Shall we talk about money?"

"You haven't changed."

"Not in any way at all," she promised.

He glanced at Freddie, who was blushing. "We have some things we'd like you to do . . ."

"For how long do you want me?" Alexandra asked.

"Will you stay the night?"

"And do anything we ask?" Freddie blurted. "Sir William says you do . . . that sort of thing."

"If I'm paid for it," Alexandra said. "But if you want something unusual . . . and for a whole night . . ." She took a deep breath; but she could always come down, she couldn't go up. "A hundred pounds." She knew Sir William had the money.

"A hundred pounds?" Freddie shouted. "That's absurd." Alexandra picked up her coat.

"She'll be worth every penny of it," Sir William said.

"I don't carry that kind of cash around with me."

"She'll take a cheque. Won't you, Alexandra?"

"A cheque?" Alexandra asked suspiciously. She wasn't quite sure what a cheque was.

"My cheque," Sir William said. "You can pay me your half later, Freddie. My cheque won't bounce, Alexandra."

Alexandra had already made her decision; she didn't have anywhere else to go. This flat was delightfully warm, it was good champagne, and Mayne was clucking happily in the kitchen. Besides, these two men would certainly be clean. It was worth taking a chance on this cheque thing. "All right," she said. "I'll just put Mayne to bed, while you two boys decide just what you want done. And then I'll cook some supper, shall I?"

"Well," Freddie commented, obviously concerned about the passage of time involved.

"You have me all night," Alexandra said. "As Sir William says, I'll deliver the goods. But we won't make it if we don't eat. Why don't you fellows strip off while I'm working?"

"Oh, indeed," Sir William agreed. "Use the spare room for the, ah, child."

Mayne and the table were both covered in Gentlemen's Relish, and the pot was all but empty. Alexandra washed the little girl's face and hands, then carried her into the spare bedroom, where a huge, soft, warm, made-up bed waited, and tucked her in with her teddy bear. "Ma," Mayne said. "I like this place."

"So do I," Alexandra said. "We'll have one like it, some day."

She took off her evening gown, kissed Mayne good night, and went through into the kitchen, wearing only her high heels, and with her hair loose past her shoulders. Freddie was in there getting another bottle of champagne, which he all but dropped. "You are a very beautiful woman," he remarked.

Sir William came in to watch her as well, and she cooked bacon and eggs. "You haven't undressed yet," she pointed out.

The two men looked at each other, then obeyed. Tunics and shirts and drawers and suspenders accumulated in the corner. They were both pretty hard already. Well, she would have been disappointed if they hadn't been. She knew she could have a fairly restful – and profitable – night if she was quick and professional. Only she had to aim higher than that, no matter how tired she was. These two men represented the sort of clientele she wanted, needed, if she was going to survive, and if she was ever going to get even with Tony the Greek. She had to give them the most memorable night of their lives.

"I want to kiss you." She turned towards Sir William, uncertain which part of her anatomy he had in mind, and he took her into his arms, held her close against him, and kissed her mouth. "I love you, Alexandra," he said. "God, how I love you."

For the second time that night she was quite taken aback, and before she could gather all her wits together, he had laid her on the settee and was on top of her. She threw one leg over the back of the settee and let the other fall on the floor, and he was inside her, holding her shoulders as he pumped up and down, gushing into her in seconds. Then he collapsed on her breasts.

She let him lie there for a few seconds, then eased herself out from beneath him, went to the bathroom. Then she returned to the lounge with two towels which she had soaked in hot water. Sir William had already rolled on his back, and she laid one of the towels on his groin and gave him a little squeeze. Had he meant what he said? She couldn't believe that.

But now he said it again. "I love you, Alexandra."

"I love you too, Sir William," she agreed. Freddie had had a bath and was smelling of deodorant and pommade. "Why, you are a handsome fellow," she said. "Think you can get it up?"

"You mean you want to have more sex?"

"You bought me for the night," she reminded him, and led him into the bedroom. "His turn."

"No." Sir William sat up. They both looked at him. "No one's entering Alexandra except me," Sir William announced.

"Now, look here," Freddie said. "I paid half."

"You haven't paid a bean," Sir William pointed out.

Alexandra felt like reminding them that neither of them had paid a bean, as yet.

"Well, I'm going to, aren't I?"

"You don't have to. Now run along home, there's a good chap."

Freddie looked at Alexandra, who wasn't sure what to do. She didn't want to upset Sir William – who remained her best bet of being paid at all. On the other hand, she didn't want to upset Freddie either; he was a potentially valuable customer. "We can't send him out like this," she protested.

"He can get dressed."

"I meant, in that state of excitement. Let me help him out, Sir Willy."

"Oh . . . all right," Sir William said.

"You can watch," Alexandra invited.

"I think you enjoyed that," she said when she was finished, going into the bathroom to shower.

"Oh, yes." Freddie followed her. "Alexandra . . ."

"Write down your phone number and I'll call you," she whispered. "Tomorrow."

He did so, got dressed; she hid the slip of paper behind the toilet, took him to the front door, closed and locked it behind him, then returned to the bedroom. Sir William was sitting up, watching her. "Alexandra, I want you."

She stood beside the bed. "You have me, Sir Willy."

"I meant, always. I want you, all for myself. I want you to do everything you did tonight, everything you can think of, to me whenever I can come to you." Alexandra frowned at him, while her brain did handsprings. "I want to watch you having orgasms," he said. "I think that is the most wonderful sight in the world."

She felt she had to advance cautiously. "Well," she

said, "I'll have an orgasm for you whenever you like, Sir Willy. You know where you can find me."

"That sleazy bar?" He caught her hands. "I don't want you to go back there, Alexandra. Not ever. I don't want you to be a whore. Alexandra, stay with me. Now and always."

"Whatever would Lady Virginia say?"

"Well, you couldn't stay here, of course. I'll get you a flat, of your own."

"A flat? Of my own?" The handsprings were back.

"Where you'd live with your daughter. And entertain only me. And any friends I might bring along from time to time."

"I couldn't afford that," Alexandra said.

"I'll pay for the flat."

"I meant I couldn't afford to work only when you were able to come."

"Silly girl, I'm asking you to be my mistress. I'll settle an income on you. You'll never have to prostitute yourself again."

Except to you and your friends, she thought. But wasn't that what she really wanted? Sir William's friends would all be like Freddie, clean, and rich. But her instincts told her she must drive a hard bargain while he was in this mood; once he had her, he might be less amenable. "How much of an income?" she asked.

"Well . . . what about twelve hundred a year?"

"Twelve hundred a year! Pounds?"

"Of course."

A hundred pounds a month! Wealth beyond her wildest dreams. "But you'd pay for the flat on top."

"Of course."

"Would it be in my name?"

"Well, of course not, my dear. You can't own property. You're only seventeen."

"We could tell everyone I'm twenty-one. They can't prove otherwise; I don't have a passport or a birth certificate, or anything. I think it should be in my name, Sir Willy. Otherwise . . . suppose something were to happen to you?"

"Nothing's going to happen to me. I'm as fit as a fiddle."

"You could be knocked down by a bus," she pointed out.

"Oh, all right. I'll put it in your name."

"How soon?"

"As soon as I find it."

"But where do I live until then?"

"You'll have to go into an hotel. Don't worry, I'll pay for it."

"With Mayne."

"Well, of course." He pulled her against him, began to kiss her breasts. "Now let's make love."

"But I can't go back to Tony's place, I won't have any clothes. Neither will Mayne."

"Well, you can go back to pick up your things."

"If I go back, I won't be able to leave again. Tony is a terrible fellow. He'll probably beat me up about tonight . . ."

"All right," he mumbled into her neck. "You can have a complete new set of clothes. And Mayne," he added, before she could speak.

"I'll need a maid."

"And a maid," Sir William said, squeezing her buttocks. "Alexandra, I'm hard as a rock. I've never done it twice in a night before. Alexandra . . ."

"You'll pay for the maid," she said.

"Yes, I'll pay for the maid. Alexandra . . ."

"Lie down," she told him. He obeyed. "Just lie there and think of me," she said. "I won't be long." She ran into the drawing room, where she'd seen a desk. She sat down and wrote rapidly, then took the headed paper into the bedroom.

"Alexandra," he wailed. "He's going down."

"Don't you think I can bring him back up again? That's what lovemaking is all about. Sign this."

"What is it?"

"Our agreement."

"For God's sake . . ." But he signed it.

"Now I am yours," she said. And you are mine, she thought, happily.

"And I'm soft as butter."

"Just lie there." She went into the spare bedroom, put the sheet of paper under Mayne's pillow, added Freddie's telephone number, just in case of emergencies, then went into the kitchen and found a jar of honey. She coated herself, front and back, from her navel to her thighs.

CHAPTER 5

Alexandra writes: *Thus was I launched, really quite inadvertently, upon my career. I should stress that I had no idea that I might be doing anything wrong, or even morally indefensible. I was concerned solely with obtaining the best possible standard of living for Mayne and myself, and there was simply no one in all the world to whom I could turn. While I had only one asset: my body. That I enjoyed using that asset can hardly be held against me.*

It took Sir William just a week to find Alexandra a flat, which was a disappointment because she enjoyed her seven days in a comfortable hotel just outside London, where he had his chauffeur take her the following morning. It was the first time she had been waited on, hand and foot, and, after she had been introduced as Sir William's niece, the staff couldn't do too much for her, supplying a cot for Mayne and every possible convenience. She even had a private bathroom.

The chambermaids and bellhops weren't as gullible as they appeared, especially when on the first evening Sir William locked the door and remained closeted with his "niece" for most of the night, but as he had tipped them all very well they didn't complain – in the euphoria of the end of the war no one was complaining about anything. Alexandra enjoyed the luxury of making love to the same man two nights running, and a man who didn't want to beat her or hurt her, but just play with her and have her play with him. In fact, that was the only way she could get him to climax, as although he spent some time inside her, gasping and going red in the face, she knew that after his exertions of the previous night he wasn't going to manage it without some serious manipulation. She wondered how old he was, but didn't care to ask at that moment.

She enjoyed going shopping even more, as soon as the stores reopened, again driven by Sir William's chauffeur, and with Sir William at her elbow. He took her to an emporium on Piccadilly named Fortnum and Mason, which she had seen before but would never have dared enter on her own, and swept her up the stairs to the dress and lingerie department. As she was still wearing her evening gown – with her coat over it both to keep out the cold and disguise the fact that she had no underclothes – and had a small child in tow, eyebrows were raised. But Sir William's chequebook answered all questions. When she saw the chequebook Alexandra remembered that he had not yet paid her for the first night, but she decided against raising that point either – he could have it on account, as it were. Certainly he spent far more than a hundred pounds on her in the shop. There were silk stockings and garter belts, lace knickers and satin petticoats; there were patent leather boots and shoes, kid gloves, and hats of every description. There was a tunic dress and a peg-top skirt and a fox fur coat, and there were day dresses and afternoon dresses . . . she got quite in the mood towards the end and was buying with total abandon. But there were no nightdresses; neither she nor Sir William wanted her to sleep in anything save her skin.

Then they went along to the children's department and fitted out Mayne as well. Sir William next took them to a smart restaurant for lunch – they were both wearing some of their new clothes when they left the store – and did not seem the least embarrassed or annoyed when Mayne spilt her ice cream down the front of her dress. "The hotel will launder it for you," he assured a horror-stricken Alexandra. It was quite heavenly, not to be criticised, as would have happened with Aunt Beryl, or to be apprehensive, as she had been all the time with Tony the Greek, or just to be plain scared of what might happen next, as she realised she had been almost all of her life, certainly since the day Mother Superior had expelled her.

But there were even better things to come, for the next day Sir William took her to a bank, and opened an account for her. He paid in one hundred pounds, and promised her that there would be another hundred pounds paid in on the first of every month.

Then the manager gave her a chequebook of her own, and showed her how to write a cheque. "How do I know there will be enough money in the bank when I come for it?" she asked.

"We will send you a statement, every month, showing all of your transactions, and the balance remaining," he explained.

"But how will I know *you* have enough money?" she insisted.

The manager allowed himself a deprecatory smile. "I think we can always promise you that, Mrs Mayne," he said.

For Alexandra, in her role as Sir William's niece, and also to throw Tony off her track, had decided to revert to her maiden name, which she much preferred to Lowndes, anyway, only adding a Mrs because of her child. "I'm not sure she's going to thank you for that when she grows up," Sir William remarked. "Mayne Mayne is a bit much."

"She can call herself whatever she likes, when she grows up," Alexandra told him. That seemed an awfully long way away, and meanwhile, she could read and reread her bank book. A hundred pounds, all of her own. She was dying to write her first cheque.

"I wouldn't touch it, if I were you," Sir William advised. "Unless you really want to buy something."

"What about the flat?" she asked. "The food and things?"

"I'll open a charge account for you at the nearest general store," he promised. "Whatever you buy will be added up, and I'll pay it at the end of the month."

Then there was the flat. It was situated down a quiet street off a busy thoroughfare, and was on the top floor, but reached by an elevator. An elevator, of her very own, Alexandra thought. "Well, you'll have to share it with all the other tenants in the building," Sir William explained. The flat itself was rather small, but it had a comfortable lounge/diner, a largish bedroom, a smaller room which was really a dressing room but in which Sir William had had placed a cot for Mayne, a bathroom, and a separate kitchenette. This was all electric, including the stove. Alexandra had never seen an electric stove before and was delighted.

She was even more delighted when Sir William took her along to the lawyer to sign the lease, which made the flat hers for the next thirty-seven years. She couldn't really understand why it had to be for thirty-seven rather than thirty-eight or fifty or forever, as she was too excited to listen to all the chat about leaseholds and freeholds, but thirty-seven years seemed amply long enough . . . she'd be fifty-four when it gave out – although of course they told the solicitor she was twenty-one – and she didn't really expect to be alive then.

Sir William next took her shopping for some more furniture, but the flat was actually quite well furnished already, and that afternoon they shared her bed. "This is the first time I have ever had anyone in a bed of my very own," she told him.

That seemed to delight him, but the next morning he informed her he was returning to Southly that afternoon. "After all," he explained, "I have celebrated the Armistice for more than a week. Ginny has been on the phone to my club asking questions."

"Will you make love to her?" Alexandra asked. She wasn't jealous, just curious.

He grinned. "As we have been separated for over a week, and it's such a special occasion, she might let me. If I'm able, after you."

"What will you do to her?"

"Why, nothing that would interest you in the least, my darling girl. Having given the signal, as it were, Ginny will arrange her nightdress round her waist, spread her legs, close her eyes, and request me to be as quick as possible."

"You mean she does it with her clothes on?"

"I have never seen Ginny without something on."

"But . . . don't you like to play with her?"

"She does not like me to touch. She regards 'that sort of thing' as 'beastly'."

"Well," Alexandra said sympathetically, "you're a bottom man, aren't you?"

"Unfortunately," he said, giving her bottom a squeeze, "Ginny regards bottoms as even more beastly than breasts. Well, in fact, she regards all sex as beastly, but she is very broad-minded and understands that as men themselves are beastly, as long as I never touch her with my hands, she lets me mount her once or twice a month. That's why she employs chambermaids who let me touch them."

"But you mustn't 'mount' them?"

"Good lord, no. That's why you were fired, you know. Not really for dropping that tray. Ginny felt you were simply too attractive."

"I know," Alexandra said, and giggled. "Would she be angry if she knew we were in bed together now?"

"She'd go stark, raving mad," Sir William said.

Alexandra thought he was being optimistic. It was difficult to imagine a woman as sexless as Lady Virginia – as he portrayed her – being wildly jealous of her husband's peccadilloes. Although, she reminded herself, she had certainly been fired, as Sir William apparently recognised, in a fit of jealousy. She was more concerned with Sir William's departure. "When will I see you again?"

"I shall get back to town once a week. I won't be able to spend the night very often, though. It'll be mostly an hour or two in the afternoon. I'll telephone to let you know." Because the flat actually had a telephone, although Alexandra didn't know who she was going to ring.

Her first reaction to the thought that Sir William was only going to be visiting her for a couple of hours a week was one of great well-being. Much as she enjoyed every facet of sexual behaviour, and every aspect of the male body, and much as she was grateful to him for raising her out of the unpleasantnesses of ordinary prostitution and setting her on her feet, the idea of having nothing to do except eat, drink, and take Mayne for walks was entrancing. She indulged herself by fulfilling a long term ambition – that of learning to speak French, a language she had long regarded as beautiful as well as sensual. Her tutor, a woman in her fifties, was agreeably surprised by Alexandra's diligence and her aptitude.

However, almost immediately, other aspects of her situation began to impinge. Anxiety over Tony the

Greek was the most important. As long as Sir William was with her she had felt not the least afraid; not even Tony the Greek would dare cross swords with Sir William Gingham-Gray, she was positive. But she was going to be quite alone from tomorrow. She got Sir William to compose an advertisement for a maid, and insert it in the newspapers. "Not *The Times*," he explained. "Housemaids don't read *The Times*. A rag like the *Daily Mail* or the *News Chronicle* is what they read. Better yet is to put a notice in your grocer's window."

The advertisement called for a respectable young lady to "do" for a young widow of moderate means, and to babysit as and when required. "How much can I pay her?" Alexandra asked.

"In London they come expensive. I suppose you may have to go as high as two hundred and fifty a year. No more, mind."

"I wouldn't dream of it," Alexandra said.

Alexandra was, however, beginning to dream of other things, as an idea took shape in her mind, an idea which grew over the next few days, when she received an amazing number of responses to her advertisement. For two days her phone never seemed to stop ringing. She arranged to meet each applicant at a tea shoppe on the corner, as she did not want to reveal her address to anyone but the eventual maid – it never occurred to her that having given a telephone number anyone could discover where she lived in a matter of minutes. They came in all shapes, sizes, ages and accents, but it took her a long time to find exactly what she wanted. Because her idea was growing all the time. For too much of her life she had been the plaything of others. Now she wanted a plaything of her own, who would also be a faithful support – because she would treat her plaything faithfully in return.

She was excited about the whole concept, and became a little despondent when after two days of interviewing she still had not discovered anyone who was remotely what she was looking for.

Anyone much older than herself was out: that thinned the ground immediately. Equally, anyone with supercilious ideas, or anyone who was determined to be strictly a housemaid and nothing else; anyone who looked down her nose at Mayne – who naturally accompanied her mother everywhere as there was as yet no one to leave her with; anyone who wasn't physically attractive. This last requirement, indeed, eliminated nine out of the first ten before they had even had a cup of tea. It wasn't until the third morning that she found what she wanted. The voice on the telephone had been so faint she had hardly heard it, but it had belonged to an Alice Smith. This seemed a suitably ordinary name. But Alexandra was delighted to discover that Alice Smith was at once very young, very blonde, and very nervous – she was also very pretty, in a crushed sort of way.

Alice was desperately thin and pale and anxious, and her dress was threadbare, although it, as well as her face and hands and nails, were clean. Alexandra bought her some cream buns to go with the tea, and she became much more cheerful. "I suppose you're already suited, Mum," she said.

"Why should I be?" Alexandra asked, trying to imagine how attractive Alice might be with another half stone of weight.

"I don't have any references," Alice explained. "I was sacked from my last job."

"Why?" Alexandra asked.

Colour crept into the pale cheeks. "I . . ." the blush deepened. "They had a son. He wanted to be familiar." She stole an anxious glance at Alexandra's face.

"The lout," Alexandra commented. "What did he do?"

"Nothing. When he tried, I slapped his face. And was sacked. If I could just work for you for a week, Mum, until you find someone more suitable, maybe I could pay the rent. Otherwise my landlady is going to throw me out."

"The wretch," Alexandra sympathised. "We can't have that. What part of England do you come from?"

"Birmingham."

Alexandra had no idea where Birmingham was. But it sounded suitably far away. "Can't you go back there?"

"Oh, no, Mum. Well, I ran away, see. If I went back, he'd beat me."

"Your father?"

"My stepfather. I had to run away. He was always coming into my room when I was changing, and things like that. And me mum wouldn't stop him. She'd just say, he fancies you."

"How dreadful," Alexandra commented. "I can see that you wouldn't want to go back. It seems to me that you don't care very much for men."

"All they want . . ." Alice gave another flush. "Well, Mum, you know."

"I do indeed," Alexandra said, sympathetically. "How much is your rent?"

"Three pounds, Mum."

Alexandra opened her handbag; she had taken the precaution of drawing some money before the interview. "Here are five pounds," she said, counting out the sovereigns.

"Oh, Mum!" Alice's eyes were as big as saucers.

"What I want you to do is go off and pay your rent, collect your things, and come to me at this address."

Alexandra wrote it down. "Oh, Mum," Alice said again.

"You realise I am trusting you to keep your word."

"Oh, yes, Mum."

"So we'll just make sure." Alexandra took out one of the sheets of paper she was finding so useful, and wrote out a receipt for the five pounds. "Now you sign it. When you come to me I'll tear this up, and the money is yours as a gift, and I'll pay you . . . two hundred pounds a year."

Alice's eyes got bigger yet. "Two hundred pound', Mum?"

"Yes. To be my maid and companion and help me look after Mayne."

Alice managed a smile at the little girl. "Oh, yes, Mum."

"You'll live in," Alexandra explained, studying her closely. "And it'll be all found. But you'll serve only me."

"Oh, yes, Mum," Alice said enthusiastically. "I'll be there in two hours."

Alexandra smiled at her. "I'll expect you at twelve. We'll have lunch together."

Alexandra hurried off to buy steaks and a bottle of wine, and wondered if she was being terribly wicked. But she had never thought of Rose or Mrs Luscumbe as being wicked, although Rose and Mrs Luscumbe had certainly been selfish and greedy. She intended to be neither of those things – she had no reason to be. She was actually being a benefactress to a poor starving waif. If she wanted something in return no one could blame her for that. And the idea of actually being the seductress instead of the seduced was entrancing. Even if she had no idea how properly to go about it.

She decided to follow her instincts. She went home, sat Mayne in front of her colouring book with her crayons, and had a hot tub. Then she put on the blood-red dressing gown which had taken her fancy at Fortnum and Mason's – she had wanted one ever since seeing Lady Virginia's – and sat in the lounge, attempting to read a newspaper, but totally unable to concentrate, she was so excited. At twelve o'clock she looked at the new wristwatch Sir William had bought her, and became quite agitated. But at three minutes past the hour the doorbell rang, and Alice was standing there, carrying a small shabby suitcase but looking much better than when Alexandra had last seen her. "Oh, Mum," she said. "I was so afraid this might be the wrong place."

"It's the right place," Alexandra assured her. "Come in, this is your home, now. It's not very big, I'm afraid, but it'll do us for the time being."

"Oh, yes, Mum," Alice said, looking around at the fresh, clean decoration.

"Now," Alexandra said. "Bring your bag in here." She led the way into the bedroom, which was at once the nicest and largest room in the flat – Sir William had seen to that, just as he had chosen the king-size double bed himself. "Do you like it?"

"Oh, Mum. It's beautiful."

Alexandra wondered if she was under the impression that it was all hers – but nobody could be that stupid. "Well, there's space in the wardrobe and an empty drawer in the bureau. Get yourself unpacked and take off those street clothes, while I cook us some lunch. Are you hungry?"

"Oh, Mum," Alice said, expressively. Alexandra fussed happily, preparing the steaks and the potatoes, and opening the wine. "Can I help you, Mum?" Alice asked. Alexandra goggled at her. Alice had put on what were obviously her working clothes: black ankle-length skirt and black long-sleeved blouse, with black stockings to go with her black boots. Over this ensemble she wore a white pinafore, very brief – bodice and skirt, and a little white cap perched on the top of her head. Alexandra's mind began to do handsprings again as ideas flooded through her brain. "I think it's just about ready to go on," she said. "Have a glass of wine." She poured two.

"I've never drunk wine before, Mum."

"Then you must learn," Alexandra told her. "Cheers."

Alice drank somewhat deeply, and gasped. "Oh, Mum!"

"It's delicious, isn't it?" Alexandra cooked the steaks while Alice wandered about the kitchen.

"It's all so nice," she said. "Do you rent it, Mum?"

"I own it. I'm a widow," Alexandra explained. "My husband was killed in the War."

"Oh, Mum."

"Now you can help me clean Mayne up." They washed Mayne's face and hands, inserted her into her chair, and had lunch. Alexandra ate sparingly, but Alice had obviously not tasted steak in some time. Alexandra also kept the girl's wine glass filled, and by the end of the meal Alice was quite giggly.

Alexandra's excitement was growing by the minute. Her victim, she thought. Her very first victim. But the first of many, she was determined on that. Although perhaps she had already captured a victim – Sir William. They washed up, cleaned Mayne up again, and put her down for her nap. "Would you like me to dust, Mum?" Alice asked.

"No, no. You can do that tomorrow. Did you have a bath this morning?" Alexandra led her into the bathroom and turned on the taps.

"Well, no, Mum. Today is Thursday."

"I bathe every day," Alexandra said. "And so must you." She took off her dressing gown, hung it on the hook behind the door. Alice hastily stepped outside. "Come back here," Alexandra commanded. "Haven't you ever seen a naked woman before?"

"Oh, Mum." She was hovering in the doorway. Alexandra held her hand and drew her back into the room.

"I am very beautiful," Alexandra pointed out.

"Oh, yes, Mum." Alice looked about to burst with embarrassment.

"I think you are very pretty too," Alexandra said. She wasn't in the least worried about the girl's fright; there was no revulsion in it, and she was in total command of the situation. "Take off your clothes. I think you could be quite beautiful too."

"Oh, Mum, I couldn't do that."

"You must do as I say," Alexandra pointed out. "Or you'll have to go." It was necessary to be cruel to be kind. "And if you go, I'll have to have my five pounds back."

"Oh, Mum!" Alice began to cry.

"No one's going to hurt you, silly goose," Alexandra said kindly. "Oh, the bath's ready." She turned off the taps. "You're not going to get into the bath with your clothes on, are you? I'll help you." Alexandra stood against her to reach behind her and untie the pinafore. Their faces were only inches apart, Alice still sniffing desperately. Alexandra kissed her on the nose. "You are I are going to be such friends," she promised.

Alexandra writes: *Obviously there will be those who will condemn my relationship with Alice. But the fact is that I wanted company, and I like sex. I enjoy it equally with either men or women. If I did not, I could hardly be as successful as I am. The point was that after so many years of loneliness, I wanted a permanent, intimate, companion – and I could hardly have employed a boy: Sir William would have had a fit. But Alice was a treasure.*

* * *

For the next couple of weeks they only went out to shop and walk Mayne. It was in any event very cold, and London was in the grip of an influenza epidemic which, according to the newspapers, was causing a huge number of deaths. Neither Alexandra nor Alice even caught a cold, as they spent much of each day in bed. Once Alice had overcome her initial fear that doing what came naturally had to be somehow wrong, she was an eager lover, and her increasingly bold explorations were a delight, while her own slender figure remained a constant source of pleasure to Alexandra – it was like having an alter ego, or a very special toy, which would respond exactly as she wished.

Her earliest plans had included a pleasant surprise for Sir William whenever next he returned to London, but it was something of a relief when he neither appeared nor telephoned for several days. At the end of a week Alexandra felt she had reached a position where she could explain the truth of the situation to Alice. By then, indeed, she thought she could have confessed herself to be the mistress of the devil, and Alice would have been happy to accept the situation. Alexandra knew that for the first time in her life the girl was actually happy. Yet she was also terrified at the prospect. "Oh, Mum!" she gasped. "The gent comes here?"

"To use my body," Alexandra said. "He is my sole support, right this minute. Oh, I mean to change that, as soon as I can. But right now, he has to be humoured in everything he wants."

"Oh, Mum!" Alice looked genuinely distressed.

"Don't worry," Alexandra said. "He isn't going to touch *you*. No fear. But he adores girl's bottoms, and you have a terrific bottom. So if he wants to play with you a little, you must let him, and pretend to enjoy it." That settled, she was impatient for Sir William to call, but it was another ten days before the phone rang. "Sir Willy," she said. "I thought you had forgotten all about me."

"Forget you?" he asked. "Oh, my darling girl. I've just been so busy. So much to be done, don't you know. But listen. I'll be in town tomorrow for a business lunch."

"And you'll stay here."

"I can't. Ginny will be with me. But I'll get to see you. The lunch should end between three and four. I have a dinner engagement at eight which means I have to be back at the flat by seven. But I'll try to get to you by four."

"Only three hours?"

"I'm afraid so, this time."

"Oh, dear," she said. But she was secretly rather relieved. She wasn't sure she could keep him going for more than three hours. She and Alice bathed after an early lunch, perfumed themselves, and then Alice dressed for the occasion as Alexandra wanted: she put on her pinafore and nothing else save for her cap and a pair of high-heeled shoes. Alexandra herself wore her crimson dressing gown. Mayne was by now beginning to show some interest in these preparations, but she was an obedient child and merely pouted when Alexandra explained that they were going to entertain and that she must stay in her room until the gentleman left. "I could entertain him too," she protested.

"You will, one day," Alexandra promised.

It was ten past four before the doorbell rang. Alice was more nervous than ever. "Suppose it's not him?" she asked. "And I open the door with nothing on."

"You do have something on," Alexandra insisted. "And it is him."

Alice went to the door while Alexandra sat on the settee and watched her. Alice released the latch and pulled the door in, gazed at Sir William. A Sir William, Alexandra realised with some concern, who had lunched well – at least on wine. Sir William gazed back at Alice. "Good God!" he commented.

Alice's pinny did not quite cover her pubic area nor was the bodice quite wide enough to hide her nipples, while her legs, which were her best feature, were utterly exposed. "Will you come in, sir?" she asked.

Sir William looked past her, as if unsure that he had the right place, and Alexandra stood up. "Sir Willy," she said.

Alice had stepped aside, and Sir William entered the apartment. Alexandra took him in her arms and gave him a long, slow, deep kiss, while Alice closed the door. Then Alexandra moved her head back. "Alice is my maid," she explained.

"Is that all she ever wears?"

"Around the flat, of course. Why wear anything more? It's not as if any other man ever comes here," Alexandra pointed out. "I hope you like her."

"I think she's charming." Sir William held out his hand. "Pleased to meet you, Alice." Alice squeezed his fingers and gave a little curtsey. "You must tell me how you came by her," Sir William said.

"When there's time," Alexandra agreed. "We don't have too much today, do we?"

"Oh, my darling girl . . ." He turned back to take her in his arms again, and just to get his mind off Alice, for the moment, Alexandra had shrugged off her dressing gown. "I am so sorry this has to be such a brief . . . is she going to stay?"

"But of course."

"I meant, in the room with us."

"Not if she embarrasses you. But I thought you might enjoy having her here. Alice and I have no secrets from each other."

"Oh," Sir William said, allowing himself to be led into the bedroom.

"Would you like anything to drink?" Alexandra asked.

"I think I've probably had enough."

"Perhaps," Alexandra agreed, undressing him, and handing each garment to the waiting Alice. He was decidedly limp, despite being in the presence of two naked women. "We are going to have to work on you."

"Oh, Alexandra, how I wish I could spend the whole night here," he said.

"We shall make it seem like a whole night," she promised, gently urging him on to the bed. She nodded to Alice, who took off her pinafore and came to stand beside him. "I think we'll just get you going first," Alexandra said. While she made love to him Alice, as instructed, stood immediately beside him. He couldn't keep his eyes from the girl's pubic curls, only inches from his face.

"I say," he muttered. "May I?"

"Whatever you wish, Sir William," Alice agreed, primly.

Sir William went for her bottom, as Alexandra had thought he would. "I think you're ready now," she said, after a few moments. Alice discreetly looked away, but she was unable to move as Sir William was still grasping her buttocks, even while surging back and forth inside Alexandra. Soon he lay gasping and flaccid. "I think we could all have a cup of tea," Alexandra told Alice, and went into the bathroom to douche.

"Where did you find her?" Sir William asked again, when she returned with a hot towel in which to wrap him.

"I advertised, and chose carefully," Alexandra told him. "She's not cheap." She listened, made sure Alice was out of earshot in the kitchen. "Three hundred a year."

"I set a limit of two-fifty."

"I know. I'll fire her if you like. But isn't she cute?" Sir William sighed, but Alexandra knew he wasn't going to forego the pleasure of playing with Alice's bottom again. "And she's a virgin, believe it or not."

"I don't."

"Well, it's true. If you play your cards right, she might let you deflower her, one day."

"You mean you wouldn't mind?"

Alexandra sat beside him. "Do you think I'd have cause to?"

"No," he said. "Never. There's only one Alexandra. Hell, coming here . . . I always wonder if you'll still be here."

"And I always am, and always will be," she reassured him.

"It's such a feeling of coming home, of relaxation . . . I never get that at Southly."

"I know," she said sympathetically. "Here's tea." Alice placed the tray on the bedside table, and withdrew; it contained only two cups. "I'll call her back in a moment," Alexandra promised. "When you're ready."

"Ready?"

"You are going to have two?" she asked.

"That'll be the day."

"You will," she assured him. "Just drink your tea. And talk to me." He wanted to do that. There was so much to be talked about. Alexandra had the feeling that his life had been hovering in a kind of limbo as long as the War was on, but now that it was over, it was possible, and necessary, to make plans again. Presumably that went for most of the people in Europe. Perhaps it even went for her. When the War had begun, she had been a delinquent, virginal schoolgirl. Now . . . but the War hadn't really affected her. Of course it had cost the lives of both Father and Mr Lowndes, and she regretted that.

But she knew she was following the path she would have done anyway, so it was probably better that they should both be dead and unaware of what she was doing. What she had to do was make sure the path led ever upwards.

Sir William's problems were on a scale difficult for her to appreciate. He worried about the huge increase in taxation, as against 1914. "Of course there's no reason for that level to be maintained now," he grumbled. "But the bastards won't reduce it, you can be certain of that." Alexandra had no idea what he was talking about; she had never paid Income Tax in her life. "But the whole country is going to the dogs," he said. "Everything is being done for the lower classes, and to hell with the people who made this country great."

Alexandra supposed he would include her in the ranks of the "lower classes". On the other hand, no one had ever done anything for her . . . except Sir William himself. So she let him ramble on for some time, lying beside him with her head on his shoulder, her breasts against his chest, and one leg thrown across his. After half an hour she felt a faint stir, and raised her head. "I think you're ready for another."

"I'll never make it twice. Not today. I haven't enough time, and I'm too damned depressed."

"But you come here to stop being depressed, Sir Willy," she pointed out. "That's what I'm here for, isn't it?"

He kissed her. "You are a darling girl, Alexandra. And I do love you, very much. But I don't think even you can do anything for me today. I'm surprised I came the first time."

"You are going to have two," Alexandra insisted. "Now, let's think of something to turn you on, really and truly. I know . . . would you like to watch me and Alice make love?"

"You and Alice? My dear girl . . . she'd never let you. Anyway, two women? It isn't possible."

"Oh, yes it is," Alexandra assured him. "Wouldn't you like to watch?"

"Well, I . . ." He was embarrassed. But she knew he did indeed want to watch.

"Sit up against the head of the bed." Alexandra got up and opened the door. "Alice!"

"You are a witch," he said. "But a most lovely witch."

"And I am your witch," she reminded him.

After that afternoon, Sir William managed to get to London at least once in every week, and he always spent a few hours at the flat. Once, indeed, he managed to spend the whole night, and the three of them shared the bed together, while Sir William managed a passable performance three times. Alexandra felt that she had made them both her sexual slaves, and her mind started to wander. Not very seriously, at first. She really was perfectly contented with Sir William and his arrangement, and with Alice. On the other hand, although she had no expenses apart from Mayne, and her hundred pounds was faithfully paid into her account every month and was beginning to mount up, she knew she was never going to get rich from Sir William's allowance. Of course the flat was also hers, and when she obtained a valuation from an estate agent she felt much wealthier, but she still didn't possess much more than a thousand pounds. Once the thought of so much money would have made her dizzy; now it seemed utterly puny. And in any event, she could only sell the flat by breaking with Sir William, which would mean the end of her allowance.

Thus she needed a stepping stone to better things. But, living the life she did, there was no way she could find one. She also, from time to time, dreamed of having a much younger lover – even someone who was handsome and virile who did not require excessive stimulation. But that too seemed an impossibility. Even when she remembered Freddie. She didn't want to risk upsetting Sir William by contacting Freddie at all, but she was upset herself when Sir William announced that he and Lady Virginia were going to Cannes that summer. "Cannes?" she shouted.

"It's on the Riviera," he explained.

"I know where it is," she snapped. She had started taking *The Tatler*. "But what do you want to go there for?" The people in *The Tatler* were all much younger and smarter than Sir William.

"Used to go every year before the War, don't you know," Sir William explained. "Now Ginny feels we should get back into the swing. I wish I could take you there, old girl. You'd love it."

"But you can't," Alexandra said sadly. She knew she'd love it too.

"Well, of course I can't. Ginny will be with me, and she knows what you look like. And we'll be meeting all of our friends . . ." He paused, somewhat lamely.

"How long will you be gone?" she asked.

"Oh, about six weeks."

"Six weeks?" she shouted.

"Now don't take on. Your allowance and bills will be paid as usual, and Alice's wages. And you'll be able to have a rest." He chucked her under the chin. "Just mind you do rest."

The day after Sir William left Alexandra telephoned Freddie. He was embarrassed because he had company. "You were going to telephone last November," he reminded her.

"Well, I've been all tied up, with Sir William."

"Don't I know it. He's been boasting about you at the club."

"Has he?" She didn't know whether to be pleased or alarmed. "Well, now he's gone off to the Riviera."

"He's left you?" Freddie at last sounded interested.

"Oh, no, he's coming back. I just thought, as he's going to be away for a while . . ."

"My dear Alexandra, you're his mistress. I can't go to bed with another man's mistress, unless he invites me to. Noblesse oblige, don't you know? It isn't as if you were his wife. That would be different. Now if you were to ask him if it would be all right . . ." Alexandra slammed the telephone on to its hook, and went to bed with Alice. But it was a long, miserable spring, as wet as English springs usually are, and now too she could hardly avoid becoming aware of the enormous tensions that were permeating English life, submerged temporarily by the War, but since the Armistice surfacing in a big way. People were always on strike. Things were hard to get. And demobilised soldiers, unemployed and many of them maimed, thronged the streets looking angry, and making everyone else angry too.

While Alice was not a totally fulfilling partner. She was as eager as ever, but only for Alexandra's arms. She seemed to feel that her relationship with Alexandra was something very special, and that their love, as she called it, transcended ordinary morals. But only *their* love. When Alexandra, feeling extremely wicked, suggested they invite the milkman in one morning and see what he was like, Alice was horrified. When Alexandra even more wickedly suggested they make advances to the girl who lived downstairs, a pretty little red-head whose husband was away a lot, Alice nearly fainted. Alexandra had not yet decided what to do about the situation – she really didn't want to get rid of Alice – when, fortunately, Sir William came home.

As he had spent the last few months gazing at young women in bathing costumes without getting anything more than his usual meagre ration from Lady Virginia, he was positively virile for the first couple of weeks after his return. Alexandra was so happy to see him she made him very happy as well. And this time she even persuaded Alice to let him mount her too. Alice was in a state of fright, and moaned terribly, but afterwards she confessed that she had rather liked it. "Think of the time you would have had with the milkman," Alexandra pointed out.

The principal cause of Alexandra's discontent was that, as Sir William's mistress, other men of his class were strictly taboo, without his permission, as Freddie had indicated. And Sir William was not likely to give his permission, she felt: he seemed inordinately jealous of her. She was therefore utterly taken aback when he arrived at the flat one afternoon and announced that they were going to a party. "A party!" she cried. "Oh, how splendid. What sort of a party?"

"It's a dinner and dance, actually."

"A dinner! My God, what am I to wear? I don't have a dinner gown." She had, as usual, been studying *The Tatler*.

"I have bought you one," Sir William said. He had left the suitcase outside in the hall, wishing to surprise her. Well, he certainly did that. The suitcase was placed on the bed, and opened, and Sir William first of all took out his dinner suit.

"You'll have to press that, Alice," Alexandra said. It obviously had not been packed by Farechild. But then she lost interest in Sir William's clothes as he lifted out the blood-red gown, which had a matching pair of knickers, and a matching pair of shoes. Apparently she was not required to wear anything else. "Oh, Sir Willie!" she screamed with excitement.

Alice was holding the gown up and stroking it. "Satin, Mum. Satin!"

"Oh, Sir Willie," Alexandra said again.

"Try it on," Sir William recommended.

Alexandra did so, a trifle nervously. But he had known her long enough, and it was virtually a perfect fit, while the decolletage was so deep she was sure her breasts would pop out every time she moved. She thought it was the most beautiful garment she had ever owned. "Oh, it's gorgeous, Mum," Alice said.

"It's got this to go with it," Sir William said, and gave her a string of pearls with a matching pearl ring.

"Are they real?" Alexandra cried.

"Of course they're real."

"And they're mine?" She couldn't believe it.

"No, they are not yours," Sir William said. "I rented them for the evening. They go back tomorrow."

"Oh!" She was quite put out. "Did you rent the dress as well?"

"No, the dress and underclothes and shoes are yours."

"Well," she said, "beggars can't be choosers, I suppose."

Sarcasm was always lost on Sir William. "Let's get on with it," he said, looking at his watch. "Or we'll be late." He put on his dinner suit while Alexandra had a quick bath and was then inserted into her gown by a wildly excited Alice. It was only after she was dressed that she realised he had also bought her a foxfur cape to go with it; she almost forgave him for the pearls. Besides, it was the first time she had ever been taken out to dinner, and she was not prepared to be upset about anything. Even the odd way Sir William was behaving. For having taken a taxi, and having arrived at their destination, he decided they were actually too early and made the cabbie drive them round the block twice before actually stopping.

They were outside another block of flats, only far more grand than Alexandra's, and were greeted by a uniformed hall porter. Then they ascended in the lift, and found themselves in the lobby of a huge apartment, which apparently occupied the entire fifth floor. In the distance Alexandra could hear music playing, but the foyer itself was empty save for a butler, who scrutinised Sir William's card, and then compared the name with a list he carried – absolute cheek, Alexandra thought. But Sir William seemed to think it was all right, and waited patiently until the butler said, "Number Four, Sir William."

"Thank you," Sir William replied, and escorted Alexandra along a corridor, off which there opened a dozen doors, numbered from one to twelve. There was a key in the lock of number four, which Sir William turned before ushering her inside. Alexandra found herself in a sumptuously furnished but otherwise very ordinary bedroom. Her disappointment returned. She couldn't believe that Sir William had gone to all this trouble and bought her this lovely gown just to have his way with her in somebody else's bedroom. Talk about kinks, she thought.
"Perhaps I should explain what we are doing," Sir William suggested, sitting down and lighting a cigar. "These are the premises of a private club, of which I am a member. It is a very private club," Sir William said, peering at her. "We meet four times a year, and dine," Sir William said. "Twelve of us."

"Twelve men?" Alexandra began to be interested.

"And twelve ladies, of course."

"Oh." Alexandra was disappointed again; the idea of being entertained by twelve men in Sir William's income bracket had been most attractive – but not if there was going to be that much competition.

"Thus you will understand that there is a certain amount of decorum to be observed." He opened a drawer and gave her a very large domino mask. "Put this on." Alexandra obeyed, studying herself in the mirror. The mask covered from her hairline to immediately above her lips – there was a space into which her nose fitted – and certainly completely hid her identity from anyone who did not know her already . . . and quite well; she supposed there had to be a lot of women with flowing black hair and a superb figure. Sir William had also put on a mask, and was equally concealed. Although she would have recognised his paunch anywhere. "Now," he said. "We behave as naturally as possible. There will be music, and it will be in order to dance with whoever asks you."

"Will they think I'm your wife?"

"Good lord, no. It is one of the rules of the club that no one will be accompanied here by his wife."

"Only his mistress," Alexandra agreed. She was still inclined to be annoyed, but was actually too intrigued. If the old bugger wanted to play it this way, she certainly wasn't going to object.

"However," Sir William continued, "it is also a rule of the club that no one must reveal his or her identity, and thus no one must remove his or her mask, throughout the evening. Even if in, ah, private with another person. I would like that understood."

"If that's the rule," Alexandra said gaily. She could hardly wait to get outside and see what the evening had to offer.

"Very well, then," Sir William said. "Now, obviously the whole purpose would be negated if you were known to have arrived with me, or indeed, which room you undressed in. At eight-thirty precisely, therefore . . ." he looked at his watch, "in thirty-three minutes from now, every light in the flat will go out and remain out for two minutes. At that time, we will leave the room by that door." He pointed at the one on the other side of the bedroom. "That leads directly into the dining room. Once we are through the door, you will turn to the left, and I will turn to the right. For the rest of the evening, we do not appear to know each other. Understood?"

"Do we reveal all when it's time to go home?"

"Good Lord, no. You will observe that the numbers on the outside of the doors are luminous. The party ends at midnight, sharp. Then the lights will go out again, and we will re-enter this room. Each couple will then leave the building at fifteen minute intervals, starting with number one. As we are number four, we will leave at one o'clock."

"So nobody has a clue," Alexandra mused. "Except the doorman and the butler. They could blackmail the lot of you."

"Antonio and Johnson are very discreet, and absolutely trustworthy," Sir William assured her.

"And that's why we had to arrive at an exact hour," Alexandra said. "So we wouldn't bump into any of the others."

"Exactly. But the arrivals are staggered over every ten minutes, otherwise the evening would drag on too long."

"So we have to wait another half an hour for the fun to begin." Alexandra sat down and crossed her legs. "Would you like to occupy your time?"

"Ah, no," Sir William said. The old bastard, she thought; he wasn't going to waste his dwindling resources on her when he might hope to have the pick of eleven other women. Well . . . she would have the pick of eleven other men. The minutes ticked away. "You are going to have a good time," Sir William assured her. "Just remember that at the end of the day you belong to me."

"And you to me," she reminded him. It was just coming

up to eight-thirty, so she gave him a kiss. Then the lights went out.

Alexandra was first to the door. She turned the handle and stepped into utter darkness. She inhaled, a variety of perfumes, turned to her left, and immediately cannoned into someone. So much for their secrecy, she thought; this man could only have come from number three beside them. Except that it was a woman. Alexandra had an enjoyable little fumble while ascertaining this, and extracted a startled exclamation, then she released her new friend and moved directly across the room. She was in the centre when the lights came on again. For a moment she was blinded, but then, so was everyone else. She blinked, and got her vision back. The room was indeed large, and one end of it was filled with a long table covered with a white cloth, on which was the most mouth-watering collection of food, both hot and cold. Close by was another white-clothed table, at which there were twenty-four place settings. There was also a large number of opened wine bottles available.

Alexandra surveyed the other guests, and discovered that the other guests were surveying her. This was for two reasons. She was isolated in the centre of the room, whereas they were still clustered outside the various doors. And, she was pleased to observe, she was by some distance both the youngest and the most beautiful woman present. The men were actually more interesting, because if three of them were clearly in Sir William's age bracket, the other eight were distinctly younger, and one of them was hardly more than thirty, she estimated: he was extremely good-looking in a dark way. She gazed at him, and he gazed back, and then a voice said over a loudspeaker, "Ladies and gentlemen, do please dine."

Presumably that was Antonio. But the sight of the

food had made Alexandra more hungry than sexy, and as she was nearest to the table she got there first. She was helping herself to hot roast pork and potatoes, and a salad, when someone squeezed her bottom. She looked round, but to her disappointment it was one of the older gentlemen. "You're a treat," he commented.

"I'm sure you are too," she said, put her plate on the dining table, poured herself a glass of wine, and sat down. The table filled very rapidly, but there was very little conversation, to begin with. Then the wine began to flow and the talk became more animated, most of it of a sexual variety. Well, she supposed, there was little else to be talked about, in these circumstances.

"You must be very young, my dear," remarked the woman sitting next to Alexandra. She was distinctly plump, and their thighs were touching.

"On, no," Alexandra said. "I'm eighteen."

"Good heavens!" the woman said, and turned away as if Alexandra might be contaminated.

"You are simply adorable," commented the man on her other side, and nuzzled her neck.

She didn't know what to do, because she didn't find him the least attractive and he didn't look very rich, either. But at that moment piped music began to play, and the man was on his feet, leading her on to the floor. He held her very close, and she could hardly move, but she endured him until the music stopped, and then started again, and she was taken over by another man. Then another, and another, until she was beginning to perspire; she was undoubtedly the most popular woman in the room. Then she changed partners again, and found herself in the arms of the young man she had noticed when first the lights had come on. He did not hold her close at all, but danced properly, with the result that their bodies only touched occasionally. "You are enchanting, mademoiselle," he said.

"And you are French."

"But of course," he agreed. "In five minutes time, the lights will go out for ten minutes. This is to enable us all to leave the room for half an hour, without revealing into which bedroom we are going. The men, of course, return to their original changing rooms. The women . . . they go wherever they are taken. Would you like to come with me?"

Alexandra held him close as they turned to the music. "Oh, yes," she said. "Oh, yes."

CHAPTER 6

The young man's intention of carrying off Alexandra was quickly obvious to everyone else in the room, and several of the others attempted to cut in before the lights went out, but he ignored them, now holding her very tightly against him. She gave a sigh of relief when at last the room was plunged into darkness. He held her hand to lead her. Several people groped at her as she passed them, but she didn't care about anyone else now. A moment later they were in his bedroom, and the door was locked. He switched on the light, still holding her hand, and then turned to face her. "My name is Gerard."

"I am Alexandra."

"What a splendid name. Let's have these off for a start." He removed his mask.

"I thought that was against the rules," Alexandra protested.

"There can be no rules between a man and a woman alone in a bedroom." She agreed with him, and took off her mask in turn. He was actually more handsome than she had hoped, and he was obviously also pleasantly surprised. "You are quite magnificent," he said, and kissed her.

She nearly swallowed his tongue in the fervour of her response, and then had her own imprisoned in turn. While he was kissing her, he lifted her from the floor, and sat her on the edge of the table. Then he parted her legs and stood between to kiss her again. She threw her legs round his thighs, locking her ankles on his buttocks and a moment later he was inside her, and inside her, and inside her. She had not supposed such a thing possible, but she had never met a man as strong as Gerard.

She hugged herself against him, arms and legs wrapped round him, while, still standing, he moved to and fro. She climaxed again just as he did, but he remained hard and inside her for several seconds, before she felt him start to dwindle, and slowly uncoiled her legs and allowed herself to slide down his body. She knew she should douche immediately; it was her habit anyway, but in this case it was surely more necessary than usual – she almost felt pregnant already. But she did not want to stop looking at him, into his eyes, as he looked back into hers. "I want you," he said.

"Again, so soon?"

"I mean, always."

"That's not possible. I wish it were."

"All things are possible. Who did you come with?"

"I cannot tell you that."

He lifted her into his arms again, and laid her on the bed. "I must know."

She sighed. But she wasn't going to refuse this man, anything. "Sir William Gingham-Gray."

"That old harpy? But of course: it is the talk of London that he has found the most marvellous mistress."

"Is that what they say?" She was delighted.

"Did you not know?" He lay beside her, kissed and played with her. "I must have you. Always."

She sighed again. "I must stay with Sir William."

"Why?"

"Because . . . because I have to live."

"I will support you."

"You?" She smiled at him. His fingers were doing

the most delightful things between her legs. He would be heaven as a lover. But how could so young a man have as much money as Sir Willy? "I like my comforts," she said.

He left the bed, and sat in a chair. "Whatever Sir William has given you, I will double it."

"Now, Gerard, really." She sat up.

"All right," he said. "I will quadruple it. Tell me what it is."

She frowned at him. He sounded so serious. She simply had to put him out of his misery. "Well," she said, "I have a flat. An apartment."

"How many bedrooms?"

"Well, one, of course. But it's in my name. And Sir William pays all of my bills."

"Of course," Gerard commented.

"And my bills include those for my daughter."

For the first time he looked concerned. "You have a daughter? By Sir William?

"Good Lord, no. I was married, when I was very young. My husband was killed in the War."

"How tragic for you. But you have a daughter. How old is she?"

"Nearly four."

"Sir William has obviously been very kind to you."

"Yes," she said. "He also pays me a hundred pounds a month pin money. That is a lot of money."

"Indeed it is. Will you come away with me? To Paris? You will adore Paris."

"I should love it, Gerard. But I cannot. I have to live. I think you are very sweet, and very handsome, and you make love divinely, but . . ."

"You have to live." He returned to the bed and knelt beside her. "I have said I will give you not less than four times what Sir William is giving you."

"Oh, Gerard . . ." she really felt sorry for him. He was so desperate. A buzzer went. "Oh," she said. "I suppose that's our signal to rejoin the others."

"I wish you to stay." Alexandra had no desire to leave, and by now he was ready again. She willingly turned on her stomach and rose on her hands and knees; she would have given him anything he wanted. But he merely wanted to enter her from behind. In that position he was even more magnificent, seemed able to stretch further and further into her. She had two orgasms before he reached his own climax, and collapsed in utter exhaustion. "I could never live without you, now," he said. "Listen. I am going back to France tomorrow. Come with me."

She sighed. "I have explained that I cannot."

"You mean you do not believe I can support you in the style to which you have become accustomed. If I prove to you that I can, will you come?"

"And be your mistress?"

"Yes. My mistress. I am sorry, but I cannot marry you."

"Because you are married already."

"Yes. Does that distress you?"

"I would have been surprised if you had not been. I would love to be your mistress, Gerard, but . . ."

"I understand. It is my business now to reassure you. Obviously I cannot do so tonight. Give me your address." She frowned at him. "So that I can write to you," he explained.

She gave him the address, and he entered it in a notebook he took from the pocket of his jacket, which was draped over a chair. Then he smiled at her. "We have missed the signal, and we obviously cannot return to the dance floor while the lights are on. So . . ." He looked at his watch. "We have another hour to midnight."

* * *

Alexandra writes: *It is a continuous source of amazement to me how things turn out. As I have said, but for that torpedo, I would probably have lived my life as a not entirely contented housewife. And now, but for Sir Willy's wish to show me off to his friends, I may well have once again wound up on the street, in view of everything that was going to happen. Instead I had met the most exciting man I was ever going to meet, and, quite unknowing, was about to embark upon that life which I have lived ever since. I am sure I cannot be blamed for wishing to replace Sir William, who would certainly need replacing, for one reason or another, before very long; it wasn't as if there was anything between us save my need for money and his for my body. But equally, I cannot be blamed for being afraid to take that decisive step until I knew exactly what I was going to.*

When Alexandra left Gerard, as the lights went out again at midnight, to regain Sir William's room, she was, for the first time in her life, she thought, utterly sated. She stood in front of the mirror and looked at herself, hair tousled, eyes sleepy, mouth puffy, and she supposed she was puffy in other places as well. Sir William was not amused. "Everyone knows you were with that French cad for two hours," he said crossly.

"How could they know that?" Alexandra asked. "When we realised that we had stayed too long and the lights were on again, we carefully did not come out until it was again dark."

"Ha!" he commented. "You silly girl, don't you realise you were the only couple missing?"

"Yes, but as no one else there knew who I was, or who I had come with, what is there to worry about? Anyway, how do you know Gerard is French?"

"What else could he be with that damned froggie

accent? And Gerard, eh? I suppose you told him your name."

"I did not," Alexandra lied primly. "He volunteered the information."

"Well, he seems to have given you a right going over," Sir William remarked. It was the first time he had ever been irritated with her, and she was glad to get home, although she wasn't rid of him; he spent the night in the apartment, and wanted to mount her. As he was pretty exhausted himself, it had to be sheer jealousy. In any event, he couldn't make it, and for the first time she didn't see that he did – she was just too tired . . . and she only wanted to think about Gerard.

Sir William left the next morning, and she slept for twelve hours. When she awoke she was still totally sated, and not even interested in Alice, who was hovering, dying to hear all about the party. Alexandra told her, which made her even more excited. Alexandra did not, however, mention Gerard. She wondered if she would ever hear from him again, and was taken aback when only a week later an official looking envelope was delivered to the flat. It was, in fact, the very first letter she had received since moving in; all her other correspondence had been accounts and statements and advices from the bank. She sat at her desk to open it, gazed at the letterhead in amazement. It was from the firm of Clos-Bruie et Fils, and the address was Abbeville, France. The letter was in English, and read:

Dear Mrs Mayne,

I have been instructed by M. Clos-Bruie Junior, to write to you as follows:

There is a house in St Germain, which is a suburb of Paris, awaiting your occupation. It is a large house, with four bedrooms, and a considerable garden, and is worth at present prices the equivalent of seven thousand pounds. The deeds will be made over to you upon your arrival in France. The servants for this house, and your maid, will be a charge on the House of Clos-Bruie. Your household accounts will be charged to Clos-Bruie; the house already has a well-stocked cellar. There is awaiting you at the house an automobile, a Panhard Drophead Coupe, which has been registered in your name. The car will be driven by a chauffeur, who will be a charge on the House of Clos-Bruie.

An account has been opened in your name in a Paris bank, with an initial deposit in French currency to the equivalent of five thousand pounds. A further five hundred pounds will be paid into this account on the first day of every month. The name of the bank will be conveyed to you upon your taking up residence in your new house.

It is my hope that these arrangements will be satisfactory to you. If they are, will you kindly communicate with my secretary, who will arrange for the transfer of yourself and your family and your possessions to France.

I wish you to know that my feelings for you have but grown since our last, and alas, only meeting, and that I earnestly hope that you will accept the above tokens of my esteem, and make me the happiest of men.

Signed for M. Clos-Bruie in his absence,
Annette Dubois, secretary.

Alexandra sat and stared at the words for several minutes. She supposed it had to be a mistake. Or a ghastly joke. He was planning to set her up as . . . a millionairess. A house worth seven thousand pounds, a car worth some hundred more, all her expenses, a bank account with five thousand pounds, and . . . she grabbed a pencil and paper to work it out. Another six thousand pounds a year! All to sleep with him? She telephoned Freddie. "There is a man who has somehow found out where I live," she explained. "And has been bothering me. I don't want to upset Sir Willy. Could you find out something about him for me?"

"What sort of a man?" Freddie asked.

"A Frenchman. His name is Gerard Clos-Bruie."

"Good God!" Freddie commented.

"Do you know him?"

"Not personally. I don't move in those circles, worse luck. I would be careful how you deal with him, Alexandra. He's very rich. He inherited his business from his father, and has done nothing but expand. I would say he is a millionaire several times over. But he also has a bad reputation where women are concerned."

"Bad in what way?" Alexandra wanted to know.

"He likes a lot of them around," Freddie told her.

"Ah," Alexandra said. But he couldn't set them all up in expensive houses, surely?

"You and Sir William still thick as thieves?" Freddie asked, hopefully.

"Oh, yes," Alexandra said.

She needed to think. Because if Freddie was telling the truth, she would be taking an enormous risk. Sir Willy might not be in the same class as Gerard, either as a lover or, apparently, financially, but he represented security. Gerard might want her now, but if he really was a fly-by-night . . . his secretary had said the house would be in her name, but that could be a trick. Once she abandoned Sir Willy she would really be out on her own. It was the first time in her life Alexandra had had a serious decision to make. Up till now things had just happened to her. She had had no say in the choice of Harry Lowndes as her husband, or of Sir Willy as her employer . . . and leaving Tony the Greek for Sir Willy had been no decision at all. But now . . . she wished there was someone with whom she could discuss it. But there wasn't. Alice would be worse than useless.

She might never have made up her mind, but for two incidents which followed in quick succession, and made her realise that Sir William did not actually represent security after all. The first was when she was walking along Oxford Street only a few days later. She had just left Selfridge's, where she had been buying underclothes, and was waiting for a taxi, when she heard a voice say, "Well, hello, Alexandra." She turned, all the blood draining from her face, and gazed at Tony the Greek. He looked different to how she remembered him; his face was pale and his hair was cut short. But it was him.

"Long time no see," he remarked. Alexandra licked her lips. "My fault," he admitted magnanimously. "They sent me up. They had a list of charges a mile long. Didn't you read about it?"

"I don't read the newspapers," Alexandra told him.

"Well, they got me, for two years. But I behaved myself. I'm on remission. I still have to behave myself. But I'm putting things back together."

"Good luck," Alexandra said.

"You are one of the things I want back," he said. "I don't blame you for trying your luck somewhere else with me not around. But now I want you back."

"If you lay a finger on me," Alexandra said, far more confidently than she felt, "I will have you back in gaol quicker than you can spit."

He looked her up and down. "Your boyfriend won't be quite so generous if you come home with slit cheeks."

Alexandra gave him her best glare, debated calling for a policeman, and saw a taxi discharging a passenger not twenty feet away. She ran for it, elbowed an elderly gentleman out of the way, and slammed the door. "Hurry," she said.

"Where to, love?"

"Just drive."

Tony was knocking on the window, but the taxi was moving away from the kerb, and she could give a sigh of relief. Then she told the driver her address.

"What's the matter with you?" Alice asked. "You look as though you've seen a ghost."

"Yes," Alexandra agreed. "I need a drink. Brandy."

Of course he would be able to find her address. The only reason he hadn't done so already was because he'd been in prison. She wanted to talk to Sir Willy about it, because this was something he surely could take care of, but to her disappointment Sir Willy didn't come the following week. Of course he had missed weeks before, but right at this time it was most annoying . . . she was afraid to go down to the West End, which was her favourite occupation. She spent a thoroughly depressed weekend, and nearly jumped out of her skin when on the Sunday afternoon the doorbell rang. Alice hurried into the lounge. "Wait," Alexandra commanded. "Find out who it is first."

Alice raised her eyebrows, but peered through the peephole. "It's a woman."

"A woman? What sort of a woman?"

"She looks very well dressed," Alice said. "I would say she is a lady." The bell trilled again.

"And you're sure she's alone?" Alexandra asked.

Alice squinted some more. "Oh, yes. There's nobody else."

"Then you can let her in."

Alice, who was wearing her black uniform, unbolted the door, and Alexandra, who was wearing her red dressing gown, gazed at Lady Virginia Gingham-Gray.

"You unutterable little wretch," Lady Virginia remarked, stalking into the room.

Alexandra got her breathing back under control, and gave a brief nod to Alice to close the door, she didn't want everyone else in the building to hear the coming row. Because obviously there was going to be one. "How nice to see you, your ladyship," she said. "After all this time. You are looking well."

Lady Virginia did not reply. Instead she walked past Alexandra and opened the bedroom door. "Well!" she remarked. She went into the kitchen, gazed at the equipment, then opened the door to the small bedroom. Mayne was on the floor playing with her dolls, of which she had seven – Alexandra liked buying dolls, she had never had any of her own. "Well!" Lady Virginia observed again.

Alexandra waited for her to return to the lounge. She was aware of a slowly growing anger. This woman was walking about her flat as if she owned it. She glanced at Alice, who was clearly terrified, having guessed who Lady Virginia had to be. But Alice would follow her lead without question, Alexandra knew. "Perhaps you'll tell me what you're looking for?" she asked politely.

"I am just obtaining the evidence of my own eyes," Lady Virginia said. "Otherwise I would never have believed it. William has lavished all of this, on you?"

"Why, yes," Alexandra said. "Sir Willy likes to come here and relax."

"Sir . . . you are impertinent, girl."

"You mean you are impertinent, barging in here like this," Alexandra pointed out.

Virginia flushed, but with anger rather than embarrassment. "You are nothing but a whore," she announced. "I will give you fifteen minutes to pack up and get out of here. Taking your brat, and that . . ." she pointed at Alice, "with you."

"You have got hold of the wrong end of the stick, Ginny," Alexandra told her, being as deliberately insolent as she could. "This apartment happens to belong to me. Not Sir Willy, and certainly not you. So now I am giving *you* one minute to leave. And don't bother to come back."

Virginia glared at her, and then swung her hand. Alexandra saw the blow coming, stepped back to avoid it, and while Virginia was off balance, delivered her own, a slap on the side of the head which turned Virginia right round and sprawled her on the carpet. Her head hit the floor, and she lay still. "Oh, my God!" Alice gasped. "You've killed her!"

Alexandra knelt beside Virginia, rolled her over, and felt her heartbeat. And a lot more besides. If a trifle overweight, Virginia was a most attractive woman. "She's only unconscious," she told Alice. "Help me." She grasped one of Virginia's arms. "Come along, do," she added, as Alice hesitated. Alice took the other arm, and between them they dragged Virginia into the bedroom; one of her shoes came off. "On to the bed," Alexandra panted. This took a great deal of heaving and pushing, but at last Virginia was rolled on to the bed. By now she was starting to sigh, and her eyes were fluttering. "Hurry," Alexandra said. "Fetch some clothes line."

Alice obeyed, running to and from the kitchen. Alexandra used the kitchen knife to cut the appropriate lengths of line and she and Alice secured Virginia's wrists to the bedposts. Virginia's eyes opened, and she heaved her body. "My God!" she said. "My head."

"I think you should fetch her ladyship a drink, Alice," Alexandra recommended. Alice hurried from the room.

Virginia realised that her wrists were secured above her head. "What on earth . . . Release me this instant!"

"If I don't, are you going to scream?" Alexandra asked.

Virginia glared at her in turn. "I will have you thrown in gaol. I will . . ."

"If you scream," Alexandra said, "and people come in here, I will have to tell them that we are making love."

"You . . ." Virginia apparently didn't know what to call her.

Alice returned with the glass of brandy. "This'll cheer you up," Alexandra said. "You hold her head, Alice." Alice obeyed, and Alexandra held Virginia's chin with one hand, squeezed, and filled Virginia's mouth with the alcohol. Virginia coughed and spat, but a good deal went down, and Alexandra continued the dosage until the glass was empty. By then Virginia's jacket and blouse were soaked, and she stank of brandy, but Alexandra reckoned that she had drunk at least half the glass.

She went to her cupboard and took out one of her new toys, a box camera she had bought for herself. She had hitherto used it principally for photos of Mayne, but she had long dreamed of taking more exotic, and erotic, snaps – she had had Alice in mind, or better yet, having Alice take photos of her. She hadn't tried it yet because she had no idea how she could get the photos developed without being arrested. But Virginia Gingham-Gray wouldn't know she didn't have a professional photographer amongst her male friends. "Now I am going to record your beauty for posterity."

For the first time Virginia realised that she was holding a camera. "You bitch," she shouted. "You bitch!"

"We need some more light," Alexandra decided. She and Alice turned on every light in the room, and then brought in the standing lamp from the lounge.

Virginia twisted and panted. "What you need is a flashlight," Alice said. "Like the professionals."

"I think we'll get a good enough picture," Alexandra

said, not really caring whether she did or not – as long as Virgina *thought* she was.

Virginia drew a long breath. "What do you want from me?" she asked.

"Just your co-operation." Alexandra, satisfied with her photography, began to release Virginia. "You're all sticky and wet with brandy. I think you need to wash up a bit." Virginia rolled off the bed, hugging herself. "It's through there," Alexandra said. "Would you like me to help you? Or Alice?"

Virginia gave her a look which should have killed her, and went into the bathroom. When she reappeared, she had regained a good deal of her composure – and her aggression.

She hastily let herself out and closed the door behind her. Alice was looking scared again, but when Alexandra began to laugh she had to laugh too.

Alexandra looked forward to laughing about the incident with Sir Willy, but she never had the opportunity, because he never came to see her again. And the following month no cheque was paid into her bank account, while the grocer on the corner presented Alexandra with his bill. "Sorry, dear," he said. "That's what I've been told to do."

Alexandra was more surprised than angry; she would never have expected Virginia to tell Sir Willy about her adventure. But at least it left her with no decision to make, and so she wrote Annette Dubois and explained that she had been out of town and thus had only just received her letter, but that she and her daughter and her maid would be delighted to come and live in France.

It was then a matter of waiting, with some apprehension, for a reply, wondering if Gerard might not have gone off the boil, or found someone else for the house in St Germain. However, a week later a reply arrived, containing a draft for five thousand francs "for removal expenses", and informing Alexandra that she would be met in Calais if she wired her date and time of arrival.

It was all frighteningly businesslike, as if she were taking up a new job – which she supposed she was. Alexandra became wildly excited, and so were Alice and Mayne. There was so much to be done, quite apart from packing up and booking their passages and arranging for their goods to be shipped. There was the bank account to be closed, and there was the flat to be put on the market. The bank manager was helpful here, and sent Alexandra to a good estate agent. He also strongly recommended that she did not transfer all her funds into francs, even if she was, as she told him, taking up a position in France for a while; she hardly considered this statement a lie. So she left her money in England, after he had assured her that no one in the whole world could touch it except herself, and certainly neither Sir William nor Lady Virginia. He then suggested that if she needed a little more between now and her departure, he would be happy to supply it, in person, by calling at her flat.

Alexandra thanked him but declined; she now regarded herself as belonging wholly to Gerard – a man she had only met once. Again she was frightened. But she took Alice and Mayne to Fortnums and bought them all new outfits so that they would make a good first impression, and wired Madame Dubois the details of their travel plans.

Then it was again just a matter of waiting, for the removal men to come and pack up their heavy goods, which Madame Dubois had instructed were to be sent in advance, care of Clos-Bruie et Fils. One or two people came to see the flat, and seemed quite interested, even if the men were more interested in the "poor young widow" with her little girl, who was being forced to sell by circumstances beyond her control. What with the excitement of the impending move, and her endeavours to learn French from a phrase book, Alexandra quite relaxed her usual watchfulness. The day before they were due to depart, and after their trunks had already been despatched, leaving them with one small suitcase each, the doorbell rang. She assumed it was another potential buyer for the flat and opened the door herself without checking to see who was actually there. Tony placed his hand on her chest and pushed, and she staggered back into the lounge, while he came in and closed the door behind himself, carefully locking it. "You can't come busting in here like this," Alexandra snapped, for the moment more angry than afraid. "I've a good mind to call the police."

"You try," he recommended. "I've come here to do a lot of busting. Your ass for a start. And then you're coming back to work for me. Indeed. You're mine, you little bitch. I don't give up what's mine." He obviously had no idea how much she had grown up over the past year, or that she had just cut her last links with England, just as he apparently supposed she was alone in the flat.

But Alice was already standing behind him, raising and lowering her eyebrows in an attempt to receive some instructions; if she had never seen Tony before in her life she could understand that he was not welcome. "If you attempt to lay a finger on me," Alexandra said, "someone is going to hit you, very hard."

"Oh, yeah?" Tony asked.

"In fact, I think someone should do that anyway," Alexandra said, peremptorily, as he came towards her. Alice got the message, and disappeared.

"I'm going to enjoy this," Tony told Alexandra, standing in front of her. "I dreamed of taking the skin off your ass all the time I was in prison." He reached out and opened her dressing gown, which, as usual around the flat, was all she was wearing. "Christ, but you just get better and better."

"So why don't you make me an offer I can't refuse?" Alexandra asked, playing for time. "Instead of trying to bully me?" Alice was back by now, carrying their largest iron frying pan, both hands wrapped around the handle.

"Because I enjoy bullying you, baby," Tony said. "And because bullying is the only thing you can understand."

"That's it," Alexandra said. "As hard as you can."

For the first time Tony appeared to realise there was someone else in the room with them. He started to turn, but Alice was already swinging as if she were playing baseball. For a small girl she had a lot of strength. The noise sounded as if someone had struck a base drum, and Tony went down as if poleaxed; the entire flat shook. "Oh, Lord," Alice said. "Do you think I hit him too hard?"

"No," Alexandra said.

"What do we do now?" Alice asked. "Call the police?"

"Not on your life," Alexandra told her. "I owe this bastard a lot more than the police can ever do to him. We are going to teach him a lesson he won't ever forget. Come on, let's hurry before he wakes up, or you'll have to hit him again."

They had the drill worked out by now. Between them, which some eager hindrance from Mayne, they dragged Tony into the bedroom and heaved him on to the bed. "This has to be good and strong," Alexandra said, as they tied his wrists and ankles to each bedpost. By now he was showing signs of regaining consciousness, but Alexandra insisted upon adding an extra line to each limb, so that he was completely trussed. "Now let's take down his pants," she said.

Alice unbuckled his belt and between them they pulled his pants and drawers down his thighs. With his legs spread they couldn't get them further than that, but Alexandra merely slit them open with the kitchen knife so that they could be pulled right off. "We don't have to worry about *him* being properly dressed when he leaves," she said. Alice and Mayne were staring at him in amazement. Even in a totally deflated state, Tony was still much larger than Sir Willy, who was the only man either of them had ever seen. Even Alexandra had forgotten how large he was. "We are going to have fun," she said.

Tony's eyes opened, and he groaned, then they opened still further as he discovered his predicament. "What the hell . . ."

Alexandra flicked his still flaccid penis. "We're going to be nice to you," she said. "In our fashion. How's your head?"

"Bloody awful," he growled, tugging on the various pieces of clothesline, without success.

"Would you like a drink?" Alexandra asked, and upended the dregs of the brandy bottle on to his face. He gasped and choked.

"Just what are you playing at?" he demanded. "You want a fuck. I'll give you one."

"I wouldn't touch you if you were the last man on earth," Alexandra told him. "We're going to cut it off."

"Big joke," Tony said.

"We'll see," Alexandra said. "Fetch the big kitchen knife, Alice."

Alice hurried off. "Now, say, wait a moment," Tony said. "It was a joke, wasn't it?"

"Oh, no," Alexandra said. Alice came back with the

kitchen knife, looking a little nervous; she didn't know if it was a joke or not – one never could tell with Alexandra.

"For God's sake," Tony shouted. "Hey, let me go."

"I think he's going to scream," Alexandra said. "I think we'll have to gag him."

"Let me go," Tony bawled. "You bitch, when I get out of here . . ."

"But you're not going to get out of here," Alexandra pointed out. "Open wide."

"You bitch! You . . ." His mouth was open and she hastily stuffed a rolled napkin in, then another. Alice had some more clothesline ready, and they tied the gag in place. Tony could only gasp and gurgle.

"We'd better blindfold him," Alexandra said. "It won't be a pretty sight." They put some more napkins over his eyes, which were rolling horribly, and tied those into place as well. Alexandra then rested the knife blade on his thigh, and he moaned and twisted, but to her amazement he was hardening. "Makes it easier," she said, and held the shaft in one hand while she touched the base with the knife blade. "Balls and all in one quick slash."

"You're not really going to?" Alice whispered.

"No, but I'm going to make him feel like it," Alexandra said. As they had spent the past week packing up and sealing their boxes, there was a large wodge of sealing wax still left. She went into the lounge and fetched this and a candle. She lit the candle, and they waited until the wax was starting to melt. Tony had almost ceased his writhing while they had been waiting for the candle to get hot, trying to hear what was going on. His nostrils had twitched at the scent of the burning wax, and he continued to make inarticulate noises at the back of his throat. Now he jerked convulsively as the hot wax landed, and again. Alexandra coated him, slowly and carefully, from glans to testicles. When it was dry and solid, the wax would be giving him very peculiar sensations. Alexandra reckoned he wouldn't be sure whether or not he *had* been castrated. "There," she said, when the penis was entirely coated with the now drying and cooling wax. She pushed the two girls outside and closed the door. "Now let's go."

"But we're not due to leave until tomorrow," Alice protested.

"Today will do," Alexandra said. They bathed and dressed themselves, fetched their suitcases, finished packing, and went downstairs. Alexandra left the front door unlocked. They took a taxi to the railway station, purchased tickets to Dover. They reached the port about five that afternoon, by which time Tony had been lying on the bed, unable to move and encased in wax, for some six hours. There was an evening sailing of the ferry, and so Alexandra changed their tickets for that one, and ten minutes before they were due to board she telephoned the woman in the flat below hers.

"This is Alexandra," she said. "I wonder if you could do something for me? I've gone away for a couple of days, and I think I've left the stove on, and the front door open. Do you think you could possibly go in and check it out for me?" The woman readily agreed, and Alexandra thanked her and hung up.

"Do you think he'll go to the police?" Alice asked, anxiously.

"Not him. If he did, they'd only laugh at him . . . and his reputation as a pimp would be ruined forever. And as a tough guy."

"He is going to be so angry," Alice said. "My God . . . if he ever catches up with us . . ."

"He's not going to," Alexandra told her. "He may be able to find out we've gone to France, but he won't know where. Nobody knows that, not even us." She watched Dover dropping astern as the ship ploughed into the calm waters of the Channel. "That's goodbye to a whole part of our lives, Alice. From here on it's up all the way."

CHAPTER 7

So here I was, Alexandra writes, *being launched into a world of which I knew nothing. Had I any idea of where it was going to lead me, I wonder if I would have risked it?*

Alexandra secured Alice and Mayne and herself rooms in a Calais hotel, and the next morning they returned to the docks at the hour they had originally intended to cross, and there found Annette Dubois waiting for them. Alexandra, for all the confidence she projected, was distinctly nervous. Madame Dubois had been most friendly and welcoming in her letters, and clearly she was in charge of Gerard's most intimate business . . . but, being so, she would also be fully aware of Alexandra's position. Yet she could not have been more charming. A small, dark woman, she spoke perfect English, kissed Alexandra on both cheeks, did the same to Alice, and gave Mayne a huge hug. "M Clos-Bruie will be entranced," she promised.

She had driven down from Paris, and it was a long drive back; it was the first time Alexandra had ever been driven by a woman, but Annette handled the car as well as any man. On the way they stopped for lunch, and Alexandra had her first taste of French bread and wine and salads, so different to anything she had ever known in England. But meanwhile her nervousness, allayed by

Annette's greeting, was now returning. "Will Gerard . . . M Clos-Bruie, be at the house?"

"Alas, no," Annette said. "He is in Switzerland at the moment. He will be back at the end of the week, eh?" She glanced at Alexandra. "But do not worry. Anything you wish, you have but to tell me, and I will arrange it for you." She gave a quick smile.

Annette had a pert rather than pretty face behind her horn-rimmed spectacles, and good legs; it was difficult to be sure about the rest of her. She was also quite old, about thirty-five, Alexandra estimated, which she found interesting: it was a female age with which she had had little contact. The drive itself was equally interesting, because everything was so different to England. They were in the suburbs of Paris before Alexandra realised it, and soon were turning in at a pair of wrought-iron gates which led off the street and along a gravel drive lined with weeping willows, up to a large house set well back from the street. "Is my house not ready?" Alexandra asked in dismay.

"But of course it is," Annette told her. "It has been ready for weeks."

"Then why are we going to an hotel?"

Annette laughed. "This is not an hotel, madame. This is your house." Before Alexandra could quite digest this fact, the car was stopping before a wide flight of stone steps which led up to a porch, and waiting for her were several people. Annette did the introductions. "This is Armand, your butler," she said. A tall, thin man, about forty-five, Alexandra estimated, with a grave expression.

"This is Madame Lucas, your housekeeper." Somewhat younger than the butler, and also thin and serious.

"Madame Morceuf, your cook." Powerfully built and red of both face and hands, but surprisingly young.

"Jean-Claude, your chauffeur." Alexandra decided she liked the look of him. He was small and swarthy, young and intense. And he obviously liked the look of her as well.

"And Lucien, the yard boy." Lucien could hardly have been more than twelve, and was so overawed at meeting his new mistress he couldn't say a word.

Annette next took Alexandra, Mayne and Alice on a tour of the house. There were actually five main bedrooms on the upper floor, each about the size of the entire London flat, and each superbly furnished with huge tester beds, soft carpets, great bureaux and wardrobes, exquisite light fixtures; each two rooms shared a bathroom, while the master bedroom was en suite. The servants apparently slept in the attic, but Alexandra immediately established that Alice would have a room on the same floor as herself. She was intrigued by the three staircases, for apart from the grand staircase, which led from the front hall to a gallery fronting the bedrooms, there was the servants' staircase, from the kitchen to the attic, and a private staircase leading up to the master suite. Downstairs were an enormous drawing room and a matching dining room; they were connected by doors which could fold right back to enlarge the room for entertaining. Again the furnishings were flawless, and expensive. To the right, glass doors gave access to a lawn, fringed in the distance by more weeping willows. Behind the dining room were the pantries and kitchens, but Alexandra was in no mood to interest herself in them; she was too excited. Because everything *was* at her command. She invited Annette to stay to dinner, and without hesitation Madame Morceuf produced a splendid meal. "I hope you will be happy here," Annette said.

"Oh, I shall," Alexandra promised.

"Then M Clos-Bruie will be happy as well," Annette

said. "Now, tomorrow morning I will come for you, and take you to the bank, eh? To sign all the papers."

"I shall look forward to that. But . . ." Alexandra's brain had been whirring throughout her tour. She needed a friend, in the opposite camp, as it were. Besides, this woman intrigued her. Of course, she realised she was going to have to be very careful: Gerard had not brought her here to seduce his secretary! "Tomorrow morning is only a few hours away. Why do you not spend the night here?"

"Here? Ooh, la-la. It would be an imposition, madame."

"I assure you that it would not be. It will be a pleasure."

Armand produced a bottle of cognac from the bar cabinet, and Alexandra and Annette each had a drink, and also gave one to Alice, who had returned from Mayne's bedroom. They sipped their brandies while Annette told them about Gerard, how he had lived a somewhat wild life as a youth, but when his father had been taken terminally ill with cancer he had turned over a new leaf, got married, and settled down to managing and indeed expanding the business, which he had done most successfully. "Since old M Clos-Bruie died," Annette said, "M Clos-Bruie has more than doubled the profits."

"Tell me about Madame Clos-Bruie," Alexandra said.

"She comes from one of the best families in France," Annette said. "She is descended from one of Napoleon's marshals. But things have not been so good since those days, eh? Her parents were happy to marry their beautiful young daughter to the rising young industrialist."

"Beautiful?" Alexandra inquired.

"Ma," Mayne said from the doorway. "I can't sleep."

"Oh, Mayne," Alexandra said. "You are a nuisance."

"I'll take her back up," Alice volunteered.

"That would be so kind of you, Alice," Alexandra agreed. "And I think it would be a good idea if you stayed until she drops off. Perhaps you could take the room adjoining hers as your own, then you can hear if she wakes again."

Alice glanced at Annette. She knew exactly what was Alexandra had in mind. But she also knew better than to be possessive with her mistress. "Of course," she agreed. "Come along, Mayne."

"She is a lovely girl," Annette murmured.

"She's very young," Alexandra reminded her.

"Is she? I would have supposed she is at least eighteen."

"Ah," Alexandra said, understanding that Annette had not been speaking of Mayne. "Yes. I suppose Alice is a lovely girl." Because Alice had filled out over the past couple of years; the careworn and half-starved waif was merely a memory.

Alexandra resumed her seat on the sofa beside Annette. "I am surrounded by beautiful women," she said. "But that is how I like to be. You were going to tell me about Madame Clos-Bruie. Is she as beautiful as I?"

"Oh, madame! How can I say? She is very different."

"I think you should show me where she is different." Alexandra stood up and held out her hand. Annette hesitated a long time, then grasped the proffered fingers.

Next morning Annette had to be away, early. She looked utterly exhausted, as well she should be, as they had hardly slept until an hour before dawn. But she also looked very happy. Alexandra was of course accompanying her, to be taken to the bank to open her account. "Now," she said, as Annette drove into the centre of Paris. "We are friends. We are intimates. We are *lovers*."

"Oh, yes, madame," Annette breathed.

"You must come down to see us whenever you have an opportunity," Alexandra pressed.

"I shall try, madame. But it will not be as often as I would like. I cannot risk my husband becoming suspicious."

"Oh, quite," Alexandra agreed. "But there is something I would like you to do for me."

"Anything, madame."

"I would like to be informed, in advance, of when Monsieur Gerard will be visiting me. You know all his appointments and intentions, I presume?"

"Well, madame, most of them."

"Then you will telephone me here, as soon as he leaves his office."

"Of course, madame."

"You are a dear, sweet lady," Alexandra said. "I just know we are going to be the best of friends."

Alexandra was well satisfied. Seducing Annette had been fun. Seducing anyone was fun. And even if the secretary would be a bit of a bore on a regular basis it was important to keep her bound entirely to them.

After their visit to the bank and the lawyer, she realised that she was a wealthy woman . . . by her previous standards. Obviously there were a great many degrees of wealth. She wanted to be up there with Gerard Clos-Bruie on her own account. But she reckoned she had time on her side.

Annette telephoned ten days later to say that Monsieur Gerard was on his way. Alexandra had used her time well. She had been at great pains to make friends with each member of her staff, spending some time with each of them, and congratulating them on their efficiency. The older people, cook and housekeeper and butler, she merely wished to please, to make them pleased with her.

The chauffeur was a very different matter. If he was not terribly handsome, he was chunkily powerful and certainly all male. And if he reminded her vaguely of Tony the Greek, he was in her employ rather than the other way around. She started taking a drive in the country every day, in her new car, with Mayne and Alice of course, and stopping by the banks of the river or a canal for a stroll and a picnic, but she was aware all the time that he was watching her, as she sat down on the grass to roll down her stockings and take off her shoes, before wading with Mayne, her skirts held high to reveal her legs. She wasn't sure whether to be apprehensive or flattered. Where she had only ever sought to have an Alice, now she was suddenly mistress of many people. That was an even more heady sensation that owning the house.

The boy Lucien she found even more interesting than Jean-Claude. He was clearly just reaching the age when he was discovering what sex was about. Equally, he was just discovering, or at least suspecting, what delightful playthings girls could be.

Alexandra writes: *I really must beg forgiveness for being at this time on what might be called an erotic high. In the most amazing fashion I had fallen on my feet, in the midst of a group of people who were absolutely mine. For someone who all her life, or so it seemed to me, had belonged to other people, this was a very heady experience. But of course, while I enjoyed flirting with them all, or doing more than that with Annette, I was always aware that if they belonged to me, I belonged to Gerard. Only he mattered.*

Her plans were immediately put into effect. On hearing from Annette, she and Alice both hastily bathed, as did Mayne. The other servants had already been warned that in no circumstances were they to venture up the stairs while Monsieur was in the house, and Alexandra left Alice and Mayne to prepare themselves while she perfumed herself and put on one of her best linen dresses. Hemlines were beginning to creep up the calf, and this was in the very latest fashion; it was impossible for her to sit down without revealing her knees. Her underwear was lace, her stockings silk; Gerard would require a vastly more sophisticated approach than poor old Sir Willy. She wondered just what relations the old reprobate was presently enjoying with Virginia, and if she was still feeding him girls to fumble first thing in the morning?

She listened to the sound of the high-powered automobile engine on the drive, and felt a pleasant excitement. It really was quite a long time since she had had any proper sex, and she knew she had to recapture the ecstacy of that night at the club. Armand opened the door as Gerard came up the front steps, and was greeted warmly. Alexandra was waiting at the arched entrance to the drawing room. "My dear!" Gerard came across the hall to her, held her hands, and kissed each in turn. "How beautiful you are. Far more beautiful than I even remembered." He was more handsome than she remembered, too. We must make the most splendid couple, she thought. Still holding her hand, but not yet having kissed her, he walked with her into the drawing room. "Do you like your new home?"

"I am enchanted, monsieur," she said. "I am enchanted with everything. I am enchanted with you."

Armand was waiting with two glasses of Pernod, Annette having told Alexandra this was Gerard's favourite aperitif. "You think of everything," Gerard said, and touched hers with his before drinking. Then, when she had also sipped, he exchanged glasses.

Alexandra was delighted. It was a sort of kiss by remote control. "Can you stay the night?" she asked. "Cook has prepared something very special."

"Alas, ma cherie, I am supposed to be attending a conference in Lille. I can stay for dinner, but I must return to my home tonight." He saw her disappointment, and put his arm round her shoulders. "Do not be sad. In another few weeks Madeleine visits her family, in Nice. She will be gone for three weeks. I will spend every night here with you."

Alexandra found that a slightly daunting thought – she had never spent twenty-one consecutive days with any man, not even her husband. But that was why she was here. "That will be perfect," she said. "But Gerard, if you must leave immediately after dinner, and it has been so very long . . ."

"Yes," he agreed, and still holding her hand, led her to the stairs. "I have dreamed of this moment since our last meeting. Sometimes I wondered if you were real."

"Now you know that I am," Alexandra told him.

"Oh, indeed. How real I . . ." He paused, because they had reached the top of the stairs, and Alice was waiting for them, and today she was fully dressed, in black skirt and blouse, black silk stockings, and black high-heeled shoes. Her white pinafore and cap formed, with her pale hair and complexion, an agreeable contrast.

"This is my personal maid, Gerard," Alexandra explained. "Or should I say, *our* personal maid?" She paused to let him know what she meant. "Her name is Alice."

"Monsieur." Alice gave a little curtsey; she had been studying French.

"Alice. I am very pleased to make your acquaintance." Gerard had recovered his sang froid, but Alexandra had no intention of letting him regain the initiative.

"And this is my daughter, Mayne," she said.

Mayne, who was now four, came out of her bedroom on cue, and also gave a curtsey. She wore a white party dress and white stockings and shoes; on her it was the black hair and eyes that made the contrast.

"What a pretty child," Gerard said, looking at Alice.

"I think so. Run along downstairs now, Mayne," Alexandra said. "Uncle Gerard and Mummy have things to discuss."

"Yes, Mummy," Mayne said obediently, having been well rehearsed, and dutifully went down the stairs.

"And so well behaved," Gerard commented.

Alexandra led him into the bedroom. "So here I am, my darling," she said. "I hope you are not disappointed."

"Disappointed? Oh, my dearest girl . . ." He took her in his arms and kissed her, and while he was doing so, lifted her from the floor. She remembered him doing that at the meeting of Sir Willy's club.

"I am so happy, Gerard," she whispered against his ear. "My only wish is to make you happy, too."

"I am already," he said. "Just looking at you." He stepped back, and encountered Alice. "What the devil . . ." Then he realised that Alice had used her last few minutes to strip, to her cap, apron, and high-heeled shoes. "Mon Dieu!"

"Will monsieur allow me?" Alice asked demurely, and removed his jacket. Gerard gazed at Alexandra, who was unbuttoning her blouse as she stepped out of her shoes.

"If she annoys you, just say so," Alexandra told him. "And we will send her away."

Gerard's mouth sagged open. Alexandra reckoned it was the first time in his life he had been entirely out of his depths.

Alice had removed his shirt and was unfastening his trousers. He stood there while she slipped them down, put one hand on her naked shoulder to balance himself as he raised each leg in turn. Alice did the same for his underpants. "If monsieur will sit down," she suggested. "I will attend to his shoes and socks." Gerard sat on the bed. Alexandra had by now finished undressing, and lay across the bed on her elbow, watching them. Alice carefully removed Gerard's socks and shoes, and then stood up. She was breathing quite heavily. "Will there be anything else, sir?" she asked. Gerard looked at Alexandra.

"Would you like anything else, now, my love?" Alexandra asked. "You can touch her, if you like."

Gerard touched Alice's breast, and she gave a little shiver. "Perhaps later," he said.

"Thank you, Alice," Alexandra said. "That will be all for now. I'll ring."

"Yes, Mum," Alice said, and left.

"What a treasure," Gerard said. "Where did you find her?"

"I have had Alice for a long time. Before I met you." Alexandra swung her legs off the bed and went to him, sat on his knees facing him, astride. "Do you prefer her to me?"

"My darling Alix . . ." His hands slid over her shoulders and down past her back to caress her buttocks. He moved his knees apart so that she had to spread her own legs, and slipped his fingers between, while he pulled his head back to smile at her. "Every woman is beautiful when in the throes of an orgasm," he said. "But your beauty redoubles."

"Oh, my darling," she said. "Do that again."

"I am the happiest woman in the world," she told him later.

"And I am the happiest man," he agreed.

They made love for an hour, and then sent for Alice. As Alexandra had imagined would be the case, Gerard thoroughly enjoyed watching two women making love, but eventually even he became exhausted. Then they bathed together and had a candlelit supper, previously arranged by Alexandra. Following which Alexandra and Alice sat with Gerard on the sofa, both wearing evening gowns, and sipped cognac. "This is the best evening I have ever had," Gerard confessed.

"I only wish you could stay longer," Alexandra said. "But it is only the first of many, I promise you that." She meant it. The omnivorous thoughts which had been clouding her mind before his arrival disappeared. The chauffeur and the boy were now nothing more than servants. Annette of course had to be humoured, whenever she could get down to the house, but that could in any event be left mainly to Alice. And as Gerard had promised, only a fortnight later he was able to come down and spend an entire three weeks. Alexandra had not forgotten her promise to Annette, however. Besides, she wanted to discover just how promiscuous Gerard was. "How many mistresses do you have?" she asked as they sat up in bed together one morning, enjoying their breakfast.

"How many? My darling girl, you are my only mistress."

"But I suppose you have a lot on the side."

"Well . . . one picks up what trifles one can, from one's friends. Or one did. But you are enough for me, now."

"What about Annette?"

"My secretary? My God! You have never met Annette." He frowned. "But you have. Did she not meet your boat, and bring you here?"

"Of course she did. I found her a very charming person."

"Charming, indeed. And most efficient. But utterly sexless. You should see that husband of hers. The pair of them think the *Perfumed Garden* is in the Vatican."

"I have never met the husband, but I think you may be wrong about her," Alexandra said.

"What are you trying to suggest? That I throw her across my desk one afternoon? I'd be arrested for rape."

"She adores you," Alexandra told him.

"Oh, come now. How do you know?"

"She has told me so."

"At your one meeting?"

"She spent the night with me, and has done so often since."

Gerard put down his coffee cup the better to turn to look at her. He had by now several times studied her making love with Alice; it was one of his most enjoyable pastimes. "You have seduced my secretary?" he asked.

"I was lonely, and upset."

"You, lonely and upset?"

"I often get lonely and upset, Besides, you were not here. But she does adore you, Gerard."

"You are the most remarkable woman I have ever met. But I really cannot consider taking on Annette as well as you . . . even if I wanted to. And with a woman like Annette, I suspect she wouldn't be satisfied with a one night stand."

"I think she would be satisfied with anything."

"You mean you would not object?"

"It is my business to make you happy, my darling. You will become bored if you have only me."

"That, never," he declared.

"Well," she teased, "what about it? Annette I mean?"

"Well . . . she is quite an attractive little thing, in a different sort of way. Is she good in bed?"

"Oh, she is. I will invite her down, and you will have her to your heart's content."

"Alix, you are a woman in a thousand."

"In a million," she told him. "Just do not forget that."

Annette, who of course knew where her boss was, was told by Alexandra on the telephone that Monsieur Gerard had some business instructions to give her, and asked her if she could drop down one evening after work. Alexandra was afraid that to tell her the truth over the phone might so terrify her she would not come. She arrived at seven, and was greeted by Alexandra. "My dearest!" Alexandra embraced her and kissed her.

"I came as soon as I could," Annette said. "But . . . where is Monsieur Clos-Bruie?"

"I have no idea. He had to go into Paris."

"Ooh, la-la. I have just come from there. I must get back."

"That is not at all necessary, Annette, dear Annette." Alexandra held her hand and led her into the drawing room. "It has been so long. As you are here, you will stay and have dinner, and then spend the night."

"But I should get back . . ."

"No, no. I do not think Gerard has gone to the office. Oh, Annette . . ." She took her in her arms and kissed her again. "I have missed you so. And so has Alice."

"Alice," Annette murmured, remembering anew that astonishing night of passion with these two beautiful women. “Oh, it has been a long time, hasn’t it, madame? Well, if you insist . . .”

“I do,” Alexandra said. “I have already told Helene to expect an extra place for dinner. But that is not for two hours yet, and as you are here . . .” Still holding Annette’s hand, she led her up the stairs and into the master bedroom, where Alice was there, already undressed. Annette gave a little squeal of pleasure, and was in her arms, with Alexandra hovering over them like a fairy godmother, every so often glancing at the inner door behind which Gerard was waiting, and listening. Within seconds Annette was in bed with Alice, whereupon Alexandra said, “Let’s really have some fun.”

This was the agreed signal, and Gerard came in. He was already undressed, and very aroused. This time Annette’s squeak was one of alarm, but before she could make up her mind what to do Gerard was on top of her. Annette was overwhelmed. “Oh, monsieur!” she gasped. “You have made me so very happy.”

“See how I always keep my word, Annette?” Alexandra asked.

Gerard was enthralled with the entertainment Alexandra had laid on for him. Next day he told Alexandra he would like to invite some of his men friends down for dinner. Alexandra arranged for Annette to spend that night as well, and the dazed guests were entertained to the meal by herself, Alice, and Annette, all naked save for as much jewellery as she could provide. The servants had been given the night off, and it was a buffet very like the club occasion on which Alexandra had first met Gerard. There were no absurdities like periods of darkness. No one was permitted to leave the room, either, but extra mattresses had been supplied and were scattered about the floor. It seemed to give Gerard as much pleasure to see Alexandra servicing other men as doing it himself, and Alexandra certainly enjoyed herself, as did Alice and Annette. By dawn even the women were exhausted. "That was the best evening of my life," Gerard told Alexandra, for the second time. "And I can speak for my friends, as well."

"I think probably of mine, too," Alexandra said. "Will we be able to do it again?"

"I am already making plans," he assured her. But his plans, and hers, came to naught. Four days later it was necessary for him to return home, as Madeleine was on her way back from her vacation, and he wished to meet her train. He kissed Alexandra and Alice goodbye – Annette had already returned to Paris – and promised to get down to them in a week or so. They stood together on the front steps to wave him goodbye. They never saw him alive again. Obviously thinking about other things than driving, he took the Arc de Triomphe roundabout at too great a speed, lost control as he entered the Champs Elysee, skidded, crashed through the plate glass window of a shop, and was killed outright.

CHAPTER 8

Against Annette's advice, Alexandra determined to attend Gerard's funeral. It was a huge affair. Annette of course went with her husband, who Alexandra now saw for the first time, and thereby understood a great many things. Alexandra went by herself in a taxi, and was quite lost in the great procession away from the Cathedral to the cemetery. She also stood discreetly at the back of the many-ringed circle round the grave, as the coffin was lowered into the ground. Throughout it all she studied Madame Clos-Bruie, a tall, slim figure, her face totally hidden beneath the black veil which descended from her black hat, but with wisps of golden hair trickling out from beneath the darkness. And became aware that Madeleine Clos-Bruie was not concentrating very hard upon the ceremony, but was instead studying the crowd of mourners.

She could only be looking for one person. Alexandra parted the men and women in front of her, and as the first clod of earth was thrown upon the coffin, stood at the graveside. The two women gazed at each other, and then Madeleine raised her veil. She really was a quite remarkably beautiful woman, and for the life of her Alexandra could not see why Gerard had not remained at home on every available opportunity. Not to be outdone, however, Alexandra momentarily raised her own veil, and the two women exchanged stares.

* * *

Gerard's death was a considerable shock. Alexandra knew she had been very close to falling in love with him, even if their relationship had been entirely one of body and business. His sudden demise left her feeling as rootless as after Harry Lowndes' sudden departure, and it took her some days to get over it. It also naturally ended their business partnership. Annette was the one who tackled this first. She had attended the reading of the Will, in her capacity as Gerard's private secretary, and came straight out to the house afterwards. "It is very disappointing," she said. "Of course we all know that Monsieur Gerard did not expect to die so soon, and I am sure had he lived a little longer, and your relationship become, how shall I say, more permanent, he would have made provision for you, madame. But there it is. There was no time."

"He had made provision for you, I hope, Annette," Alexandra said.

"Oh, well, madame . . ." Annette blushed prettily. "He has bequeathed me five thousand francs. Again, I cannot help but feel that had *our* relationship, as created by you, been allowed by fate to become established, I might have done very well also. But there it is. And I am afraid I have lost my job. The new Managing Director, Monsieur Clos-Bruie's cousin, has already informed me that my services will no longer be required."

"Oh, Annette!" Alexandra cried, genuinely distressed. "I am so sorry for you."

"I have my husband to support me, madame, and I have no doubt I will soon secure another position. It is you I worry about." She became very businesslike. "I have made up here a survey of your financial position, which I have converted into pounds." She knew that Alexandra had no grasp of francs and exchange rates. "You will immediately have to let all of your servants go. That will bring down your overheads, but of course you cannot contemplate living in this house without servants. However, if you place it on the market I believe you may well receive about seven thousand pounds for it. You have some seven thousand pounds in your bank account, and by selling the car and your jewellery you should obtain a thousand more. You will thus have a capital of fifteen thousand pounds, which, properly invested, should bring you in about seven hundred pounds a year. This should be sufficient for yourself and the little girl to live on, in a modest fashion, of course. I am afraid you will have to let Alice go as well." She sighed. "I would offer the girl employment myself, but I doubt my husband would permit it. Madame, are you listening to me?"

Alexandra was in fact listening very hard, and not accepting a word of it. Had she been gang-raped, lost a husband, submitted to Tony the Greek and his customers and then to Sir William, to wind up struggling to live on seven hundred pounds a year . . . and without Alice? She regarded the girl virtually as a sister. Anyway, give up this house, and the car, and the servants? "Madame?" Annette was asking.

"Would you not like to continue working, for me instead of Gerard, Annette?"

"Oh, madame, I wish it were possible, but . . ."

"I think the first thing we must do is have a party like the one Gerard threw."

"Madame, you cannot afford it."

"You have not yet turned over your office to your replacement?"

"Well, no, madame, I have been given a week's notice."

"Then you will be able to obtain a list of the names and addresses of everyone who was at that party. I also wish the names and addresses of all of Gerard's friends and acquaintances. Can you do that for me?"

"Well, of course, madame, but . . ."

Alexandra kissed her. "Let me worry about how it will be paid for. I would like that list tomorrow."

Alexandra writes: *I suppose I was filled with a kind of death or glory emotion. I had not set out to be a prostitute; it had just happened. Now I had had a glimpse of the heights that could be achieved, simply by the use of my body. And my brains, to be sure. But again, I was not thinking in terms of prostitution. That would be a stopgap, and conducted at the very highest level, until I could find another protector. I did not presume that would be difficult. I was still, remember, only twenty, I knew my beauty and my allure, and I never doubted my ability. But there was more. For the first time in my life I would be absolutely free, to pick and choose, and to indulge my every fantasy. I can hardly be blamed, I consider, for not regarding what I was planning as either criminal or immoral. As far as I was concerned, it was me, and Mayne and Alice, whom I regarded as totally my responsibility, against the world. I saw no reason why I should not emerge the victor from that battle.*

I suppose there will be many who will regard me as the most reprehensible of women. But I was driven by three urgent necessities. Firstly, if I was going to create the most exclusive brothel in Paris – which was my intention – I needed staff. Secondly, my staff had to be utterly subservient to me, and faithful to me, in every possible way; I could only accomplish this – at least until I could prove to them all that they were going to become wealthy as long as they worked for me – by binding them to me, both physically and emotionally. And thirdly, I had already become attached to these people. Having lived such an intensely lonely life up to that moment, I really wanted to create this utterly intimate circle, in which all of us would desire each other, and hopefully love each other, and even more hopefully profit together – always with me as the mistress controlling both the others and events, of course.

Courageously, Alexandra summoned Gerard's loyal staff and during a frank and lengthy interview told them what her plans for the future entailed. To her surprise and delight she received the full support of Annette, Armand, Madame Lucas, now to be called Jeanne, Jean-Claude her chauffeur – and even the twelve-year-old Lucien. Only Madame Morcerf declined to become involved, though she too was tempted by the money Alexandra promised would be theirs to share, and requested to be allowed to stay on in her capacity as cook.

Now, she began attending to business. Annette brought her a list of the names and addresses of the men who had attended Gerard's party, and those of all the other acquaintances that she could discover. It was Annette's opinion that Gerard's best friend had been a man called Philippe Duclos, and it was on him that Alexandra first called, telephoning for an appointment in his office. "My dear Alexandra." He kissed both her hands. "I caught a glimpse of you at the funeral, but everything was so rushed . . ."

"And it would not have done for you to be seen talking to Gerard's mistress," Alexandra said.

"Well . . . undoubtedly my wife would have noticed. And now . . . you must be desolated."

"Of course. But life must go on."

"Indeed. And now you seek a new protector. My dear girl, I should be overjoyed to fill that role, but . . . I am afraid I could not do so on Gerard's scale. I am but an advocate."

"I would not dream of imposing upon you," Alexandra told him. "I do not seek another protector, as I have no need of protection."

Philippe frowned. "Then why have you come to see me?"

"I have come to ask if you enjoyed that evening at my house."

"My dear girl, I shall never forget it."

"Would you like another one? I have greatly expanded my repertoire . . . and my staff. Of course, with Gerard gone, I am afraid I will have to make a small charge . . ."

Philippe licked his lips. "How much?"

"Well . . . the evening itself, with all you can eat or drink, and a performance, twenty English pounds."

"You are very expensive."

"It will be the best evening you have ever had. Far more so than the last time. Only the best champagne and caviar, and the show alone is worth twenty."

"And are there any extras?"

"Oh, indeed. For a further ten pounds you may have the use of one of my bedrooms, and any one of my people, male or female, for the remainder of the night."

Philippe was still frowning. "Did you say, male *or* female?"

"I am very broad-minded," Alexandra said. "If you wish more than one to attend you, it will be of course another ten pounds."

"And suppose I wished you, my dear Alexandra?"

"I am double."

They gazed at each other. "I would like to have you at my disposal, for a whole night," Philippe said at last.

"Would you, Philippe? What do you wish to do to me?"

"I will tell you that on the night."

"You mean you wish to make a firm booking now? Would you not prefer to wait and see what else I have to offer?"

"It is you I wish," he said. "You said I may command you as I choose?"

"Certainly."

"I wish only you."

"You can only have me after the meal and the entertainment," Alexandra explained. "I have my duty to my other clientele."

"Very well. I will bring forty pounds with me."

She had hoped he would pay her there and then, or at least the equivalent in francs. But she would have to trust him, and from the way he was looking at her she did not suppose she was taking any risk. She stood up and held out her hand. "The evening starts on Friday, at eight. Dinner will be served at nine, the entertainment will be at ten, and at eleven I am yours."

Philippe kissed her fingers. "Friday at eight." Alexandra was quite excited; Philippe had a very intense look about him. Not that she had too much time to think about him.

She spent a busy three days visiting every man on her list, and found that the majority were very interested indeed. If they all came it was going to be a very busy, and profitable, evening.

The evening, as expected, was a tremendous success. They took three hundred and seventy-three pounds in cash. The meal and drinks had cost fifty, and Alexandra shared out twenty to each of her staff, a total of two hundred and thirty, leaving her with a net profit of one hundred and forty-three for the night. With a party once a fortnight and sufficient customers during the week, it seemed that she could rely upon a steady weekly profit of well over a hundred pounds. As her total outgoings were somewhat less than a hundred a month, including staff wages, she was clearly going to be well ahead if she could have two of her evenings a month. But as they were expensive for the customers, they would have to be something no man could resist, if she was going to keep her clientele happy, and paying.

The first evening had most certainly been that. But it would be a mistake merely to attempt to repeat it. There was also the question of new blood. All matters to be pondered. There was also the matter of her other assets to be attended to. She telephoned her London bank, and was put through to the manager. "Mrs Mayne?" He sounded at once astonished and excited. "May I ask where you are calling from?"

"This is an overseas call," Alexandra explained. "Has my flat been sold as yet?"

"Ah . . . no, I'm afraid it hasn't. Overseas, you say?"

"Far, far away," Alexandra said, beginning to feel just a little suspicious.

"I see. Will you be coming back in the near future?"

"Should I?"

"Well, you see . . . do you remember how you left your flat?"

"I do."

"Well, you see . . . the police would like to discuss it with you."

"Why?"

"Well, you see, the, ah, man you left there has filed charges against you, of assault and battery."

"Of all the cheek," Alexandra said. "Do you know who he was? He was the biggest pimp in London."

"I'm afraid the whole world knows who he is, now, Mrs Mayne. Certainly all London. The young lady you telephoned to release him was so distressed by what she found that she ran out into the street shouting for help, and it so happened that one of the people she accosted was a newspaper photographer, who happened to have his, ah, equipment with him."

"Good heavens!" Alexandra was intrigued. "Do you mean that he was in the papers?"

"In every possible sense, Mrs Mayne. So you see, the police would like to hear your side of the story."

Alexandra had no intention of becoming mixed up with the police again. As for putting herself any place where Tony could possibly get hold of her . . . "Well, I don't think I shall be returning to England in the foreseeable future. Does this mean I can't sell my flat?"

"Well, no, of course not. But if you do not come back, you may have a little problem passing contracts."

"Can't a solicitor do it on my behalf?"

"Well, I suppose so. Look, would you like me to come . . . ah, to wherever you are, to explain the position more fully? You're not too far away, are you?"

"They can't touch my money, can they?" Alexandra asked.

"Oh, indeed not."

"Than what is my balance?"

"Ah . . . hold on a moment." He was quickly back. "Just over a thousand pounds."

"Oh, good." She had not revealed the existence of that little nest egg to Annette, nor did she intend to now. "I tell you what, Mr Cody, you just hang on to that money for me, and make sure it gets its interest, and I'll be in touch about us meeting up."

"But you must give me your address."

"Why?"

"Well, if there is an offer for the flat . . ."

"I'll call you, regularly. Promise. 'Bye." She told Alice

about it and they had a good laugh. But then Alice became serious.

"Does this mean we can never go home?" she asked anxiously.

"Of course we can go back to England," Alexandra said. As far as she was concerned, home was wherever she happened to be. "We just have to give this a little time to die down. And for Tony to be arrested again, and locked up."

CHAPTER 9

Annette was now working full-time as Alexandra's secretary, as well, of course, as being available whenever one of their clients required her services. "It is Madame Clos-Bruie," she whispered in alarm one day, putting her hand over the telephone mouth piece.

Alexandra, who was sitting at her desk doing her accounts, frowned at her. "She has said so?"

"No, no. But I recognise her voice. She wishes to speak to you. To Madame Mayne. What are we to do?"

"Why, let me speak with her, of course." Annette gulped and placed the telephone on Alexandra's desk. "This is Madame Mayne," Alexandra said. "May I ask who is speaking?"

There was a momentary hesitation, then the quiet voice said, "My name is Madeleine Clos-Bruie. I am the widow of Gerard Clos-Bruie."

"Ah," Alexandra said. "I saw you, at Gerard's funeral."

"Then you acknowledge your relationship with my late husband, madame?"

"Of course. I was his mistress. Believe me, I mourn him as much as yourself, madame."

Annette's eyebrows were bobbing up and down like yo-yos.

"I am sure you do, madame," Madeleine Clos-Bruie agreed. "As we have so much in common, I thought perhaps we should meet."

"Nothing would give me greater pleasure, madame."

"Will you call at my town house, whenever is convenient?"

"No, madame. I think it would be preferable for us to meet on, shall I say, neutral ground. Why do we not lunch together, at Maxim's?"

There was a moment's silence. Then Madeleine Clos-Bruie said, "If you wish. Shall we say . . . tomorrow at one? Shall I book a table for two?"

"No, no, madame," Alexandra said. "I will book. Tomorrow, at one." She replaced the phone, and looked at Annette.

"Ooh, la-la," Annette squealed. "What is going to happen?"

"Whatever it is, I am sure it will be very enjoyable. Just tell me one thing: this house is inalienably in my name, is it not?"

"Oh, yes, madame. Monsieur Gerard was very careful about that."

"And the car, and everything?"

"Everything, madame."

"Well, then, we have nothing to fear from Madame Clos-Bruie, have we?"

Next day Alexandra was in a state of tremendous excitement. She checked off the appointments – there were four in the afternoon, one for her, one for Alice, one for Francoise, and one for Lucien, who was proving very popular. "Well," she told Annette, "if by any chance I am not back by four you will have to take mine."

"He will be very disappointed," Annette said. She knew she was not in the same class as her employer.

"Tell him I will only charge him half the next time," Alexandra said.

She dressed with great care, wearing a wine-coloured

suit with a frilly white satin blouse, wine-coloured court shoes, and white gloves. A wine-coloured picture hat completed the ensemble. "You look magnificent," Annette exclaimed, clapping her hands, while Alice fussed around making sure everything was just so, and Mayne jumped up and down with glee.

Alexandra agreed with them. She had Jean-Claude drive her, wearing full livery, and swept into Maxim's ten minutes late. "Madame Mayne," the maitre d' exclaimed when he heard her name. "Madame Clos-Bruie is waiting for you."

She was shown to the discreet table she had reserved, giving no indication that this was the first time she had ever been in the famous restaurant, although Madeleine Clos-Bruie was obviously known here. Madeleine also wore a suit, but hers was black, as befitted a recent widow; the colour showed off her pale skin and yellow hair to perfection. Her blouse, however, was an exact match of Alexandra's, as both women recognised at a glance. "We have similar tastes in everything," Alexandra remarked as they sat down. "I am sorry I am late. There is so much to be done, every day."

"I am sure there is. I wish I could say the same."

Alexandra ordered an aperitif, and studied the menu and her guest at the same time. "You are finding life empty," she suggested.

"Perhaps." They ordered.

"If there is anything I can do to help," Alexandra remarked.

"You," Madeleine said. "Yes, perhaps you can help. You can tell me what you gave to my husband that I did not."

Alexandra gazed at her. "Looking at you, madame, I find that a very difficult question to answer."

Madeleine gave a slight flush. "You are very beautiful. And completely different to me in colouring."

"Perhaps. But I am not *more* beautiful than you, madame."

"Thank you. However, my husband spent a great deal of money on you."

"Yes, he did. And I am grateful. Madame, may I speak frankly?"

"I hope that you will."

"Well, in the first place, there are some men who find it absolutely necessary to have more than one woman at a time. After all, monogamy is a strictly Christian point of view, is it not? And Christians total less than a quarter of the world's human population."

"That is true," Madeleine said thoughtfully.

"Had he been born a Muslim, Gerard would have been able to maintain a harem." Alexandra smiled at Madeleine. "I think it would have been a great pleasure to be in a harem with you, madame." Madeleine raised her eyebrows, and again gave a faint flush. "But there is a second reason for men to seek sex apart from their wives, however beautiful," Alexandra went on.

"Yes?" Suddenly Madeleine was tense.

"Well, it is possible for a man to desire services which perhaps his wife may not wish to render." Alexandra popped a mouthful of coquille into her mouth and chewed vigorously. "I do not of course wish to pry into your marital affairs."

"It is why you are here. Why we are both here," Madeleine said. "Did my husband wish to use you . . . unnaturally?"

"No, he did not, madame." Alexandra frowned. Gerard, for all his virility, had been utterly orthodox in his requirements. "Did he ask such things of you?"

"I . . . I could not respond to him as I should."

"You could not climax," Alexandra said.

"You understand this?"

"Of course."

"He was too gentle, perhaps. And you wished something more. Tell me."

Madeleine raised her head. "How can I speak to you, you of all people, of this?"

"Because I, alone of all people, can help you, madame. Madeleine." Alexandra rested her hand on top of hers. "Believe me. Helping people is my business. Oh, yes," she insisted as Madeleine looked sceptical. "Now let me see . . . you are imagining that you are frigid. There is no such woman, in my experience. But you were, as you said, unable to respond to your husband. It could be to do with something that happened when you were a girl? Tell me about it," Alexandra coaxed.

Madeleine continued to toy with her food. But Alexandra knew she was going to confess, because it was something she desperately wanted to do. "I was an only child," she said at last. "We were very close, my parents and I. When we were on holiday, we often shared the same room. And when they thought I was asleep . . ." She blushed most prettily.

"They made love," Alexandra said. "And that put you off sex."

"No, no," Madeleine said, and blushed even more deeply. "I adored listening to them and watching them, while I pretended to be asleep. Then when we were at home I would try to watch them. I even used to look through the keyhole of their bedroom." She raised her head, her eyes enormous. "Was I not a monster?"

"Of course not. But . . ." Alexandra was puzzled.

"I once asked Gerard if he would install a mirror, on the ceiling of our bedroom, and he was shocked." She glanced at Alexandra. "Do you have a mirror in your bedroom?"

The penny dropped. "You wish to see, as well as feel! Of course! And if you do not see, you cannot feel! Of course."

"Does *that* not make me a monster?"

"It makes you unusual. Voyeurism is considered a male vice, as a rule. But . . . you must let me put things right for you."

Madeleine's head jerked. "You?"

"Of course. I believe I can cure your affliction. I know I can." She could not remember ever having been so excited before: Madeleine was by some distance the most beautiful woman she had ever met.

"Why should you wish to help me?" Madeleine asked.

Because I want to get my hands on your body, Alexandra thought. And because you will earn me a fortune. She smiled. "I think I owe it to you."

"To be cured of this affliction . . ." Madeleine sighed. "But I do not see how it can be done. Anyway, I no longer have a husband."

"You mean you do not have a lover, either?"

"Of course I do not." Madeleine was clearly shocked at the suggestion.

"Well, there is nothing wrong in having a lover, certainly when you do not have a husband. Will you trust me?"

"Why should I do that? *How* can I do that?"

"Simply because I know how much you must have loved Gerard, and because I loved him too."

Madeleine played with her flan. "You will wish to be paid."

"Not a penny," Alexandra insisted. "I wish only to help you. But . . . you must come and visit with me."

Madeleine gave her another long stare. "For how long?"

"It is impossible to say, for certain. But I would estimate that if you were to come to my house for an entire weekend, Friday night to Monday morning . . . this coming weekend would be very convenient." It was not one of her Friday party nights.

"Can I really trust you?" Madeleine asked.

"I think you and I are going to be the very best of friends," Alexandra assured her. Because we are going to be lovers, she thought. "I will send my chauffeur for you at six o'clock on Friday," she said.

Alexandra writes: *Would you believe that I genuinely wanted to help Madeleine? That I felt a certain guilt for having been able to make her husband happy where she could not? I also wanted to make love to her, I admit it freely. She was a most beautiful person. And in the event, it was one of the happiest and most fruitful ambitions of my life.*

She hurried home and sent Jean-Claude out to buy the biggest mirror he could find. When he returned, she had all the men mount it on the ceiling of her bedroom. Then she told all the girls that on Friday night none of them must close their doors when entertaining clients, and she had all the hinges oiled. They were intrigued.

On Friday afternoon she had Jean-Claude dress in his livery to go and fetch Madeleine, and waited alone in the drawing room until she heard the car returning. Armand, dressed in his black suit, opened the door and invited Madeleine into the house. Jean-Claude carried her valise. Madeleine stood in the hall and looked around herself. "This is a beautiful house," she said, as Alexandra appeared in the drawing room doorway. "Did Gerard give it to you?"

"Yes, he did. Will you not come in?" Madeleine entered the drawing room. This evening she was wearing a plain dress, in green trimmed with black, the skirt short enough to reveal her calves, which were every bit as good as the rest of her. "Would you like an aperitif?"

"Thank you."

Alexandra nodded at Armand, who promptly produced two glasses of Pernod. "Do you live here alone?" Madeleine asked.

"Oh, no. There are my servants, of course, who are also my friends. You will meet them all later. Then I have a daughter. You will meet her soon enough. And I do a great deal of entertaining." Madeleine raised her eyebrows. Alexandra gestured her to the settee, and sat beside her. "I do not wish to have any secrets from you," she said. "I wish you to understand that my friends pay me to be entertained. There are, in fact, some of my friends here now, being entertained."

Madeleine nodded. "I saw the cars outside. You mean you are a whore."

"I would prefer the word courtesan. After all, many of the greatest and most famous women in history, and especially here in France, have been courtesans. Think of Diane de Poitiers, or Ninon l'Enclos, or Madame Recamier . . ."

"You are well read," Madeleine observed.

"Reading is my greatest pleasure. Well, almost."

"I trust there is no chance of our conversation being interrupted by one of your 'guests'."

"None in the slightest. But . . . would you not like to look at some of them?" Madeleine raised her eyebrows, and Alexandra got up and held out her hand.

* * *

She took off her shoes and had Madeleine do the same, then led her up the stairs and along the gallery, their stockinged feet silent on the carpet. The first door was just ajar. Alexandra pushed it in, and beckoned Madeleine to look, at Alice and a client, rolling about on the bed. Madeleine stared for several seconds, then gulped and stepped back. Alexandra showed her three more rooms. Madeleine was panting by now, and stepped back rather sharply.

Alexandra put her fingers on her lips, and led her back to her own room.

"Now, here is where I entertain *my* clients. Would you not like to be a client?"

Madeleine's head jerked. "What do you mean? I am a woman."

"We cater for all tastes. Do you like the mirror?"

Madeleine looked up. "My God! Did you . . . make love with Gerard in here?"

"Of course. Now, would you not like to make love beneath that mirror?"

"Make love? With whom?

"Well, why not with me?"

"With you?"

Alexandra kissed her, lightly, on the lips. "You really do something to me. From the moment I first saw you, at Gerard's funeral, I wanted to have you." She looked into Madeleine's eyes. "Do you think that is very wicked, at a funeral?"

"Are you a lesbian?"

"I am a woman who enjoys sex. I have fallen in love with men. I fell in love with Gerard. Now I have fallen in love with you. Desperately." She kissed her again. "Would you like to join our little group?"

"And become a whore, you mean?"

"I hope to wean you away from your stereotyped

thinking, someday," Alexandra said. "But yes, if that is how you wish to put it. Remembering always that we do it for pleasure. Making the clients pay is simply to finance our way of life. And you can always do it beneath a mirror like this. I will have a room fitted up especially for you."

"You are a devil," Madeleine commented.

"Then is hell not a lovely place?" Alexandra asked, and began to undress her.

They got up at seven, showered, and went downstairs. Helene had put on her usual marvellous meal, and Armand poured only the choicest wines. When the meal was finished, Alexandra escorted Madeleine into the drawing room. "We must give ourselves time to digest," she said. "Then . . . I think Jean-Claude is the one for you."

"The chauffeur? My God!"

"You will love every minute of it. Now, tell me about Nicole Dubois."

"Nicole? Do you know her?"

"I have never met her. But Philippe is one of my most regular customers. He says it is because he can get no satisfaction at home."

"Hmmm. I have often wondered about that. Nicole is a strange girl."

"In what way? They have three children, have they not?"

"Oh, yes, but that was some time ago. The eldest is seven and the youngest four."

"So she must have liked sex, once."

"I think she still likes sex."

"But not with Philippe?"

"It is strange, but I do not think she has a lover. Or has ever had one."

"You mean *she* is a lesbian?"

"I do not think that either. Her name is never linked with anyone. She has no close friends, spends a great deal of time by herself. I think she does a lot of gardening . . ."

"Philippe told me that."

"And for the rest, she reads. She spends a lot of time in her bedroom, reading. She plays no games, belongs to no women's clubs, and as I have said, has no close friends. Because Gerard and Philippe were good friends, I tried to see a lot of her, but it always seemed to bore her when I called. So I stopped."

"Hm," Alexandra said thoughtfully. "Is she good-looking?"

"Well . . . I would describe her as handsome." Madeleine shot her a glance. "You are not going to attempt to seduce *her*?"

"Why not?"

"You are insatiable."

Alexandra smiled. "And you are jealous. Already. But there is no need to be. I promise you that when I have 'seduced' Nicole, as you put it, I will share her with you."

"My God!"

"Would you not like that? The whole object of your being here, my dearest Madeleine, is to free your mind as well as your body from the absurd social mores in which you live. I have never even seen this woman Nicole. You have. So tell me honestly . . . would you not like to be in bed with her, naked? Do you not suppose you would enjoy it?"

Madeleine ate very busily.

Alexandra writes: *My intention, of course, was to make mine the most exclusively high-class brothel in Paris, and that meant the world. I could only do this by employing exclusively high-class women. But I thought it best not to tell Madeleine this at that moment: she was not completely mine yet. But she soon was.*

By Monday morning Madeleine was utterly exhausted, but also, Alexandra estimated, happier than at any previous time in her life. "You will come again next weekend," Alexandra told her. "I do not think your treatment is quite complete. But listen . . . Friday night is one of my party nights. Will you not attend? You will enjoy it, I promise."

"How can I?" Madeleine asked. "Most of your clients were Gerard's friends."

"Have you ever had an affair with any of them?"

"Of course not."

"Well, then . . . you shall come as the masked wonder."

"They would be certain to recognise me?"

"I assure you they will not. And I will not let you be alone with any of them either. How about it?"

Madeleine was obviously sorely tempted.

Alexandra was very pleased with herself. She was not only having the time of her life, but she was gradually creating a unique kind of brothel, one staffed only by a hand-picked – literally – elite.

But before she could take her plans any further, she received a remarkable indication of what the future might hold for her. The day after Madeleine had gone home, Alexandra was in bed, feeling quite exhausted by the weekend's activities, and lazily planning her Friday night's programme, when Armand appeared. "There is a gentleman downstairs to see you, madame."

Alexandra sat up. "A gentleman? A client, you mean? I am not entertaining any clients today, Armand."

"The gentleman did not indicate that he wishes to be a client, madame. He merely says that he wishes to see you upon a most urgent matter. He has sent up his card."

Alexandra studied the card. Signor Pertinelli, with an Italian address. She looked at Armand. "He is very well dressed, madame."

Alexandra sighed. "I suppose I had better see him. There may be some profit in it for us. Thank you, Armand, I will be down in a minute." She had a quick shower, put on her favourite blood-red dressing gown and slippers, left her hair loose and did not bother with make-up, as she knew she would be all a-glow from the hot water, and went downstairs. To pause in dismay; Signor Pertinelli looked distinctly like an undertaker, from both his height and thin build, his somewhat cadaverous face, and his dark clothes.

On the other hand, he also looked delighted to see her. "Madame Mayne?" He bent over her hand, touched it with his lips. "You are even more beautiful than I had been led to expect. And this house, so elegant. His excellency will be pleased."

"I think you had better sit down, signor." Alexandra did so herself, crossing her knees so that the dressing gown fell away from her legs. "And tell me what you are talking about."

"I am an emissary for his excellency Signor d'Annunzio," Pertinelli explained. Alexandra had heard the name, but she could not at the moment remember where. "His excellency is on a visit to Paris, Madame, and seeks an evening's entertainment. He has heard your name mentioned with regard to this."

Now she was back in her depths. "What exactly does Signor d'Annunzio have in mind?"

"Madame?" Pertinelli was at a loss for words.

"I mean, signor, does he wish to visit me in the

afternoon, or at night? Does he wish me, or one of my girls? Or both? Does he wish to visit us for one hour or two? Would he like a meal? Would he like any additional entertainment? These are all matters to be decided."

"You are very efficient, madame," Pertinelli said. "But Signor d'Annunzio wishes to visit you, not one of your girls. He will come to you, and he will spend the night. He will dine with you. You will close your establishment's doors for that night. There will be no need for you to provide any additional entertainment."

"Your client wishes to hire my entire establishment, for the night, and have dinner?" She wanted to get it right.

"That is correct, madame."

"It will be very expensive."

Pertinelli gave a deprecatory wave of his hand. "Name your price."

"Well . . ." She wished she had had the time to work it out. She had grossed some three hundred and fifty pounds from each of her evenings. But that had been with all her girls and boys participating. If this Italian lunatic wanted just her . . . but if he wanted her entire house to himself he was in effect hiring the rest of her staff as well, even if he wasn't intending to use them. Then there was to be no entertainment . . . but she had offered to lay on an entertainment . . . she took a deep breath, but she could always come down. "Four hundred English pounds."

Pertinelli nodded. "And when will this be?"

Alexandra cursed herself for not asking more. "I could manage tomorrow night."

"Tomorrow night it shall be." Pertinelli stood up, kissed her hand again. "Signor d'Annunzio will be here at eight, and he will dine at nine. He will depart at eight o'clock on Thursday morning. Good day to you, madame."

* * *

Alexandra wasn't at all sure whether she was awake or dreaming; it had never occurred to her that there was a man who would pay four hundred pounds for the enjoyment of a single whore, even for a night – and even for her! Not even Gerard had done anything like that. Of course, Gerard had actually bought her, lock, stock and barrel, for a much larger sum. But she didn't want to belong to any man so completely again – and she wouldn't ever need to, if there were sufficient more like this Signor d'Annunzio. She called the household together to tell them what was happening. "Just who is this man, anyway?"

"He is a very famous Italian poet, madame," Armand said. "But he is also a war hero. An aviator."

"A friend of Mussolini's," Jean-Claude added.

Alexandra had only the vaguest idea who Mussolini was.

"Now he rules Fiume," Jeanne said.

"It is a seaport at the head of the Adriatic Sea," Annette explained. "Signor d'Annunzio has become its ruler."

"You mean he is a prince?" Alexandra was intrigued.

"I do not think he is a prince, madame," Annette said. "He is more of an adventurer. Fiume is in dispute between Italy and the Serbo-Croats. There was some talk of it being handed over to the Serbo-Croats by the League of Nations. So Signor d'Annunzio gathered a band of mercenaries and seized the city, defying anyone to turn him out."

"Good heavens! Did anyone try?"

"Not as yet." And now he is coming to visit me, Alexandra thought, and braced herself for an encounter with a demi-god. She considered long and carefully what to wear, and in the end plumped for the utmost modesty, and wore knickers, although nothing else, beneath her pale green dinner gown, but the gown had less decolletage than most of her clothes. Helene was told to prepare her best meal, regardless of expense, and Armand to decant some bottles of his finest wine. Then it was a matter of waiting, until Signor d'Annunzio was announced.

He arrived at eight sharp. Alexandra elected to receive him in the downstairs drawing room, and for the occasion she had all her staff dress as either maids or butlers, so that to reach her he had to pass a guard of honour of beautiful women, as well as Jean-Claude and Lucien. Then Armand threw open the doors, and announced: "His excellency Signor d'Annunzio."

Alexandria was on her feet, facing the doors as they swung inwards, and with difficulty stopped herself from gasping. Her demi-god was half a head shorter than herself, had a totally insignificant body, was absolutely bald, and wore a patch over one eye – but not even the black patch was the least romantic. However, he was at least dressed in a dinner suit.

D'Annunzio, on the contrary, seemed pleased with what he was looking at. "Pertinelli is an honest fellow," he remarked. "They are hard to find."

"Indeed, signor," Alexandra said, and escorted him upstairs. "Would you care for a drink?"

Armand was waiting with a tray. D'Annunzio sniffed the first glass presented to him. "This is Bollinger."

Alexandra looked at Armand. "The gentleman is correct, madame."

"I am always correct," d'Annunzio announced. "I only drink Krug."

"I am sorry," Alexandra said. "Your man did not inform me of this. Do we have any Krug, Armand?" She had never heard of it but she assumed it was champagne.

"I'm afraid not, madame. I can obtain some."

"Then you had better do so."

D'Annunzio waved his hand. "It is not important. My doctor tells me I drink too much of it, anyway."

"Ah," Alexandra said. "I think you had better leave us, Armand. I assume you still wish dinner at nine, signor?"

"Of course. I always eat at nine." D'Annunzio followed her into her bedroom, sat down, legs spread. "Uncover me, madame."

Alexandra hitched up her skirt and knelt before him.

Annette and Alice saw Signor d'Annunzio off at eight o'clock the next morning, and then went in to Alexandra's bedroom. Alice drew the blinds while Annette stood at the bed and gazed at Francoise, one of the new girls, and Alexandra. "He's gone," she told them.

"Thank God for that." Alexandra sat up, pushing hair from her eyes. "Francoise?"

Francoise had been on her face. Now she rose to her knees. "I thought he was never going to stop," she said.

"So did I. What a man."

"Now tell the truth, you enjoyed it," Alice said,

"Well . . . is the money still there?"

It was lying on the dressing table. Annette counted it. "He must be very rich."

"Coffee," Alexandra said. "I want a gallon of black coffee. And then a hot bath."

"I will see to it." Alice hurried from the room.

"The money is all here," Annette said. "Would you like me to bank it?"

"Yes, please. And while you are out . . . see if you can obtain a list of all the most wealthy men in Europe. There must be some kind of international *Who's Who* available."

CHAPTER 10

It would require several volumes to list the men, and women, whom Alexandra and her entourage claim to have serviced over the next five years. But she had certain favourites.

One of her greatest thrills was when she received a telephone call from Nathalie Barney. Alexandra had of course heard of Miss Barney, an American heiress who lived at 20 rue Jacob, and had created, before the War, the most famous literary salon in Paris. All the leading poets and authors had gathered there, although her most memorable occasion had been when the future spy, Mata Hari, had arrived naked, riding a white horse. Those days were done now, of course, but Nathalie's reputation as a lesbian was as great as ever. Now she invited the hardly less famous Madame Alexandra to call. Alexandra was intrigued, because she also knew that Nathalie was about fifty, and she had never been to bed with a woman of that age.

In the event she was agreeably surprised, because even at fifty Nathalie Barney remained a very beautiful woman. She had refused to follow fashion and crop her tumbling golden hair, and Alexandra had never cut her hair either – no matter what the current mode. It actually was a tea party, at which several other women were present, and not all of them were pleased to discover that the newcomer to their little circle was the most famous courtesan in Paris, but Nathalie found it all very amusing, and of course Alexandra was invited to stay on after the party was over. "I wish to hear all about your life," Nathalie told her. "Is it true that all prostitutes are lesbians?"

"I am not all prostitutes," Alexandra told her. "And I am not a lesbian. I do not believe in words like that. I am what I am. I love having sex with men. But I also love having sex with women."

"And do you never get emotionally involved?"

"Of course I do. When I am in bed with someone, man or woman, I love only him. Or her. I would die for him. Or her. But when it is over, well . . . until the next time."

"I can love only one person," Nathalie said.

Presumably, Alexandra thought, she also meant, at a time, even if the time might be slightly longer; she had certainly had a succession of lovers. "Then obviously you cannot wish to love me," she suggested, teasing.

"I should very much like to love you," Nathalie said. "I am sure we have much to learn from each other. But I would need you all for myself."

"That is not possible," Alexandra told her.

"Is it money? I have enough for us both. You will never want."

"I have too many people dependent on me," Alexandra explained.

Nathalie stroked a finger down the side of Alexandra's jaw. "You are so very beautiful."

"And as I am here . . ." Alexandra suggested.

The affair was too torrid to last. Alexandra soon discovered that Nathalie could be a thorough nuisance, varying from threatening suicide to turning up at the house at all hours of the day and night and loudly demanding to see her, whether she was engaged or not. She tried interesting her in one of the girls, but Nathalie wanted only Alexandra. It was a long six months until her new friend tired of her and fell in love with someone else.

Her male friends included several actors. Charles Chaplin visited her establishment several times, but although he was one of the best lovers she had ever had, he spent so much time talking about himself she became bored. Gary Cooper was another Hollywood actor who visited her while filming on the Continent. He was so well endowed Alexandra tried to get him to give up the screen and work for her, but he also refused.

There were also literary giants. F Scott Fitzgerald was taken to Alexandra's by his friend Ernest Hemingway, but was too nervous to perform. Hemingway himself came often enough, but would never attend any of the Friday night soirees after his first, at which he was frankly shocked. He preferred long private sessions with Alexandra. Bertrand Russell spent a weekend with Alexandra, but not at her house; he told her he wished to study her sexual habits and took her off to Switzerland, where she had a thoroughly exhilarating time.

Her most famous caller, however, was Prince Carol of Romania. His visit was quite an event, because she was informed of it by the Minister of the Interior – a regular client – who warned her that there would have to be certain adjustments for the night. This consisted of refusing all appointments, and indeed, barring the house to all except her staff. Then the establishment was taken over by secret service men who searched everywhere, and quite put even the girls off sex. But as a lover Carol was a disappointment, seeming to prefer catching glimpses of himself in one of the many mirrors which adorned

Alexandra's bedroom than to getting on with the job. Nor was he any great shakes when fully aroused. But he paid very well.

By 1929 Alexandra was rich as well as famous. She had always preferred to salt her money away rather than spend it, and she had no need to buy clothes or jewels, or even motor cars, as these were bestowed on her by her admirers. When she wished a holiday, she merely suggested to one of her clients, who happened to live, or have a home, in an exotic part of the world, that she would like to spend some time with him at *his* place, free of charge. Leaving the House was no longer a problem. Annette, now in her early forties, managed the financial side of the business with tremendous efficiency, and Madeleine Clos-Bruie, who had given up all pretence and moved into the House, proved an efficient and popular substitute madame. Thus Alexandra was enabled to travel to America and the West Indies, to various parts of Europe, to the Far East, and even to Japan, as the guest of amorous businessmen. While her bank balance grew.

She returned to British Guiana, and travelled up to the ranch. She made the journey incognito, and in fact there was no one to connect the beautiful, sophisticated, richly dressed and bejewelled widow Mayne, travelling with her equally attractive daughter, with the unfortunate young woman of that same name who had left the colony in disgrace a dozen years before. The one person who might have made the connection, Mrs Brand, had died. Alexandra's purpose in returning had been to see if the ranch remained hers, but apparently it did not; Jonathan Mayne had not owned the land, only leased it from the Government, and any lease not worked for a specified number of years returned to the Government.

It had been re-leased, and the new operators were very polite.

Alexandra merely told them all that she was a distant relative of Jonathan. She toyed with the idea of finding Rose, or David Lamb, supposing they were still there, to enjoy a look-at-me now triumph, and then decided against it: why stir up old memories? She returned to Paris.

She sold the London flat, by the expedient of placing it in the hands of good agents; apparently her treatment of Tony the Greek had now been long forgotten, although, she hoped, not by Tony the Greek. She did not get much for the flat, as the lease was now down to twenty-five years, but she just wanted to be rid of it.

There were of course, problems, from time to time. To cater for her large and ever-growing clientele, Alexandra needed a large and ever-growing staff. Obviously it was impossible to have them all living on the premises, even if she did add on a staff wing in the garden which could sleep a dozen. Thus she found herself increasingly having to rely on casual labour. These might be bored housewives or eager schoolgirls, or real professionals who were available at night. This meant of course that the old intimate control which she had exerted over her "people", as she called them, was lost, and although she interviewed, and often sampled, every new applicant herself, it was still difficult to maintain the old discipline, and more important the old loyalty, which she had first created. These outside recruits talked, or more likely boasted, about the organisation to which they now belonged, and inevitably there were visits from the gendarmarie, but these were usually not annoying; no French prefect of police was going to prosecute the most famous brothel in the country.

More serious, there was the risk of disease, and

Alexandra found herself forced to employ a doctor on a full-time basis.

There was the clear young voice on the telephone, who requested the pleasure of calling upon Madame Alexandra, for the night. "A whole night?" queried Annette, who handled the bookings, and on whom the youthfulness of the caller's voice had registered. "You realise that this is very expensive."

"What is the cost?" the boy inquired.

"For a whole night? This depends upon what you wish."

"What can I have?"

"There are two choices. You may come at eight, and dine with Madame Alexandra and then spend the night. This will cost the equivalent of one hundred English pounds. The alternative is to come at eleven, having dined. This will cost only eighty pounds."

"I understand. I will come for dinner."

"The fee must be paid in cash. In advance."

"Of course."

"Very well, we will expect you on Wednesday night, at eight. May I have your name, monsieur?"

"Jacques will be sufficient. I shall be there."

"What do you make of it?" Annette asked Alexendra, when she showed her the booking.

"I am intrigued," Alexandra confessed.

For the occasion she wore her new deep red evening gown with its plunging decolletage, front and back; her back, indeed, was naked to the curve of her buttocks. She also added all of her best jewellery and spent some time over her hair, which was more black and lustrous and wavy than ever, and as it now also reached the curve of her buttocks, made up for the absence of material.

Helene laid on the best of dinners. There were, of course, clients calling at the house every night, but Alexandra's special guests were received in one of the upstairs rooms which had been converted into a dining room, and it was here that she waited to receive the young man. She *was* actually quite intrigued. No man not already established and wealthy could afford her fees. The late 1920's was far before the advent of the enormously wealthy young pop star or money-market millionaire. Even the occasional youthful actor like Gable or Cooper had been at least her age, while their visits had always been heralded by the announcement of their name and status, as if that alone should be sufficient to have her rolling on the carpet at their feet.

And for all their size and glamour, they had been distinctly inadequate lovers, although Alexandra never doubted that she could have trained Cooper on into becoming quite useful. But here was a man who sounded younger than either of those, and who had not even deigned to give her his name!

She listened to the sound of various automobiles arriving, the murmer of voices from downstairs as the girls welcomed their guests; they would all be sitting down to a general dinner before pairing off, and felt her heart give a pleasant pit-a-pat as there were feet on her private staircase, and a moment later the double doors were thrown open by Armand, who announced, "Lieutenant Jacques Peyraud to call upon Madame."

Alexandra stood up, and gazed at the young man who was standing in the doorway. Young man? she thought: this was a boy, certainly not a day over eighteen. He wore the uniform of a cadet at the Saumur Military Academy. And looked very nervous. She went towards him, her arm outstretched. "Monsieur."

He kissed her hand. "I am honoured, madame." His

voice at least was steady. "May I say that you are even more beautiful than I had expected?"

Alexandra smiled. "You may say that whenever you wish." She nodded to Armand, who closed the doors. "A glass of wine?"

"Thank you."

She poured two – unlike Tony the Greek, she always served her clients with the very best – gave him his, and then brushed her glass against it. Then she sat down, on the settee, and patted the space beside her. The settee had been carefully designed so that it was impossible for two people to share it without their thighs touching. "How long have you been at the Academy?" she asked.

"Three months, madame."

"Three months. Good heavens!" She realised that he could be even younger than she had first supposed. "But you are enjoying life there."

"Why, yes, madame. But . . . how can you tell?"

"With the sort of allowance your father is giving you, I would have thought you would enjoy life anywhere."

"My allowance is no greater than that of any other cadet at the Academy, madame."

Alexandra raised her eyebrows. "You amaze me. Have you robbed a bank?"

He flushed. "I am sworn to secrecy."

"But then, Jacques, so am I, regarding anything any one of my guests may say to me in private." She squeezed his hand, then lifted it and rested it against her breast. He gave a little shiver, the whole length of his body. "Tell me," she invited, speaking in little more than a whisper.

He licked his lips. "You are so famous, madame, so discussed, so . . ."

"Am I really?" Alexandra was delighted. "Even by schoolboys? I beg your pardon, Jacques, I meant cadets."

She knew he wasn't going to take offence; she was still holding his hand against her breast.

"Oh, yes, madame. And so it became understood amongst my colleagues that we all shared a single dream, to be able to spend a night in your arms."

"I think that is enchanting," Alexandra told him.

"But none of us had sufficient money. So it was agreed, that each cadet – there are two hundred of us – would subscribe the equivalent of ten English shillings from his allowance. Then when the money was accumulated, lots would be drawn, and the winner would . . ." he gazed at her, "have the night."

Alexandra kissed him on the lips. "I think that is even more enchanting," she said. "And I give you my word that this is a night you will never forget."

He was anxious. "You understand that I am sworn to tell my comrades everything that happens."

Alexandra smiled at him. "Why, you are welcome to do so, my dear Jacques." Who knows, she thought, one or two of them might be future clients – when they become generals. "And now, let us eat. You have made me very impatient."

He was flattered, but she was telling the truth. The old excitement, which had been less in evidence in the past couple of years, was back. Helene had laid on her usual outstanding meal, designed as much to make the rich old gentlemen who normally sampled it both tipsy and indigested, and thus render Alexandra's evening the more easy. But this night Alexandra carefully monitored what Jacques ate and drank. "You must not spoil your appetite," she told him. "For love."

The meal over, she led him into her bedroom, closed the door, and turned to face him, She had already released everything that needed releasing, and now a simple shrug of her shoulders had the gown sliding past her hips to lie around her ankles. She stepped out of it, and out of her shoes at the same time; as usual when working, she wore no underclothes. Jacques stared at her, absolutely petrified. "You must relax," she said. "You must think only of love." She went to him, took him in her arms, and kissed his mouth, forcing it open to find his tongue. "Let me undress you," she said, and took off his uniform. Then she knelt before him and took him into her mouth. He gasped, and held on to her head. "Madame," he panted. "Madame, you will . . ." He was already past the point of no return.

Jacques' face was the picture of misery. "I am dishonoured," he groaned. "To have failed even to enter . . . oh, madame. I shall kill myself."

"Silly boy," Alexandra said. "Are you incapable of making it more than once in a night? At your age? Come to bed." She led him back into the bedroom, made him lie on the bed, lay down on top of him, kissed his mouth and shook her hair all over his face, while her breasts slid up and down his chest. His arms went round her, hesitantly. She felt him come down on her, while his groin banged into her buttocks. "Oh," he gasped. "Oh!" When they were both clearly exhausted, Alexandra rang the bell. "Annette," she said, when her secretary, wrapped in a dressing gown and looking somewhat bleary-eyed – she also had entertained a client the previous night – entered her room, "I have decided that Lieutenant Peyraud shall be a guest of the establishment, for last night."

Annette opened her mouth and then closed it again. "One hundred pounds?"

"Yes. Will you fetch the money, please?"

"Oh, madame," Jacques protested. "I cannot let you."

"But you must. However . . ." Alexandra kissed him. "I look forward to entertaining one of your comrades, in the near future. But . . . there will be no more refunds."

Alexandra personally enjoyed her life so much she might never have thought of giving it up, had it not been for 1929. It was not merely the Wall Street crash, although that was serious enough, as during the following year its effects began to permeate Europe and cause a general tightening of financial belts.

But then four events, one after the other, took place which caused a radical reappraisal of her situation.

The first was when the Minister of the Interior, an old and favoured client, telephoned and asked for an appointment for a dear friend of his, who happened to be in Paris and wished to sample all the delights of the most famous city in the world. "What sort of thing is he looking for?" Alexandra asked.

"An evening with you, my dear Alexandra," the Minister said.

"I take it this gentleman knows the price?" Alexandra checked.

"Do not worry about that. He is very wealthy. Alexandra, I must warn you . . . he is English."

"Ah," Alexandra said.

Alexandra did not entertain Englishmen very often, although they sometimes came as guests of one of her regulars. But she did know that they were nearly always on the lookout for something unusual. This did not bother her in the least, from a moral point of view. But she herself, now that she was thirty, had no desire to accommodate a stranger's perversities, and so she arranged to have Francoise and Georges – the prettiest of her young boys – standing by, as well as Annette to wield a cane, to cater for whatever odd tastes her visitor might have. But she received him alone, as usual, arranging her features in a polite smile as Armand opened the door, and announced, "Sir William Gingham-Gray."

Alexandra's jaw dropped, and she hastily brought it up again. But then, Sir William was also totally taken aback, and indeed she thought he might be going to faint; he had aged considerably since last she had seen him. "Sir Willy!" she cried.

"Alexandra!" She was in his arms and he was kissing her with desperate anxiety. "Oh, my dearest, darling girl," he said. "If you knew how much I have missed you. I was a fool, to let you go. I have been so worried about you. But here . . ." He looked around him. "To find you working in a brothel!"

Alexandra held his hand and led him to the settee. "I do not work here, Sir Willy. I own it."

"You . . . good God!"

"I always intended to rise to the top," she reminded him.

"Of course you did. Well . . . do you still have that sweet little girl, Alice?"

"Of course. I also have half a dozen other sweet little girls, and half a dozen more sweet but rather big girls, any one of whom is at your beck and call."

"But not you."

Alexandra kissed him on the nose. "Of course, me, silly. I just thought you might prefer someone new."

"I want you. Oh, how I want you. Alexandra . . ." He touched her shoulder, and she obligingly slipped down the straps of her gown so that he could fondle her breasts. "You are still the most beautiful woman in the world."

"Why, Sir Willy, you say the nicest things. Shall we

eat?" She led him into the adjacent room where the table was laid.

"Alexandra, would you take everything off?" She stepped out of her gown, laid it over a chair. "And could we be served by naked girls? I would so like to be served by Alice, naked."

"I think that can be arranged." Alexandra rang the bell and Armand came in. "My guest would like to be served by two of the girls, Armand. Alice certainly, and . . ." She glanced at Sir William. "Do you like them young and slim, or somewhat more voluptuous?"

"Well, Alice is still slim, isn't she?"

"Oh, indeed."

"Then, I'd like a large blonde."

"Ask Madeleine to join us, Armand. They will serve, and they should be undressed." Armand bowed, and left.

"I can hardly believe this is happening," Sir William said.

"There is something I must tell you. The fee you paid was for me alone. It is an extra twenty-five pounds for each of the girls."

Sir William pulled a face. "I see you haven't changed."

"Wouldn't you be sorry if I had?"

"Yes," he agreed. "I would be sorry. All right. Fifty pounds extra. You're sure this girl Madeleine is worth it?"

"Madeleine is worth a lot more than twenty-five pounds. I am letting you have her cheap because you are one of my oldest customers."

He paid up, then took her in his arms to kiss her and hold her body against his.

Madeleine arrived. "Oh," Sir William said. "Oh, by George!" Madeleine, as usual when she was entertaining, had piled her golden hair on the top of her head, exposing at once her utterly beautiful face, and at the same time seeming doubly to expose her equally magnificent body. Sir William seemed quite overwhelmed.

It was Madeleine he really wanted, although out of loyalty to old times' sake he stroked Alexandra's and Alice's bottoms. Alexandra was monitoring his progress, and within a few moments he was as hard as she had ever seen him. "Now's the time," she decided, and rolled Madeleine onto her back on a velvet settee. Sir Willy gasped with anticipation, and then fell forward on to Madeleine's breasts, humping up and down.

Alexandra and Alice watched, patting Sir William on the bottom to encourage him on. His face was invisible, but his breathing grew louder and louder, and then an anguished expression crossed Madeleine's face. "Alexandra!" she gasped. "Alexandra!"

It went against all of Alexandra's instincts to cut off a man in his stride, as it were, and especially Sir Willy, but if he might do himself an injury . . . She patted him, on the shoulder. "Maybe you're not going to make it after all, Sir Willy," she said. "Maybe you should stop now."

"No," he panted, still rising and falling. "No. I'm going to make it. I always . . ." He gave a gasp and collapsed.

"Alexandra!" Madeleine screamed. "Get him off me!"

Alexandra and Alice rolled Sir William on to his back. His face was purple, but the colour was slowly subsiding, and he had stopped panting. "Sir Willy!" Alexandra knelt beside him, felt for a pulse or a heartbeat.

"Oh, my God! He's dead," Alice said.

"Ring for Dr Ferrand," Alexandra told her. Alice ran for the telephone. "And then get me the Minister," Alexandra shouted. She took Madeleine in her arms. "Are you all right?"

"Yes," Madeleine said. "I am all right." But she was shaking.

"Thank God it was you," Alexandra said. Madeleine pulled her head back to look at her. "There is no one else could have handled it," Alexandra explained. "Save myself."

The Minister came himself, and agreed that the whole thing had to be hushed up, both because it would be bad for business and because it would be bad for protocol. He agreed even more whole-heartedly when Alexandra told him how she and Sir Willy had been friends before, and of Lady Virginia's hatred for her. The body was dressed and taken out into the woods, and the story was put about that Sir William had died of a heart attack while out walking. The scandal was therefore very minor, Alexandra's staff being sworn to secrecy. Yet it had a distinct effect upon all of them, not least herself; it made her realise that as quite a few of her clientele were elderly gentlemen seeking to recapture the powers of their youth, this kind of disaster might not be the last.

The second incident occurred soon after, when Mayne came into her bedroom one Saturday morning, and as she usually did, climbed into bed beside her. Alexandra had had a long night, and was only half awake. She put her arm round the girl's shoulders, and hugged her against herself. "Ma," Mayne said. "I want to work."

Alexandra sat up to gaze at her, perhaps seeing her for the first time in several years, however close they had been in that time. Mayne was all but fifteen years old, and an extremely well-developed young woman. While she was almost as beautiful as her mother, her hair tawny rather than midnight, her face perhaps slightly more aquiline. "You're only fourteen years old."

"I'm going to be fifteen in three months time."

"Even I didn't lose my virginity until I was fifteen," Alexandra reminded her.

"Things were different then," Mayne pointed out.

It was a difficult consideration. Mayne was a most lovely child, and she was a virgin. She was therefore worth a great deal of money. But Alexandra, however amoral, didn't really want to sell her own daughter. On the other hand, she reflected, she was running a business, to which it appeared Mayne might very well succeed. So she stifled her conscience, and at the following Friday night party offered Mayne. Mayne herself was delighted, as she stood on the table wearing a pair of sheer harem pants and nothing else, and slowly turned round before the gasping gazes of some twenty clients.

They accepted that she was going to be expensive, but also, once they understood that she was Alexandra's daughter, they went for it, and Mayne was finally knocked down at a hundred and twenty pounds. Alexandra felt quite weepy as Mayne was escorted off to bed – the man was old enough to be her grandfather. But apparently the girl enjoyed every minute of it, and from then on took a leading part in all the proceedings. But her debut coming on top of Sir William's untimely death left Alexandra feeling very old.

The third occurrence took place late in 1930. Alexandra often went shopping on the Champs Elysees, and after visiting the shops would lunch at her favourite café, where she was so well known. She was sitting with an aperitif one morning, with Madeleine, who enjoyed the Champs Elysees more than anyone else, when she observed a man looking at her. There was nothing unusual in this; men were always gazing at Alexandra, and any of her women who happened to be with her, and Alexandra, as was her usual habit, looked back at him with a half-smile – he might turn out to be a possible client. But when she looked again, she realised that there was something familiar about his face. For several minutes she could not place it, then she slowly realised who it was.

For a moment she felt quite disturbed, his presence brought back so many memories. And then she reflected that it had all been a very long time ago, and was not something to cause her the least worry now. In fact, she realised, if *he* had never happened, *she* would not be sitting here now, rich, famous and indestructible. As for him . . . clearly he was recognising her as well, without having the slightest idea what to do about it. She called the waiter. "Maurice, that gentlemen having a coffee over there. Is he English?"

"Oh, yes, madame. Very English."

"That's what I thought. Would you ask him if he would care to have a cognac with us?"

"Of course, madame." Maurice scuttled off.

Madeleine raised her eyebrows. She had never known Alexandra to solicit business on the street before. "An old friend," Alexandra explained.

The man spoke with Maurice for several minutes, before getting up and coming across. "Forgive me for staring at you," he said in very bad French.

"Why not try English," Alexandra suggested. "We both speak it. You're David Lamb."

He gave a little gasp. "Then you're . . ."

"Alexandra Mayne," Alexandra said. "It's been a long time."

David sat down. "I . . ." He licked his lips, gave Madeleine an anxious glance.

"Oh, this is Madeleine Clos-Bruie," Alexandra said.

"She's a friend of mine." David shook hands. He looked terribly embarrassed. "It was a long time ago," Alexandra reminded him. "Oh, I hated your guts, for a while. But I've learned that everything turns out for the best, if you're determined that it should."

"You must have had an interesting experience together," Madeleine remarked.

"I'll tell you about it, some time," Alexandra volunteered.

"What are you doing in Paris?" she asked.

"I'm on a trip. With my wife." He gave a somewhat anxious glance along the street.

Maurice brought the cognac. "I think you should sit down to drink that," Alexandra suggested. "And tell me what you've been doing these past fifteen years."

"Well . . . working, I suppose. I joined up in 1918, but I didn't actually get to France. Then I became an accountant. I still am an accountant. But you . . ."

"Well, I suppose I have been working as well," Alexandra said.

"But . what . . . I mean, have you lived in Paris long?"

"About ten years. I like it here."

"It's very exciting." He finished his cognac. "It's been simply great seeing you again . . ."

"Why rush off?"

"Well, my wife . . ."

"Have you told her about me?"

"Oh, good lord, no. It's just . . . well, she's very jealous. And you're a very beautiful woman."

"How nice of you to say that. I was hoping you and I might have a nice long chat."

"I would love that, of course. But . . ."

"Doesn't your wife ever do anything on her own?"

"Well, yes, she does." He gave Madeleine another anxious glance. "It's only in the afternoon, I'm afraid."

"The afternoon suits me perfectly," Alexandra said.

"Well, Miriam has a friend living in Paris. She's going to take tea with her the day after tomorrow."

"How long will she be at this tea?"

"Oh . . . a couple of hours, I suppose."

"And what will you be doing in this time?"

"I thought I'd take a stroll around Paris. We could meet . . ."

"My car will pick you up. Here. At what time?"

"Well, three-thirty. But . . . your car?"

"This one." Jean-Claude was just pulling the car into the kerb. "Three-thirty, the day after tomorrow."

"Gosh, Alexandra, that sounds smashing. I'm so looking forward to it."

"Don't tell your wife," she recommended.

"He doesn't have any money," Madeleine pointed out. "That's obvious."

"So, he'll be my charity of the year. We are old friends."

"He took your virginity?"

"However did you guess?"

Madeleine shrugged. "Something about the way you looked at each other."

"It wasn't at all what you think," Alexandra said. "In fact, it was all rather horrible."

"It usually is, the first time."

"This was far worse. I'll you about it some time."

As usual the thought of a sexual conquest had Alexandra feeling pleasantly excited, especially as this was a *re*conquest. The memory of what they had endured together made the prospect even more entrancing. Presumably he was not still the prude he had been as a boy. On the Thursday she cancelled her two bookings, handing them over to Madeleine, so as to leave herself quite free. She had a light lunch and a single glass of wine, a long hot shower, then dressed herself in a summer frock and waited. At a quarter to four Jean-Claude drew up in the yard. There were several cars there already, belonging to clients and those of her staff who drove themselves, but the house was quiet as everyone was occupied, and Jean-Claude showed David up the private staircase which emerged outside Alexandra's boudoir. Alexandra herself opened the door for him, and Jean-Claude hastily withdrew. "I'm in a complete fog," David confessed.

Perhaps he hadn't changed that much, after all, Alexandra thought. "About what?" she asked, as she drew him into the room, and closed the door.

"This place, you . . . everything. This room."

"Well," Alexandra said, "this is my boudoir."

"You mean you live here?"

"I own here."

"This place? It's an hotel?"

"Why do you ask so many questions? No, it is not an hotel. It is my house. Now, aren't you going to kiss me?"

"But . . . your husband . . .?"

"I do not have a husband. And your wife does not know where you are, nor will she ever. So you can do what you like. To me. Won't you enjoy that?"

He looked positively frightened. "Just like that?"

"I know, it would be better with soft lights and sweet music. But as it is the middle of the afternoon we cannot have the soft lights, and as you only have just over an hour, it would be wasting precious time for us to listen to sweet music. So, if you will not kiss me, I will kiss you." She put both arms round his neck and kissed him on the mouth. It took her several seconds to get him to part his lips, and then he hastily withdrew.

"Alexandra . . . why did you bring me here?"

"To make love. Don't you want to? I have thought of you, often, since that horrible day. Have you thought of me?"

"Well . . . yes. I have. I often wondered what had happened to you. You married a chap called Lowndes, didn't you?"

"That's right. But he died in the War. So I'm not married to anyone now. I'm my own boss, and I can do whatever I like. And as I have said, so can you, within reason."

"But we have only just met, after fifteen years."

"Oh, really," Alexandra said, beginning to feel irritated. "What are fifteen years? The last time I saw you, we were not having a good experience. I think we should see if we can improve on that."

He sat down, his shoulders hunched. "If you knew how much that day haunts me."

"It was a long time ago. You must get over it." She sat beside him.

"You mean you don't, well . . . dream of it?"

"I have many other things to dream about," Alexandra assured him.

"I dream of it," he said.

"Therefore you dream of me," Alexandra pointed out.

"Yes, and it is magnificent to see you again, and see you looking so well. So prosperous. But to meet you, and then . . . well . . ."

"The way time is passing, we may as well have had the soft music," Alexandra said. "Well, what do you wish to do with me?"

"I thought we would talk, and . . ."

"How long are you in Paris?"
"For two more days."
"And will your wife be out on her own again?"
"I'm afraid not."
"And you wish to talk!"
"Oh, Alexandra, you have changed."
"And you have not. Well, we have talked. Now, do you wish to make love to me, or do you wish to go home and wait for your wife?"
"Alexandra! I'm not sure I could do anything. It's all been so sudden."
"You've had two days to prepare."
"Yes. But I didn't know, well . . . it's not very usual for women to want to make love, is it? Especially in the middle of the afternoon."
"Your wife does not like to make love in the middle of the afternoon?"
"Well, of course not. Love-making is for at night. In the dark. Isn't it?"
"You know something, you need to be one of my clients," Alexandra told him. "I would make you a much happier man."
"Clients? Are you a solicitor?"
Alexandra laughed. "You could put it that way. But I don't actually solicit. I run the best house in Paris. Everyone knows this. Men come from all over the world to visit Alexandra's. And they pay a great deal for the privilege, I can tell you. That's why I am very rich. And you, I was going to take for free, for old times' sake. And all you wish to do is talk. I will be a laughing stock."
David's mouth had been opening and closing in consternation as she spoke. "The best house in Paris? Do you mean you're a . . . well . . .?"
"Yes, David, I'm a whore. I prefer to think of myself as a courtesan. But if I am a whore, I am one of the

most successful whores who have ever lived. Does that shock you?"

She could tell that it did. His mouth opened and shut all over again, and he hastily stood up. "I must go."

"Because it is against your principles to go with a whore?

She was angry. And now she had made him angry as well. "How dare you?" he snapped. "You . . . you . . ."

"Whore?" He glared at her, then turned and left the room. Alexandra stood at the balustrade as he went down the stairs. "Jean-Claude," she called. "Take this gentleman back to where you picked him up. And then come back here. To me."

She told herself that David's attitude was that of a total, prudish, prurient fool. Yet it rankled. She *was* a whore, and her daughter was a whore. No matter that they both enjoyed the life enormously, and that because of their enjoyment she was growing enormously rich. She remained a whore. A woman beyond the pale of polite society. A woman men were ashamed to mention to their wives. And where was it going to end? At thirty she was still as lovely as she had ever been, perhaps more so, but she knew it was not going to last very much longer. And she had sufficient money put by to retire, whenever she chose. But retire to what? Sex was her life, the very foundation of her being. Although she did not know it, the solution to her problem, as it seemed, appeared before the end of the year.

Again it was her friend, the Minister, who was responsible. He telephoned her one day to say that he had an old and distinguished acquaintance, the Count of Eboli, visiting Paris, and the Count was very anxious to call on the famous Alexandra Mayne. "You are sure he is fit?"

Alexandra asked. She didn't wish a repetition of the Sir William catastrophe.

"For his age, the Count is one of the healthiest men I have ever known."

"His age? What is his age?"

"Well . . . he fought in the Spanish American War, you understand. As a colonel."

Alexandra knew she would have to look the Spanish-American War up, but she had at least learned that her prospective customer was Spanish. "Very well," she sighed.

When she consulted the encyclopaedia, Alexandra discovered that the Spanish-American War had been fought in 1898, that is, two years before she had been born. She also discovered that one seldom became a colonel much under the age of thirty-five, which meant that her prospective client had to be at least sixty-seven years old. She instructed Helene to prepare a very simple meal, and determined to serve nothing but dry white wine.

But in the event, she was pleasantly surprised. Pedro d'Eboli was a tall, spare man, obviously, as the Minister had claimed, very fit, and did not look much over fifty. He was also charm itself, kissed her hand, and said, "I have heard so much about you, Senora Mayne, but nothing that has been said does you sufficient justice."

"You are a flatterer," Alexandra told him, as she led him to the settee. She was wearing a red evening gown, as usual, cut low in both front and back, and of course, no underwear, although she did not suppose he could immediately tell this. "Do you often come to Paris?"

"Not often enough, obviously. I used to visit this beautiful city with some regularity, but three years ago my wife died, and for a while I lost my taste for the cosmopolitan life."

"I am so very sorry," Alexandra said, resting her hand on his arm.

"It was three years ago. Now . . . now I wish to live again. And where better could I begin than here?"

"We shall do our best," Alexandra promised him, and signalled Armand, hovering in the doorway, to bring in the champagne cocktails. "To a pleasant evening."

"To a memorable one," the Count corrected. He watched Armand withdraw, closing the doors behind himself. "Now, I understand there are certain financial matters to be settled, before the evening can properly begin."

"I'm afraid so," Alexandra agreed. "You wish to spend the night?"

"Of course."

"Then . . . a hundred pounds."

"And what does that buy me?"

"A gourmet meal, all the wine you can drink, and me."

"When you say, you, what do you mean?" His gaze was as direct as his questions.

"What you are looking at, Count. Would you like to see what you are looking at?"

"That is not necessary. The gown conceals just enough to make me sure it is worth concealing. And all of that is mine, for the night?"

Alexandra began to feel a little concerned. "My skin must not be marked in any way that will not fade in half an hour."

"May I kiss you?"

"Of course."

"Your mouth? I have heard that . . . well, certain women reserve their lips for their true lovers."

"I am not a certain woman, Count. I am Alexandra Mayne. Any man who comes to my bed is my true lover."

She smiled at him. "At least until he leaves it again." She put her arms round his neck and kissed him, deeply and slowly. While she did that, his hands slid lightly over the front of her gown, tickling her nipples, and then round the back to find the bare flesh of her shoulders. She thought he might grow on her.

"Shall we eat?" she asked.

"If that is what you wish, certainly."

He held her chair for her, while Armand hurried in with the food and wine. "I have never been to Spain," she confessed.

"I am sure you would enjoy it," he commented. "In the summer. It can be very cold in the winter. At least where I live."

"Where is that?"

"Northeast of Madrid. I have an estate." He smiled, looking into his glass. "I grow grapes."

"You are a wine grower?"

"It is a hobby."

"And you do not like mine."

"It is . . . uninteresting?"

"I assure you, it is not my best. It is just that some of my guests find good wines a little hard to digest, and that spoils their evening."

"I shall not find it so," Pedro de Eboli promised. Alexandra told Armand to bring on the best Margaux he had. She was finding her latest client an increasingly interesting companion. "Very good," Pedro observed. "A good vintage, too. But you know, I still prefer my own rioja. I should like you to taste it."

"I would be pleased to do so."

"Hm," he said. "Hm."

They finished the meal. "I also have some very good port," Alexandra said. "Would you like some?"

"Very much. Tell your fellow to bring the decanter, and then leave us, not to return."

"He has not yet cleared the table," Alexandra pointed out.

"I do not want the table cleared."

"As you wish." Alexandra gave the necessary instructions, and Armand withdrew, closing the doors behind him.

"He will not come back?" Pedro asked.

"Not until I send for him."

"Good." Pedro leaned back and surveyed the remains of the meal.

"Shall I pour your port?" Alexandra asked.

"I shall pour it. I would like you to take off your gown, and anything else you may be wearing." Alexandra slipped her shoulder straps off and allowed her dress to slide past her thighs to the floor. Then she stepped out of her shoes. "You are quite beautiful," Pedro said.

"Thank you."

"Now I would like you to lie on the table."

Alexandra looked at the various dishes, especially one on which there remained most of a large jellied consomme. "It would have been easier to have Armand clear it first," she said.

"But I wish you to lie on the dishes. If any are broken, I will pay for them. I wish to place your bottom here . . ." He gestured at the jelly.

"Am I to lie on my back or my front?" Alexandra asked.

"On your back."

"I see. Excuse me a moment." She went into the bedroom, leaving the door open so that he could see what she was doing, and tied her hair up in a scarf. Then she returned to the dining room, and climbed on to the table, settling herself on her back, her head resting on an empty plate, her bottom on the plate of jelly, which squished between her thighs and bubbled out in front.

Pedro went away a thoroughly satisfied customer, Alexandra thought. But she was totally taken aback when he telephoned two days later. "He says he does not wish an appointment, as such," Annette explained. "He wishes to speak with you personally."

It was in the morning, and Alexandra was still in bed. She raised her eyebrows, got up, and went to the telephone extension in her boudoir. "I would like you to have dinner with me," Pedro explained.

Alexandra checked her diary. "I am free next Thursday night. I will expect you at eight."

"I mean, I would like to take you out to dinner."

"Me?"

"What is wrong with that?"

"Well . . . evenings are when I work."

"Do you never take time off?"

"Never," Alexandra lied.

"Very well. I will hire you for the evening, as before. Only, you will come out with me."

"But that is a waste of money," she told him. "You will be paying for dinner, twice."

"That is surely my concern?"

"Of course. I will expect you next Thursday at eight."

She felt almost like a young girl again, and the girls were as excited as herself. "I wonder where he'll take you?" Madeleine asked.

Pedro took her to Maxim's. They had an excellent dinner, and then he took her back to the House, and they made love again until the small hours. This time his sex was more straightforward, but he seemed more pleased with her than ever. He took her out twice the following week. "He is becoming a permanency," Annette remarked when the same thing happened the next week. "He has so far spent a thousand pounds on you this month."

Alexandra reflected that he was old enough to know what he wanted to do with his money, but she was yet at once exhilarated and apprehensive. She had had several clients who had clearly been far more wealthy than the Count, but none of them had become regular fixtures, as it were. She knew there had to be something at the end of it. "I am returning to Spain next week," Pedro said, over their next dinner table.

"Oh! I shall be sorry to see you go."

"I should like you to visit me there. It would be better if you did not actually accompany me. I will pay your fare, of course, but I would like you to come down in a week."

"Now, Pedro . . ."

"I know you said you never took time off. So, name your price, for a fortnight's stay at my home in Spain."

"My God!" she cried. "It will be astronomical. I work afternoons as well, you know."

"Name it."

"Well . . . I could not possibly leave town for two weeks for less than two thousand pounds."

Pedro wrote her a cheque. "Pedro," she said. "Do not be a fool. I am a whore. I am well known as a whore. People will know that you have entertained a whore in your family home." She had accepted such hospitality in the past from various of her clients, but none of them had been a Spanish count, with all the weight of family and history that entailed.

"I am not interested in people," he told her. "I am interested in you. I leave Paris tomorrow. I will expect you in a week."

* * *

"What am I to do?" Alexandra asked Annette and Madeleine.

Annette shrugged; she had already banked the cheque. "It is his money, and his reputation. Go, and enjoy yourself."

"And tell us all about it when you come back," Madeleine said.

Alexandra took the train down to Irun. Here, as Pedro had promised, there was a car waiting for her, a Rolls-Royce, which took her to the southeast, through Pamplona. She sat in the back and gazed at the liveried chauffeur as she was driven over steadily deteriorating roads in a welter of dust. "Do you speak English?" she asked at last, some time after leaving Pamplona.

"A leetle, senora."

"When do we reach Eboli?"

"We have been on Eboli for the past fifteen minutes, senora."

Sure enough she now saw the vines clinging to the rolling hills, and a few minutes later the castle came into view. Alexandra caught her breath, because it *was* a castle, built on a hillside overlooking a ravine, with castellated towers, high walkways, and a drive up, beside the ravine, to a huge gateway, above which a portcullis hung menacingly. "The Count of Eboli lives here?" she asked incredulously.

"It is his home, senora," the chauffeur told her. "The Counts of Eboli have lived here for centuries."

Beyond the portcullis and the gate there was an extensive courtyard, and there Pedro waited to greet her, accompanied by a dozen excited dogs, of every variety from mastiffs to spaniels, along with several servants, who fussed over the bags. "I had not expected a castle," Alexandra confessed.

"All Spanish counts live in castles," Pedro said with a smile. Alexandra was lost in wonder as she was escorted through a vast baronial hall, and along corridors and up staircases adorned with suits of armour and splendid paintings, presumably of past Counts and Countesses of Eboli, on the walls, and into a huge bedroom. "This is the room with the view," Pedro told her, and led her to the picture window, which looked out, beyond the ravine, at the hills and mountains beyond. In the near distance, in the next valley, there was a sizeable village. "All you can see is Eboli," he told her.

"You mean, you own it?"

"It has belonged to my family for many hundreds of years."

"You own the village?"

"The inhabitants are my tenants."

"I didn't know there was an estate like this anywhere in the world, nowadays."

"But of course there are, hundreds of them, in Iberia, in Eastern Europe . . . there are quite a few in Great Britain as well. Here in Spain, the politicians of the left are always muttering about changing things, but we pay little attention to such matters. Now, I am sure you feel like a bath. Will you join me for a cocktail before dinner?" He was so certain. He had not even touched her, save for a formal kiss on each cheek. And there was a smiling maid to help her with her toilette. Alexandra had to remind herself that she had to measure up in her own behaviour. But surely he had not invited her here simply as a guest?

He did not come to her room that night. Next morning, he took her riding over the estate, delighted to discover that she was an expert horsewoman. "I learned to ride without benefit of saddle or stirrups, on the Guianese savannah," she told him.

"I would like to hear your life story."

"Warts and all?" she laughed.

"Every single one." They returned to the castle for lunch, and after the meal retired to his bedroom, which also looked out across the valley. There he undressed her, and then himself. "To have you here, in my own bedroom, naked, has been my dream from the moment I first saw you. I do not wish you to leave, Alexandra."

She kissed him, and they made love. Then, as he raised the matter again, she told him her entire life story. As he knew who and what she was, she didn't see that he could be in any way upset, and he wasn't. When she was finished, he lay facing her for several seconds, then he said, "I meant what I said, just now. I do not wish you to leave."

"Oh, Pedro, I would love to stay. I can think of nowhere finer. But . . . I'm a little young to retire. And you would soon tire of me."

"That could never happen," he said. "Besides, I am a little old to tire of my wife."

CHAPTER 11

Alexandra was completely taken aback. "You cannot be serious," she protested.

"I understand that it will mean a complete change of lifestyle for you," Pedro agreed. "But . . . you are over thirty, my dearest girl, and surely something of a change will be inevitable in a few years' time."

"I meant, from your point of view. I'm a whore."

"We have been through all of this before. I have no children. Perhaps you will give me a child. I should like that. But certainly there is no one to criticise what I do, no one who matters, anyway."

"But society . . ."

"I have not moved in Spanish society since the death of my wife. I have no great desire to resume doing so. If you wish us to, of course . . ."

"Oh, Pedro," she said, and kissed him. "You will have to give me time to think about it."

"Of course," he agreed.

Alexandra did not need all that much time. Little Alexandra Mayne, born in the backwoods of British Guiana, and doomed to a life of prostitution, Countess of Eboli! The thought was an irresistibly heady one. And certainly life on Eboli, as displayed to her by Pedro and his employees, was at once delightful and excitingly different to anything she had ever known. She returned to Paris with her mind half made up, but then it was necessary to consult her women.

To her gratification, they were nearly all in favour. Alexandra, however, having experienced various ups and downs during her life, had no intention of abandoning the House altogether. Her decision was made the easier by Mayne's desire to remain in the business. Thus she retained the house, and an interest in the profits, merely promoting Madeleine to be Madame, a position for which the magnificent blonde woman was eminently fitted. She was tempted to take one or two of her favourites with her, as she doubted Pedro would entirely be able to satisfy her, and in the end opted for Francoise, who now that she was approaching twenty-one was an utterly beautiful girl. Alexandra's relationship with Alice was no longer what it had once been, and in any event Alice had grown very fond of Parisian life. Of course, there was always the prospect of breaking in one or two of the black-haired and -eyed senoritas on the estate, but Alexandra knew she had to make her way in this new society slowly and carefully. She would have liked to take Lucien as well, but she didn't want to make Pedro jealous, so she shelved that idea for the time being, retaining it as a thought for the future: Pedro was getting on.

The wedding itself was celebrated at the castle. Alexandra shut up the House so that all of her staff could journey down for the occasion, and Pedro gave his people a holiday, so that everyone enjoyed a great fiesta. The whole affair had been conducted with as much secrecy as possible, but even so the news got out very rapidly, and almost immediately the papers began their campaign. Slightly confused in the beginning, they soon ferreted out the truth, and "Count of Eboli marries mysterious stranger" changed to "Count of Eboli marries Parisian courtesan"; none of them were the least afraid of a libel suit where Alexandra was so well known. This reportage only upset her for fear that it would upset Pedro, but he merely laughed.

Alexandra was more concerned with making her mark in her immediate surroundings. The people on the estate were no problem; that their employer had elected to spend his declining years with a beautiful young woman who merely amused them. The people in the village were more difficult, and the nuns in the nearby convent the biggest problem of all, but Alexandra went out of her way to call on them and subscribe to their good works, and slowly but surely won them over.

Domestically, it was a time of great bliss. There was Spanish to be learned – Alexandra found this surprisingly easy – Pedro to be amused, the estate to interest herself in, and Francoise to keep her company whenever she became bored, or sexually frustrated. In the beginning she had expected that Pedro, like Sir Willy, would rather enjoy having a beautiful and nubile second string to his bow, as it were, all with the willing consent of his wife. But Pedro never made any advances to Francoise, and to prevent *her* from becoming sexually frustrated, Alexandra had to give her permission to take up with one of the stable lads. For the time being, however, they were both quite happy, and Alexandra enjoyed enormously being the Countess of Eboli, and staying in the best hotels whenever Pedro decided to visit Madrid or the Balearics, or the Riviera or Italy. She could not help but be aware, however, that all was not well with Spain, or that Pedro was worried about the political situation. They had hardly been married a year when there was an upheaval, a left wing government was elected to power, and the King and Queen fled the country. Alphonso XIII abdicated, and Spain officially became a republic. "Where does that leave us?" Alexandra asked. "You, I mean, Pedro."

"I will have to pay more taxes," he agreed.

"I meant, can you go on being a count?" She dearly wanted to go on being a countess.

"Why not?"

"Well . . . do they have counts in republics?"

"They have counts in France, don't they?"

"Why, so they do." She felt greatly relieved.

Over the next four years Alexandra did her best to ignore all political problems. There continued to be no shortage of money, from her point of view, and the servants and villagers became more and more pleased with her, while she was welcome at the convent whenever she chose, and indeed the nuns often came to tea at the castle. She also had a great deal to occupy her in her own life. In September 1935 Mayne celebrated her nineteenth birthday. Except for the tawny streaks in her hair she was a carbon copy of her mother at that age, and Alexandra was delighted. She was also just about the most famous whore in Paris, but Alexandra was beginning to wonder if she should not be married. She considered that every woman should marry, and have a child, or she would not be properly fulfilling her role *as* a woman; she even gave her blessing when Francoise wished to marry her stable boy, whom Pedro promptly made head groom.

But Mayne was apparently totally disinterested in men save as physical objects. Alexandra supposed her upbringing had a good deal to do with that, and brooded, but Madeleine was reassuring. "She has just not met the right man," she pointed out. "She will, one of these days."

* * *

There were changes at the House, however. Alice received a proposal of marriage. Alexandra was delighted. The old intimacy had long become diluted by all the other intimacies Alexandra had accumulatd, and she was relieved to think that her earliest playmate was about to settle into domestic bliss.

Her true intimate nowadays was Madeleine.

Madeleine had taken up visiting the castle twice a year. This was in any event necessary, as although Alexandra visited Paris, and the House, also twice a year, these were always frenetically active social occasions. When Madeleine came down she was able to bring Alexandra up to date with what was really happening, especially financially. They were also able to make love and thoroughly enjoy themselves, and the holiday did Madeleine good. She was at the castle in July 1936, as Paris was busily emptying for the summer holidays and there was not a lot of custom at the House. She wished principally to discuss Mayne, as did Alexandra. Mayne often came down for the summer as well, but this time she had elected to go to Italy with a friend. "A boyfriend?" Alexandra asked, hopefully.

"A girl."

"One of us?"

"I don't think she is a prostitute. As to whether she likes girls more than boys, I would say yes."

"Have you met her?"

"Once. At a restaurant. She seems awfully upper crust. Mayne is quite smitten."

"What are we going to do?" Alexandra wondered. "Do you think this friend knows what Mayne does?"

"I have no idea."

"It is going to turn out a disaster," Alexandra grumbled.

"I will have to come back up with you, and have a serious talk with her."

"Well, there's no hurry," Madeleine pointed out. "She's not coming back until the end of August, and I am so looking forward to my time here.

Next morning they and Francoise went for a ride. "This place is so peaceful," Madeleine said. "The journey here, ugh. Everyone was so unpleasant. And there were slogans written up all over the place."

"Spain is in a mess," Alexandra agreed. "But as you say, it is all peaceful here."

"I hope you are right," Francoise said. "Miguel told me yesterday that there have been men in the village saying there has been fighting, both in the north and in the south. They say that army units have mutinied against the Government."

"Good heavens! But there are no army units around Eboli."

"These men have been saying that the Count is a member of the Falange Party, and is a supporter of the army mutiny. They say it is a plot to take over the government and bring back the king. They were telling the villagers that the Count should be arrested, and shot. They are saying that all Falangists should be shot, because they are Fascists."

"I hope they were thrown out," Alexandra said angrily.

"I think they are still there," Francoise said.

They had just topped a rise from where they could look down on the village, at the distant houses. Alexandra had intended to ride in there today. But now . . . she drew rein. "I think we should go home," she suggested. "And find out what this is all about."

They rode home very quickly, and Alexandra found Pedro

in his study, and on the telephone, but he waved her to a chair while he carried on a conversation, which, as she listened, she found most disturbing, for it was all about troop concentrations and political affairs. When at last he hung up, she was on the edge of her seat, her riding crop clutched tightly in her hands. "Now my darling girl, what is the matter?" He smiled at her.

"Pedro, what is happening?"

"It is very simple, really, my dear. You are probably unaware of it, here on Eboli, but over the past few months this country has descended into a state of near anarchy. In places like Madrid and Barcelona there is about one political murder a night. The Left murders members of the Right, and as the judiciary is in the hands of the Left, the Right can obtain no justice, and thus have to murder their opponents as well. This is a situation which cannot possibly last."

"And you are of the Right, a member of the Falangist Party."

"It would be difficult to be a Communist and own an estate like Eboli."

"And what is happening with these soldiers?"

"Well, as I was saying, the army commanders have finally decided that the government is incompetent, and have determined to take over the country."

"But . . . that is a revolution."

"It will be very quick, and then we will restore the monarchy, get rid of all these socialists and communists, and put Spain back on her feet again." He frowned at her. "You have no sympathy for such people, surely?"

Alexandra had never thought about social classes before. But all of her clients came from at least the middle class, and she was now an aristocrat. "Of course I do not. But Pedro, Francoise told me there are men in the village, speaking against you."

"Well, I suppose it is something we shall have to put up with. There will be a troop of cavalry here tomorrow. I have sent for them."

"Pedro, I'm frightened."

"Do not be. We are perfectly safe. And as I say, the cavalry will be here tomorrow." He cocked his head. "There is the lunch gong, and you are still in your habit."

Alexandra took a deep breath, and knew that she had to get over her panic. She was the Countess of Eboli. "I will go and wash my hands. Is it not possible for me to eat in my habit?"

"It really is not proper," Pedro said severely. "Go and change. I will tell Alfredo to hold the meal for fifteen minutes. Run along now." Just as if he were her father, Alexandra thought. But then, he was old enough to be her father. And at least his total confidence was reassuring.

She hurried up to her room, where her maid was waiting with a change of clothing, and regained the dining room exactly fifteen minutes late. Madeleine had also changed, but luncheon was a subdued meal, for all the Count's attempts at conversation. "I have invited two of the sisters for tea," Alexandra said as they sipped their cognacs and coffee. "Do you think they will come?"

"Why should they not?"

"At five o'clock," Alexandra said, and stood up. "Will you retire?"

"Not this afternoon, my dear. I think I shall go down to the village and see what is happening there."

"You will be careful, Pedro."

"These are my people. Madeleine." He kissed Alexandra on the forehead, and left the room.

Madeleine and Alexandra gazed at each other, but there were still the butler and two footmen fussing about. “Siesta,” Alexandra said, and led the way to the stairs.

They made love, and then showered, and dressed, both in party frocks, Madeleine’s in pale green and Alexandra’s in deep blue. They were downstairs and waiting when the pony trap came through the gates, and the two sisters got down. Angelina really was a very lovely girl, with clipped features and deep, dark eyes. Esmerelda was overweight and suffered from having too stern a face. “Whatever do you think is happening, Countess?” said Esmerelda.

“There is trouble everywhere,” Alexandra said.

“I meant in the village. There is so much noise.”

“In the village?” Alexandra rang her golden bell, and one of the maids appeared. “Where is Alfredo?”

“I do not know, Countess.”

“Well, I wish you to find him. I wish to know what is the cause of the noise in the village. And you may serve tea.”

“I am sure there is nothing to worry about,” Angelina said.

“Find Alfredo,” Alexandra snapped.

“Yes, Countess.” The maid withdrew.

“Shall I pour?” Madeleine asked, determined not to be distracted from the matter in hand. “One lump, or two?”

“Three for Sister Esmerelda,” Angelina giggled. “She has a sweet tooth.”

Madeleine poured the tea, but at that moment the maid returned. “Alfredo is not here, Countess,” she said. “I think he has gone to the village.”

“Of all the effrontery!” Alexandra got up and went to the window. “Listen to that noise? Oh, my God!” The two nuns and Madeleine hurried to stand beside her, and watch the crowd of people marching up the road towards the castle gates. "Quickly," Alexandra said. "Juanita, close the gates."

"I, Countess?"

She was clearly going to be useless. "Madeleine, come with me," Alexandra snapped.

Francoise appeared. "There is a mob at the gates!" she cried. "Oh, where is Miguel? He went with the Count to the village."

Now the noise was very close, punctuated by the explosions of firearms. They could even make out the words being shouted: "Get the Fascist bitches!"

The two sisters ran for the stairwell, apparently with some idea of regaining their pony and trap and escaping. Francoise fled for the back of the house, with the maid. Madeleine started for the stairs, then checked herself, as Alexandra had not yet moved. "Alix!" she shouted. "They will lynch you!" As they must have already lynched Pedro, Alexandra thought. It had been so long since she had come face to face with any physical violence, except in the play-acting of her various tableaux – not since Tony the Greek. She had coped with that well enough, but she knew this was something entirely different. There were simply too many of them. "Oh, Alix," Madeleine said. She came back down the stairs and ran to embrace her friend. They held each other close, and listened to screams coming from the yard.

They released each other and went to the window, looked down to see the crowd of men, and women and children, surging through the gate, carrying Juanita, who had made some attempt to carry out her mistress's orders. She was being tossed from arms to arms, in the air, as if she were a toy, while her hair flailed and she screamed again and again. Then they saw the mob stop, as it sighted the pony and trap, and the two nuns desperately scrambling in. Juanita was forgotten, thrown to the ground and trampled as the human animals ran forward. Sister Esmerelda stood up on the driving seat and snapped her whip at them, but someone caught the thong and plucked it, and her, forward. She fell into their midst, struggling and shouting. Alexandra felt Madeleine's fingers biting into her arm.

Sister Esmeralda was dragged to her feet, her habit already torn away. Now her cowl was ripped from her head, and the mob jeered at her shaven head. They threw her amongst themselves as they had done with Juanita, each man or each woman seizing hold of any article of clothing they could reach, so that in a few moments she was naked, her white body gleaming in the afternoon sunlight, promising all manner of delights as she was thrown down and the first man, having already dropped his trousers, knelt between her legs.

Then it was the turn of Angelina, who had remained sitting on the driving seat, apparently paralysed with fear, while her friend was being assaulted. "Oh, no," Madeleine whispered. Hands reached up and pulled Angelina down. She made no effort to resist them, stood there as they ripped the clothes from her body as well. Unlike Esmeralda she was small breasted and slender, her beauty lying in her face and her legs. But the people surrounding her had no interest in beauty . . . only in the fact that she was a woman. And a nun.

"Alexandra . . ." Francoise stood in the inner doorway, her face ashen, trembling.

Alexandra drew a long breath. "They are only men," she said. It was important to remember that; a moment later the mob was in the house.

Alexandra made herself stand still. She listened to the shattering of glass and crockery, the obscene laughter which flowed all around her, the ripping sound as the

Count's priceless drapes were torn from the walls, the crack of breaking wood as his exquisite furniture was kicked and thrown into pieces. She heard Francoise screaming on the far side of the room, but Madeleine, like herself, made no sound. The pair of them, so beautiful, so elegantly, flawlessly dressed, indeed gave the mob pause for a moment's reflection, and almost a spark of hope seeped into Alexandra's breast. Then she was surrounded by foetid breaths and clawing hands, which tore the pearls from her neck and sent them scattering over the parquet, to be grovelled after by some of the men, while others ripped the dress from her shoulders. She was lifted from the floor by several pairs of hands, which at the same time dragged the lace knickers from her hips, while their owners shrieked and howled their lust. She found herself on the floor, her legs held apart, while man after man sought an entry, and those who were waiting pulled her nipples and squeezed her breasts.

It was what might come after that concerned her, as she thanked God that Mayne had elected not to visit her this summer. And that immediate future was rushing at her soon enough, as even the men grew tired of raping her, and she was seized by the arms and dragged to her feet, to gaze at Madeleine and Francoise, bodies pink and white and bruised from their manhandling, hair clouding across their faces, breasts heaving as they panted, and realised she could look no different. "Bring the bitch," someone shouted, and with a chorus of obscene laughter she was taken back to the window, where her stomach rolled as she saw that Angelina had been crucified against the barn door, by knives thrust through her arms and shoulders. But Esmeralda was suffering even more, as she had the larger breasts. These the women were engaged in cutting away, cackling as they did so. Francoise, also dragged across the room to stand beside them, vomited.

And Alexandra realised that, much as she had resolved to die without granting her assailants a word, much less begging, she had to try to save her friends. "Please," she shouted above the din. "It is I you wish. I am the Countess of Eboli. These are but visitors. They are French. They have nothing to do with Spain."

She might as well have shouted to the breeze. Francoise had been identified as the wife of Miguel, a man much hated in the village. She was given to the women, and screamed in desperation as they slashed at her body with their knives before throwing her in a corner to bleed to death. Alexandra and Madeleine remained in the hands of the men, who wished to shave them. First of all their hair was cropped until it was short as a boy's, then their heads were gone over with a pair of sheers. The same was done to their pubic region with a great deal of obscene comment and laughter. As if it mattered; they were both too bruised and exhausted to care. The women then demanded them. But the men refused. "We will have them again tomorrow," they shouted, and dragged the two women back into the house and down to a cellar, where they were thrown upon the floor and locked in.

They lay together for some time. Noise only distantly reached them, but it did seem as if the castle was being thoroughly looted. All manner of thoughts tumbled through Alexandra's mind. She had had so much, and had left it behind to reach after even more. To be brought to this unbelievable situation. Pedro was dead. She had never pretended that she loved him, but he had been kind to her, as well as amazingly generous, and he had given her a glimpse of the lifestyle she wanted to make her own. Now that too was vanished. And Francoise. Poor, innocent Francoise. She had made Francoise what she was, in the genuine belief that was the way to happiness and prosperity. Francoise had certainly been both happy and prosperous, down to today. Now there were only Madeleine and herself left. For how long? But then her old spirit reasserted itself. She was alive, and relatively unharmed. She was not just going to lie down and wait trembling for death to come to her. She forced herself to her knees, and stroked Madeleine's bald scalp. "Are you all right?"

Madeleine raised her head, then let it sink to the floor again. "Are they going to kill us?"

"I'm afraid they may, when they get tired of us. But there is always the chance they may simmer down a little overnight."

"God, I'm thirsty," Madeleine muttered.

Alexandra stood up and looked around her. There was very little light in the cellar, although it had still been light outside when they had been imprisoned. But she knew these cellars very well. This one contained wine, although the marauding villagers had not apparently realised this; it was not the main wine cellar, but a subsidiary where some especially choice vintages were stored. "We could get drunk, I suppose," she said. And then remembered that at the far end there was a washbasin. She went down the passageway between two racks and turned on the taps, and to her delight water gushed out. "Let's clean ourselves up, first," she suggested. Madeleine joined her and they washed each other, scooping water over each other as if they had been children. "Do you suppose Pedro is dead?" Madeleine asked.

"Almost certainly."

"Then you are the Dowager Countess of Eboli."

"If Eboli is still standing tomorrow, yes. We'll celebrate." She took a bottle from the nearest rack, opened it; each cellar contained corkscrew and tasting cup, hanging by cords from the ceiling. They drank the bottle between them, and then another, and then lay on the floor and slept, for the moment oblivious to anything that was going on around them.

Alexandra awoke at what she guessed was about dawn. It was utterly dark in the cellar, but she could hear a good deal of movement from above them. She sat up to listen; her immediate fear was that the mob might fire the castle; then there would be no hope for them at all. But these sounds were more ordered; some of the tramping feet even had a military thud to them. She shook Madeleine. "Wake up. I think soldiers have arrived."

"Whose soldiers?"

"Does it matter? They have to be better than the mob." She went to the door and banged on it with her fists. "Hello," she shouted. "Down here!"

For a moment she thought no one had heard her, then she listened to boots clumping on the stairs outside. "Who is in there?" someone demanded.

"The Countess of Eboli and a friend," Alexandra replied.

There was a muttered consultation. Then the voice said, "Unlock the door."

"We are locked in," Alexandra told him. "Is there no key?"

"The key is gone. Stand away. We will break it down."

Alexandra and Madeleine retreated behind the nearest wine rack, and the door trembled to the blows being hurled at it. Then someone thought of shooting out the lock, and the cellar reverberated to the explosions while chunks of wood flew in every direction. A few minutes later the door burst in and the women were confronted by half a dozen soldiers and a sergeant. The group were entirely taken aback by the sight of the two naked, hairless female bodies, and although all armed with rifles and bayonets, insensibly moved closer together as if they were looking at ghosts. "I'm afraid we have been the victims of the mob," Alexandra explained.

"Then I do not understand how you are alive," the sergeant said. "Out there . . ." Ge gestured with his thumb.

"We have seen it," Alexandra told him.

"Do you think we could have something to eat?" Madeleine asked. "And may we be allowed to find ourselves something to wear?"

The sergeant considered, briefly, then nodded. His men formed a protective squad around Alexandra and Madeleine, pressing as close as they could. "Have you dispersed the mob?" Alexandra asked, as they climbed the stairs.

"We have sent them home, yes," the sergeant said. "Most of them are guilty of murder."

"You do not understand the truth of the matter, senora. The Falange has taken up arms against the government. Your husband was a known Falangist. The people were very angry when they discovered this."

"And you consider they are justified in tearing him to pieces? With my servants? And two nuns?"

"It is civil war, now, Countess. These things happen in a civil war."

Alexandra gave up, and turned her attention to finding something to wear. Her bedroom had been thoroughly looted, but the women had gone for her ball gowns and formal dresses, rather than casual wear. What clothes were left had been scattered across the floor, many of them torn into pieces, as were her bedclothes. But she did find a pair of knickers, a pair of slacks, and a shirt, and even a bandanna in which she could conceal her bald head. Now all she wanted to do was get out of this castle and this accursed country, back to Paris and the House, and hibernate until her hair grew again. She opened the door, and found a soldier leaning against the wall, smoking a cigarette. But he had a rifle slung on his shoulder. "You must stay inside," he told her.

"I wish to see my friend."

"She is in her room."

Alexandra kept her temper under control. "When do I get something to eat?"

"I do not know."

"Then I suggest you go and find out. I am starving."

"You are a prisoner. You are a member of the Falange."

"I have only the vaguest idea what the Falange is," Alexandra told him. "And even if I were a member of it, is it your policy to starve your prisoners to death?"

The soldier considered this, then marched to the top of the stairs. "The Countess wishes food," he bawled.

There was an indeterminate reply from the depths of the house, but a few minutes later another soldier appeared with a tray on which were bread and sausages. "I also wish coffee," Alexandra said. "And my friend."

The soldiers muttered at each other, but both Madeleine and coffee were produced. Madeleine had found a dress which was torn but was adequate; she also had tied up her head. "Food," she said, and ate wolfishly. Alexandra joined her; she was no less hungry. The soldiers watched them with great interest. "Are we prisoners?" Madeleine asked between mouthfuls.

"It looks as if we are. Trouble is, there seems to be nobody in real authority."

But even as she spoke she heard the growl of a car engine in the courtyard. She got up to go to the window, but was checked by the guard. "You eat," he recommended.

Madeleine raised her eyebrows, and Alexandra sat

down again. They drank their coffee and listened to distant commands and the stamping of boots. Then there were feet on the stairs. "You stand," the soldier said. "The Colonel comes."

"Authority at last," Alexandra said. but she didn't know why she was so relieved; this man could very easily order them to be shot.

They stood together, away from the table, and facing the door, and a few minutes later the Colonel appeared. He wore brown boots and cross belts and a high peaked cap, and he gave them a perfunctory salute. "Which of you is the Countess of Eboli?"

"I am the Countess of Eboli," Alexandra told him.

"Then I must offer you my condolences, Countess." He stared at her, apparently taking in her beauty in for the first time.

"Thank you. May I ask what is to happen to me, and my friend?"

The Colonel looked at Madeleine for the first time as well. "Your friend is Spanish?"

"My friend is French. As I am English."

The Colonel nodded, as if he already knew that. "But you lived in Paris before marrying the Count."

"Yes. I have a house there. I wish to return there, with my friend. Is this possible?"

"I have heard of this house." Alexandra glanced at Madeleine, who again raised her eyebrows. "I have always wished to visit there," the Colonel went on. "But . . . it is very expensive, I understand."

"Sometimes," Alexandra said cautiously.

"But now . . ." The Colonel smiled. "The house has come to me. Am I not right?"

Alexandra sighed; she was a mass of aches and pains, and she had had enough sex in the past twenty-four hours – even for her. "That is possible, Senor Colonel. Are you addressing me as Senora the Countess, or as Madame Mayne?"

"I think I would prefer Madame Mayne, Countess."

"Then there will be a charge. And for my friend."

His turn to raise his eyebrows. "You are my prisoners. I have power of life and death over you."

Alexandra shrugged. "So did the mob. We had supposed we would be dead by now. It is in your power to kill us, but would that give you any satisfaction? It is in your power to rape us, but would *that* give you much satisfaction? When it is in our power to make you the happiest man alive?"

The Colonel considered. "You can do this?"

"Of course. It is our profession. But there must be a charge."

"You are my prisoners," he said again.

"We cannot perform properly, without a charge," Alexandra told him. "But there are many forms of charges. Neither Madame Clos-Bruie nor I are Spanish. We have no knowledge of, or interest in, Spanish politics. I married the Count of Eboli because he paid me to do so; he bought me, as he might have bought me in a slave market." That was a little unfair on Pedro, but he was dead, and it was her business to stay alive. The Colonel was licking his lips at the thought of being able to go to a slave market and purchase two such marvellous creatures as stood before him. "And since then he has treated me a slave," Alexandra continued, warming to her theme. "He has even, as you see, made me bring one of my ladies down from Paris to satisfy his insatiable lust. As for beating . . . how do you suppose we have survived the beating we received from the villagers? Simply because what they did to us was nothing compared with that the count did to us every day."

The captain scratched his head. "You should have been on the stage," Madeleine remarked, in French.

"Why, someone once said that to me, long ago," Alexandra said, and found herself wondering what had happened to that nice young man, her very first customer . . . and she did not even know his name. She wondered if he had returned to the corner of the Haymarket a few nights later, and driven away in disgust when she had not been there? How long ago it seemed.

But she needed to concentrate on the business in hand. "You have had a hard life," said the Colonel.

"That is why the only payment I am asking of you, for the service of myself and Madame Clos-Bruie, is a safe-conduct to the French border," Alexandra said.

"That is all?"

"And some money to get us there. Just our fares to the border. I usually charge four hundred English pounds a session, for each of us. So you will see that you are getting a bargain. And I promise you that you will have the experience of a lifetime." He did.

CHAPTER 12

Alexandra and Madeleine were just happy to get home. Fortunately, it remained high summer, and Paris was empty – business, as always during July and August, was very slow. Equally, Alexandra did not publicise her return, and no one outside the House knew she was back at all, much less permanently. Annette and Jeanne were of course horrified to see her bald head and at what she had to tell them, while Jean-Claude clenched his fists and vowed vengeance, as did Lucien, once he had got over his grief at the news of Francoise's death.

For Alexandra it was a time for lying in her own bed, or sitting in the garden in the sun. Ostensibly she was waiting for her hair to grow back, but in her heart she knew that she had been vastly more upset by what had happened than she could let even Madeleine understand. It was not the death of Pedro or the loss of her new-found aristocracy. She had known Pedro was going to die some time soon, and she had equally known that would entail a return to Paris. But the quite ghastly upsurge of animal-like violence had frightened her. She had never supposed that any people could act that way. Not even the men who had raped her so many years before had actually threatened her life, or wanted to mutilate her. But slowly she put the memory behind her, greatly assisted by the return of Mayne in the autumn. Mayne had of course read of the outbreak of the Spanish Civil War in the newspapers, and had cabled Paris to find out if her mother was safe. Alexandra had just returned, and she cabled back to say she was. Now Mayne for the first time learned the truth of what had happened, and like the others, she was devastated, far more than Alexandra, by the death of Pedro, who she had come to regard as the father she had never known.

With Mayne was her girlfriend, Sarah Bryan, who turned out to be English. Mayne admitted that they were lovers. Sarah, who was a few years older, was in the middle of a very messy divorce from her wealthy husband, and had fled to Paris to escape the publicity. The reason for the divorce was an affair she had had with another woman, also married, who had returned to *her* husband. Alexandra found it all rather intriguing, and wondered if Sarah would be interested in joining her staff: the English girl was extremely attractive. Short and plump and blonde, in the strongest contrast to Mayne, who took after her mother in build, Sarah looked deliciously cuddly. But she was entirely off men. She had genuinely fallen for Mayne, and Mayne was enjoying being adored. Alexandra considered the situation, and decided against overreacting. She remembered women like Nathalie Barney, and had no doubt that Sarah would go off the boil soon enough. She still wanted Mayne to have a sufficiently meaningful relationship with a man, at some time in her life. But there was time; Mayne was only twenty. By that winter both Alexandra and Madeleine were sufficiently recovered to welcome back their old clients. Though she had no wish to continue further association with Spain, she had no objection to Italy, and when she was visited by Count Alessandro di Marti, Alexandra made him most welcome. He invited her, along with Mayne (who would not be parted from Sarah) to Venice, to see the famous Carnival.

On a subtly April evening, a delighted Alexandra, with her two companions, found themselves in St Mark's Square.

"There is someone I want you to meet," Sandro told her, as he hurried her through the crowds. "Where are we going?" she asked.

"My palazzo."

"To meet your special friend."

"Yes. He is here incognito, you understand." He escorted her down various sidestreets, all crowded with enthusiastic people, until they arrived at the side door of a rather large building. Like all Venetian palazzos it looked sadly in need of repair, but once the door was opened for them by a liveried footman they found themselves in a palace indeed. The garden was luxurious, canopied to keep off any rain, and festooned with fairy lights. There were quite a few people here, men and women, in costume, but while they all carried masks, few had them on at the moment. Amongst them waiters wandered with trays of drinks and canapés.

All heads turned at the sight of Alexandra, but she kept her mask on and Sandro hurried her through the throng with only a few scattered introductions. Inside the building, in a vast drawing room filled with statues, Alexandra might have supposed she was surrounded by more costumery, but these were all uniforms, mostly in black. Dominating the room was a heavy-set man with a pronounced five-o'clock shadow, the more prominent because he had a big chin and kept thrusting it out, as he equally kept drawing deep breaths to inflate his chest, causing his uniform tunic to swell. Alexandra knew immediately who it had to be: she had seen sufficient photographs of Mussolini. She also realised immediately what was going to be involved – she had read enough about the dictator's sexual habits. "You must excuse me for a moment," she told Sandro.

"But Il Duce is waiting to speak with you."

Mussolini had seen their entrance, and was beckoning them over. Sandro muttered. He held her elbow to escort her forward. "Duce," he said. "The Countess Mayne."

Alexandra wasn't in a curtseying mood, so she offered her hand while giving a slight bow, without lowering either her head or her eyes. Mussolini stared at her, then allowed his eyes to droop, down her body and back up again. "I am honoured, Duce," Alexandra said.

Mussolini made a remark in Italian. "The Duce reciprocates, Alexandra," Sandro interpreted. "He says he has heard much about you."

"From you, no doubt," Alexandra said.

"He wishes to see your face."

Alxandra obligingly lifted her mask, for a moment, then let it fall back into place. "Now, may I be excused?"

Sandro interpreted, and Mussolini gave a shout of laughter while replying. "Il Duce says that you may be excused," Sandro said. "He says he will be excused with you. Is that not droll?"

Alexandra shrugged. "Where is the cloak-room?" Sandro spoke to Mussolini, who gave another shout of laughter, before seizing Alexandra's arm and escorting her to an inner doorway. Here there were armed guards, but these parted as their leader waved his arm, and he marched her along a corridor leading away from the reception rooms. He spoke to her, but without Sandro, who had been left behind, she had no idea what he was saying. Then he opened a door, and she found herself pushed into a man's toilet. There were three men already in there, but at the sight of the Duce, equipped with a woman, they hastily left, bowing and saluting.

Before she had worked out what he was going to do, he had dropped his breeches around his ankles, put his hands under her buttocks to lift her out of the basin, and was inside her. She threw her arms round his neck to hold herself there, at the same time reflecting with some annoyance that as he had not commanded her to strip, or kissed her, or even looked at her very closely, she could have been anyone rather than the most famous courtesan in Europe. He was very quick, but she enjoyed it thoroughly. Then he released her, sitting her back in the basin, made a remark in Italian, and left, pulling up his breeches as he did so. Alexandra washed herself, eased herself out of the basin, and straightened her clothes. The door swung in, and Sandro stood there, beaming. "The Duce is very pleased," he said. "He said I must give you this." It was a thousand lira note.

"Am I allowed to rejoin the party?" Alexandra was disgusted.

"No, no, you cannot do that," Sandro said. "My wife is here."

"Does she know who I am?"

"No, but she might find out."

"I see." Alexandra was by now feeling definitely annoyed. "Well, at least point her out to me."

Sandro escorted her along the corridor, and from the entrance to the reception room pointed out a willowy woman with long golden hair; she looked like a pale imitation of Madeleine. "She is some years younger than I," Sandro said proudly. "And comes from a very wealthy family."

"Ah," Alexandra commented. "But . . . she saw me when I came in. I remember that one looking at me."

"Well, yes, she did. But you see, I told her I was under

orders to bring the most famous whore in Paris, who just happens to be in Venice, here for Mussolini. She does not like that sort of thing, of course, but Mussolini always gets what he wishes, and she understands this."

"Let me get this straight," Alexandra said. "You visited me in Paris on behalf of Mussolini?"

He pinched her bottom. "Not the first time, of course. But when I told Il Duce of the marvellous creature I had found, with her daughter . . . you will have to bring Mayne tomorrow. But in the morning. Duce returns to Rome before lunch."

"You mean," Alexandra said. "In addition to everything else, you are Mussolini's pimp." He frowned at her, unsure whether or not she was joking. "Does your wife know about that?"

"Well, of course not. Alexandra, you are not going to make trouble, I hope. Because I must warn you, we do not put up with that sort of thing, here in Fascist Italy."

"Of course you do not, Sandro. If I make trouble your thugs will pour castor oil down my throat. So I will just crawl away with my tail between my legs. Is that not what you wish?"

"I will make it up to you," he promised. "But it would be best for you to go home now, yes. I will expect you and your daughter at ten tomorrow morning."

"Surely Il Duce doesn't want me again?"

"He wants your daughter."

"She's a big girl," Alexandra said. "She'll come on her own." Because, she thought, I have things to do, you little Fascist bastard.

She returned to the hotel. She went up to her suite, opened the door, and made the waiter wait while she wrote a note, which she gave him to deliver. "It is very important that the note is delivered," she told him. "I will give you a thousand lira now, and if I get the right reply, I'll give you another thousand. You understand?"

"Oh, yes, signora." He hurried off.

She told the girls her plan for the day. Both Mayne and Sarah had a role to play. "Ugh!" Mayne said. "He sounds revolting."

"It'll be over so quickly you won't even know it's happened," Alexandra asssured her.

They packed – they only had one small case each – and left the bags with the hall porter. Sandro turned up at half-past nine, and Alexandra gave him a great big kiss. "Well, thank God you're in a good mood, today," he said.

"I am always in a good mood," she assured him. "Here is Mayne, all ready for you. Or at least, for Il Duce."

As it was a warm day, Mayne was wearing a summer frock and showing a lot of leg. "Duce will be enchanted," Sandro said enthusiastically.

"Well, mind she's back here by eleven."

"Oh, Duce is leaving at eleven," Sandro said, and then frowned. "Why does Mayne have to be back then?"

"Because I met some friends last night, and I'm entertaining them to lunch," Alexandra told him. "In fact, I wonder if you and your wife would like to join us?"

Sandro looked scandalised. "I'm afraid that will not be possible. My wife and I are lunching with her sister."

"After dropping Mussolini at the station? You had better hope the train is on time."

"Italian trains are always on time," Sandro said stiffly. "Duce has seen to that."

"I'm glad to hear it. Well, I'll say ta-ta. Sarah and I have things to do. Oh, by the way, how exactly are you going to introduce Mayne to your wife?"

"Giovanna, my wife, will not be there. She is spending

the morning at the Ludovici Gallery. There is a painting she is interested in. There is nothing for you to worry your pretty little head about."

"I'm so glad," Alexandra said.

Giovanna di Marti was easy to find; she was accompanied by the director as she looked at the paintings he obviously expected her to buy. Alexandra looked at some paintings herself, while she moved closer to them, and then chose her moment to find herself standing beside the Countess. "Why," she said. "How nice to see you again." Giovanna di Marti gazed at her, eyebrows arched. She had never seen Alexandra's face, of course, but she had seen Alexandra, and clearly she was trying to remember where and when. "You've forgotten me," Alexandra said, roguishly. "I'm Alexandra d'Eboli. We met in Paris, last year."

Clearly Giovanna did not remember, but she was not going to snub an obvious aristocrat. "Of course," she said. "How nice."

"And are you enjoying the Carnival?"

Giovanna gave a faint shrug. "It is really rather a bore."

"Absolutely," Alexandra agreed. "But it is so good to see you again. Shall we take a coffee together?"

"Well . . . I am supposed to be meeting my husband . . ."

"At your sister's for lunch. He told me."

"You have seen Sandro?"

"Indeed. He was at the station seeing Il Duce off when I arrived, a little while ago."

"Oh." Giovanna was clearly confused. "Well . . ."

"I am staying at the Intercontinental," Alexandra said. "I keep a suite there, you know."

"Oh." This time Giovanna's tone revealed that she was impressed. "Well, perhaps . . ."

"There is lots of time," Alexandra assured her, and tucked Giovanna's arm beneath her own as they left the gallery and strolled towards the hotel. "Have you decided to buy?"

"Well . . ." Giovanna said, "as a matter of fact . . ."

Alexandra kept the conversation on art until they reached the hotel, where she was greeted by a smiling manager. They took the lift, and Alexandra ushered Giovanna into the sitting room, which was presently empty, although there were several half-filled glasses of champagne to be seen, and some noise from the next room. "My daughter," Alexandra explained. "She is entertaining. However, as they are drinking champagne, why not? It is better than the coffee."

She poured, with her back turned, dropping several of the sleeping pills she had bought that morning into one of the glasses. Alexandra had dissolved the pills into a paper handkerchief before going to the gallery, and the powder merely increased the bubbles. Giovanna never noticed, as she was clearly trying to decide how to leave again as soon as she could without being rude. But she took the glass. "Well, here's to old friends," Alexandra said, and drank deeply.

"Oh . . . yes." Giovanna also drank, and Alexandra refilled her glass. "No, really, I must be on my way," Giovanna protested. "I didn't really expect to be drinking champagne."

"It's good for you," Alexandra assured her. "Let's go see what Sarah is doing."

She went to the bedroom door, and after a moment's hesitation, Giovanna followed her, stumbling as she did so. "Countess," she muttered. "Countess . . ."

Alexandra opened the door to reveal a naked Sarah and two naked officers, in bed together. "Aren't they a pretty sight?" she asked. Giovanna stared at them in consternation, turned, and gave a little sigh. Alexandra caught her before she could fall, and half lifted, half carried her to the other bed. "I'm afraid she's been over-indulging. Help me undress her. Just be careful not to tear anything."

"You sure dislike this dame," Ken commented.

"I sure dislike her husband. And her husband's boss," Alexandra said. "But she's the one who's picking up the tab. Now listen, I really am grateful. Next time you're in Paris, come to the House and you can have a freebie, with any one of my girls you choose."

"I choose you."

"Then I'll expect you," she told him.

They caught the train to Vienna, both to throw Sandro off their track and to be across the border in the quickest possible time. But there was no pursuit. Indeed, Alexandra did not suppose she would ever hear from Sandro again.

Later that year Ken Wilmot called for his reward, and told her that he and Dunning had had an absolute ball. "I don't reckon this continent is big enough to hold both you and that woman, Alix. Why don't you emigrate to the States?"

"Paris is where it's at," she told him. "I'm not going anywhere." But as that summer wore on, the drums began to beat.

Alexandra was more interested in the news coming out of Spain than out of Germany. She was delighted that Franco had triumphed, not because she had anything but distaste for Fascism, but because she hated the ugly face of the Communists, as illustrated to her, more, and besides, she wanted Pedro to be avenged. However, she had no desire to return south of the Pyrenees, even supposing she had a reason. But she had to become interested in what was happening beyond the Rhine, as her clients began to reveal considerable agitation. Like so many other people, she and Madeleine were on the Champs Elysees when war was declared that September, listening to the news and gazing at the sky as if expecting the first bombers to appear overhead at any moment. But after that, despite the catastrophe of Poland, the whole business seemed remote, and her own business thrived that winter, as it seemed every Frenchman who could raise the fee wanted to have an evening at Madame Alexandra's before the roof fell in. The bombing raids were a nuisance, but in the suburbs they were not a danger, while when the fighting began in Norway it seemed more remote than ever. She was devastated when, lying in bed with Sarah Bryan, who had now joined her staff, on the morning of 10 May 1940, she was interrupted by a frantic Mayne, to say that the Germans had invaded Belgium, Holland and France. Alexandra telephoned her principal client at the Foreign Ministry, Jacques Dalneau. "There is nothing to be afraid of, Alexandra," Jacques said reassuringly. "It is all part of our master plan. The Nazis will be defeated."

Alexandra was prepared to believe him; not all of her girls were as convinced, and over the next few weeks she began to feel they were right, as news trickled in of the continued Allied defeats, of the flight of the British Army from Dunkirk, and as a steady but growing stream of people began to leave Paris. It took her some time to get through to the Ministry, and in fact before she managed it, Jacques called her. This was a different, highly agitated, Jacques. "Alexandra, you must leave immediately."

"Leave Paris?"

"Everyone is leaving Paris. The Government is leaving Paris. We are going to Bordeaux. Listen, pack up and go to Bordeaux. I will find you a house, and you can set up shop there."

"You mean France has been defeated?"

"For the moment, yes. Now, I must rush. I will see you in Bordeaux. But Alexandra, hurry."

Alexandra replaced the phone and faced a circle of anxious faces. She repeated what the Minister had told her, and there was a chorus of alarm. Alexandra clapped her hands for silence. "I have made my decision," she said. "I am remaining in Paris. I am not afraid of the Germans. We have entertained enough Germans in the House, have we not? So, for me, it is business as usual. However, I am forcing no one to remain with me. Anyone who wishes may pack up and leave. I will give anyone who is going a travelling allowance. Regretfully, I feel all of the men should go. But remember that there is a place for you here, when the Germans have gone away again, eh? Now, you must make your decisions, quickly." She went upstairs to her boudoir and sat at her desk, took out her cash box, and waited. Several of the girls came at once, clearly terrified. Alexandra paid them and kissed them goodbye.

Lucien arrived, with Georges and Alphonse and Jean-Claude. "We cannot leave you, Madame."

"You must. You are men of military age. You may well be arrested. But . . ." she smiled at them, "I will expect you back."

"I will stay, Madame," Armand said. "I am sixty-three years old. They can hardly say I am of military age. And you will need a man about the place."

"Oh, yes, Armand," she said, gratefully.

Nicole telephoned. "Philippe says we must leave Paris, Alix. Are you leaving Paris?"

"I am staying. Germans need sex too, you know."

"I don't want to go," Nicole said.

"What about the children?"

"God knows. They aren't here. Michel is in the army, and I don't even know if he is alive. Anna is in South America. Louis is in Africa. If I stayed, could I come to live with you?"

"Of course, my dear. But if you stay, will not Philippe be very angry?"

Nicole sighed. "I will have to let you know."

But Nicole, after all, elected to go with her husband, and Alexandra was left with eight people. Armand and Helene stayed, as of course did Madeleine; Madeleine was forty-one, now, but she remained an exceptionally beautiful woman, and she was Alexandra's closest friend. Mayne also stayed, although Alexandra would have preferred her to go, just in case something went wrong, and Sarah elected to stay with her. Having got over her dislike for men, Sarah was one of the most enthusiastic and hard-working of Alexandra's staff. The remaining two were Mala, a twenty-six-year-old brunette, and Lucie, a sixteen-year-old who had only joined the staff the previous year.

They all went down on 14 June to watch the German army march into Paris, standing amidst the weeping crowds as the jackboots thundered on the Champs Elysees, then Alexandra hurried them home. Several of the soldiers had spotted the group of extremely attractive women, and she did not want to get them into trouble before the occupation even began. As she had anticipated, she was having her breakfast the next morning when a staff car flying the swastika came down the drive and drew up in front of the house. Armand opened the door, while Alexandra drank her coffee and waited, although she did put on a dressing gown. A few minutes later she heard feet on the stairs and Armand knocked. "Excuse me, Madame, but a Colonel Stoeppner wishes a word with you."

"Then show him in, Armand." Alexandra did not get up, but smiled at the Colonel as he came through the door. "I do not usually entertain in the mornings," she told him. "But I suppose for the conquerors of Paris I must make an exception."

The Colonel, a tall, handsome man who revealed a bald head as he saluted and then removed his cap, appeared rather tense. "This is a fine house you have here, Countess," he said in excellent French.

"It is the best House in Paris, Colonel. Will you have a cup of coffee?"

The Colonel sat opposite her, gazing at her breasts, which were half exposed as the dressing gown fell open. "I have orders to place your establishment out of bounds."

Alexandra poured coffee. "You are shutting me down?"

"Out of bounds to all Frenchmen, and all enlisted German soldiers. As of now this brothel is reserved for German officers, only."

"Really, Colonel, I do not think of my house as a brothel. Rather as a place where men may forget their troubles. However, as you wish, I shall admit only German officers."

"You have a tariff?"

Alexandra got up and went to her desk. This time the dressing gown was disarranged sufficiently for him to obtain a glimpse of her legs. She opened a drawer, took out one of her printed sheets of paper, and returned to give it to him, remained standing beside him while he read it. He was obviously finding it difficult to concentrate. "You are very professional, Countess."

"That is why I am successful."

"You are also very expensive." He brushed the paper with his hand. "Two hundred English pounds for a night, with you? How old are you, Countess?"

"I shall be forty in December," Alexandra said.

"And you seriously expect a man to pay two hundred pounds for this privilege?"

"If the woman happens to be Alexandra Mayne, yes," Alexandra told him. "Why do you not judge for yourself?" She shrugged the dressing gown from her shoulders, let it slither past her thighs to the floor. "Well?"

"I do not have two hundred pounds, Countess."

Alexandra smiled, and stood against him to unbutton his tunic; immediately she felt his arm go round her to caress her buttocks. "I am prepared to allow you a trial run, Colonel."

"My officers cannot pay your prices," Stoeppner explained. "But they must have sexual relief. I am sure you understand this. As of now you will halve these prices."

"Halve them?" Alexandra shouted.

"That is correct."

Alexandra thrust her hands into her hair. "I think you can let the Colonel perform his own ablutions, Mayne," she said. "And dress himself." She waited for him to leave, then lay down again with a thump. "This is going to be a long war," she said.

In fact it was a successful one. Alexandra still believed in quality rather than quantity, having sampled both Tony the Greek's idea of prostitution and her own. But there could be no doubt that during the next couple of months the House was more popular than it had ever been; Alexandra had to insist that they would accept no clients between four in the morning and noon, or they would have had no sleep. For the rest of the day there were never less than a dozen men on the premises, and as she had only five women available she had to shorten the permitted time. Thus she was not out of pocket at all, as having halved her prices, she halved the time bought by each client as well. Business was indeed so brisk she recruited a couple of new girls, who came from surprisingly good families, fallen upon hard times since the German occupation. She entirely abandoned her "entertainments", of course; not only did the Germans not seem the least interested, but she could not spare the time.

Mayne was uneasy about the situation. "The Germans are going to lose, aren't they?" she asked.

"Well, I suppose so," Alexandra said.

"Then, won't we be charged with treason?"

"For doing what?"

"Sleeping with the enemy."

"We are whores, darling," Alexandra pointed out. "Our business is sleeping with men. We can't be expected to determine whether they are friends or enemies. It isn't as if we were doing it for free."

And in fact there were some difficulties. Sarah had an English passport, and it was with great difficulty that Alexandra kept her from being deported to a German internment camp. More serious was the visit from the Gestapo. "Are any of your girls Jewish, Countess?" inquired the man in the leather coat.

"I should not think so," Alexandra said. It had never occurred to her to ask, but she did know that owing to their strict upbringing prostitution was an occupation Jewish girls would turn to only in the last extremity.

"Nevertheless, they must be inspected," the man said. "Assemble them before me, please, Countess." Alexandra duly did so; it was eleven in the morning, and they had all just woken up and were taking breakfast. The Gestapo officer made them all strip and himself examined them, with great care.

The girls submitted patiently, but Alexandra was outraged; the lout hadn't paid for the privilege he was enjoying. "What exactly is it you are looking for?" she inquired.

"There are characteristics . . ."

"Stuff and nonsense," she said. "I shall report this to Colonel Stoeppner."

"The Colonel has no authority over the Gestapo."

"Then you have nothing to worry about, have you?" Alexandra inquired.

He flushed. "And what of yourself, Countess? I find your complexion a little darker than normal."

"That is because, in addition to being a countess," Alexandra explained, "I am an Indian princess."

"An *Indian*?"

"An American Indian. A *Red* Indian," Alexandra said triumphantly.

"I shall have to report this, Countess."

"By all means do so," Alexandra agreed. "American Indians were the original Aryans." That seemed to confuse him, and in fact she heard nothing further on that subject. But as the summer wore on and France surrendered, she began to realise that she was going to have to remain on good terms with the Germans for a very long time; they and their Italian allies were supreme in Europe, west of Russia. Her own situation seemed satisfactory enough, as she continued to be very busy, and as she entertained generals as well as captains and lieutenants, and even the odd field-marshal. Nor was life under the Germans at all difficult for the Countess Mayne. She accepted much of her payment in kind, and was never short of either food or drink. Of course it was galling to be forbidden to leave Paris, and it was distressing to see and hear of the iron grip which was slowly descending on the whole country, even that portion of it ruled by the Vichy Government: no one could be blind to the fact that people were being shot on a daily basis, or that the country was being bled white.

But she had made her decision to sit it out, and now she knew she must abide by it. She warned her girls to do nothing to offend, and wait for either Britain to make peace, when presumably things would be more relaxed, or for a miracle to happen. She certainly meant Mayne and herself to survive, and did not see what was going to stop them doing that, when she was awakened one morning that autumn, at eight o'clock, by an alarmed Armand. "There are men here insisting upon being admitted, madame," he said.

Alexandra had not got to bed until four, and was very sleepy. "What men? We admit no one at this hour."

"These are Italians, madame. Their leader insists upon seeing you, or he says he will burn the building down. His name is Alessandro di Marti."

CHAPTER 13

Alexandra leapt out of bed, put on her dressing gown. Her brain was racing. "You had better let the gentlemen in, Armand," she said, "before they do something stupid. But as soon as you have done that, telephone Colonel Stoeppner and tell him we are being attacked by a bunch of drunken Italians." Armand hurried off. Alexandra washed her face and drew a brush through her hair, then faced her boudoir door as it burst open,

Sandro was supported by half a dozen junior officers. "You bitch!" he said by way of greeting.

Alexandra raised her eyebrows. "You are trespassing, Sandro."

"Trespassing? In a whorehouse!" He gave a shout of laughter.

"This house is out of bounds to anyone, unless he is a German officer," Alexandra said quietly. "If you are in any doubt of that, you had better telephone Military Headquarters."

For a moment he frowned at her, then he snorted. "I have not come here to fuck you, whore. I have come here to take the skin from your ass."

Alexandra drew a sharp breath. She could not doubt he meant what he was saying. She had to stall. "Before you do anything stupid, Sandro," she said. "I think you should know that last night I slept with Field-Marshal von Rundstedt. I believe he is coming back tonight . . ."

which was a lie, but Sandro couldn't possibly know that. "It is my ass he is after, Sandro. And what are you so angry about, anyway? That your wife had sex with a few friends of mine?"

"Aha!" He pointed. "Then you admit it."

"Well, obviously, as it took place in my hotel suite."

"I wish their names and addresses."

"Now you know I cannot give you those, Sandro. You yourself told me that anything went during Carnival?"

"Giovanna says they were Americans, from their accents, and the hotel staff say they were naval officers, from their uniforms. Therefore they were off USS *Michigan*. Do not trouble to deny it."

"I am not troubling to deny it."

"Their names."

"As you have found out so much, I would have thought you would have found out those as well, by now."

"There are nearly a hundred officers on that ship."

"Are you suggesting your wife had a hundred men?"

Sandro glared at her, while his men shifted their feet uneasily. They knew he had lost control of the situation.

"Now, I suggest you all leave," Alexandra said. "Before the Gestapo get here."

Sandro's knees gave way and he sat in a chair. "You do not understand. My wife has left me."

"But you had nothing to do with it."

"She made me confess that it was I took you to Venice to meet Il Duce. That I had been to this House. That I had been unfaithful."

"I thought all Italian men were unfaithful?" Alexandra asked, interested. "Well, all men, really. But Italian men more than most."

"Not when they are married to Giovanna della Rovere."

"Aristocracy, is she?"

"The most aristocratic family in Europe."

Alexandra thought that was a debatable point, but now was not the time. "Can't Musso help?"

"Musso? Oh, you mean Il Duce? My dear Alexandra, he is as afraid of the della Roveres as the rest of us. Now she says she is going to have the marriage annulled. What am I to do? I will have no money . . ."

"But you're a di Marti," Alexandra said encouragingly. "You own that fabulous palazzo in Venice."

"I still have no money. My family lost all of its money, years ago. Now I have only the title."

"Surely you could sell the palazzo?"

"I cannot sell my family home," Sandro said, with dignity. "That would be unthinkable."

"Well, I'm sorry, Sandro. But I don't like being treated like a nothing, and that is how you treated me."

"Alexandra . . ." He leapt up, ran forward, and seized her hand. "If my marriage is annulled . . . will you marry me?"

"How can your marriage be annulled? You're a Roman Catholic."

"We cannot be divorced. But the marriage can be annulled."

"On what grounds? You must have consummated it."

"There are many grounds for annulling a marriage, if one has enough money and a good lawyer, and a friend in the Vatican. They will find out that Giovanna and I are related."

"Are you?"

"I do not think so. But they will find it out just the same. Alexandra, my darling Alexandra, will you not make me the happiest man in the world?"

"I'd love to do that, Sandro. But I can't marry you."

"Why not? I have just been appointed commander-in-chief of the Seventh Army. We guard the northeast frontier. You will be the wife of a commanding general. Does that not please you?"

"It sounds wonderful." She really did wish to get rid of him just as quickly as possible. "But I'm already married."

"What? You did not tell me this."

"You never asked me."

"What is the name of the man?" Sandro demanded, looking from left to right as if expecting to see an outraged husband emerging from the closet.

"David Mayne," Alexandra explained. "That's my name, Mayne."

"But . . ." Sandro looked dumbfounded. "Did you not marry the Count of Eboli?"

"Yes." Alexandra hung her head. "Bigamously. Oh, not intentionally so, you understand. I thought David was dead. But he wasn't, and two years ago he came back. Well, when I refused to give up this life he went off again. But we are still married."

"And where is he now?"

"In England. He's in the British Army. So you see . . . I'd love to marry you, Sandro. But I can't."

Sandro's shoulders sagged, and he turned, and left the room, his henchmen behind him. They hardly looked at the girls, gathered in an anxious group at the far end of the gallery.

Over the next year Alexandra lived a very full life. It was also very financially rewarding, even if – presuming that the Nazis *were* going to lose the War – she did not know what she was going to do with the mountain of German marks she was accumulating. Her real wealth was in a Swiss bank account, and was accumulating interest all the time. As the year wore on, however, it became less and less likely that the Nazis *would* lose it. Certainly the

Germans seemed to be going from strength to strength, and when they invaded Russia in the summer of 1941 and gained a succession of huge victories, it seemed that the entire continent of Europe, barring Britain, would soon be theirs.

Nor, according to what the French newspapers were permitted to say by the German censors, was there the slightest hope of the British holding out for more than another couple of months. So obviously they had to regard the situation as permanent.

She was therefore the more taken aback when, that August, as she sat in her garden before lunch one day, reading a novel, a voice said, "Hist, Madame Mayne."

Alexandra's head jerked. There was someone in the bushes just inside her wall. And his voice was familiar! "Who are you?" she asked. She was not the least afraid; the entire household was within earshot, and since Sandro's invasion of the previous year Stoeppner kept an armed guard on the front gate to make sure she received no other uninvited guests.

"Lucien, madame."

"Lucien!" she cried in delight, getting up.

"Hush, madame. No one must know I am here."

Alexandra sat down again. "How did you get in?" she asked.

"I came over the wall during the night," Lucien said. "I have crouched in these bushes for nine hours, waiting for you."

"Are you an escaped prisoner?"

"No. I am an English agent."

"You mean you are a spy. You will be shot."

"Will you betray me, madame?"

"Well, of course I will not betray you. But someone

is sure to. You must get away from here as quickly as possible. I will help you."

"I knew this, madame. That is why I am here. There are many of us needing help."

Alexandra looked at the wall. "Are they all hiding behind there?"

"There is only me today, madame. But the others will be coming. Seeking your help."

"Oh, no," Alexandra said. "Oh, no, no, no, no, no. I will help you, Lucien, because you are one of *my* people. But I will help no one else."

"But you must, madame. Do you want to be regarded as a traitor, a collaborator, after the war?"

"I have never betrayed anyone. As for collaborating . . . I am a whore. This is well known."

"You are also both an English and a French citizen. When Britain and France have won the war, there will be questions asked."

"That seems a remote possibility, right now," Alexandra pointed out.

"They will win the War, madame. There can be no doubt about that. If it takes a hundred years, they will win it."

"I'm sure you're right," Alexandra agreed. "But I'm also sure you'll agree that in a hundred years' time I'm unlikely to be around to answer any questions."

"You refuse to help? Your own kith and kin?"

Alexandra was tempted to remind him that her Guyanese Amerindian kith and kin, treated as they were as children by the Colonial Office, were not involved in this War, and could hope for no benefit from it, while her English kith and kin had never offered her the smallest welcome into their society. Yet he did strike a chord, oddly enough. "What would you wish me to do?"

"We would like to use your establishment as a safe house."

"I do not understand you. We?"

"The Allies, madame. There are many English servicemen, principally airmen, loose in the occupied countries, Holland, Belgium and France itself, endeavouring to evade capture by the Germans. I am part of an organisation which attempts to get these men out of the country, into Spain, from where they can be sent back to England. However, there is often a considerable delay between stages, and naturally Paris, as the rail centre of France, is where our people have to wait on many occasions. Thus we have to have somewhere safe where they can stay until the next stage of their journey can be arranged."

"Don't you realise that for fourteen hours in every day my house is full of German officers?"

"That is what makes it so safe. The Germans would never dream of searching it, now that it is so well established as an army brothel."

"My house is not a brothel," Alexandra snapped. "It is a House of Rest and Relaxation. If you expect me to help you, you will have to be polite."

"But you will help me? It will be very simple. You have a large number of rooms. When one of my people comes to you, you will simply install him in a room, and he will stay there, until he receives orders to proceed. All you have to do is feed him. Can you trust your people?"

Alexandra considered. Her own people, of course; they would die for her. But the two new girls . . . yet they seemed whole-heartedly anti-Nazi. "But how are your people to get to me? There is a guard on my front door."

"They will come over the wall, just as I did. All you

have to made sure of is that they are not immediately betrayed."

"And what happens when *I* am betrayed?"

"Then you will die with honour, madame."

It occurred to Alexandra that Lucien had grown up further than she had ever expected, or wished him to. "I find that very encouraging. But as you here, Lucien, dear, dear Lucien . . ."

The girls were all delighted to see Lucien again, and also to have a man they actually liked. He had an exhausting couple of hours, while eating at the same time, and telling Alexandra of his adventures. "Now I serve de Gaulle," he said proudly. "And Churchill, of course."

"You are a very brave man, Lucien," Mayne said, her eyes shining.

"I am doing my duty, as must you all."

"What about Georges and Jean-Claude?" Madeleine asked. "Do they serve De Gaulle, too?"

"Alas, madame, Georges is dead."

"Oh!" Alexandra was startled; she had been very fond of Georges. "And Jean-Claude?"

"I do not know, madame. We became separated. But if he is alive, I know that he will be serving De Gaulle as well."

Two weeks later, the first evader arrived.

They came at night, but a signalling system had been set up, and they were able to make their presence known in the house. They then remained, as Lucien had done, concealed in the bushes at the bottom of the garden until the last German had gone home, when they were brought into the house, fed and bathed, and put to bed in one of the spare servant rooms on the attic floor, where they remained until the next stage of their transport was arranged. This sometimes took several days, and although in the beginning Alexandra was highly nervous as long as one of them was in her house, she soon got used to it. Time passed relatively peacefully.

She was awakened one morning by a series of crashes and bangs which seemed to be shaking the house to its foundations. An earthquake! she thought, and leapt out of bed, reaching for her robe. But before she could put it on, the door burst open, and her room was filled with armed men in black uniforms. "For God's sake!" she shouted. "We are not open until two."

The commander of the invaders – he was a captain she had never seen before, very young and stiff looking, with yellow hair – came up to her, looked her up and down, slowly. "You are the woman who calls herself the Countess Mayne?"

"I *am* the Countess Mayne."

"You are under arrest."

"On what charge?"

"You will be informed of the charge in due course. You will come with us."

Alexandra listened to more screams and shouts of outrage from the gallery. "You are arresting my girls as well?"

"Everyone in this house is under arrest, Countess."

"That is outrageous." Alexandra went to her desk, picked up the telephone.

The Captain followed her. "Just what do you think you are doing, Countess?"

"I am telephoning Colonel Stoeppner. He will be very angry about this."

The officer hit her across the thigh with his swagger-stick. The pain quite took Alexandra's breath away, and she dropped the receiver. Then she instinctively turned towards him, to receive a poke in the stomach which again winded her, so that she fell to her knees. "There will be no telephone calls, Countess."

Alexandra was half thrown down the stairs, and with the others, was herded out of the front door and into the waiting black maria. Four of the SS men got in the back of the van with them, and said again, "No speaking."

As they all carried heavy rubber truncheons no one felt like disobeying, while one sat at the end of the van with a sub-machine gun on his lap, so there was no possibility of a concerted attempt to overpower them. Alexandra could only stare at Madeleine and Mayne and then at Sarah, willing them to be silent. She was more worried about Mala and Lucie, who were clearly terrified, while she was at the same time attempting to think of a way to get them out of this mess. There had to be one, if she could only think. But thought was difficult with the raging pain in her thigh and belly, and before she had arrived at any solution they reached Gestapo headquarters. Here most of the staff, male and female, turned out to watch the naked girls being herded inside. A captain, accompanied by an older man wearing the insignia of a colonel, entered the room. The guards immediately stood to attention. "This is an outrage!" said Alexandra, determined not to show her very real fear. "I demand to know with what we are charged."

The colonel stepped up to her. "You are the Countess Mayne?"

"Yes," Alexandra said. "That lout knew who I was."

The colonel looked her up and down, obviously appreciating what he was seeing. "In there," he said, pointing at an inner doorway. Alexandra glanced at Madeleine and Mayne, willing them to be patient, and followed him. The inner room contained a desk, behind which the colonel sat, and two chairs. Alexandra was not invited to sit, so she remained standing before the desk, slowly becoming aware that the room was in fact a torture chamber; there were manacles attached to the wall, and a variety of whips and canes and other objects she could not identify hanging from hooks. The colonel smiled at her expression. "Yes, it would pay you to be honest with me, Countess. My name is Colonel Hassner, and I am in charge of this investigation. Now listen carefully. You are accused of running a staging post for the Underground Railway, which endeavours to assist enemy airmen to escape from France. What I want from you are the names and descriptions of the Resistance people who have been controlling you. Give me those, and we can forget all about your involvement in the matter."

"You must take me for a fool," Alexandra said. "In the first place, I am not involved in anything; in the second place, I am not controlled by any member of the Underground, and I do not know any members of the Resistance; and in the third place, I would not give you their names even if I did know any of them."

The colonel regarded her for several seconds, then shrugged again. "Then I will have an entertaining morning."

"It would in your own best interests, Colonel, to inform my fiancé of what is happening. Otherwise it may go very hard with you."

The colonel frowned. "Whores do not have fiancés."

"I do," Alexandra pointed out. "His name is General Count Alessandro di Marti, Commander-in-Chief of the Italian Seventh Army."

"You expect me to believe that?"

"Well," Alexandra said. "Why do you not get hold of the general and find out. He is in command of northeast Italy and Dalmatia. His address is the Palazzo Marti, Venice." She could only pray he had not been moved.

The colonel considered, while Alexandra waited, endeavouring to look as nonchalant as possible. "Have my secretary telephone Venice, Carl," the colonel decided. "If she can obtain General di Marti, have the call put through to this office."

The telephone jangled. For a moment Alexandra didn't hear it, because of the jangling of fear in her own ears. Then her eyes opened as Carl picked up the receiver. Carl looked at his superior. "It is General Di Marti, Herr Colonel."

"Sandro!" Alexandra shouted.

Hassner glanced at her, then gestured to his men, before picking up the phone. "Yes, General," Hassner was saying. "Yes, she is here with me now. There are serious charges . . . it is very irregular, General. Yes. Very well." He put his hand over the mouthpiece. "He wishes to speak with you. I trust you will be circumspect, Countess."

She picked up the phone. "Sandro!" she sobbed. "Oh, Sandro."

"I am told you are in some kind of trouble with the police. Why do you expect me to help you?"

"Oh, Sandro, these men are trying to stop us getting married. I know that is what they are doing."

"Getting married?"

Alexandra took a long breath; the Germans of course could only hear her end of the conversation, at least in this room. It was all or nothing now. "Sandro! You do still wish us to be married?"

"Well . . . of course I do, Alix. But you said you could not marry me, because you had a husband living."

"I have just heard that dear David is dead. So I am counting the hours," Alexandra said. "I have my passage booked to Venice. With my girls."

"Your . . . ah, your daughter and that delightful Englishwoman?"

"There are actually ten of us. Including my cook and my butler. I could not possibly travel without my cook and butler."

"My dear Alix, I cannot possibly support ten people."

"You don't have to. I will support them. I am a very wealthy woman," Alexandra pointed out. "My money is in Switzerland. It is just a matter of drawing it out."

"Alix! You are a treasure."

"So, will you instruct this colonel to let us go, please?"

"Well . . . what is the charge?"

"He says I have been sheltering Allied airmen at the House."

"That is a very serious offence, Alix. Have you done this?"

"I have absolutely no idea. I keep telling this man this. Men come to my house, for sex. I do not inquire into their antecedents, their nationality, or their politics. And if they wish to stay for two or three days, who am I to argue, as long as they pay the fee? I know I have broken the law, the German law. They wanted the house reserved for their officers alone. But what was I to do, Sandro? There were not enough of them to pay the bills." She relied upon the likelihood that he would be so confused by now he would not start asking why she did not use the money in Switzerland. "So I started accepting other clients. I am sorry, but I had to do it."

"Hm," Sandro said. "They will shut you down, Alix."

"I do not mind about that, Sandro darling, as I wish to come to Venice anyway." The Germans saw a smile spread slowly on Alexandra's lovely face. Then:

"He wants to speak to you," Alexandra said, and held out the phone.

CHAPTER 14

"Oh, my darling!" Sandro hugged and kissed Alexandra on the Venice Railway Station. "To have you here, to know that we are going to be married . . ."

"It is good for me too," Alexandra told him. "Now let me introduce my people." Several of them Sandro had met before, of course, on his visits to the House. But Alexandra could tell that he was very taken by Mala. "Now they are all yours," she told him. She did not want to have to cope with him all on her own. Having been released by the Gestapo into Sandro's custody. Alexandra felt safer after the marriage ceremony – a quiet affair held in St Marks, but she had little enthusiasm for her husband's company.

"At least," she told Madeleine, we could hardly be in a safer place than here in Venice." Or so it seemed that spring, while that the Allies were winning could not be doubted. Sandro was able to tell them about the German debacle at Stalingrad, and about the surrender of the entire Axis forces in North Africa. He was sad about this because it involved so many Italians, but he wanted the War to end as much as anyone, and was delighted when the British and the Americans invaded Sicily. His attitude surprised and worried Alexandra, as it smacked of treason, but Sandro merely smiled and told her that things were getting better and better. She understood something of what he meant when the Allies invaded Italy itself, and the Italian Government promptly surrendered. "It is fantastic," Sandro told the women. "There was a meeting of the Fascist Grand Council, and Mussolini was deposed. Oh, I would have given anything to have been there, to have seen his face. Now he is under arrest. He will undoubtedly be tried as a war criminal."

Alexandra waited until they were alone in their bedroom before she asked him, "I thought Il Duce was your friend? Are you not a Fascist?"

"Il Duce was never my friend," Sandro declared. "He was my master."

"Whom you obeyed slavishly."

"Well, does one not obey one's master slavishly?" Alexandra had no good rejoinder to that, as she had certainly obeyed the only master she had ever had, Tony the Greek, slavishly. But that didn't make her feel any the more happy with Sandro's volte face; he had not confronted Mussolini personally. "As for being a Fascist," her husband went on. "I was a Fascist when it was necessary to be a Fascist. Now it is necessary to be something else. When the right moment arrives. For the time being I have given Field-Marshal Kesselring my personal assurance that I, and the troops under my command, will remain loyal to our German allies, and fight to the last bullet."

"But you intend to betray them."

"Of course. The Germans have lost this war. They are only continuing to fight because they have committed too many crimes to surrender. But I have committed no crime. The moment it becomes possible, I will surrender my command."

But the Allied advance up the peninsular took much longer than expected, as Kesselring and his troops fought with brilliant tenacity. Sandro began to worry that they might summon him and his men to take their turn in defending places like Monte Cassino or counter-attacking at Anzio, but the Germans were not prepared to trust even "loyal" Italians that far, and besides, he was needed to guard the top of the Adriatic against any sudden irruption of the Yugoslav guerillas. To his far greater dismay, the Germans also pulled off a spectacular rescue of Mussolini from the mountain hotel at which he was being held captive, and installed him in Milan as head of a new Fascist Italian State. Sandro hastened to greet his old master. "And you had better come too," he told Alexandra. "Il Duce remembers you fondly."

"He remembers my body," Alexandra grumbled.

"I thought you were no longer a friend of his, Sandro," Mayne said.

"He is my master," Sandro told her. "He is all of our master. We cannot forget this."

They drove in Sandro's official staff car to Milan, and were shown into the palazzo appropriated by Mussolini as his headquarters. There, although Sandro was dressed in full uniform as a general, his left breast a mass of medal ribbons – where he had earned them Alexandra could not imagine – they were kept waiting for half an hour before being shown into a huge office, where there were several other officers as well as armed guards, and seated behind the desk at the far end of the room, beneath the huge windows, Mussolini himself. Alexandra was astonished: the great bull of a man she remembered from four years ago seemed to have shrunk; only the bald head and jutting, unshaven chin were recognisable. Until he spoke. Then his voice was as harsh and angry as she recalled. Sandro had stood to attention and given the Fascist salute. "Duce!"

"Traitor," Mussolini growled.

"Duce?" Sandro's voice shook. Alexandra and Mayne were standing immediately behind him, and they touched hands in apprehension.

Mussolino slapped his desk. "I have here copies of correspondence between you and Badoglio, concerning the coup mounted against me. And concerning the intended surrender of your command to the Allies."

Alexandra caught her breath; could Sandro have been so foolish as to put his plans into writing? "They must be forgeries, Duce," Sandro protested. "I have never written anything like that. I am your most faithful servant."

"You are a liar and a coward as well as a traitor." Mussolini snapped his fingers. "Take this carrion out. Have him tried, find him guilty, and condemn him to death. Bring the warrant to me to sign."

"No!" Sandro shrieked, and to Alexandra's horror, sank to his knees, his hands clasped before his chest. "I beg of you, Duce. I am innocent. I am your servant. Take away my rank, give me a rifle, and send me into the front line. I will happily die for you."

Mussolino got up and came round his desk. He stood in front of Sandro, and began tearing the medal ribbons from his chest. "Cowardly swine. Yes, I do reduce you to the ranks. But you will still be shot." Four of the guards had to drag the weeping Sandro from the room; he was incapable of movement. Alexandra and Mayne remained standing, motionless, before the desk. Mussolini peered at them. "You are the Parisian whore," he said.

"I am Alexandra Mayne," Alexandra said. "Countess of Eboli, Countess di Marti."

"That shit married you? Well, you must be glad to be rid of him." His eyes moved up and down her body. Then he stood close to her and moved his hand up and down her body as well, squeezing her breasts through her dress. "God, but you are still the loveliest creature," he muttered. "What do you want?" he suddenly roared, as the door opened. The officer muttered in the Duce's ear. He turned to Alexandra. "You think you have won a battle, eh, whore? This husband of yours, this lying, cheating, cowardly wretch, has begged for clemency. He is prepared to buy his freedom."

Alexandra caught her breath. "He has no money."

"But *you* have money, Contessa. Your husband says you have a fortune in a bank in Switzerland. Do you not wish to ransom your husband's life, Contessa?" Mussolini inquired, his voice suddenly soft.

Alexandra looked at Mayne. They both knew Sandro for what he was, and they both loathed him. And it had cost him not a penny to save their lives from the Gestapo – rather had he gained a good many pennies. But he *had* saved their lives.

"I will pay three hundred thousand Swiss francs for Sandro's life, Duce."

"Don't make me laugh. You have much more than that."

Alexandra bit her lip. "Very well. Five hundred thousand." Half her fortune. "There is no more."

"You are nearly as big a liar as your husband, Contessa. According to Sandro, you have a million Swiss francs in that account. Now, I am a generous man. I do not wish you to starve. You will pay eight hundred thousand francs for your husband's life. That will leave you with two hundred thousand for yourself."

"I cannot live on the income from two hundred thousand Swiss francs," Alexandra protested.

"You will have to use the capital."

"And then I will be left with nothing."

"The capital will enable you to make a fresh start. In Venice, if you wish. I give you permission to open a brothel in Venice. There. Am I not generous?"

Alexandra looked at Mayne, who waggled her eyebrows. She sighed. "Very well, Duce. Eight hundred thousand Swiss francs. Am I allowed to take my husband home with me?"

"No. He will still have to be tried. Only I shall make sure that he is acquitted. But you have not yet paid the money."

Alexandra arranged for the money to be transferred to Genoa, and drew out the remaining two hundred thousand at the same time. There seemed little point in leaving it in a Swiss bank, and she needed it to tide her over until she could become established again.

"We'll have to recruit some new girls," Madeleine said. But suddenly, for Alexandra, the heart had gone out of the whole business. It seemed even more futile when they received news that Sandro had after all been condemned by the courts, found guilty, and shot. Alexandra was outraged, more by the way she had been cheated out of her money than by Sandro's death.

It was necessary to live, however, and apparently they had the run of Sandro's palazzo, as if he did have relatives, they were in the south and on the Allied side. They did some business, principally thanks to Mayne and Sarah, and just about made ends meet. But when, the following June, news was received of the Allied landing in Normandy, Alexandra herself became restless. She became even more restless when the Allies made yet another landing, in the Riviera, thus eliminating German rule there as well. The Riviera seemed very close. When she heard that Paris was in Allied hands . . . "But the Germans still control north Italy," Madeleine argued. "We'll never get to the border."

"It will be better than staying here," Alexandra argued. "The Russians are coming from the east. I do not wish to have to wind up under some Commissar who will probably have us shot anyway." She made her plans, but it was difficult to contemplate moving during the winter, and by the next spring the situation had entirely changed, as the Germans in Italy finally collapsed, and on 30 April British troops entered Venice.

They stood on the drive and looked at the ruins of the House; it had been burned. "Oh, Ma," Mayne said, and put her arm round Alexandra's shoulders.

"Who would have done this, madame?" Armand asked.

"It must have been the Germans," Madeleine commented. Sarah began to cry while Helene looked ready to burst with indignation.

Alexandra could not recall ever feeling so depressed. She remembered when Gerard had died, and Annette had suggested she sell everything and live quietly with Alice and Mayne, and she had thought, have I been gang-raped, suffered Tony the Greek, and been everyone's plaything, to try to eke out an existence on the fringes of society? Then she had tossed her head and got to work. And succeeded beyond her wildest dreams. Now, having suffered even more, she was in a worse position, as she did not even have a house to sell, and she was twenty-five years older . . . and she did not know where to turn.

She faced them next morning. "I am sorry," she said. "But we have reached the end of the road. I did not think I would ever come to this, but I can no longer support you. I am not sure I can support myself. I propose to go back to England, where things are cheaper, I believe. But I cannot take you all with me. Mayne?"

"Oh, I will come with you, of course, Mama. I'll keep the wolf from the door."

Alexandra squeezed her hand, but the fact was that Mayne herself was twenty-nine years old, and if she had to walk the London streets she was going to age very rapidly. "What will you do, Madeleine?"

"I have an aunt," Madeleine said. "I think she has a pretty good idea what I have been doing these last twenty-odd years, so I don't know if she will take me in, but . . . there is nowhere else. Oh, Alexandra . . ." She burst into tears.

Most of the others looked about to weep as well, even Armand. But then Alexandra felt the same way. Her head jerked when there was a knock on the door. "Who is it?"

"It is the Manager, Madame Mayne."

"We are paid up to the end of the week," Alexandra said, opening the door.

"Oh, yes, madame. That is not a problem. But there is a man here to see you. He has been searching for you for several days, madame."

"Don't tell me we're going to be arrested all over again," Mayne said.

"Stay here," Alexandra told them, and went downstairs.

She didn't like the look of the man at all. He was well dressed, but he had officialdom written all over him, and he peered at her bad-temperedly. "Madame Alexandra Mayne? I am Monsieur Pierre Joubert." He gave her his card, and Alexandra deduced that he was a lawyer. "I am here as a representative of Senor Esteban Cordillo, of Madrid."

"I've never heard of him," Alexandra said. Although the name was actually familiar.

"Will you deny that you were once married to Count Pedro d'Eboli, of Eboli, in northern Spain?"

"Well . . . I was, yes." What in the name of God are they suing me for now? she wondered.

"Therefore, madame, your correct title is the Countess d'Eboli. Is that not true?"

"Only in a manner of speaking," Alexandra said defensively. "When I was a widow, I married Count di Marti."

M Joubert almost smiled. "So you are twice a countess. How fortunate for you. However, my business, as representative of Senor Cordillo, is with the Countess d'Eboli. I have some papers here for you to sign . . ." He spread them on the table.

"I am not signing anything," Alexandra told him.

Joubert frowned. "Do you not wish to take possession of your estate?"

Alexandra sat down. "What estate?"

"Why, the late Count's estate. He left a will, which left everything to you, Countess. Now, there were of course complications," Joubert went on. "There were some blood relatives of the Count, and they contested the will, claiming that the Count was of unsound mind when he made it. Senor Cordillo disputed this, of course. The case dragged on for some years, but it was finally decided in the Count's favour. That was three months ago, madame. But by then you had disappeared. It has taken me three months to track you down."

"I'm sorry about that," Alexandra said dazedly, trying to think straight. "Are you trying to tell me that the Count left me some money?"

"Well, Countess, you understand that the expenses have been very heavy . . . however," Joubert said brightly. "There was sufficient money in cash to pay the various fees, and the estate itself is untouched." Alexandra began to feel faint. Joubert bent over his papers. "Six hundred hectares . . ." He peered at her. "That is approximately one thousand, five hundred acres, you understand. The castle of Eboli, the village of Eboli, and the Eboli bodega. The house in Madrid and the house in Alicante and the finca outside Javea. The apartment in Paris and the permanent hotel suite in London. The two Rolls-Royces, the four Mercedes, and the Ferarri. The nine hundred and twenty-four horses. The yacht in Castellon. And of course the various bank accounts, but these are details which will be supplied by Senor Cordillo. Are you sure you do not remember him, your husband's man of affairs?"

"I remember Senor Cordillo," Alexandra said. "My late husband said he was absolutely trustworthy, and devoted to the name of Eboli."

"Well, Countess, I would say that he has proved that. Wouldn't you?"

"I should mention that I am a little short of funds at the moment," Alexandra remarked.

"My dear Countess. The value of your inheritance has been estimated, loosely, you understand, at the quivalent of five million, eight hundred and forty-seven thousand, six hundred and three pounds, seventeen shillings, and six pence halfpenny. In these circumstances the House of Joubert will be happy to extend you as much credit as you may require until you have your affairs in your own hands."

"You're so kind," Alexandra said.

Alexandra went upstairs. "There has been a change of plan," she announced. "Instead of splitting up, here is what we are going to do today. We are going to go out now, and go shopping on the Champs Elysees. I know there is not much available, but we must do the best we can to get some decent clothes together. Then we shall go to Maxim's and have a champagne lunch. Then we are going to take the train for Bayonne and Irun. Does that not sound a nice programme?"

QUESTIONNAIRE

Please tick the appropriate boxes to indicate your answers

1. Where did you get this book?
Bought in supermarket ☐ please name ______________________
Bought at book exchange or second hand shop ☐
Borrowed from a friend ☐ Other (please indicate)______________

2. Did you enjoy reading it?
A lot ☐ A little ☐ Not at all ☐

3. What did you particularly like about this book?
Believeable characters ☐ Easy to read ☐ Good value for money ☐
Enjoyable locations ☐ Interesting story ☐ Modern setting ☐

4. What did you particularly dislike about this book?

____

5. Would you buy another book by this author?
Yes ☐ Maybe ☐ No ☐

6. What other kinds of books do you enjoy reading?
Horror ☐ Puzzle books ☐ Historical fiction ☐ Romantic fiction ☐
Crime/Detective ☐ Cookery ☐ Other (please indicate)______________

7. Who are your favourite authors?

____

And now a little about you –

8. How old are you?
Under 25 ☐ 25–34 ☐ 35–44 ☐ 45–54 ☐ 55–64 ☐ Over 65 ☐

9. What is your marital status?
Single ☐ Married/living with partner ☐ Widowed ☐ Separated/divorced ☐

10. What is your current occupation?
Employed full-time ☐ Employed part-time ☐ Student ☐
Housewife full-time ☐ Unemployed ☐ Retired ☐

11. Do you have children? If so, how many and how old are they?

____

12. What is your annual household income?
Under £10,000 ☐ £10–20,000 ☐ £20–30,000 ☐
£30–40,000 ☐ Over £40,000 ☐

Miss/Mrs/Ms ______________________________________
Address____
____
______________________________ Postcode ____________

Thank you for completing this questionnaire. Now tear it out – put it in an envelope and send it to:

Robinson Publishing Limited
FREEPOST LON 3335
LONDON
W8 4BR

No stamp is required! (Freepost valid in the UK only, address must be written as shown.) Offer ends December 1996.